HENRIETTA TEMPLE: A LOVE STORY
BY

Benjamin Disraeli

FOREWORD

Benjamin Disraeli was a British politician who twice served as the Prime Minister and also became the Earl of Beaconsfield. Disraeli is noted for being influential as a politician and as a novelist.

Henrietta Temple: A Love Story

BOOK I.

CHAPTER I.

THE family of Armine entered England with William the Norman. Ralph d'Armyn was standard-bearer of the Conqueror, and shared prodigally in the plunder, as appears by Doomsday Book. At the time of the general survey the family of Ermyn, or Armyn, possessed numerous manors in Nottinghamshire, and several in the shire of Lincoln. William D'Armyn, lord of the honour of Armyn, was one of the subscribing Barons to the Great Charter. His predecessor died in the Holy Land before Ascalon. A succession of stout barons and valiant knights maintained the high fortunes of the family; and in the course of the various struggles with France they obtained possession of several fair castles in Guienne and Gascony. In the Wars of the Roses the Armyns sided with the house of Lancaster. Ferdinand Armyn, who shared the exile of Henry the Seventh, was knighted on Bosworth Field, and soon after created Earl of Tewkesbury. Faithful to the Church, the second Lord Tewkesbury became involved in one of those numerous risings that harassed the last years of Henry the Eighth. The rebellion was unsuccessful, Lord Tewkesbury was beheaded, his blood attainted, and his numerous estates forfeited to the Crown. A younger branch of the family, who had adopted Protestantism, married the daughter of Sir Francis Walsingham, and attracted, by his talents in negotiation, the notice of Queen Elizabeth. He was sent on a secret mission to the Low Countries, where, having greatly distinguished himself, he obtained on his return the restoration of the family estate of Armine, in Nottinghamshire, to which he retired after an eminently prosperous career, and amused the latter years of his life in the construction of a family mansion, built in that national style of architecture since described by the name of his royal mistress, at once magnificent and convenient. His son, Sir Walsingham Armine, figured in the first batch of baronets under James the First.

During the memorable struggle between the Crown and the Commons, in the reign of the unhappy Charles, the Armine family became distinguished Cavaliers. The second Sir Walsingham raised a troop of horse, and gained great credit by charging at the head of his regiment and defeating Sir Arthur Haselrigg's Cuirassiers. It was the first time that that impenetrable band had been taught to fly; but the conqueror was covered with wounds. The same Sir Walsingham also successfully defended Armine House against the Commons, and commanded the cavalry at the battle of Newbury, where two of his brothers were slain. For these various services and sufferings Sir Walsingham was advanced to the dignity of a baron of the realm, by the title of Lord Armine, of Armine, in the county of Nottingham. He died without issue, but the baronetcy devolved on his youngest brother, Sir Ferdinando.

The Armine family, who had relapsed into popery, followed the fortunes of the second James, and the head of the house died at St. Germain. His son, however, had been prudent enough to remain in England and support the new dynasty, by which means he contrived to secure his title and estates. Roman Catholics, however, the Armines always remained, and this circumstance accounts for this once-distinguished family no longer figuring in the history of their country. So far, therefore, as the house of Armine was concerned, time flew during the next century with immemorable wing. The family led a secluded life on their estate, intermarrying only with the great Catholic families, and duly begetting baronets.

At length arose, in the person of the last Sir Ferdinand Armine, one of those extraordinary and rarely gifted beings who require only an opportunity to influence the fortunes of their nation, and to figure as a Cæsar or an Alcibiades. Beautiful, brilliant, and ambitious, the young and restless Armine quitted, in his eighteenth year, the house of his fathers, and his stepdame of a country, and entered the Imperial service. His blood and creed gained him a flattering reception; his skill and valour soon made him distinguished. The world rang with stories of his romantic bravery, his gallantries, his eccentric manners, and his political intrigues, for he nearly contrived to be elected King of Poland. Whether it were disgust at being foiled in this high object by the influence of Austria, or whether, as was much whispered at the time, he had dared to urge his insolent and unsuccessful suit on a still more delicate subject to the Empress Queen herself, certain it is that Sir Ferdinand suddenly quitted the Imperial service, and appeared at Constantinople in person. The man whom a point of honour prevented from becoming a Protestant in his native country had no scruples about his profession of faith at Stamboul: certain it is that the English baronet soon rose high in the favour of the Sultan, assumed the Turkish dress, conformed to the Turkish customs, and finally, led against Austria a division of the Turkish army. Having gratified his pique by defeating the Imperial forces in a sanguinary engagement, and obtaining a favourable peace for the Porte, Sir Ferdinand Armine doffed his turban, and suddenly reappeared in his native country. After the sketch we have given of the last ten years of his life, it is unnecessary to observe that Sir Ferdinand Armine immediately became what is called fashionable; and, as he was now in Protestant England, the empire of fashion was the only one in which the young Catholic could distinguish himself. Let us then charitably set down to the score of his political disabilities the fantastic dissipation and the frantic prodigality in which the liveliness of his imagination and the energy of his soul exhausted themselves. After three startling years he married the Lady Barbara Ratcliffe, whose previous divorce from her husband, the Earl of Faulconville, Sir Ferdinand had occasioned. He was, however, separated from his lady during the first year of their more hallowed union, and, retiring to Rome, Sir Ferdinand became apparently devout. At the end of a year he offered to transfer the whole of his property to the Church, provided the Pope would allow him an annuity and make him a cardinal. His Holiness not deeming it fit to consent to the proposition, Sir Ferdinand quitted his capital in a huff, and, returning to England, laid claim to the peerages of Tewkesbury and Armine. Although assured of failing in these claims, and himself perhaps as certain of ill success as his lawyers, Sir Ferdinand nevertheless expended upwards of 60,000L. in their promotion, and was amply repaid for the expenditure in the gratification of his vanity by keeping his name before the public. He was never content except when he was astonishing mankind; and while he was apparently exerting all his efforts to become a King of Poland, a Roman cardinal, or an English peer, the crown, the coronet, and the scarlet hat were in truth ever secondary points with him, compared to the sensation throughout Europe which the effort was contrived and calculated to ensure.

On his second return to his native country Sir Ferdinand had not re-entered society. For such a man, society, with all its superficial excitement, and all the shadowy variety with which it attempts to cloud the essential monotony of its nature, was intolerably dull and commonplace. Sir Ferdinand, on the contrary, shut himself up in Armine, having previously announced to the world that he was going to write his memoirs. This history, the construction of a castle, and the prosecution of his claims before the House of Lords, apparently occupied his time to his satisfaction, for he remained quiet for several years, until, on the breaking out of the French Revolution, he hastened to Paris, became a member of the Jacobin Club, and of the National Convention. The name of Citizen Armine appears among the regicides. Perhaps in this vote he avenged the loss of the crown of Poland, and the still more mortifying repulse he may have received from the mother of Marie Antoinette. After the execution of the royal victims, however, it was discovered that Citizen Armine had made them an offer to save their lives and raise an insurrection in La Vendue, provided he was made Lieutenant-general of the kingdom. At his trial, which, from the nature of the accusation and the character of the accused, occasioned to his gratification a great sensation, he made no effort to defend himself, but seemed to glory in the chivalric crime. He was hurried to the guillotine, and met his fate with the greatest composure, assuring the public with a mysterious air, that had he lived four-and-twenty hours longer everything would have been arranged, and the troubles which he foresaw impending for Europe prevented. So successfully had Armine played his part, that his mysterious and doubtful career occasioned a controversy, from which only the appearance of Napoleon distracted universal attention, and which, indeed, only wholly ceased within these few years. What were his intentions? Was he or was he not a sincere Jacobin? If he made the offer to the royal family, why did he vote for their death? Was he resolved, at all events, to be at the head of one of the parties? A middle course would not suit such a man; and so on. Interminable were the queries and their solutions, the pamphlets and the memoirs, which the conduct of this vain man occasioned, and which must assuredly have appeased his manes. Recently it has been discovered that the charge brought against Armine was perfectly false and purely malicious. Its victim, however, could not resist the dazzling celebrity of the imaginary crime, and he preferred the reputation of closing his career by conduct which at once perplexed and astonished mankind, to a vindication which would have deprived his name of some brilliant accessories, and spared him to a life of which he was perhaps wearied.

By the unhappy victim of his vanity and passion Sir Ferdinand Armine left one child, a son, whom he had never seen, now Sir Ratcliffe. Brought up in sadness and in seclusion, education had faithfully developed the characteristics of a reserved and melancholy mind. Pride of lineage and sentiments of religion, which even in early youth darkened into bigotry, were not incompatible with strong affections, a stern sense of duty, and a spirit of chivalric honour. Limited in capacity, he was, however, firm in purpose. Trembling at the name of his father, and devoted to the unhappy parent whose presence he had scarcely ever quitted, a word of reproach had never escaped his lips against the chieftain of his blood, and one, too, whose career, how little soever his child could sympathise with it, still maintained, in men's mouths and minds, the name and memory of the house of Armine. At the death of his father Sir Ratcliffe had just attained his majority, and he succeeded to immense estates encumbered with mortgages, and to considerable debts, which his feelings of honour would have compelled him to discharge, had they indeed been enforced by no other claim. The estates of the family, on their restoration, had not been entailed; but, until Sir Ferdinand no head of the house had abused the confidence of his ancestors, and the vast possessions of the house of Armine had descended unimpaired; and unimpaired, so far as he was concerned, Sir Ratcliffe determined they should remain. Although, by the sale of the estates, not only the encumbrances and liabilities might have been discharged, but himself left in possession of a moderate independence, Sir Ratcliffe at once resolved to part with nothing. Fresh sums were raised for the payment of the debts, and the mortgages now consumed nearly the whole rental of the lands on which they were secured. Sir Ratcliffe obtained for himself only an annuity of three hundred per annum, which he presented to his mother, in addition to the small portion which she had received on her first marriage; and for himself, visiting Armine Place for the first time, he roamed for a few days with sad complacency about that magnificent demesne, and then, taking down from the walls of the magnificent hall the sabre with which his father had defeated the Imperial host, he embarked for Cadiz, and shortly after his arrival obtained a commission in the Spanish service.

Although the hereditary valour of the Armines had descended to their forlorn representative, it is not probable that, under any circumstances, Sir Ratcliffe would have risen to any eminence in the country of his temporary adoption. His was not one of those minds born to command and to create; and his temper was too proud to serve and to solicit. His residence in Spain, however, was not altogether without satisfaction. It was during this sojourn that he gained the little knowledge of life and human nature he possessed; and the creed and solemn manners of the land harmonised with his faith and habits. Among these strangers, too, the proud young Englishman felt not so keenly the degradation of his house; and sometimes, though his was not the fatal gift of imagination, sometimes he indulged in day dreams of its rise. Unpractised in business, and not gifted with that intuitive quickness which supplies experience and often baffles it, Ratcliffe Armine, who had not quitted the domestic hearth even for the purposes of education, was yet fortunate enough to possess a devoted friend: and this was Glastonbury, his tutor, and confessor to his mother. It was to him that Sir Ratcliffe intrusted the management of his affairs, with a confidence which was deserved; for Glastonbury sympathised with all his feelings, and was so wrapped up in the glory of the family, that he had no greater ambition in life than to become their historiographer, and had been for years employed in amassing materials for a great work dedicated to their celebrity.

When Ratcliffe Armine had been absent about three years his mother died. Her death was unexpected. She had not fulfilled two-thirds of the allotted period of the Psalmist, and in spite of many sorrows she was still beautiful. Glastonbury, who communicated to him the intelligence in a letter, in which he vainly attempted to suppress his own overwhelming affliction, counselled his immediate return to England, if but for a season; and the unhappy Ratcliffe followed his advice. By the death of his mother, Sir Ratcliffe Armine became possessed, for the first time, of a small but still an independent income; and having paid a visit, soon after his return to his native country, to a Catholic nobleman to whom his acquaintance had been of some use when travelling in Spain, he became enamored of one of his daughters, and his passion being returned, and not disapproved by the father, he was soon after married to Constance, the eldest daughter of Lord Grandison.

CHAPTER II.

Armine Described.

AFTER his marriage Sir Ratcliffe determined to reside at Armine. In one of the largest parks in England there yet remained a fragment of a vast Elizabethan pile, that in old days bore the name of Armine Place. When Sir Ferdinand had commenced building Armine Castle, he had pulled down the old mansion, partly for the sake of its site and partly for the sake of its materials. Long lines of turreted and many-windowed walls, tall towers, and lofty arches, now rose in picturesque confusion on the green ascent where heretofore old Sir Walsingham had raised the fair and convenient dwelling, which he justly deemed might have served the purpose of a long posterity. The hall and chief staircase of the castle and a gallery alone were finished, and many a day had Sir Ferdinand passed in arranging the pictures, the armour, and choice rarities of these magnificent apartments. The rest of the building was a mere shell; nor was it in all parts even roofed in. Heaps of bricks and stone and piles of timber appeared in every direction; and traces of the sudden stoppage of a great work might be observed in the temporary saw-pits still remaining, the sheds for the workmen, and the kilns and furnaces, which never had been removed. Time, however, that had stained the neglected towers with an antique tint, and had permitted many a generation of summer birds to build their sunny nests on all the coignes of vantage of the unfinished walls, had exercised a mellowing influence even on these rude accessories, and in the course of years they had been so drenched by the rain, and so buffeted by the wind, and had become so covered with moss and ivy, that they rather added to then detracted from the picturesque character of the whole mass.

A few hundred yards from the castle, but situate on the same verdant rising ground, and commanding, although well sheltered, an extensive view over the wide park, was the fragment of the old Place that we have noticed. The rough and undulating rent which marked the severance of the building was now thickly covered with ivy, which in its gamesome luxuriance had contrived also to climb up a remaining stack of tall chimneys, and to spread over the covering of the large oriel window. This fragment contained a set of pleasant chambers, which, having been occupied by the late baronet, were of course furnished with great taste and comfort; and there was, moreover, accommodation sufficient for a small establishment. Armine Place, before Sir Ferdinand, unfortunately for his descendants, determined in the eighteenth century on building a feudal castle, had been situate in famous pleasure-grounds, which extended at the back of the mansion over a space of some hundred acres. The grounds in the immediate vicinity of the buildings had of course suffered severely, but the far greater portion had only been neglected; and there were some indeed who deemed, as they wandered through the arbour-walks of this enchanting wilderness, that its beauty had been enhanced even by this very neglect. It seemed like a forest in a beautiful romance; a green and bowery wilderness where Boccaccio would have loved to woo, and Watteau to paint. So artfully had the walks been planned, that they seemed interminable, nor was there a single point in the whole pleasaunce where the keenest eye could have detected a limit. Sometimes you wandered in those arched and winding walks dear to pensive spirits; sometimes you emerged on a plot of turf blazing in the sunshine, a small and bright savannah, and gazed with wonder on the group of black and mighty cedars that rose from its centre, with their sharp and spreading foliage. The beautiful and the vast blended together;

and the moment after you had beheld with delight a bed of geraniums or of myrtles, you found yourself in an amphitheatre of Italian pines. A strange exotic perfume filled the air: you trod on the flowers of other lands; and shrubs and plants, that usually are only trusted from their conservatories, like sultanas from their jalousies, to sniff the air and recall their bloom, here learning from hardship the philosophy of endurance, had struggled successfully even against northern winters, and wantoned now in native and unpruned luxuriance. Sir Ferdinand, when he resided at Armine, was accustomed to fill these pleasure-grounds with macaws and other birds of gorgeous plumage; but these had fled away with their master, all but some swans which still floated on the surface of a lake, which marked the centre of this paradise. In the remains of the ancient seat of his fathers, Sir Ratcliffe Armine and his bride now sought a home.

The principal chamber of Armine Place was a large irregular room, with a low but richly-carved oaken roof, studded with achievements. This apartment was lighted by the oriel window we have mentioned, the upper panes of which contained some ancient specimens of painted glass, and having been fitted up by Sir Ferdinand as a library, contained a collection of valuable books. From the library you entered through an arched door of glass into a small room, of which, it being much out of repair when the family arrived, Lady Armine had seized the opportunity of gratifying her taste in the adornment. She had hung it with some old-fashioned pea-green damask, that exhibited to a vantage several copies of Spanish paintings by herself, for she was a skilful artist. The third and remaining chamber was the dining-room, a somewhat gloomy chamber, being shadowed by a neighbouring chestnut. A portrait of Sir Ferdinand, when a youth, in a Venetian dress, was suspended over the old-fashioned fireplace; and opposite hung a fine hunting piece by Schneiders. Lady Armine was an amiable and accomplished woman. She had enjoyed the advantage of a foreign education under the inspection of a cautious parent: and a residence on the Continent, while it had afforded her many graces, had not, as unfortunately sometimes is the case, divested her of those more substantial though less showy qualities of which a husband knows the value. She was pious and dutiful: her manners were graceful, for she had visited courts and mixed in polished circles, but she had fortunately not learnt to affect insensibility as a system, or to believe that the essence of good breeding consists in showing your fellow-creatures that you despise them. Her cheerful temper solaced the constitutional gloom of Sir Ratcliffe, and indeed had originally won his heart, even more than her remarkable beauty: and while at the same time she loved a country life, she possessed in a lettered taste, in a beautiful and highly cultivated voice, and in a scientific knowledge of music and of painting, all those resources which prevent retirement from degenerating into loneliness. Her foibles, if we must confess that she was not faultless, endeared her to her husband, for her temper reflected his own pride, and she possessed the taste for splendour which was also his native mood, although circumstances had compelled him to stifle its gratification.

Love, pure and profound, had alone prompted the union between Ratcliffe Armine and Constance Grandison Doubtless, like all of her race, she might have chosen amid the wealthiest of the Catholic nobles and gentry one who would have been proud to have mingled his life with hers; but, with a soul not insensible to the splendid accidents of existence, she yielded her heart to one who could repay the rich sacrifice only with devotion. His poverty, his pride, his dangerous and hereditary gift of beauty, his mournful life, his illustrious lineage, his reserved and romantic mind, had at once attracted her fancy and captivated her heart. She shared all his aspirations and sympathised with all his hopes; and the old glory of the house of Armine, and its revival and restoration, were the object of her daily thoughts, and often of her nightly dreams. With these feelings Lady Armine settled herself at her new home, scarcely with a pang that the whole of the park in which she lived was let out as grazing ground, and only trusting, as she beheld the groups of ruminating cattle, that the day might yet come for the antlered tenants of the bowers to resume their shady dwellings. The good man and his wife who hitherto had inhabited the old Place, and shown the castle and the pleasaunce to passing travellers, were, under the new order of affairs, promoted to the respective offices of serving-man and cook, or butler and housekeeper, as they styled themselves in the village. A maiden brought from Grandison to wait on Lady Armine completed the establishment, with her young brother, who, among numerous duties, performed the office of groom, and attended to a pair of beautiful white ponies which Sir Ratcliffe drove in a phaeton. This equipage, which was remarkable for its elegance, was the especial delight of Lady Armine, and certainly the only piece of splendour in which Sir Ratcliffe indulged. As for neighbourhood, Sir Ratcliffe, on his arrival, of course received a visit from the rector of his parish, and, by the courteous medium of this gentleman, he soon occasioned it to be generally understood that he was not anxious that the example of his rector should be followed. The intimation, in spite of much curiosity, was of course respected. Nobody called upon the Armines. This happy couple, however, were too much engrossed with their own society to require amusement from any other sources than themselves. The honeymoon was passed in wandering in the pleasure-grounds, and in wondering at their own marvellous happiness. Then Lady Armine would sit on a green bank and sing her choicest songs, and Sir Ratcliffe repaid her for her kindness with speeches softer even than serenades. The arrangement of their dwelling occupied the second month; each day witnessed some felicitous yet economical alteration of her creative taste. The third month Lady Armine determined to make a garden.

'I wish,' said her affectionate husband, as he toiled with delight in her service, 'I wish, my dear Constance, that Glastonbury was here; he was such a capital gardener.'

'Let us ask him, dear Ratcliffe; and, perhaps, for such a friend we have already allowed too great a space of time to elapse without sending an invitation.'

'Why, we are so happy,' said Sir Ratcliffe, smiling; 'and yet Glastonbury is the best creature in the world. I hope you will like him, dear Constance.'

'I am sure I shall, dear Ratcliffe. Give me that geranium, love. Write to him, to-day; write to Glastonbury to-day.'

CHAPTER III.

Arrival of Glastonbury.

ADRIAN GLASTONBURY was a younger son of an old but decayed English family. He had been educated at a college of Jesuits in France, and had entered at an early period of life the service of the Romish Church, whose communion his family had never quitted. At college young Glastonbury had been alike distinguished for his assiduous talents and for the extreme benevolence of his disposition. His was one of those minds to which refinement is natural, and which learning and experience never deprive of simplicity. Apparently his passions were not violent; perhaps they were restrained by his profound piety. Next to his devotion, Glastonbury was remarkable for his taste. The magnificent temples in which the mysteries of the Deity and saints he worshipped were celebrated developed the latent predisposition for the beautiful which became almost the master sentiment of his life. In the inspired and inspiring paintings that crowned the altars of the churches and the cathedrals in which he ministered, Glastonbury first studied art; and it was as he glided along the solemn shade of those Gothic aisles, gazing on the brave groining of the vaulted roofs, whose deep and sublime shadows so beautifully contrasted with the sparkling shrines and the delicate chantries below, that he first imbibed that passion for the architecture of the Middle Ages that afterwards led him on many a pleasant pilgrimage with no better companions than a wallet and a sketch-book. Indeed, so sensible was Glastonbury of the influence of the early and constant scene of his youth on his imagination, that he was wont to trace his love of heraldry, of which he possessed a remarkable knowledge, to the emblazoned windows that perpetuated the memory and the achievements of many a pious founder.

When Glastonbury was about twenty-one years of age, he unexpectedly inherited from an uncle a sum which, though by no means considerable, was for him a sufficient independence; and as no opening in the service of the Church at this moment offered itself, which he considered it a duty to pursue, he determined to gratify that restless feeling which seems inseparable from the youth of men gifted with fine sensibilities, and which probably arises in an unconscious desire to quit the commonplace and to discover the ideal. He wandered on foot throughout the whole of Switzerland and Italy; and, after more than three years' absence, returned to England with several thousand sketches, and a complete Alpine Hortus Siccus. He was even more proud of the latter than of having kissed the Pope's toe. In the next seven years the life of Glastonbury was nearly equally divided between the duties of his sacred profession and the gratification of his simple and elegant tastes. He resided principally in Lancashire, where he became librarian to a Catholic nobleman of the highest rank, whose notice he had first attracted by publishing a description of his Grace's residence, illustrated by his drawings. The duke, who was a man of fine taste and antiquarian pursuits, and an exceedingly benevolent person, sought Glastonbury's acquaintance in consequence of the publication, and from that moment a close and cherished intimacy subsisted between them. In the absence of the family, however, Glastonbury found time for many excursions; by means of which he at last completed drawings of all our cathedrals. There remained for him still the abbeys and the minsters of the West of England, a subject on which he was ever eloquent. Glastonbury performed all these excursions on foot, armed only with an ashen staff which he had cut in his early travels, and respecting which he was superstitious; so that he would have no more thought of journeying without this stick than most other people without their hat. Indeed, to speak truth, Glastonbury had been known to quit a house occasionally without that necessary appendage, for, from living much alone, he was not a little absent; but instead of piquing himself on such eccentricities, they ever occasioned him mortification. Yet Glastonbury was an universal favourite, and ever a welcome guest. In his journeys he had no want of hosts; for there was not a Catholic family which would not have been hurt had he passed them without a visit. He was indeed a rarely accomplished personage. An admirable scholar and profound antiquary, he possessed also a considerable practical knowledge of the less severe sciences, was a fine artist, and no contemptible musician. His pen, too, was that of a ready writer; if his sonnets be ever published, they will rank among the finest in our literature.

Glastonbury was about thirty when he was induced by Lady Barbara Armine to quit a roof where he had passed some happy years, and to undertake the education of her son Ratcliffe, a child of eight years of age. From this time Glastonbury in a great degree withdrew himself from his former connexions, and so completely abandoned his previous mode of life, that he never quitted his new home. His pupil repaid him for his zeal rather by the goodness of his disposition and his unblemished conduct, than by any remarkable brilliancy of talents or acquirements: but Ratcliffe, and particularly his mother, were capable of appreciating Glastonbury; and certain it is, whatever might be the cause, he returned their sympathy with deep emotion, for every thought and feeling of his existence seemed dedicated to their happiness and prosperity.

So great indeed was the shock which he experienced at the unexpected death of Lady Barbara, that for some time he meditated assuming the cowl; and if the absence of his pupil prevented the accomplishment of this project, the plan was only postponed, not abandoned. The speedy marriage of Sir Ratcliffe followed. Circumstances had prevented Glastonbury from being present at the ceremony. It was impossible for him to retire to the cloister without seeing his pupil. Business, if not affection, rendered an interview between them necessary. It was equally impossible for Glastonbury to trouble a bride and bridegroom with his presence. When, however, three months had elapsed, he began to believe that he might venture to propose a meeting to Sir Ratcliffe; but while he was yet meditating on this step, he was anticipated by the receipt of a letter containing a warm invitation to Armine.

It was a beautiful sunshiny afternoon in June. Lady Armine was seated in front of the Place looking towards the park, and busied with her work; while Sir Ratcliffe, stretched on the grass, was reading to her the last poem of Scott, which they had just received from the neighbouring town.

'Ratcliffe, my dear,' said Lady Armine, 'some one approaches.'

'A tramper, Constance?'

'No, no, my love; rise; it is a gentleman.'

'Who can it be?' said Sir Ratcliffe, rising; 'perhaps it is your brother, love. Ah! no, it is—it is Glastonbury!'

And at these words he ran forward, jumped over the iron hurdle which separated their lawn from the park, nor stopped his quick pace until he reached a middle-aged man of very prepossessing appearance, though certainly not unsullied by the dust, for assuredly the guest had travelled far and long.

'My dear Glastonbury,' exclaimed Sir Ratcliffe, embracing him, and speaking under the influence of an excitement in which he rarely indulged, 'I am the happiest fellow alive. How do you do? I will introduce you to Constance directly. She is dying to know you, and quite prepared to love you as much as myself. O! my dear Glastonbury, you have no idea how happy I am. She is a perfect angel.'

'I am sure of it,' said Glastonbury, seriously.

Sir Ratcliffe hurried his tutor along. 'Here is my best friend, Constance,' he eagerly exclaimed. Lady Armine rose and welcomed Mr. Glastonbury very cordially. 'Your presence, my dear sir, has, I assure you, been long desired by both of us,' she said, with a delightful smile.

'No compliments, believe me,' added Sir Ratcliffe; 'Constance never pays compliments. She fixed upon your own room herself. She always calls it Mr. Glastonbury's room.'

'Ah! madam,' said Mr. Glastonbury, laying his hand very gently on the shoulder of Sir Ratcliffe, and meaning to say something felicitous, 'I know this dear youth well; and I have always thought whoever could claim this heart should be counted a very fortunate woman.'

'And such the possessor esteems herself,' replied Lady Armine with a smile.

Sir Ratcliffe, after a quarter of an hour or so had passed in conversation, said: 'Come, Glastonbury, you have arrived at a good time, for dinner is at hand. Let me show you to your room. I fear you have had a hot day's journey. Thank God, we are together again. Give me your staff; I will take care of it; no fear of that. So, this way. You have seen the old Place before? Take care of that step. I say, Constance,' said Sir Ratcliffe, in a suppressed voice, and running back to his wife, 'how do you like him?'

'Very much indeed.'

'But do you really?'

'Really, truly.'

'Angel!' exclaimed the gratified Sir Ratcliffe.

CHAPTER IV.

Progress of Affairs at Armine.

LIFE is adventurous. Events are perpetually occurring, even in the calmness of domestic existence, which change in an instant the whole train and tenor of our thoughts and feelings, and often materially influence our fortunes and our character. It is strange, and sometimes as profitable as it is singular, to recall our state on the eve of some acquaintance which transfigures our being; with some man whose philosophy revolutionises our mind; with some woman whose charms metamorphose our career. These retrospective meditations are fruitful of self-knowledge. The visit of Glastonbury was one of those incidents which, from the unexpected results that they occasion, swell into events. He had not been long a guest at Armine before Sir Ratcliffe and his lady could not refrain from mutually communicating to each other the gratification they should feel could Glastonbury be induced to cast his lot among them. His benevolent and placid temper, his many accomplishments, and the entire affection which he evidently entertained for everybody that bore the name, and for everything that related to the fortunes of Armine, all pointed him out as a friend alike to be cherished and to be valued. Under his auspices the garden of the fair Constance soon flourished: his taste guided her pencil, and his voice accompanied her lute. Sir Ratcliffe, too, thoroughly enjoyed his society: Glastonbury was with him the only link, in life, between the present and the past. They talked over old times together; and sorrowful recollections lost half their bitterness, from the tenderness of his sympathetic reminiscences. Sir Ratcliffe, too, was conscious of the value of such a companion for his gifted wife. And Glastonbury, moreover, among his many accomplishments, had the excellent quality of never being in the way. He was aware that young people, and especially young lovers, are not averse sometimes to being alone; and his friends, in his absence, never felt that he was neglected, because his pursuits were so various and his resources so numerous that they were sure he was employed and amused.

In the pleasaunce of Armine, at the termination of a long turfen avenue of purple beeches, there was a turreted gate, flanked by round towers, intended by Sir Ferdinand for one of the principal entrances of his castle. Over the gate were small but convenient chambers, to which you ascended by a winding stair-. case in one of the towers; the other was a mere shell. It was sunset; the long vista gleamed in the dying rays, that shed also a rich breadth of light over the bold and baronial arch. Our friends had been examining the chambers, and Lady Armine, who was a little wearied by the exertion, stood opposite the building, leaning on her husband and his friend.

'A man might go far, and find a worse dwelling than that portal,' said Glastonbury, musingly. 'Me-thinks life might glide away pleasantly enough in those little rooms, with one's books and drawings, and this noble avenue for a pensive stroll.'

'I wish to heaven, my dear Glastonbury, you would try the experiment,' said Sir Ratcliffe.

'Ah! do, Mr. Glastonbury,' added Lady Armine, 'take pity upon us!'

'At any rate, it is not so dull as a cloister,' added Sir Ratcliffe; 'and say what they like, there is nothing like living among friends.'

'You would find me very troublesome,' replied Glastonbury, with a smile; and then, turning the conversation, evidently more from embarrassment than distaste, he remarked the singularity of the purple beeches.

Their origin was uncertain; but one circumstance is sure: that, before another month had passed, Glastonbury was a tenant for life of the portal of Armine Castle, and all his books and collections were safely stowed and arranged in the rooms with which he had been so much pleased.

The course of time for some years flowed on happily at Armine. In the second year of their marriage Lady Armine presented her husband with a son. Their family was never afterwards increased, but the proud father was consoled by the sex of his child for the recollection that the existence of his line depended upon the precious contingency of a single life. The boy was christened Ferdinand. With the exception of an annual visit to Lord Grandison, the Armine family never quitted their home. Necessity as well as taste induced this regularity of life. The affairs of Sir Ratcliffe did not improve. His mortgagees were more strict in their demands of interest than his tenants in payment of their rents. His man of business, who had made his fortune in the service of the family, was not wanting in accommodation to his client; but he was a man of business; he could not sympathise with the peculiar feelings and fancies of Sir Ratcliffe, and he persisted in seizing every opportunity of urging on him the advisability of selling his estates. However, by strict economy and temporary assistance from his lawyer, Sir Ratcliffe, during the first ten years of his marriage, managed to carry on affairs; and though occasional embarrassments sometimes caused him fits of gloom and despondency, the sanguine spirit of his wife, and the confidence in the destiny of their beautiful child which she regularly enforced upon him, maintained on the whole his courage. All their hopes and joys were indeed centred in the education of the little Ferdinand. At ten years of age he was one of those spirited and at the same time docile boys, who seem to combine with the wild and careless grace of childhood the thoughtfulness and self-discipline of maturer age. It was the constant and truthful boast of his parents, that, in spite of all his liveliness, he had never in the whole course of his life disobeyed them. In the village, where he was idolised, they called him 'the little prince;' he was so gentle and so generous, so kind and yet so dignified in his demeanour. His education was remarkable; for though he never quitted home, and lived in such extreme seclusion, so richly gifted were those few persons with whom he passed his life, that it would have been difficult to have fixed upon a youth, however favoured by fortune, who enjoyed greater advantages for the cultivation of his mind and manners. From the first dawn of the intellect of the young Armine, Glastonbury had devoted himself to its culture; and the kind scholar, who had not shrunk from the painful and patient task of impregnating a young mind with the seeds of knowledge, had bedewed its budding promise with all the fertilising influence of his learning and his taste. As Ferdinand advanced in years, he had participated in the accomplishments of his mother; from her he derived not only a taste for the fine arts, but no unskilful practice. She, too, had cultivated the rich voice with which Nature had endowed him, and it was his mother who taught him not only to sing, but to dance. In more manly accomplishments, Ferdinand could not have found a more skilful instructor than his father, a consummate sportsman, and who, like all his ancestors, was remarkable for his finished horsemanship and the certainty of his aim. Under a roof, too, whose inmates were distinguished for their sincere piety and unaffected virtue, the higher duties of existence were not forgotten; and Ferdinand Armine was early and ever taught to be sincere, dutiful, charitable, and just; and to have a deep sense of the great account hereafter to be delivered to his Creator. The very foibles of his parents which he imbibed tended to the maintenance of his magnanimity. His illustrious lineage was early impressed upon him, and inasmuch as little now was left to them but their honour, so it was doubly incumbent upon him to preserve that chief treasure, of which fortune could not deprive them, unsullied.

This much of the education of Ferdinand Armine. With great gifts of nature, with lively and highly cultivated talents, and a most affectionate and disciplined temper, he was adored by the friends who nevertheless had too much sense to spoil him. But for his character, what was that? Perhaps, with all their anxiety and all their care, and all their apparent opportunities for observation, the parent and the tutor are rarely skilful in discovering the character of their child or charge. Custom blunts the fineness of psychological study: those with whom we have lived long and early are apt to blend our essential and our accidental qualities in one bewildering association. The consequences of education and of nature are not sufficiently discriminated. Nor is it, indeed, marvellous, that for a long time temperament should be disguised and even stifled by education; for it is, as it were, a contest between a child and a man.

There were moments when Ferdinand Armine loved to be alone, when he could fly from all the fondness of his friends, and roam in solitude amid the wild and desolate pleasure-grounds, or wander for hours in the halls and galleries of the castle, gazing on the pictures of his ancestors. He ever experienced a strange satisfaction in beholding the portrait of his grandfather. He would sometimes stand abstracted for many minutes before the portrait of Sir Ferdinand in the gallery, painted by Reynolds, before his grandfather left England, and which the child already singularly resembled. But was there any other resemblance between them than form and feature? Did the fiery imagination and the terrible passions of that extraordinary man lurk in the innocent heart and the placid mien of his young descendant? No matter now! Behold, he is a light-hearted and airy child! Thought passes over his brow like a cloud in a summer sky, or the shadow of a bird over the sunshiny earth; and he skims away from the silent hall and his momentary reverie to fly a kite or chase a butterfly!

CHAPTER V.

A Domestic Scene.

YEARS glided away without any remarkable incidents in the life of young Ferdinand. He seldom quitted home, except as companion to Glastonbury in his pedestrian excursions, when he witnessed a different kind of life from that displayed in the annual visit which he paid to Grandison. The boy amused his grandfather, with whom, therefore, he became a favourite. The old Lord, indeed, would have had no objection to his grandson passing half the year with him; and he always returned home with a benediction, a letter full of his praises, and a ten-pound note. Lady Armine was quite delighted with these symptoms of affection on the part of her father towards her child, and augured from them important future results. But Sir Ratcliffe, who was not blessed with so sanguine a temperament as his amiable lady, and who, unbiassed by blood, was perhaps better qualified to form an opinion of the character of his father-in-law, never shared her transports, and seldom omitted an opportunity of restraining them.

'It is all very well, my dear,' he would observe, 'for Ferdinand to visit his relations. Lord Grandison is his grandfather. It is very proper that he should visit his grandfather. I like him to be seen at Grandison. That is all very right. Grandison is a first-rate establishment, where he is certain of meeting persons of his own class, with whom circumstances unhappily,' and here Sir Ratcliffe sighed, 'debar him from mixing; and your father, Constance, is a very good sort of man. I like your father, Constance, you know, very much. No person ever could be more courteous to me than he has ever been. I have no complaints to make of him, Constance; or your brother, or indeed of any member of your family. I like them all. Persons more kind, or more thoroughly bred, I am sure I never knew. And I think they like us. They appear to me to be always really glad to see us, and to be unaffectedly sorry when we quit them. I am sure I should be very happy if it were in my power to return their hospitality, and welcome them at Armine: but it is useless to think of that. God only knows whether we shall be able to remain here ourselves. All I want to make you feel, my love, is, that if you are building any castle in that little brain of yours on the ground of expectations from Grandison, trust me you will be disappointed, my dear, you will, indeed.' 'But, my love—'

'If your father die to-morrow, my dear, he will not leave us a shilling. And who can complain? I cannot. He has always been very frank. I remember when we were going to marry, and I was obliged to talk to him about your portion; I remember it as if it were only yesterday; I remember his saying, with the most flattering smile in the world, "I wish the 5,000L., Sir Ratcliffe, were 50,000L., for your sake; particularly as it will never be in my power to increase it."'

'But, my dear Ratcliffe, surely he may do something for his favourite, Ferdinand?'

'My dear Constance, there you are again! Why favourite? I hate the very word. Your father is a good-natured man, a very good-natured man: he is one of the best-natured men I ever was acquainted with. He has not a single care in the world, and he thinks nobody else has; and what is more, my dear, nobody ever could persuade him that anybody else has. He has no idea of our situation; he never could form an idea of it. If I chose to attempt to make him understand it he would listen with the greatest politeness, shrug his shoulders at the end of the story, tell me to keep up my spirits, and order another bottle of Madeira in order that he might illustrate his precept by practice. He is a good-natured selfish man. He likes us to visit him because you are gay and agreeable, and because I never asked a favour of him in the whole course of our acquaintance: he likes Ferdinand to visit him because he is a handsome fine-spirited boy, and his friends congratulate him on having such a grandson. And so Ferdinand is his favourite; and next year I should not be surprised were he to give him a pony: and perhaps, if he die, he will leave him fifty guineas to buy a gold watch.'

'Well, I dare say you are right, Ratcliffe; but still nothing that you can say will ever persuade me that Ferdinand is not papa's decided favourite.'

'Well! we shall soon see what this favour is worth,' retorted Sir Ratcliffe, rather bitterly.

'Regularly every visit for the last three years your father has asked me what I intended to do with Ferdinand. I said to him last year more than I thought I ever could say to anyone. I told him that Ferdinand was now fifteen, and that I wished to get him a commission; but that I had no influence to get him a commission, and no money to pay for it if it were offered me. I think that was pretty plain; and I have been surprised ever since that I ever could have placed myself in such a degrading position as to say so much.'

'Degrading, my dear Ratcliffe!' said his wife.

'I felt it as such; and such I still feel it.'

At this moment Glastonbury, who was standing at the other end of the room examining a large folio, and who had evidently been uneasy during the whole conversation, attempted to quit the room.

'My dear Glastonbury,' said Sir Ratcliffe, with a forced smile, 'you are alarmed at our domestic broils. Pray, do not leave the room. You know we have no secrets from you.'

'No, pray do not go, Mr. Glastonbury,' added Lady Armine: 'and if indeed there be a domestic broil,' and here she rose and kissed her husband, 'at any rate witness our reconciliation.'

Sir Ratcliffe smiled, and returned his wife's embrace with much feeling.

'My own Constance,' he said, 'you are the dearest wife in the world; and if I ever feel unhappy, believe me it is only because I do not see you in the position to which you are entitled.'

'I know no fortune to be compared to your love, Ratcliffe; and as for our child, nothing will ever persuade me that all will not go right, and that he will not restore the fortunes of the family.'

'Amen!' said Glastonbury, closing the book with a reverberating sound. 'Nor indeed can I believe that Providence will ever desert a great and pious line!'

CHAPTER VI.

Containing Another Domestic Scene.

LADY ARMINE and Glastonbury were both too much interested in the welfare of Sir Ratcliffe not to observe with deep concern that a great, although gradual, change had occurred in his character during the last five years. He had become moody and querulous, and occasionally even irritable. His constitutional melancholy, long diverted by the influence of a vigorous youth, the society of a charming woman, and the interesting feelings of a father, began to reassert its ancient and essential sway, and at times even to deepen into gloom. Sometimes whole days elapsed without his ever indulging in conversation; his nights, once tranquil, were now remarkable for their restlessness; his wife was alarmed at the sighs and agitation of his dreams. He abandoned also his field sports, and none of those innocent sources of amusement, in which it was once his boast their retirement was so rich, now interested him. In vain Lady Armine sought his society in her walks, or consulted him about her flowers. His frigid and monosyllabic replies discouraged all her efforts. No longer did he lean over her easel, or call for a repetition of his favourite song. At times these dark fits passed away, and if not cheerful, he was at least serene. But on the whole he was an altered man; and his wife could no longer resist the miserable conviction that he was an unhappy one.

She, however, was at least spared the mortification, the bitterest that a wife can experience, of feeling that this change in his conduct was occasioned by any indifference towards her; for, averse as Sir Ratcliffe was to converse on a subject so hopeless and ungrateful as the state of his fortune, still there were times in which he could not refrain from communicating to the partner of his bosom all the causes of his misery, and these, indeed, too truly had she divined.

'Alas!' she would sometimes say as she tried to compose his restless pillow; 'what is this pride to which you men sacrifice everything? For me, who am a woman, love is sufficient. Oh! my Ratcliffe, why do you not feel like your Constance? What if these estates be sold, still we are Armines! and still our dear Ferdinand is spared to us! Believe me, love, that if deference to your feelings has prompted my silence, I have long felt that it would be wiser for us at once to meet a necessary evil. For God's sake, put an end to the torture of this life, which is destroying us both. Poverty, absolute poverty, with you and with your love, I can meet even with cheerfulness; but indeed, my Ratcliffe, I can bear our present life no longer; I shall die if you be unhappy. And oh! dearest Ratcliffe, if that were to happen, which sometimes I fear has happened, if you were no longer to love me—'

But here Sir Ratcliffe assured her of the reverse.

'Only think,' she would continue, 'if when we married we had voluntarily done that which we may now be forced to do, we really should have been almost rich people; at least we should have had quite enough to live in ease, and even elegance. And now we owe thousands to that horrible Bagster, who I am sure cheated your father out of house and home, and I dare say, after all, wants to buy Armine for himself.'

'He buy Armine! An attorney buy Armine! Never, Constance, never! I will be buried in its ruins first. There is no sacrifice that I would not sooner make—'

'But, dearest love, suppose we sell it to some one else, and suppose after paying every thing we have thirty thousand pounds left. How well we could live abroad on the interest of thirty thousand pounds?'

'There would not be thirty thousand pounds left now!'

'Well, five-and-twenty, or even twenty. I could manage on twenty. And then we could buy a commission for dear Ferdinand.'

'But to leave our child!'

'Could not he go into the Spanish service? Perhaps you could get a commission in the Spanish Guards for nothing. They must remember you there. And such a name as Armine! I have no doubt that the king would be quite proud to have another Armine in his guard. And then we could live at Madrid; and that would be so delightful, because you speak Spanish so beautifully, and I could learn it very quickly. I am very quick at learning languages, I am, indeed.'

'I think you are very quick at everything, dear Constance. I am sure you are really a treasure of a wife; I have cause every hour to bless you; and, if it were not for my own sake, I should say that I wish you had made a happier marriage.'

'Oh! do not say that, Ratcliffe; say anything but that, Ratcliffe. If you love me I am the happiest woman that ever lived. Be sure always of that.'

'I wonder if they do remember me at Madrid!'

'To be sure they do. How could they forget you; how could they forget my Ratcliffe? I daresay you go to this day by the name of the handsome Englishman.'

'Pooh! I remember when I left England before, I had no wife then, no child, but I remembered who I was, and when I thought I was the last of our race, and that I was in all probability going to spill the little blood that was spared of us in a foreign soil, oh, Constance, I do not think I ever could forget the agony of that moment. Had it been for England, I would have met my fate without a pang. No! Constance, I am an Englishman: I am proud of being an Englishman. My fathers helped to make this country what it is; no one can deny that; and no consideration in the world shall ever induce me again to quit this island.'

'But suppose we do not quit England. Suppose we buy a small estate and live at home.'

'A small estate at home! A small, new estate! Bought of a Mr. Hopkins, a great tallow-chandler, or some stock-jobber about to make a new flight from a Lodge to a Park. Oh no! that would be too degrading.'

'But suppose we keep one of our own manors?'

'And be reminded every instant of every day of those we have lost; and hear of the wonderful improvements of our successors. I should go mad.'

'But suppose we live in London?'

'Where?'

'I am sure I do not know; but I should think we might get a nice little house somewhere.'

'In a suburb! a fitting lodgment for Lady Armine. No! at any rate we will have no witnesses to our fall.'

'But could not we try some place near my father's?'

'And be patronised by the great family with whom I had the good fortune of being connected. No! my dear Constance, I like your father very well, but I could not stand his eleemosynary haunches of venison, and great baskets of apples and cream-cheeses sent with the housekeeper's duty.'

'But what shall we do, dear Ratcliffe?'

'My love, there is no resisting fate. We must live or die at Armine, even if we starve.'

'Perhaps something will turn up. I dreamed the other night that dear Ferdinand married an heiress. Suppose he should? What do you think?'

'Why, even then, that he would not be as lucky as his father. Good night, love!'

CHAPTER VII.

Containing an Unexpected Visit to London, and Its Consequences.

THE day after the conversation in the library to which Glastonbury had been an unwilling listener, he informed his friends that it was necessary for him to visit the metropolis; and as young Ferdinand had never yet seen London, he proposed that he should accompany him. Sir Ratcliffe and Lady Armine cheerfully assented to this proposition; and as for Ferdinand, it is difficult to describe the delight which the anticipation of his visit occasioned him. The three days that were to elapse before his departure did not seem sufficient to ensure the complete packing of his portmanteau: and his excited manner, the rapidity of his conversation, and the restlessness of his movements were very diverting.

'Mamma! is London twenty times bigger than Nottingham? How big is it, then? Shall we travel all night? What o'clock is it now? I wonder if Thursday will ever come? I think I shall go to bed early, to finish the day sooner. Do you think my cap is good enough to travel in? I shall buy a hat in London. I shall get up early the very first morning, and buy a hat. Do you think my uncle is in London? I wish Augustus were not at Eton, perhaps he would be there. I wonder if Mr. Glastonbury will take me to see St. Paul's! I wonder if he will take me to the play. I'd give anything to go to the play. I should like to go to the play and St. Paul's! What fun it will be dining on the road!'

It did indeed seem that Thursday would never come; yet it came at last. The travellers were obliged to rise before the sun, and drive over to Nottingham to meet their coach; so they bid their adieus the previous eve. As for Ferdinand, so fearful was he of losing the coach, that he scarcely slept, and was never convinced that he was really in time, until he found himself planted in breathless agitation outside of the Dart light-post-coach. It was the first time in his life that he had ever travelled outside of a coach. He felt all the excitement of expanding experience and advancing manhood. They whirled along: at the end of every stage Ferdinand followed the example of his fellow-travellers and dismounted, and then with sparkling eyes hurried to Glastonbury, who was inside, to inquire how he sped. 'Capital travelling, isn't it, sir? Did the ten miles within the hour. You have no idea what a fellow our coachman is; and the guard, such a fellow our guard! Don't wait here a moment. Can I get anything for you? We dine at Mill-field. What fun!'

Away whirled the dashing Dart over the rich plains of our merry midland; a quick and dazzling vision of golden corn-fields and lawny pasture land; farmhouses embowered in orchards and hamlets shaded by the straggling members of some vast and ancient forest. Then rose in the distance the dim blue towers, or the graceful spire, of some old cathedral, and soon the spreading causeways announced their approach to some provincial capital. The coachman flanks his leaders, who break into a gallop; the guard sounds his triumphant bugle; the coach bounds over the noble bridge that spans a stream covered with craft; public buildings, guildhalls, and county gaols rise on each side. Rattling through many an inferior way they at length emerge into the High Street, the observed of all observers, and mine host of the Red Lion, or the White Hart, followed by all his waiters, advances from his portal with a smile to receive the 'gentlemen passengers.'

'The coach stops here half an hour, gentlemen: dinner quite ready!'

'Tis a delightful sound. And what a dinner! What a profusion of substantial delicacies! What mighty and iris-tinted rounds of beef! What vast and marble-veined ribs! What gelatinous veal pies! What colossal hams! Those are evidently prize cheeses! And how invigorating is the perfume of those various and variegated pickles! Then the bustle emulating the plenty; the ringing of bells, the clash of thoroughfare, the summoning of ubiquitous waiters, and the all-pervading feeling of omnipotence, from the guests, who order what they please, to the landlord, who can produce and execute everything they can desire. 'Tis a wondrous sight. Why should a man go and see the pyramids and cross the desert, when he has not beheld York Minster or travelled on the Road! Our little Ferdinand amid all this novelty heartily enjoyed himself, and did ample justice to mine host's good cheer. They were soon again whirling along the road; but at sunset, Ferdinand, at the instance of Glastonbury, availed himself of his inside place, and, wearied by the air and the excitement of the day, he soon fell soundly asleep.

Several hours had elapsed, when, awaking from a confused dream in which Armine and all he had lately seen were blended together, he found his fellow-travellers slumbering, and the mail dashing along through the illuminated streets of a great city. The streets were thickly thronged. Ferdinand stared at the magnificence of the shops blazing with lights, and the multitude of men and vehicles moving in all directions. The guard sounded his bugle with treble energy, and the coach suddenly turned through an arched entrance into the court-yard of an old-fashioned inn. His fellow-passengers started and rubbed their eyes.

'So! we have arrived, I suppose,' grumbled one of these gentlemen, taking off his night-cap.

'Yes, gentlemen, I am happy to say our journey is finished,' said a more polite voice; 'and a very pleasant one I have found it. Porter, have the goodness to call me a coach.'

'And one for me,' added the gruff voice.

'Mr. Glastonbury,' whispered the awe-struck Ferdinand, 'is this London?'

'This is London: but we have yet two or three miles to go before we reach our quarters. I think we had better alight and look after our luggage. Gentlemen, good evening!'

Mr. Glastonbury hailed a coach, into which, having safely deposited their portmanteaus, he and Ferdinand entered; but our young friend was so entirely overcome by his feelings and the genius of the place, that he was quite unable to make an observation. Each minute the streets seemed to grow more spacious and more brilliant, and the multitude more dense and more excited.

Beautiful buildings, too, rose before him; palaces, and churches, and streets, and squares of imposing architecture; to his inexperienced eye and unsophisticated spirit their route appeared a never-ending triumph. To the hackney-coachman, however, who had no imagination, and who was quite satiated with metropolitan experience, it only appeared that he had had an exceeding good fare, and that he was jogging up from Bishopsgate Street to Charing Cross.

When Jarvis, therefore, had safely deposited his charge at Morley's Hotel, in Cockspur Street, and extorted from them an extra shilling, in consideration of their evident rustication, he bent his course towards the Opera House; for clouds were gathering, and, with the favour of Providence, there seemed a chance about midnight of picking up some helpless beau, or desperate cabless dandy, the choicest victim, in a midnight shower, of these public conveyancers.

The coffee-room at Morley's was a new scene of amusement to Ferdinand, and he watched with great diversion the two evening papers portioned out among twelve eager quidnuncs, and the evident anxiety which they endured, and the nice diplomacies to which they resorted, to obtain the envied journals. The entrance of our two travellers so alarmingly increasing the demand over the supply, at first seemed to attract considerable and not very friendly notice; but when a malignant half-pay officer, in order to revenge himself for the restless watchfulness of his neighbour, a political doctor of divinity, offered the journal, which he had long finished, to Glastonbury, and it was declined, the general alarm visibly diminished. Poor Mr. Glastonbury had never looked into a newspaper in his life, save the County Chronicle, to which he occasionally contributed a communication, giving an account of the digging up of some old coins, signed Antiquarius; or of the exhumation of some fossil remains, to which he more boldly appended his initials.

In spite of the strange clatter in the streets, Ferdinand slept well, and the next morning, after an early breakfast, himself and his fellow-traveller set out on their peregrinations. Young and sanguine, full of health and enjoyment, innocent and happy, it was with difficulty that Ferdinand could restrain his spirits as he mingled in the bustle of the streets. It was a bright sunny morning, and although the end of June, the town was yet quite full.

'Is this Charing Cross, sir? I wonder if we shall ever be able to get over. Is this the fullest part of the town, sir? What a fine day, sir! How lucky we are in the weather! We are lucky in everything! Whose house is that? Northumberland House! Is it the Duke of Northumberland's? Does he live there? How I should like to see it! Is it very fine? Who is that? What is this? The Admiralty; oh! let me see the Admiralty! The Horse Guards! Oh! where, where? Let us set our watches by the Horse Guards. The guard of our coach always sets his watch by the Horse Guards. Mr. Glastonbury, which is the best clock, the Horse Guards, or St. Paul's? Is that the Treasury? Can we go in? That is Downing Street, is it? I never heard of Downing Street. What do they do in Downing Street? Is this Charing Cross still, or is it Parliament Street? Where does Charing Cross end, and where does Parliament Street begin? By Jove, I see Westminster Abbey!'

After visiting Westminster Abbey and the two Houses of Parliament, Mr. Glastonbury, looking at his watch, said it was now time to call upon a friend of his who lived in St. James's Square. This was the nobleman with whom early in life Glastonbury had been connected, and with whom and whose family he had become so great a favourite, that, notwithstanding his retired life, they had never permitted the connexion entirely to subside. During the very few visits which he had made to the metropolis, he always called in St. James's Square and his reception always assured him that his remembrance imparted pleasure.

When Glastonbury sent up his name he was instantly admitted, and ushered up stairs. The room was full, but it consisted only of a family party. The mother of the Duke, who was an interesting personage, with fine grey hair, a clear blue eye, and a soft voice, was surrounded by her great-grandchildren, who were at home for the Midsummer holidays, and who had gathered together at her rooms this morning to consult upon amusements. Among them was the heir presumptive of the house, a youth of the age of Ferdinand, and of a prepossessing appearance. It was difficult to meet a more amiable and agreeable family, and nothing could exceed the kindness with which they all welcomed Glastonbury. The Duke himself soon appeared. 'My dear, dear Glastonbury,' he said, 'I heard you were here, and I would come. This shall be a holiday for us all. Why, man, you bury yourself alive!'

'Mr. Armine,' said the Duchess, pointing to Ferdinand.

'Mr. Armine, how do you do? Your grandfather and I were well acquainted. I am glad to know his grandson. I hope your father, Sir Ratcliffe, and Lady Armine are well. My dear Glastonbury, I hope you have come to stay a long time. You must dine with us every day. You know we are very old-fashioned people; we do not go much into the world; so you will always find us at home, and we will do what we can to amuse your young friend. Why, I should think he was about the same age as Digby? Is he at Eton? His grandfather was. I shall never forget the time he

cut off old Barnard's pig-tail. He was a wonderful man, poor Sir Ferdinand! he was indeed.'
While his Grace and Glastonbury maintained their conversation, Ferdinand conducted himself
with so much spirit and propriety towards the rest of the party, and gave them such a lively and
graceful narrative of all his travels up to town, and the wonders he had already witnessed, that
they were quite delighted with him; and, in short, from this moment, during his visit to London
he was scarcely ever out of their society, and every day became a greater favourite with them.
His letters to his mother, for he wrote to her almost every day, recounted all their successful
efforts for his amusement, and it seemed that he passed his mornings in a round of sight-seeing,
and that he went to the play every night of his life. Perhaps there never existed a human being
who at this moment more thoroughly enjoyed life than Ferdinand Armine.

In the meantime, while he thought only of amusement, Mr. Glastonbury was not inattentive to
his more important interests; for the truth is that this excellent man had introduced him to the
family only with the hope of interesting the feelings of the Duke in his behalf. His Grace was a
man of a generous disposition. He sympathised with the recital of Glastonbury as he detailed to
him the unfortunate situation of this youth, sprung from so illustrious a lineage, and yet cut off
by a combination of unhappy circumstances from almost all those natural sources whence he
might have expected support and countenance. And when Glastonbury, seeing that the Duke's
heart was moved, added that all he required for him, Ferdinand, was a commission in the army,
for which his parents were prepared to advance the money, his Grace instantly declared that he
would exert all his influence to obtain their purpose.

Mr. Glastonbury was, therefore, more gratified than surprised when, a few days after the
conversation which we have mentioned, his noble friend informed him, with a smile, that he
believed all might be arranged, provided his young charge could make it convenient to quit
England at once. A vacancy had unexpectedly occurred in a regiment just ordered to Malta, and
an ensigncy had been promised to Ferdinand Armine. Mr. Glastonbury gratefully closed with the
offer. He sacrificed a fourth part of his moderate independence in the purchase of the
commission and the outfit of his young friend, and had the supreme satisfaction, ere the third
week of their visit was completed, of forwarding a Gazette to Armine, containing the
appointment of Ferdinand Armine as Ensign in the Royal Fusiliers.

CHAPTER VIII.

A Visit to Glastonbury's Chamber.

IT WAS arranged that Ferdinand should join his regiment by the next Mediterranean packet, which was not to quit Falmouth for a fortnight. Glastonbury and himself, therefore, lost no time in bidding adieu to their kind friends in London, and hastening to Armine. They arrived the day after the Gazette. They found Sir Ratcliffe waiting for them at the town, and the fond smile and cordial embrace with which he greeted Glastonbury more than repaid that good man for all his exertions. There was, notwithstanding, a perceptible degree of constraint both on the part of the baronet and his former tutor. It was evident that Sir Ratcliffe had something on his mind of which he wished to disburden himself; and it was equally apparent that Glastonbury was unwilling to afford him an opportunity. Under these rather awkward circumstances, it was perhaps fortunate that Ferdinand talked without ceasing, giving his father an account of all he had seen, done, and heard, and of all the friends he had made, from the good Duke of——-to that capital fellow, the guard of the coach.

They were at the park gates: Lady Armine was there to meet them. The carriage stopped; Ferdinand jumped out and embraced his mother. She kissed him, and ran forward and extended both her hands to Mr. Glastonbury. 'Deeds, not words, must show our feelings,' she said, and the tears glittered in her beautiful eyes; Glastonbury, with a blush, pressed her hand to his lips. After dinner, during which Ferdinand recounted all his adventures, Lady Armine invited him, when she rose, to walk with her in the garden. It was then, with an air of considerable confusion, clearing his throat, and filling his glass at the same time, that Sir Ratcliffe said to his remaining guest,

'My dear Glastonbury, you cannot suppose that I believe that the days of magic have returned. This commission, both Constance and myself feel, that is, we are certain, that you are at the bottom of it all. The commission is purchased. I could not expect the Duke, deeply as I feel his generous kindness, to purchase a commission for my son: I could not permit it. No! Glastonbury,' and here Sir Ratcliffe became more animated, 'you could not permit it, my honour is safe in your hands?' Sir Ratcliffe paused for a reply.

'On that score my conscience is clear,' replied Glastonbury.

'It is, then,—it must be then as I suspect,' rejoined Sir Ratcliffe. 'I am your debtor for this great service.'

'It is easy to count your obligations to me,' said Glastonbury, 'but mine to you and yours are incalculable.'

'My dear Glastonbury,' said Sir Ratcliffe, pushing his glass away as he rose from his seat and walked up and down the room, 'I may be proud, but I have no pride for you, I owe you too much; indeed, my dear friend, there is nothing that I would not accept from you, were it in your power to grant what you would desire. It is not pride, my dear Glastonbury; do not mistake me; it is not pride that prompts this explanation; but—but—had I your command of language I would explain myself more readily; but the truth is, I—I—I cannot permit that you should suffer for us, Glastonbury, I cannot indeed.'

Mr. Glastonbury looked at Sir Ratcliffe steadily; then rising from his seat he took the baronet's arm, and without saying a word walked slowly towards the gates of the castle where he lodged, and which we have before described. When he had reached the steps of the tower he withdrew his arm, and saying, 'Let me be pioneer,' invited Sir Ratcliffe to follow him. They accordingly entered his chamber.

It was a small room lined with shelves of books, except in one spot, where was suspended a portrait of Lady Barbara, which she had bequeathed him in her will. The floor was covered with so many boxes and cases that it was not very easy to steer a course when you had entered. Glastonbury, however, beckoned to his companion to seat himself in one of his two chairs, while he unlocked a small cabinet, from a drawer of which he brought forth a paper.

'It is my will,' said Glastonbury, handing it to Sir Ratcliffe, who laid it down on the table.

'Nay, I wish you, my dear friend, to peruse it, for it concerns yourself.'

'I would rather learn its contents from yourself, if you positively desire me,' replied Sir Ratcliffe.

'I have left everything to our child,' said Glastonbury; for thus, when speaking to the father alone, he would often style the son.

'May it be long before he enjoys the 'bequest,' said Sir Ratcliffe, brushing away a tear; 'long, very long.'

'As the Almighty pleases,' said Glastonbury, crossing himself. 'But living or dead, I look upon all as Ferdinand's, and hold myself but the steward of his inheritance, which I will never abuse.'

'O! Glastonbury, no more of this I pray; you have wasted a precious life upon our forlorn race. Alas! how often and how keenly do I feel, that had it not been for the name of Armine your great talents and goodness might have gained for you an enviable portion of earthly felicity; yes, Glastonbury, you have sacrificed yourself to us.'

'Would that I could!' said the old man, with brightening eyes and an unaccustomed energy of manner. 'Would that I could! would that any act of mine, I care not what, could revive the fortunes of the house of Armine. Honoured for ever be the name, which with me is associated with all that is great and glorious in man, and [here his voice faltered, and he turned away his face] exquisite and enchanting in woman!

'No, Ratcliffe,' he resumed, 'by the memory of one I cannot name, by that blessed and saintly being from whom you derive your life, you will not, you cannot deny this last favour I ask, I entreat, I supplicate you to accord me: me, who have ever eaten of your bread, and whom your roof hath ever shrouded!'

'My friend, I cannot speak,' said Sir Ratcliffe, throwing himself back in the chair and covering his face with his right hand; 'I know not what to say; I know not what to feel.'

Glastonbury advanced, and gently took his other hand. 'Dear Sir Ratcliffe,' he observed, in his usual calm, sweet voice, 'if I have erred you will pardon me. I did believe that, after my long and intimate connection with your house; after having for nearly forty years sympathised as deeply with all your fortunes as if, indeed, your noble blood flowed in these old veins; after having been honoured on your side with a friendship which has been the consolation and charm of my existence; indeed, too great a blessing; I did believe, more especially when I reminded myself of the unrestrained manner in which I had availed myself of the advantages of that friendship, I did believe, actuated by feelings which perhaps I cannot describe, and thoughts to which I cannot now give utterance, that I might venture, without offence, upon this slight service: ay, that the offering might be made in the spirit of most respectful affection, and not altogether be devoid of favour in your sight.'

'Excellent, kind-hearted man!' said Sir Ratcliffe, pressing the hand of Glastonbury in his own; 'I accept your offering in the spirit of perfect love. Believe me, dearest friend, it was no feeling of false pride that for a moment influenced me; I only felt-'

'That in venturing upon this humble service I deprived myself of some portion of my means of livelihood: you are mistaken. When I cast my lot at Armine I sank a portion of my capital on my life; so slender are my wants here, and so little does your dear lady permit me to desire, that, believe me, I have never yet expended upon myself this apportioned income; and as for the rest, it is, as you have seen, destined for our Ferdinand. Yet a little time and Adrian Glastonbury must be gathered to his fathers. Why, then, deprive him of the greatest gratification of his remaining years? the consciousness that, to be really serviceable to those he loves, it is not necessary for him to cease to exist.'

'May you never repent your devotion to our house!' said Sir Ratcliffe, rising from his seat. 'Time was we could give them who served us something better than thanks; but, at any rate, these come from the heart.'

CHAPTER IX.

The Last Day and the Last Night.

IN THE meantime, the approaching I departure of Ferdinand was the great topic of interest at Armine, It was settled that his father should accompany him to Falmouth, where he was to embark; and that they should pay a visit on their way to his grandfather, whose seat was situate in the west of England. This separation, now so near at hand, occasioned Lady Armine the deepest affliction; but she struggled to suppress her emotion. Yet often, while apparently busied with the common occupations of the day, the tears trickled down her cheek; and often she rose from her restless seat, while surrounded by those she loved, to seek the solitude of her chamber and indulge her overwhelming sorrow. Nor was Ferdinand less sensible of the bitterness of this separation. With all the excitement of his new prospects, and the feeling of approaching adventure and fancied independence, so flattering to inexperienced youth, he could not forget that his had been a very happy home. Nearly seventeen years of an innocent existence had passed, undisturbed by a single bad passion, and unsullied by a single action that he could regret. The river of his life had glided along, reflecting only a cloudless sky. But if he had been dutiful and happy, if at this moment of severe examination his conscience were serene, he could not but feel how much this enviable state of mind was to be attributed to those who had, as it were, imbued his life with love; whose never-varying affection had developed all the kindly feelings of his nature, had anticipated all his wants, and listened to all his wishes; had assisted him in difficulty and guided him in doubt; had invited confidence by kindness, and deserved it by sympathy; had robbed instruction of all its labour, and discipline of all its harshness.

It was the last day; on the morrow he was to quit Armine. He strolled about among the mouldering chambers of the castle, and a host of thoughts and passions, like clouds in a stormy sky, coursed over his hitherto serene and light-hearted breast. In this first great struggle of his soul some symptoms of his latent nature developed themselves, and, amid the rifts of the mental tempest, occasionally he caught some glimpses of self-knowledge. Nature, that had endowed him with a fiery imagination and a reckless courage, had tempered those dangerous, and, hitherto, those undeveloped and untried gifts, with a heart of infinite sensibility. Ferdinand Armine was, in truth, a singular blending of the daring and the soft; and now, as he looked around him and thought of his illustrious and fallen race, and especially of that extraordinary man, of whose splendid and ruinous career, that man's own creation, the surrounding pile, seemed a fitting emblem, he asked himself if he had not inherited the energies with the name of his grandsire, and if their exertion might not yet revive the glories of his line. He felt within him alike the power and the will; and while he indulged in magnificent reveries of fame and glory and heroic action, of which career, indeed, his approaching departure was to be the commencement, the association of ideas led his recollection to those beings from whom he was about to depart. His fancy dropped like a bird of paradise in full wing, tumbling exhausted in the sky: he thought of his innocent and happy boyhood, of his father's thoughtful benevolence, his sweet mother's gentle assiduities, and Glastonbury's devotion; and he demanded aloud, in a voice of anguish, whether Fate could indeed supply a lot more exquisite than to pass existence in these calm and beauteous bowers with such beloved companions.

His name was called: it was his mother's voice. He dashed away a desperate tear, and came forth with a smiling face. His mother and father were walking together at a little distance.

'Ferdinand,' said Lady Armine, with an air of affected gaiety, 'we have just been settling that you are to send me a gazelle from Malta.' And in this strain, speaking of slight things, yet all in some degree touching upon the mournful incident of the morrow, did Lady Armine for some time converse, as if she were all this time trying the fortitude of her mind, and accustoming herself to a catastrophe which she was resolved to meet with fortitude.

While they were walking together, Glastonbury, who was hurrying from his rooms to the Place, for the dinner hour was at hand, joined them, and they entered their home together. It was singular at dinner, too, in what excellent spirits everybody determined to be. The dinner also, generally a simple repast, was almost as elaborate as the demeanour of the guests, and, although no one felt inclined to eat, consisted of every dish and delicacy which was supposed to be a favourite with Ferdinand. Sir Ratcliffe, in general so grave, was to-day quite joyous, and produced a magnum of claret which he had himself discovered in the old cellars, and of which even Glastonbury, an habitual water-drinker, ventured to partake. As for Lady Armine, she scarcely ever ceased talking; she found a jest in every sentence, and seemed only uneasy when there was silence. Ferdinand, of course, yielded himself to the apparent spirit of the party; and, had a stranger been present, he could only have supposed that they were celebrating some anniversary of domestic joy. It seemed rather a birth-day feast than the last social meeting of those who had lived together so long, and loved each other so dearly.

But as the evening drew on their hearts began to grow heavy, and every one was glad that the early departure of the travellers on the morrow was an excuse for speedily retiring.

'No adieus to-night!' said Lady Armine with a gay air, as she scarcely returned the habitual embrace of her son. 'We shall be all up to-morrow.'

So wishing his last good night with a charged heart and faltering tongue, Ferdinand Armine took up his candle and retired to his chamber. He could not refrain from exercising an unusual scrutiny when he had entered the room. He held up the light to the old accustomed walls, and threw a parting glance of affection at the curtains. There was the glass vase which his mother had never omitted each day to fill with fresh flowers, and the counterpane that was her own handiwork. He kissed it; and, flinging off his clothes, was glad when he was surrounded with darkness and buried in his bed.

There was a gentle tap at his door. He started.

'Are you in bed, my Ferdinand?' inquired his mother's voice.

Ere he could reply he heard the door open, and observed a tall white figure approaching him. Lady Armine, without speaking, knelt down by his bedside and took him in her arms. She buried her face in his breast. He felt her tears upon his heart. He could not move; he could not speak. At length he sobbed aloud.

'May our Father that is in heaven bless you, my darling child; may He guard over you; may He preserve you!' Very weak was her still, solemn voice. 'I would have spared you this, my darling. For you, not for myself, have I controlled my feelings. But I knew not the strength of a mother's love. Alas! what mother has a child like thee? O! Ferdinand, my first, my only-born: child of love and joy and happiness, that never cost me a thought of sorrow; so kind, so gentle, and so dutiful! must we, oh! must we indeed part?'

'It is too cruel,' continued Lady Armine, kissing with a thousand kisses her weeping child. 'What have I done to deserve such misery as this? Ferdinand, beloved Ferdinand, I shall die.'

'I will not go, mother, I will not go,' wildly exclaimed the boy, disengaging himself from her embrace and starting up in his bed. 'Mother, I cannot go. No, no, it never can be good to leave a home like this.'

'Hush! hush! my darling. What words are these? How unkind, how wicked it is of me to say all this! Would that I had not come! I only meant to listen at your door a minute, and hear you move, perhaps to hear you speak, and like a fool,—how naughty of me! never, never shall I forgive myself-like a miserable fool I entered.'

'My own, own mother, what shall I say? what shall I do? I love you, mother, with all my heart and soul and spirit's strength: I love you, mother. There is no mother loved as you are loved!'

"Tis that that makes me mad. I know it. Oh! why are you not like other children, Ferdinand? When your uncle left us, my father said, "Good-bye," and shook his hand; and he—he scarcely kissed us, he was so glad to leave his home; but you-tomorrow; no, not to-morrow. Can it be to-morrow?'

'Mother, let me get up and call my father, and tell him I will not go.'

'Good God! what words are these? Not go! 'Tis all your hope to go; all ours, dear child. What would your father say were he to hear me speak thus? Oh! that I had not entered! What a fool I am!'

'Dearest, dearest mother, believe me we shall soon meet.'

'Shall we soon meet? God! how joyous will be the day.'

'And I—I will write to you by every ship.'

'Oh! never fail, Ferdinand, never fail.'

'And send you a gazelle, and you shall call it by my name, dear mother.'

'Darling child!'

'You know I have often stayed a month at grand-papa's, and once six weeks. Why! eight times six weeks, and I shall be home again.'

'Home! home again! eight times six weeks; a year, nearly a year! It seems eternity. Winter, and spring, and summer, and winter again, all to pass away. And for seventeen years he has scarcely been out of my sight. Oh! my idol, my beloved, my darling Ferdinand, I cannot believe it; I cannot believe that we are to part.'

'Mother, dearest mother, think of my father; think how much his hopes are placed on me; think, dearest mother, how much I have to do. All now depends on me, you know. I must restore our house.'

'O! Ferdinand, I dare not express the thoughts that rise upon me; yet I would say that, had I but my child, I could live in peace; how, or where, I care not.'

'Dearest mother, you unman me.'

'It is very wicked. I am a fool. I never, no! never shall pardon myself for this night, Ferdinand.'

'Sweet mother, I beseech you calm yourself. Believe me we shall indeed meet very soon, and somehow or other a little bird whispers to me we shall yet be very happy.'

'But will you be the same Ferdinand to me as before? Ay! There it is, my child. You will be a man when you come back, and be ashamed to love your mother. Promise me now,' said Lady Armine, with extraordinary energy, 'promise me, Ferdinand, you will always love me. Do not let them make you ashamed of loving me. They will joke, and jest, and ridicule all home affections. You are very young, sweet love, very, very young, and very inexperienced and susceptible. Do not let them spoil your frank and beautiful nature. Do not let them lead you astray. Remember Armine, dear, dear Armine, and those who live there. Trust me, oh! yes, indeed believe me, darling, you will never find friends in this world like those you leave at Armine.'

'I know it,' exclaimed Ferdinand, with streaming eyes; 'God be my witness how deeply I feel that truth. If I forget thee and them, dear mother, may God indeed forget me.'

'My Ferdinand,' said Lady Armine, in a calm tone, 'I am better now. I hardly am sorry that I did come now. It will be a consolation to me in your absence to remember all you have said. Good night, my beloved child; my darling child, good night. I shall not come down to-morrow, dear. We will not meet again; I will say good-bye to you from the window. Be happy, my dear Ferdinand, and as you say indeed, we shall soon meet again. Eight-and-forty weeks! Why what are eight-and-forty weeks? It is not quite a year. Courage, my sweet boy! let us keep up each other's spirits. Who knows what may yet come from this your first venture into the world? I am full of hope. I trust you will find all that you want. I packed up everything myself. Whenever you want anything write to your mother. Mind, you have eight packages; I have written them down on a card and placed it on the hall table. And take the greatest care of old Sir Ferdinand's sword. I am very superstitious about that sword, and while you have it I am sure you will succeed. I have ever thought that had he taken it with him to France all would have gone right with him. God bless, God Almighty bless you, child. Be of good heart. I will write you everything that takes place, and, as you say, we shall soon meet. Indeed, after to-night,' she added in a more mournful tone, 'we have naught else to think of but of meeting. I fear it is very late. Your father will be surprised at my absence.' She rose from his bed and walked up and down the room several times in silence; then again approaching him, she folded him in her arms and quitted the chamber without again speaking.

CHAPTER X.

The Advantage of Being a Favourite Grandson.

THE exhausted Ferdinand found consolation in sleep. When he woke the dawn was just breaking. He dressed and went forth to look, for the last time, on his hereditary woods. The air was cold, but the sky was perfectly clear, and the beams of the rising sun soon spread over the blue heaven. How fresh, and glad, and sparkling was the surrounding scene! With what enjoyment did he inhale the soft and renovating breeze! The dew quivered on the grass, and the carol of the wakening birds, roused from their slumbers by the spreading warmth, resounded from the groves. From the green knoll on which he stood he beheld the clustering village of Armine, a little agricultural settlement formed of the peasants alone who lived on the estate. The smoke began to rise in blue curls from the cottage chimneys, and the church clock struck the hour of five. It seemed to Ferdinand that those labourers were far happier than he, since the setting sun would find them still at Armine: happy, happy Armine!

The sound of carriage wheels roused him from his reverie. The fatal moment had arrived. He hastened to the gate according to his promise, to bid farewell to Glastonbury. The good old man was up. He pressed his pupil to his bosom, and blessed him with a choking voice.

'Dearest and kindest friend!' murmured Ferdinand. Glastonbury placed round his neck a small golden crucifix that had belonged to Lady Barbara. 'Wear it next your heart, my child,' said he; 'it will remind you of your God, and of us all.' Ferdinand quitted the tower with a thousand blessings.

When he came in sight of the Place he saw his father standing by the carriage, which was already packed. Ferdinand ran into the house to get the card which had been left on the hall table for him by his mother. He ran over the list with the old and faithful domestic, and shook hands with him. Nothing now remained. All was ready. His father was seated. Ferdinand stood a moment in thought. 'Let me run up to my mother, sir?' 'You had better not, my child,' replied Sir Ratcliffe, 'she does not expect you. Come, come along.' So he slowly seated himself, with his eyes fixed on the window of his mother's chamber; and as the carriage drove off the window opened, and a hand waved a white handkerchief. He saw no more; but as he saw it he clenched his hand in agony.

How different was this journey to London from his last! He scarcely spoke a word. Nothing interested him but his own feelings. The guard and the coachman, and the bustle of the inn, and the passing spectacles of the road, appeared a collection of impertinences. All of a sudden it seemed that his boyish feelings had deserted him. He was glad when they arrived in London, and glad that they were to stay in it only a single day. Sir Ratcliffe and his son called upon the Duke; but, as they had anticipated, the family had quitted town. Our travellers put up at Hatchett's, and the following night started for Exeter in the Devonport mail. Ferdinand arrived at the western metropolis having interchanged with his father scarcely a hundred sentences. At Exeter, after a night of most welcome rest, they took a post-chaise and proceeded by a cross-road to Grandison. When Lord Grandison, who as yet was perfectly unacquainted with the revolutions in the Armine family, had clearly comprehended that his grandson had obtained a commission without either troubling him for his interest, or putting him in the disagreeable predicament of refusing his money, there were no bounds to the extravagant testimonials of his affection, both towards his son-in-law and his grandson. He seemed quite proud of such relations; he patted Sir Ratcliffe on his back, asked a thousand questions about his darling Constance, and hugged and slobbered over Ferdinand as if he were a child of five years old. He informed all his guests daily (and the house was full) that Lady Armine was his favourite daughter, and Sir Ratcliffe his favourite son-in-law, and Ferdinand especially his favourite grandchild. He insisted upon Sir Ratcliffe always sitting at the head of his table, and always placed Ferdinand on his own right hand. He asked his butler aloud at dinner why he had not given a particular kind of Burgundy, because Sir Ratcliffe Armine was here.

'Darbois,' said the old nobleman, 'have not I told you that Clos de Vougeot is always to be kept for Sir Ratcliffe Armine? It is his favourite wine. Clos de Vougeot directly to Sir Ratcliffe Armine. I do not think, my dear madam [turning to a fair neighbour], that I have yet had the pleasure of introducing you to my son-in-law, my favourite son-in-law, Sir Ratcliffe Armine. He married my daughter Constance, my favourite daughter, Constance. Only here for a few days, a very, very few days indeed. Quite a flying visit. I wish I could see the whole family oftener and longer. Passing through to Falmouth with his son, this young gentleman on my right, my grandson, my favourite grandson, Ferdinand. Just got his commission. Ordered for Malta immediately. He is in the Fusileers, the Royal Fusileers. Very difficult, my dear madam, in these days to obtain a commission, especially a commission in the Royal Fusileers. Very great interest required, very great interest, indeed. But the Armines are a most ancient family, very highly connected, very highly connected; and, between you and me, the Duke of——would do anything for them.

Come, come, Captain Armine, take a glass of wine with your old grandfather.'

'How attached the old gentleman appears to be to his grandson!' whispered the lady to her neighbour.

'Delightful! yes!' was the reply, 'I believe he is the favourite grandson.'

In short, the old gentleman at last got so excited by the universal admiration lavished on his favourite grandson, that he finally insisted on seeing the young hero in his regimentals; and when Ferdinand took his leave, after a great many whimpering blessings, his domestic feelings were worked up to such a pitch of enthusiasm, that he absolutely presented his grandson with a hundred-pound note.

'Thank you, my dear grandpapa,' said the astonished Ferdinand, who really did not expect more than fifty, perhaps even a moiety of that more moderate sum; 'thank you, my dear grandpapa; I am very much obliged to you, indeed.'

'I wish I could do more for you; I do, indeed,' said Lord Grandison; 'but nobody ever thinks of paying his rent now. You are my grandson, my favourite grandson, my dear favourite daughter's only child. And you are an officer in his Majesty's service, an officer in the Royal Fusiliers, only think of that! It is the most unexpected thing that ever happened to me. To see you so well and so unexpectedly provided for, my dear child, has taken a very great load off my mind; it has indeed. You have no idea of a parent's anxiety in these matters, especially of a grandfather. You will some day, I warrant you,' continued the noble grandfather, with an expression between a giggle and a leer; 'but do not be wild, my dear Ferdinand, do not be too wild at least. Young blood must have its way; but be cautious; now, do; be cautious, my dear child. Do not get into any scrapes; at least, do not get into any serious scrapes; and whatever happens to you,' and here his lordship assumed even a solemn tone, 'remember you have friends; remember, my dear boy, you have a grandfather, and that you, my dear Ferdinand, are his favourite grandson.'

This passing visit to Grandison rather rallied the spirits of our travellers. When they arrived at

Falmouth, they found, however, that the packet, which waited for government despatches, was not yet to sail. Sir Ratcliffe scarcely knew whether he ought to grieve or to rejoice at the reprieve; but he determined to be gay. So Ferdinand and himself passed their mornings in visiting the mines, Pendennis Castle, and the other lions of the neighbourhood; and returned in the evening to their cheerful hotel, with good appetites for their agreeable banquet, the mutton of Dartmoor and the cream of Devon.

At length, however, the hour of separation approached; a message awaited them at the inn, on their return from one of their rambles, that Ferdinand must be on board at an early hour on the morrow. That evening the conversation between Sir Ratcliffe and his son was of a graver nature than they usually indulged in. He spoke to him in confidence of his affairs. Dark hints, indeed, had before reached Ferdinand; nor, although his parents had ever spared his feelings, could his intelligent mind have altogether refrained from guessing much that had never been formally communicated. Yet the truth was worse even than he had anticipated. Ferdinand, however, was young and sanguine. He encouraged his father with his hopes, and supported him by his sympathy. He expressed to Sir Ratcliffe his confidence that the generosity of his grandfather would prevent him at present from becoming a burden to his own parent, and he inwardly resolved that no possible circumstance should ever induce him to abuse the benevolence of Sir Ratcliffe.

The moment of separation arrived. Sir Ratcliffe pressed to his bosom his only, his loving, and his beloved child. He poured over Ferdinand the deepest, the most fervid blessing that a father ever granted to a son. But, with all this pious consolation, it was a moment of agony.

BOOK II.

CHAPTER I.

Partly Retrospective, yet Very Necessary to be Perused.

EARLY five years had elapsed between the event which formed the subject of our last chapter and the recall to England of the regiment in which Captain Armine now commanded a company. This period of time had passed away not unfruitful of events in the experience of that family, in whose fate and feelings I have attempted to interest the reader. In this interval Ferdinand Armine had paid one short visit to his native land; a visit which had certainly been accelerated, if not absolutely occasioned, by the untimely death of his cousin Augustus, the presumptive heir of Grandison. This unforeseen event produced a great revolution in the prospects of the family of Armine; for although the title and an entailed estate devolved to a distant branch, the absolute property of the old lord was of great amount; and, as he had no male heir now living, conjectures as to its probable disposition were now rife among all those who could possibly become interested in it. Whatever arrangement the old lord might decide upon, it seemed nearly certain that the Armine family must be greatly benefited. Some persons even went so far as to express their conviction that everything would be left to Mr. Armine, who everybody now discovered to have always been a particular favourite with his grandfather. At all events, Sir Ratcliffe, who ever maintained upon the subject a becoming silence, thought it as well that his son should remind his grandfather personally of his existence; and it was at his father's suggestion that Ferdinand had obtained a short leave of absence, at the first opportunity, to pay a hurried visit to Grandison and his grandfather.

The old lord yielded him a reception which might have flattered the most daring hopes. He embraced Ferdinand, and pressed him to his heart a thousand times; he gave him his blessing in the most formal manner every morning and evening; and assured everybody that he now was not only his favourite but his only grandson. He did not even hesitate to affect a growing dislike for his own seat, because it was not in his power to leave it to Ferdinand; and he endeavoured to console that fortunate youth for his indispensable deprivation by mysterious intimations that he would, perhaps, find quite enough to do with his money in completing Armine Castle, and maintaining its becoming splendour. The sanguine Ferdinand returned to Malta with the conviction that he was his grandfather's heir; and even Sir Ratcliffe was almost disposed to believe that his son's expectations were not without some show of probability, when he found that Lord Grandison had absolutely furnished him with the funds for the purchase of his company.

Ferdinand was fond of his profession. He had entered it under favourable circumstances. He had joined a crack regiment in a crack garrison. Malta is certainly a delightful station. Its city, Valetta, equals in its noble architecture, if it even do not excel, any capital in Europe; and although it must be confessed that the surrounding region is little better than a rock, the vicinity, nevertheless, of Barbary, of Italy, and of Sicily, presents exhaustless resources to the lovers of the highest order of natural beauty. If that fair Valetta, with its streets of palaces, its picturesque forts and magnificent church, only crowned some green and azure island of the Ionian Sea, Corfu for instance, I really think that the ideal of landscape would be realised.

To Ferdinand, who was inexperienced in the world, the dissipation of Malta, too, was delightful. It must be confessed that, under all circumstances, the first burst of emancipation from domestic routine hath in it something fascinating. However you may be indulged at home, it is impossible to break the chain of childish associations; it is impossible to escape from the feeling of dependence and the habit of submission. Charming hour when you first order your own servants, and ride your own horses, instead of your father's! It is delightful even to kick about your own furniture; and there is something manly and magnanimous in paying our own taxes. Young, lively, kind, accomplished, good-looking, and well-bred, Ferdinand Armine had in him all the elements of popularity; and the novelty of popularity quite intoxicated a youth who had passed his life in a rural seclusion, where he had been appreciated, but not huzzaed. Ferdinand was not only popular, but proud of being popular. He was popular with the Governor, he was popular with his Colonel, he was popular with his mess, he was popular throughout the garrison. Never was a person so popular as Ferdinand Armine. He was the best rider among them, and the deadliest shot; and he soon became an oracle at the billiard-table, and a hero in the racquet-court. His refined education, however, fortunately preserved him from the fate of many other lively youths: he did not degenerate into a mere hero of sports and brawls, the genius of male revels, the arbiter of roistering suppers, and the Comus of a club. His boyish feelings had their play; he soon exuded the wanton heat of which a public school would have served as a safety-valve. He returned to his books, his music, and his pencil. He became more quiet, but he was not less liked. If he lost some companions, he gained many friends; and, on the whole, the most boisterous wassailers were proud of the accomplishments of their comrade; and often an invitation to a mess dinner was accompanied by a hint that Armine dined there, and that there was a chance of hearing him sing. Ferdinand now became as popular with the Governor's lady as with the Governor himself, was idolised by his Colonel's wife, while not a party throughout the island was considered perfect without the presence of Mr. Armine.

Excited by his situation, Ferdinand was soon tempted to incur expenses which his income did not justify. The facility of credit afforded him not a moment to pause; everything he wanted was furnished him; and until the regiment quitted the garrison he was well aware that a settlement of accounts was never even desired. Amid this imprudence he was firm, however, in his resolution never to trespass on the resources of his father. It was with difficulty that he even brought himself to draw for the allowance which Sir Ratcliffe insisted on making him; and he would gladly have saved his father from making even this advance, by vague intimations of the bounty of Lord Grandison, had he not feared this conduct might have led to suspicious and disagreeable enquiries. It cannot be denied that his debts occasionally caused him anxiety, but they were not considerable; he quieted his conscience by the belief that, if he were pressed, his grandfather could scarcely refuse to discharge a few hundred pounds for his favourite grandson; and, at all events, he felt that the ultimate resource of selling his commission was still reserved for him. If these vague prospects did not drive away compunction, the qualms of conscience were generally allayed in the evening assembly, in which his vanity was gratified. At length he paid his first visit to England. That was a happy meeting. His kind father, his dear, dear mother, and the faithful Glastonbury, experienced some of the most transporting moments of their existence, when they beheld, with admiring gaze, the hero who returned to them. Their eyes were never satiated with beholding him; they hung upon his accents. Then came the triumphant visit to Grandison; and then Ferdinand returned to Malta, in the full conviction that he was the heir to fifteen thousand a year.

Among many other, there is one characteristic of capitals in which Valetta is not deficient: the facility with which young heirs apparent, presumptive, or expectant, can obtain any accommodation they desire. The terms; never mind the terms, who ever thinks of them? As for

Ferdinand Armine, who, as the only son of an old baronet, and the supposed future inheritor of Armine Park, had always been looked upon by tradesmen with a gracious eye, he found that his popularity in this respect was not at all diminished by his visit to England, and its supposed consequences; slight expressions, uttered on his return in the confidence of convivial companionship, were repeated, misrepresented, exaggerated, and circulated in all quarters. We like those whom we love to be fortunate. Everybody rejoices in the good luck of a popular character; and soon it was generally understood that Ferdinand Armine had become next in the entail to thirty thousand a year and a peerage. Moreover, he was not long to wait for his inheritance. The usurers pricked up their ears, and such numerous proffers of accommodation and assistance were made to the fortunate Mr. Armine, that he really found it quite impossible to refuse them, or to reject the loans that were almost forced on his acceptance.

Ferdinand Armine had passed the Rubicon. He was in debt. If youth but knew the fatal misery that they are entailing on themselves the moment they accept a pecuniary credit to which they are not entitled, how they would start in their career! how pale they would turn! how they would tremble, and clasp their hands in agony at the precipice on which they are disporting! Debt is the prolific mother of folly and of crime; it taints the course of life in all its dreams. Hence so many unhappy marriages, so many prostituted pens, and venal politicians! It hath a small beginning, but a giant's growth and strength. When we make the monster we make our master, who haunts us at all hours, and shakes his whip of scorpions for ever in our sight. The slave hath no overseer so severe. Faustus, when he signed the bond with blood, did not secure a doom more terrific. But when we are young we must enjoy ourselves. True; and there are few things more gloomy than the recollection of a youth that has not been enjoyed. What prosperity of manhood, what splendour of old age, can compensate for it? Wealth is power; and in youth, of all seasons of life, we require power, because we can enjoy everything that we can command. What, then, is to be done? I leave the question to the schoolmen, because I am convinced that to moralise with the inexperienced availeth nothing.

The conduct of men depends upon their temperament, not upon a bunch of musty maxims. No one had been educated with more care than Ferdinand Armine; in no heart had stricter precepts of moral conduct ever been instilled. But he was lively and impetuous, with a fiery imagination, violent passions, and a daring soul. Sanguine he was as the day; he could not believe in the night of sorrow, and the impenetrable gloom that attends a career that has failed. The world was all before him; and he dashed at it like a young charger in his first strife, confident that he must rush to victory, and never dreaming of death.

Thus would I attempt to account for the extreme imprudence of his conduct on his return from England. He was confident in his future fortunes; he was excited by the applause of the men, and the admiration of the women; he determined to gratify, even to satiety, his restless vanity; he broke into profuse expenditure; he purchased a yacht; he engaged a villa; his racing-horses and his servants exceeded all other establishments, except the Governor's, in breeding, in splendour, and in number. Occasionally wearied with the monotony of Malta, he obtained a short leave of absence, and passed a few weeks at Naples, Palermo, and Rome, where he glittered in brilliant circles, and whence he returned laden with choice specimens of art and luxury, and followed by the report of strange and flattering adventures. Finally, he was the prime patron of the Maltese opera, and brought over a celebrated Prima Donna from San Carlo in his own vessel.

In the midst of his career, Ferdinand received intelligence of the death of Lord Grandison. Fortunately, when he received it he was alone; there was no one, therefore, to witness his blank dismay when he discovered that, after all, he was not his grandfather's heir! After a vast number of trifling legacies to his daughters, and their husbands, and their children, and all his favourite friends, Lord Grandison left the whole of his property to his grand-daughter Katherine, the only remaining child of his son, who had died early in life, and the sister of the lately deceased Augustus.

What was to be done now? His mother's sanguine mind, for Lady Armine broke to him the fatal intelligence, already seemed to anticipate the only remedy for this 'unjust will.' It was a remedy delicately intimated, but the intention fell upon a fine and ready ear. Yes! he must marry; he must marry his cousin; he must marry Katherine Grandison. Ferdinand looked around him at his magnificent rooms; the damask hangings of Tunis, the tall mirrors from Marseilles, the inlaid tables, the marble statues, and the alabaster vases that he had purchased at Florence and at Rome, and the delicate mats that he had himself imported from Algiers. He looked around and he shrugged his shoulders: 'All this must be paid for,' thought he; 'and, alas! how much more!' And then came across his mind a recollection of his father and his cares, and innocent Armine, and dear Glastonbury, and his sacrifice. Ferdinand shook his head and sighed.

'How have I repaid them,' thought he. 'Thank God, they know nothing. Thank God, they have only to bear their own disappointments and their own privations; but it is in vain to moralise. The future, not the past, must be my motto. To retreat is impossible; I may yet advance and conquer. Katherine Grandison: only think of my little cousin Kate for a wife! They say that it is not the easiest task in the world to fan a lively flame in the bosom of a cousin. The love of cousins is proverbially not of a very romantic character. 'Tis well I have not seen her much in my life, and very little of late. Familiarity breeds contempt, they say. Will she dare to despise me?' He glanced at the mirror. The inspection was not unsatisfactory. Plunged in profound meditation, he paced the room.

CHAPTER II.

In Which Captain Armine Achieves with Rapidity a Result
Which Always Requires Great Deliberation.

It so happened that the regiment in which Captain Armine had the honour of commanding a company was at this time under orders of immediate recall to England; and within a month of his receipt of the fatal intelligence of his being, as he styled it, disinherited, he was on his way to his native land, This speedy departure was fortunate, because it permitted him to retire before the death of Lord Grandison became generally known, and consequently commented upon and enquired into. Previous to quitting the garrison, Ferdinand had settled his affairs for the time without the slightest difficulty, as he was still able to raise any money that he required.

On arriving at Falmouth, Ferdinand learnt that his father and mother were at Bath, on a visit to his maiden aunt, Miss Grandison, with whom his cousin now resided. As the regiment was quartered at Exeter, he was enabled in a very few days to obtain leave of absence and join them. In the first rapture of meeting all disappointment was forgotten, and in the course of a day or two, when this sentiment had somewhat subsided, Ferdinand perceived that the shock which his parents must have necessarily experienced was already considerably softened by the prospect in which they secretly indulged, and which various circumstances combined in inducing them to believe was by no means a visionary one.

His cousin Katherine was about his own age; mild, elegant, and pretty. Being fair, she looked extremely well in her deep mourning. She was not remarkable for the liveliness of her mind, yet not devoid of observation, although easily influenced by those whom she loved, and with whom she lived. Her maiden aunt evidently exercised a powerful control over her conduct and opinions; and Lady Armine was a favourite sister of this maiden aunt. Without, therefore, apparently directing her will, there was no lack of effort from this quarter to predispose Katherine in favour of her cousin. She heard so much of her cousin Ferdinand, of his beauty, and his goodness, and his accomplishments, that she had looked forward to his arrival with feelings of no ordinary interest. And, indeed, if the opinions and sentiments of those with whom she lived could influence, there was no need of any artifice to predispose her in favour of her cousin. Sir Ratcliffe and Lady Armine were wrapped up in their son. They seemed scarcely to have another idea, feeling, or thought in the world, but his existence and his felicity; and although their good sense had ever preserved them from the silly habit of uttering his panegyric in his presence, they amply compensated for this painful restraint when he was away. Then he was ever, the handsomest, the cleverest, the most accomplished, and the most kind-hearted and virtuous of his sex. Fortunate the parents blessed with such a son! thrice fortunate the wife blessed with such a husband!

It was therefore with no ordinary emotion that Katherine Grandison heard that this perfect cousin Ferdinand had at length arrived. She had seen little of him even in his boyish days, and even then he was rather a hero in their Lilliputian circle.

Ferdinand Armine was always looked up to at Grandison, and always spoken of by her grandfather as a very fine fellow indeed; a wonderfully fine fellow, his favourite grandson, Ferdinand Armine: and now he had arrived. His knock was heard at the door, his step was on the stairs, the door opened, and certainly his first appearance did not disappoint his cousin Kate. So handsome, so easy, so gentle, and so cordial; they were all the best friends in a moment. Then he embraced his father with such fervour, and kissed his mother with such fondness: it was evident that he had an excellent heart. His arrival indeed, was a revolution. Their mourning days seemed at once to disappear; and although they of course entered society very little, and never frequented any public amusement, it seemed to Katherine that all of a sudden she lived in a round of delightful gaiety. Ferdinand was so amusing and so accomplished! He sang with her, he played with her; he was always projecting long summer rides and long summer walks. Then his conversation was so different from everything to which she had ever listened. He had seen so many things and so many persons; everything that was strange, and everybody that was famous. His opinions were so original, his illustrations so apt and lively, his anecdotes so inexhaustible and sparkling! Poor inexperienced, innocent Katherine! Her cousin in four-and-twenty hours found it quite impossible to fall in love with her; and so he determined to make her fall in love with him. He quite succeeded. She adored him. She did not believe that there was anyone in the world so handsome, so good, and so clever. No one, indeed, who knew Ferdinand Armine could deny that he was a rare being; but, had there been any acute and unprejudiced observers who had known him in his younger and happier hours, they would perhaps have remarked some difference in his character and conduct, and not a favourable one. He was indeed more brilliant, but not quite so interesting as in old days; far more dazzling, but not quite so apt to charm. No one could deny his lively talents and his perfect breeding, but there was a restlessness about him, an excited and exaggerated style, which might have made some suspect that his demeanour was an effort, and that under a superficial glitter, by which so many are deceived, there was no little deficiency of the genuine and sincere. Katherine Grandison, however, was not one of those profound observers. She was easily captivated. Ferdinand, who really did not feel sufficient emotion to venture upon a scene, made his proposals to her when they were riding in a green lane: the sun just setting, and the evening star glittering through a vista. The lady blushed, and wept, and sobbed, and hid her fair and streaming face; but the result was as satisfactory as our hero could desire. The young equestrians kept their friends in the crescent at least two hours for dinner, and then had no appetite for the repast when they had arrived.

Nevertheless the maiden aunt, although a very particular personage, made this day no complaint, and was evidently far from being dissatisfied with anybody or anything. As for Ferdinand, he called for a tumbler of champagne, and secretly drank his own health, as the luckiest fellow of his acquaintance, with a pretty, amiable, and high-bred wife, with all his debts paid, and the house of Armine restored.

CHAPTER III.

Which Ferdinand Returns to Armine.

IT WAS settled that a year must elapse from the death of Lord Grandison before the young couple could be united: a reprieve which did not occasion Ferdinand acute grief. In the meantime the Grandisons were to pass at least the autumn at Armine, and thither the united families proposed soon to direct their progress. Ferdinand, who had been nearly two months at Bath, and was a little wearied of courtship, contrived to quit that city before his friends, on the plea of visiting London, to arrange about selling his commission; for it was agreed that he should quit the army.

On his arrival in London, having spoken to his agent, and finding town quite empty, he set off immediately for Armine, in order that he might have the pleasure of being there a few days without the society of his intended; celebrate the impending first of September; and, especially, embrace his dear Glastonbury. For it must not be supposed that Ferdinand had forgotten for a moment this invaluable friend; on the contrary, he had written to him several times since his arrival: always assuring him that nothing but important business could prevent him from instantly paying him his respects.

It was with feelings of no common emotion, even of agitation, that Ferdinand beheld the woods of his ancient home rise in the distance, and soon the towers and turrets of Armine Castle. Those venerable bowers, that proud and lordly house, were not then to pass away from their old and famous line? He had redeemed the heritage of his great ancestry; he looked with unmingled complacency on the magnificent landscape, once to him a source of as much anxiety as affection. What a change in the destiny of the Armines! Their glory restored; his own devoted and domestic hearth, once the prey of so much care and gloom, crowned with ease and happiness and joy; on all sides a career of splendour and felicity. And he had done all this! What a prophet was his mother! She had ever indulged the fond conviction that her beloved, son would be their restorer. How wise and pious was the undeviating confidence of kind old Glastonbury in their fate! With what pure, what heart-felt delight, would that faithful friend listen to his extraordinary communication!

His carriage dashed through the park gates as if the driver were sensible of his master's pride and exultation. Glastonbury was ready to welcome him, standing in the flower-garden, which he had made so rich and beautiful, and which had been the charm and consolation of many of their humbler hours.

'My dear, dear father!' exclaimed Ferdinand, embracing him, for thus he ever styled his old tutor. But Glastonbury could not speak; the tears quivered in his eyes and trickled down his faded cheek. Ferdinand led him into the house.

'How well you look, dear father!' continued Ferdinand; 'you really look younger and heartier than ever. You received all my letters, I am sure; and yours, how kind of you to remember and to write to me! I never forgot you, my dear, dear friend. I never could forget you. Do you know I am the happiest fellow in the world? I have the greatest news in the world to tell my Glastonbury—and we owe everything to you, everything. What would Sir Ratcliffe have been without you? what should I have been? Fancy the best news you can, dear friend, and it is not so good as I have got to tell. You will rejoice, you will be delighted! We shall furnish a castle! by

Jove we shall furnish a castle! We shall indeed, and you shall build it! No more gloom; no more care. The Armines shall hold their heads up again, by Jove they shall! Dearest of men, I dare say you think me mad. I am mad with joy. How that Virginian creeper has grown! I have brought you so many plants, my father! a complete Sicilian Hortus Siccus. Ah, John, good John, how is your wife? Take care of my pistol-case. Ask Louis; he knows all about everything. Well, dear Glastonbury, and how have you been? How is the old tower? How are the old books, and the old staff, and the old arms, and the old everything? Dear, dear Glastonbury!'

While the carriage was unpacking, and the dinner-table prepared, the friends walked in the garden, and from thence strolled towards the tower, where they remained some time pacing up and down the beechen avenue. It was evident, on their return, that Ferdinand had communicated his great intelligence. The countenance of Glastonbury was radiant with delight.

Indeed, although he had dined, he accepted with readiness Ferdinand's invitation to repeat the ceremony; nay, he quaffed more than one glass of wine; and, I believe, even drank the health of every member of the united families of Armine and Grandison. It was late before the companions parted, and retired for the night; and I think, before they bade each other good night, they must have talked over every circumstance that had occurred in their experience since the birth of Ferdinand.

CHAPTER IV.

In Which Some Light Is Thrown on the Title of This Work.

HOW delicious after a long absence to wake on a sunny morning and find ourselves at home! Ferdinand could scarcely credit that he was really again at Armine. He started up in his bed, and rubbed his eyes and stared at the unaccustomed, yet familiar sights, and for a moment Malta and the Royal Fusiliers, Bath and his betrothed, were all a dream; and then he remembered the visit of his dear mother to this very room on the eve of his first departure. He had returned; in safety had he returned, and in happiness, to accomplish all her hopes and to reward her for all her solicitude. Never felt anyone more content than Ferdinand Armine, more content and more grateful.

He rose and opened the casement; a rich and exhilarating perfume filled the chamber; he looked with a feeling of delight and pride over the broad and beautiful park; the tall trees rising and flinging their taller shadows over the bright and dewy turf, and the last mists clearing away from the distant woods and blending with the spotless sky. Everything was sweet and still, save, indeed, the carol of the birds, or the tinkle of some restless bellwether. It was a rich autumnal morn. And yet with all the excitement of his new views in life, and the blissful consciousness of the happiness of those he loved, he could not but feel that a great change had come over his spirit since the days he was wont to ramble in this old haunt of his boyhood. His innocence was gone. Life was no longer that deep unbroken trance of duty and of love from which he had been roused to so much care; and if not remorse, at least to so much compunction. He had no secrets then. Existence was not then a subterfuge, but a calm and candid state of serene enjoyment. Feelings then were not compromised for interests; and then it was the excellent that was studied, not the expedient. 'Yet such I suppose is life,' murmured Ferdinand; 'we moralise when it is too late; nor is there anything more silly than to regret. One event makes another: what we anticipate seldom occurs; what we least expected generally happens; and time can only prove which is most for our advantage. And surely I am the last person who should look grave. Our ancient house rises from its ruins; the beings I love most in the world are not only happy, but indebted to me for their happiness; and I, myself, with every gift of fortune suddenly thrown at my feet, what more can I desire? Am I not satisfied? Why do I even ask the question? I am sure I know not. It rises like a devil in my thoughts, and spoils everything. The girl is young, noble, and fair, and loves me. And her? I love her, at least I suppose I love her. I love her at any rate as much as I love, or ever did love, woman. There is no great sacrifice, then, on my part; there should be none; there is none; unless indeed it be that a man does not like to give up without a struggle all his chance of romance and rapture.

'I know not how it is, but there are moments I almost wish that I had no father and no mother; ay! not a single friend or relative in the world, and that Armine were sunk into the very centre of the earth. If I stood alone in the world methinks I might find the place that suits me; now everything seems ordained for me, as it were, beforehand. My spirit has had no play. Something whispers me that, with all its flush prosperity, this is neither wise nor well. God knows I am not heartless, and would be grateful; and yet if life can afford me no deeper sympathy than I have yet experienced, I cannot but hold it, even with all its sweet reflections, as little better than a dull delusion.'

While Ferdinand was thus moralising at the casement, Glastonbury appeared beneath; and his appearance dissipated this gathering gloom. 'Let us breakfast together,' proposed Ferdinand. 'I have breakfasted these two hours,' replied the hermit of the gate. 'I hope that on the first night of your return to Armine you have proved auspicious dreams.'

'My bed and I are old companions,' said Ferdinand, 'and we agreed very well. I tell you what, my dear Glastonbury, we will have a stroll together this morning and talk over our plans of last night. Go into the library and look over my sketch-books: you will find them on my pistol-case, and I will be with you anon.'

In due time the friends commenced their ramble. Ferdinand soon became excited by Glastonbury's various suggestions for the completion of the castle; and as for the old man himself, between his architectural creation and the restoration of the family to which he had been so long devoted, he was in a rapture of enthusiasm, which afforded an amusing contrast to his usual meek and subdued demeanour.

'Your grandfather was a great man,' said Glastonbury, who in old days seldom ventured to mention the name of the famous Sir Ferdinand: 'there is no doubt he was a very great man. He had great ideas. How he would glory in our present prospects! 'Tis strange what a strong confidence I have ever had in the destiny of your house. I felt sure that Providence would not desert us. There is no doubt we must have a portcullis.'

'Decidedly, a portcullis,' said Ferdinand; 'you shall make all the drawings yourself, my dear Glastonbury, and supervise everything. We will not have a single anachronism. It shall be perfect.'

'Perfect,' echoed Glastonbury; 'really perfect. It shall be a perfect Gothic castle. I have such treasures for the work. All the labours of my life have tended to this object. I have all the emblazonings of your house since the Conquest. There shall be three hundred shields in the hall. I will paint them myself. Oh! there is no place in the world like Armine!'

'Nothing,' said Ferdinand; 'I have seen a great deal, but after all there is nothing like Armine.'

'Had we been born to this splendour,' said Glastonbury, 'we should have thought little of it. We have been mildly and wisely chastened. I cannot sufficiently admire the wisdom of Providence, which has tempered, by such a wise dispensation, the too-eager blood of your race.'

'I should be sorry to pull down the old place,' said Ferdinand.

'It must not be,' said Glastonbury; 'we have lived there happily, though humbly.'

'I would we could move it to another part of the park, like the house of Loretto,' said Ferdinand with a smile.

'We can cover it with ivy,' observed Glastonbury, looking somewhat grave.

The morning stole away in these agreeable plans and prospects. At length the friends parted, agreeing to meet again at dinner. Glastonbury repaired to his tower, and Ferdinand, taking his gun, sauntered into the surrounding wilderness.

But he felt no inclination for sport. The conversation with Glastonbury had raised a thousand thoughts over which he longed to brood. His life had been a scene of such constant excitement since his return to England, that he had enjoyed little opportunity of indulging in calm self-communion; and now that he was at Armine, and alone, the contrast between his past and his present situation struck him so forcibly that he could not refrain from falling into a reverie upon his fortunes. It was wonderful, all wonderful, very, very wonderful. There seemed indeed, as Glastonbury affirmed, a providential dispensation in the whole transaction. The fall of his family, the heroic, and, as it now appeared, prescient firmness with which his father had clung, in all their deprivations, to his unproductive patrimony, his own education, the extinction of his mother's house, his very follies, once to him a cause of so much unhappiness, but which it now seemed were all the time compelling him, as it were, to his prosperity; all these and a thousand other traits and circumstances flitted over his mind, and were each in turn the subject of his manifold meditation. Willing was he to credit that destiny had reserved for him the character of restorer; that duty indeed he had accepted, and yet——

He looked around him as if to see what devil was whispering in his ear. He was alone. No one was there or near. Around him rose the silent bowers, and scarcely the voice of a bird or the hum of an insect disturbed the deep tranquillity. But a cloud seemed to rest on the fair and pensive brow of Ferdinand Armine. He threw himself on the turf, leaning his head on one hand, and with the other plucking the wild flowers, which he as hastily, almost as fretfully, flung away.

'Conceal it as I will,' he exclaimed, 'I am a victim; disguise them as I may, all the considerations are worldly. There is, there must be, something better in this world than power and wealth and rank; and surely there must be felicity more rapturous even than securing the happiness of a parent. Ah! dreams in which I have so oft and so fondly indulged, are ye, indeed, after all, but fantastical and airy visions? Is love indeed a delusion, or am I marked out from men alone to be exempted from its delicious bondage? It must be a delusion. All laugh at it, all jest about it, all agree in stigmatising it the vanity of vanities. And does my experience contradict this harsh but common fame? Alas! what have I seen or known to give the lie to this ill report? No one, nothing. Some women I have met more beautiful, assuredly, than Kate, and many, many less fair; and some have crossed my path with a wild and brilliant grace, that has for a moment dazzled my sight, and perhaps for a moment lured me from my way. But these shooting stars have but glittered transiently in my heaven, and only made me, by their evanescent brilliancy, more sensible of its gloom. Let me believe then, oh! let me of all men then believe, that the forms that inspire the sculptor and the painter have no models in nature; that that combination of beauty and grace, of fascinating intelligence and fond devotion, over which men brood in the soft hours of their young loneliness, is but the promise of a better world, and not the charm of this one.

'But, what terror in that truth! what despair! what madness! Yes! at this moment of severest scrutiny, how profoundly I feel that life without love is worse than death! How vain and void, how flat and fruitless, appear all those splendid accidents of existence for which men struggle, without this essential and pervading charm! What a world without a sun! Yes! without this transcendent sympathy, riches and rank, and even power and fame, seem to me at best but jewels set in a coronet of lead!

'And who knows whether that extraordinary being, of whose magnificent yet ruinous career this castle is in truth a fitting emblem—I say, who knows whether the secret of his wild and restless course is not hidden in this same sad lack of love? Perhaps while the world, the silly, superficial world, marvelled and moralised at his wanton life, and poured forth its anathemas against his heartless selfishness, perchance he all the time was sighing for some soft bosom whereon to pour his overwhelming passion, even as I am!

'O Nature! why art thou beautiful? My heart requires not, imagination cannot paint, a sweeter or a fairer scene than these surrounding bowers. This azure vault of heaven, this golden sunshine, this deep and blending shade, these rare and fragrant shrubs, yon grove of green and tallest pines, and the bright gliding of this swan-crowned lake; my soul is charmed with all this beauty and this sweetness; I feel no disappointment here; my mind does not here outrun reality; here there is no cause to mourn over ungratified hopes and fanciful desires. Is it then my destiny that I am to be baffled only in the dearest desires of my heart?'

At this moment the loud and agitated barking of his dogs at some little distance roused Ferdinand from his reverie. He called them to him, and soon one of them obeyed his summons, but instantly returned to his companion with such significant gestures, panting and yelping, that Ferdinand supposed that Basto was caught, perhaps, in some trap: so, taking up his gun, he proceeded to the dog's rescue.

To his surprise, as he was about to emerge from a berceau on to a plot of turf, in the centre of which grew a large cedar, he beheld a lady in a riding-habit standing before the tree, and evidently admiring its beautiful proportions.

Her countenance was raised and motionless. It seemed to him that it was more radiant than the sunshine. He gazed with rapture on the dazzling brilliancy of her complexion, the delicate regularity of her features, and the large violet-tinted eyes, fringed with the longest and the darkest lashes that he had ever beheld. From her position her hat had fallen back, revealing her lofty and pellucid brow, and the dark and lustrous locks that were braided over her temples. The whole countenance combined that brilliant health and that classic beauty which we associate with the idea of some nymph tripping over the dew-bespangled meads of Ida, or glancing amid the hallowed groves of Greece. Although the lady could scarcely have seen eighteen summers, her stature was above the common height; but language cannot describe the startling symmetry of her superb figure.

There is no love but love at first sight. This is the transcendent and surpassing offspring of sheer and unpolluted sympathy. All other is the illegitimate result of observation, of reflection, of compromise, of comparison, of expediency. The passions that endure flash like the lightning: they scorch the soul, but it is warmed for ever. Miserable man whose love rises by degrees upon the frigid morning of his mind! Some hours indeed of warmth and lustre may perchance fall to his lot; some moments of meridian splendour, in which he basks in what he deems eternal sunshine. But then how often overcast by the clouds of care, how often dusked by the blight of misery and misfortune! And certain as the gradual rise of such affection is its gradual decline and melancholy setting. Then, in the chill, dim twilight of his soul, he execrates custom; because he has madly expected that feelings could be habitual that were not homogeneous, and because he has been guided by the observation of sense, and not by the inspiration of sympathy.

Amid the gloom and travail of existence suddenly to behold a beautiful being, and as instantaneously to feel an overwhelming conviction that with that fair form for ever our destiny must be entwined; that there is no more joy but in her joy, no sorrow but when she grieves; that in her sigh of love, in her smile of fondness, hereafter all is bliss; to feel our flaunty ambition fade away like a shrivelled gourd before her vision; to feel fame a juggle and posterity a lie; and to be prepared at once, for this great object, to forfeit and fling away all former hopes, ties, schemes, views; to violate in her favour every duty of society; this is a lover, and this is love! Magnificent, sublime, divine sentiment! An immortal flame burns in the breast of that man who adores and is adored. He is an ethereal being. The accidents of earth touch him not. Revolutions of empire, changes of creed, mutations of opinion, are to him but the clouds and meteors of a stormy sky. The schemes and struggles of mankind are, in his thinking, but the anxieties of pigmies and the fantastical achievements of apes. Nothing can subdue him. He laughs alike at loss of fortune, loss of friends, loss of character. The deeds and thoughts of men are tor him equally indifferent. He does not mingle in their paths of callous bustle, or hold himself responsible to the airy impostures before which they bow down. He is a mariner who, on the sea of life, keeps his gaze fixedly on a single star; and if that do not shine, he lets go the rudder, and glories when his barque descends into the bottomless gulf.

Yes! it was this mighty passion that now raged in the heart of Ferdinand Armine, as, pale and trembling, he withdrew a few paces from the overwhelming spectacle, and leant against a tree in a chaos of emotion. What had he seen? What ravishing vision had risen upon his sight? What did he feel? What wild, what delicious, what maddening impulse now pervaded his frame? A storm seemed raging in his soul, a mighty wind dispelling in its course the sullen clouds and vapours of long years. Silent he was indeed, for he was speechless; though the big drop that quivered on his brow and the slight foam that played upon his lip proved the difficult triumph of passion over expression. But, as the wind clears the heaven, passion eventually tranquillises the soul. The tumult of his mind gradually subsided; the flitting memories, the scudding thoughts, that for a moment had coursed about in such wild order, vanished and melted away, and a feeling of bright serenity succeeded, a sense of beauty and of joy, and of hovering and circumambient happiness. He advanced, and gazed again; the lady was still there. Changed indeed her position; she had gathered a flower and was examining its beauty.

'Henrietta!' exclaimed a manly voice from the adjoining wood. Before she could answer, a stranger came forward, a man of middle age but of an appearance remarkably prepossessing. He was tall and dignified, fair, with an aquiline nose. One of Ferdinand's dogs followed him barking. 'I cannot find the gardener anywhere,' said the stranger; 'I think we had better remount.'

'Ah, me! what a pity!' exclaimed the lady.

'Let me be your guide,' said Ferdinand, advancing.

The lady rather started; the gentleman, not at all discomposed, courteously welcomed Ferdinand, and said, 'I feel that we are intruders, sir. But we were informed by the woman at the lodge that the family were not here at present, and that we should find her husband in the grounds.'

'The family are not at Armine,' replied Ferdinand; 'I am sure, however, Sir Ratcliffe would be most happy for you to walk about the grounds as much as you please; and as I am well acquainted with them, I should feel delighted to be your guide.'

'You are really too courteous, sir,' replied the gentleman; and his beautiful companion rewarded Ferdinand with a smile like a sunbeam, that played about her countenance till it finally settled into two exquisite dimples, and revealed to him teeth that, for a moment, he believed to be even the most beautiful feature of that surpassing visage.

They sauntered along, every step developing new beauties in their progress and eliciting from his companions renewed expressions of rapture. The dim bowers, the shining glades, the tall rare trees, the luxuriant shrubs, the silent and sequestered lake, in turn enchanted them, until at length, Ferdinand, who had led them with experienced taste through all the most striking points of the pleasaunce, brought them before the walls of the castle.

'And here is Armine Castle,' he said; 'it is little better than a shell, and yet contains something which you might like to see.'

'Oh! by all means,' exclaimed the lady.

'But we are spoiling your sport,' suggested the gentleman.

'I can always kill partridges,' replied Ferdinand, laying down his gun; 'but I cannot always find agreeable companions.'

So saying, he opened the massy portal of the castle and they entered the hall. It was a lofty chamber, of dimensions large enough to feast a thousand vassals, with a dais and a rich Gothic screen, and a gallery for the musicians. The walls were hung with arms and armour admirably arranged; but the parti-coloured marble floor was so covered with piled-up cases of furniture that the general effect of the scene, was not only greatly marred, but it was even difficult in some parts to trace a path.

'Here,' said Ferdinand, jumping upon a huge case and running to the wall, 'here is the standard of Ralph d'Ermyn, who came over with the Conqueror, and founded the family in England. Here is the sword of William d'Armyn, who signed Magna Carta. Here is the complete coat armour of the second Ralph, who died before Ascalon. This case contains a diamond-hilted sword, given by the Empress to the great Sir Ferdinand for defeating the Turks; and here is a Mameluke sabre, given to the same Sir Ferdinand by the Sultan for defeating the Empress.'

'Oh! I have heard so much of that great Sir Ferdinand,' said the lady. 'He must have been the most interesting character.'

'He was a marvellous being,' answered her guide, with a peculiar look, 'and yet I know not whether his descendants have not cause to rue his genius.'

'Oh! never, never!' said the lady; 'what is wealth to genius? How much prouder, were I an Armine, should I be of such an ancestor than of a thousand others, even if they had left me this castle as complete as he wished it to be!'

'Well, as to that,' replied Ferdinand, 'I believe I am somewhat of your opinion; though I fear he lived in too late an age for such order of minds. It would have been better for him perhaps if he had succeeded in becoming King of Poland.'

'I hope there is a portrait of him,' said the lady; 'there is nothing I long so much to see.'

'I rather think there is a portrait,' replied her companion, somewhat drily. 'We will try to find it out. Do not you think I make not a bad cicerone?'

'Indeed, most excellent,' replied the lady.

'I perceive you are a master of your subject,' replied the gentleman, thus affording Ferdinand an easy opportunity of telling them who he was. The hint, however, was not accepted.

'And now,' said Ferdinand, 'we will ascend the staircase.'

Accordingly they mounted a large spiral staircase which filled the space of a round tower, and was lighted from the top by a lantern of rich, coloured glass on which were emblazoned the arms of the family. Then they entered the vestibule, an apartment spacious enough for a salon; which, however, was not fitted up in the Gothic style, but of which the painted ceiling, the gilded panels, and inlaid floor were more suitable to a French palace. The brilliant doors of this vestibule opened in many directions upon long suites of state chambers, which indeed merited the description of shells. They were nothing more; of many the flooring was not even laid down; the walls of all were rough and plastered.

'Ah!' said the lady, 'what a pity it is not finished!'

'It is indeed desolate,' observed Ferdinand; 'but here perhaps is something more to your taste.' So saying, he opened another door and ushered them into the picture gallery.

It was a superb chamber nearly two hundred feet in length, and contained only portraits of the family, or pictures of their achievements. It was of a pale green colour, lighted from the top; and the floor, of oak and ebony, was partially covered with a single Persian carpet, of fanciful pattern and brilliant dye, a present from the Sultan to the great Sir Ferdinand. The earlier annals of the family were illustrated by a series of paintings by modern masters, representing the battle of Hastings, the siege of Ascalon, the meeting at Runnymede, the various invasions of France, and some of the most striking incidents in the Wars of the Roses, in all of which a valiant Armyn prominently figured. At length they stood before the first contemporary portrait of the Armyn family, one of Cardinal Stephen Armyn, by an Italian master. This great dignitary was legate of the Pope in the time of the seventh Henry, and in his scarlet robes and ivory chair looked a papal Jupiter, not unworthy himself of wielding the thunder of the Vatican. From him the series of family portraits was unbroken; and it was very interesting to trace, in this excellently arranged collection, the history of national costume. Holbein had commemorated the Lords Tewkesbury, rich in velvet, and golden chains, and jewels. The statesmen of Elizabeth and James, and their beautiful and gorgeous dames, followed; and then came many a gallant cavalier, by Vandyke. One admirable picture contained Lord Armine and his brave brothers, seated together in a tent round a drum, on which his lordship was apparently planning the operations of the campaign. Then followed a long series of un-memorable baronets, and their more interesting wives and daughters, touched by the pencil of Kneller, of Lely, or of Hudson; squires in wigs and scarlet jackets, and powdered dames in hoops and farthingales.

They stood before the crowning effort of the gallery, the masterpiece of Reynolds. It represented a full-length portrait of a young man, apparently just past his minority. The side of the figure was alone exhibited, and the face glanced at the spectator over the shoulder, in a favourite attitude of Vandyke. It was a countenance of ideal beauty. A profusion of dark brown curls was dashed aside from a lofty forehead of dazzling brilliancy. The face was perfectly oval; the nose, though small was high and aquiline, and exhibited a remarkable dilation of the nostril; the curling lip was shaded by a very delicate mustache; and the general expression, indeed, of the mouth and of the large grey eyes would have been perhaps arrogant and imperious, had not the extraordinary beauty of the whole countenance rendered it fascinating.

It was indeed a picture to gaze upon and to return to; one of those visages which, after having once beheld, haunt us at all hours and flit across our mind's eye unexpected and unbidden. So great was the effect that it produced upon the present visitors to the gallery, that they stood before it for some minutes in silence; the scrutinising glance of the gentleman was more than once diverted from the portrait to the countenance of his conductor, and the silence was eventually broken by our hero.

'And what think you,' he enquired, 'of the famous Sir Ferdinand?'

The lady started, looked at him, withdrew her glance, and appeared somewhat confused. Her companion replied, 'I think, sir, I cannot err in believing that I am indebted for much courtesy to his descendant?'

'I believe,' said Ferdinand, 'that I should not have much trouble in proving my pedigree. I am generally considered an ugly likeness of my grandfather.'

The gentleman smiled, and then said, 'I hardly know whether I can style myself your neighbour, for I live nearly ten miles distant. It would, however, afford me sincere gratification to see you at Ducie Bower. I cannot welcome you in a castle. My name is Temple,' he continued, offering his card to Ferdinand. 'I need not now introduce you to my daughter. I was not unaware that Sir Ratcliffe Armine had a son, but I had understood he was abroad.'

'I have returned to England within these two months,' replied Ferdinand, 'and to Armine within these two days. I deem it fortunate that my return has afforded me an opportunity of welcoming you and Miss Temple. But you must not talk of our castle, for that you know is our folly. Pray come now and visit our older and humbler dwelling, and take some refreshment after your long ride.'

This offer was declined, but with great courtesy. They quitted the castle, and Mr. Temple was about to direct his steps towards the lodge, where he had left his own and his daughter's horses; but Ferdinand persuaded them to return through the park, which he proved to them very satisfactorily must be the nearest way. He even asked permission to accompany them; and while his groom was saddling his horse he led them to the old Place and the flower-garden.

'You must be very fatigued, Miss Temple. I wish that I could persuade you to enter and rest yourself.'

'Indeed, no: I love flowers too much to leave them.'

'Here is one that has the recommendation of novelty as well as beauty,' said Ferdinand, plucking a strange rose, and presenting it to her. 'I sent it to my mother from Barbary.'

'You live amidst beauty.'

'I think that I never remember Armine looking so well as to-day.'

'A sylvan scene requires sunshine,' replied Miss Temple. 'We have been most fortunate in our visit.'

'It is something brighter than the sunshine that makes it so fair,' replied Ferdinand; but at this moment the horses appeared.

CHAPTER V.

In Which Captain Armine Is Very Absent during Dinner.

YOU are well mounted,' said Mr. Temple to Ferdinand.

"Tis a barb. I brought it over with me.'

"Tis a beautiful creature,' said Miss Temple.

'Hear that, Selim,' said Ferdinand; 'prick up thine ears, my steed. I perceive that you are an accomplished horsewoman, Miss Temple. You know our country, I dare say, well?'

'I wish to know it better. This is only the second summer that we have passed at Ducie.'

'By-the-bye, I suppose you know my landlord, Captain Armine?' said Mr. Temple.

'No,' said Ferdinand; 'I do not know a single person in the county. I have myself scarcely been at Armine for these five years, and my father and mother do not visit anyone.'

'What a beautiful oak!' exclaimed Miss Temple, desirous of turning the conversation.

'It has the reputation of being planted by Sir Francis Walsingham,' said Ferdinand. 'An ancestor of mine married his daughter. He was the father of Sir Walsingham, the portrait in the gallery with the white stick. You remember it?'

'Perfectly: that beautiful portrait! It must be, at all events, a very old tree.'

'There are few things more pleasing to me than an ancient place,' said Mr. Temple.

'Doubly pleasing when in the possession of an ancient family,' added his daughter.

'I fear such feelings are fast wearing away,' said Ferdinand.

'There will be a reaction,' said Mr. Temple.

'They cannot destroy the poetry of time,' said the lady.

'I hope I have no very inveterate prejudices,' said Ferdinand; 'but I should be sorry to see Armine in any other hands than our own, I confess.'

'I never would enter the park again,' said Miss Temple.

'So far as worldly considerations are concerned,' continued Ferdinand, 'it would perhaps be much better for us if we were to part with it.'

'It must, indeed, be a costly place to keep up,' said Mr. Temple.

'Why, as for that,' said Ferdinand, 'we let the kine rove and the sheep browse where our fathers hunted the stag and flew their falcons. I think if they were to rise from their graves they would be ashamed of us.'

'Nay!' said Miss Temple, 'I think yonder cattle are very picturesque. But the truth is, anything would look well in such a park as this. There is such a variety of prospect.'

The park of Armine indeed differed materially from those vamped-up sheep-walks and ambitious paddocks which are now honoured with the title. It was, in truth, the old chase, and little shorn of its original proportions. It was many miles in circumference, abounding in hill and dale, and offering much variety of appearance. Sometimes it was studded with ancient timber, single trees of extraordinary growth, and rich clumps that seemed coeval with the foundation of the family. Tracts of wild champaign succeeded these, covered with gorse and fern. Then came stately avenues of sycamore or Spanish chestnut, fragments of stately woods, that in old days doubtless reached the vicinity of the mansion house; and these were in turn succeeded by modern coverts. At length our party reached the gate whence Ferdinand had calculated that they should quit the park. He would willingly have accompanied them. He bade them farewell with regret, which was softened by the hope expressed by all of a speedy meeting.

'I wish, Captain Armine,' said Miss Temple, 'we had your turf to canter home upon.'

'By-the-bye, Captain Armine,' said Mr. Temple, 'ceremony should scarcely subsist between country neighbours, and certainly we have given you no cause to complain of our reserve. As you are alone at Armine, perhaps you would come over and dine with us to-morrow. If you can manage to come early, we will see whether we may not contrive to kill a bird together; and pray remember we can give you a bed, which I think, all things considered, it would be but wise to accept.'

'I accept everything,' said Ferdinand, smiling; 'all your offers. Good morning, my dearest sir; good morning, Miss Temple.'

'Miss Temple, indeed!' exclaimed Ferdinand, when he had watched them out of sight. 'Exquisite, enchanting, adored being! Without thee what is existence? How dull, how blank does everything even now seem! It is as if the sun had just set! Oh! that form! that radiant countenance! that musical and thrilling voice! Those tones still vibrate on my ear, or I should deem it all a vision! Will to-morrow ever come? Oh! that I could express to you my love, my overwhelming, my absorbing, my burning passion! Beautiful Henrietta! Thou hast a name, methinks, I ever loved. Where am I? what do I say? what wild, what maddening words are these? Am I not Ferdinand Armine, the betrothed, the victim? Even now, methinks, I hear the chariot-wheels of my bride. God! if she be there; if she indeed be at Armine on my return: I'll not see her; I'll not speak to them; I'll fly. I'll cast to the winds all ties and duties; I will not be dragged to the altar, a miserable sacrifice, to redeem, by my forfeited felicity, the worldly fortunes of my race. O Armine, Armine! she would not enter thy walls again if other blood but mine swayed thy fair demesne: and I, shall I give thee another mistress, Armine? It would indeed be treason! Without her I cannot live. Without her form bounds over this turf and glances in these arbours I never wish to view them. All the inducements to make the wretched sacrifice once meditated then vanish; for Armine, without her, is a desert, a tomb, a hell. I am free, then. Excellent logician! But this woman: I am bound to her. Bound? The word makes me tremble. I shiver: I hear the clank of my fetters. Am I indeed bound? Ay! in honour. Honour and love! A contest! Pah! The Idol must yield to the Divinity!'

With these wild words and wilder thoughts bursting from his lips and dashing through his mind; his course as irregular and as reckless as his fancies; now fiercely galloping, now pulling up into a sudden halt, Ferdinand at length arrived home; and his quick eye perceived in a moment that the dreaded arrival had not taken place. Glastonbury was in the flower-garden on one knee before a vase, over which he was training a creeper. He looked up as he heard the approach of Ferdinand. His presence and benignant smile in some degree stilled the fierce emotions of his pupil. Ferdinand felt that the system of dissimulation must now commence; besides, he was always careful to be most kind to Glastonbury. He would not allow that any attack of spleen, or even illness, could ever justify a careless look or expression to that dear friend.

'I hope, my dear father,' said Ferdinand, 'I am punctual to our hour?'

'The sun-dial tells me,' said Glastonbury, 'that you have arrived to the moment; and I rather think that yonder approaches a summons to our repast. I hope you have passed your morning agreeably?'

'If all days would pass as sweet, my father, I should indeed be blessed.'

'I, too, have had a fine morning of it. You must come to-morrow and see my grand emblazonry of the Ratcliffe and Armine coats; I mean it for the gallery.' With these words they entered the Place.

'You do not eat, my child,' said Glastonbury to his companion.

'I have taken too long a ride, perhaps,' said Ferdinand: who indeed was much too excited to have an appetite, and so abstracted that anyone but Glastonbury would have long before detected his absence.

'I have changed my hour to-day,' continued Glastonbury, 'for the pleasure of dining with you, and I think to-morrow you had better change your hour and dine with me.'

'By-the-bye, my dear father, you, who know everything, do you happen to know a gentleman of the name of Temple in this neighbourhood?'

'I think I heard that Mr. Ducie had let the Bower to a gentleman of that name.'

'Do you know who he is?'

'I never asked; for I feel no interest except about proprietors, because they enter into my County History. But I think I once heard that this Mr. Temple had been our minister at some foreign court. You give me a fine dinner and eat nothing yourself. This pigeon is savoury.'

'I will trouble you. I think there once was a Henrietta Armine, my father?'

'The beautiful creature!' said Glastonbury, laying down his knife and fork; 'she died young. She was a daughter of Lord Armine; and the Queen, Henrietta Maria, was her godmother. It grieves me much that we have no portrait of her. She was very fair, her eyes of a sweet light blue.'

'Oh! no; dark, my father; dark and deep as the violet.'

'My child, the letter-writer, who mentions her death, describes them as light blue. I know of no other record of her beauty.'

'I wish they had been dark,' said Ferdinand recovering himself; 'however, I am glad there was a Henrietta Armine; 'tis a beautiful name.'

'I think that Armine makes any name sound well,' said Glastonbury. 'No more wine indeed, my child. Nay! if I must,' continued he, with a most benevolent smile, 'I will drink to the health of Miss Grandison!'

'Ah!' exclaimed Ferdinand.

'My child, what is the matter?' inquired Glastonbury.

'A gnat, a fly, a wasp! something stung me,' said Ferdinand.

'Let me fetch my oil of lilies,' said Glastonbury; ''tis a specific'

'Oh, no! 'tis nothing, only a fly: sharp at the moment; nothing more.'

The dinner was over; they retired to the library. Ferdinand walked about the room restless and moody; at length he bethought himself of the piano, and, affecting an anxiety to hear some old favourite compositions of Glastonbury, he contrived to occupy his companion. In time, however, his old tutor invited him to take his violoncello and join him in a concerto. Ferdinand of course complied with his invitation, but the result was not satisfactory. After a series of blunders, which were the natural result of his thoughts being occupied on other subjects, he was obliged to plead a headache, and was glad when he could escape to his chamber.

Rest, however, no longer awaited him on his old pillow. It was at first delightful to escape from the restraint upon his reverie which he had lately experienced. He leant for an hour over his empty fireplace in mute abstraction. The cold, however, in time drove him to bed, but he could not sleep; his eyes indeed were closed, but the vision of Henrietta Temple was not less apparent to him. He recalled every feature of her countenance, every trait of her conduct, every word that she had expressed. The whole series of her observations, from the moment he had first seen her until the moment they had parted, were accurately repeated, her very tones considered, and her very attitudes pondered over. Many were the hours that he heard strike; he grew restless and feverish. Sleep would not be commanded; he jumped out of bed, he opened the casement, he beheld in the moonlight the Barbary rose-tree of which he had presented her a flower. This consoling spectacle assured him that he had not been, as he had almost imagined, the victim of a dream. He knelt down and invoked all heavenly and earthly blessings on Henrietta Temple and his love. The night air and the earnest invocation together cooled his brain, and Nature soon delivered him, exhausted, to repose.

CHAPTER VI.

In Which Captain Armine Pays His First Visit to Ducie.

YES! it is the morning. Is it possible? Shall he again behold her? That form of surpassing beauty: that bright, that dazzling countenance; again are they to bless his entranced vision? Shall he speak to her again? That musical and thrilling voice, shall it again sound and echo in his enraptured ear?

Ferdinand had reached Armine so many days before his calculated arrival, that he did not expect his family and the Grandisons to arrive for at least a week. What a respite did he not now feel this delay! if ever he could venture to think of the subject at all. He drove it indeed from his thoughts; the fascinating present completely engrossed his existence. He waited until the post arrived; it brought no letters, letters now so dreaded! He jumped upon his horse and galloped towards Ducie.

Mr. Temple was the younger son of a younger branch of a noble family. Inheriting no patrimony, he had been educated for the diplomatic service, and the influence of his family had early obtained him distinguished appointments. He was envoy to a German court when a change of ministry occasioned his recall, and he retired, after a long career of able and assiduous service, comforted by a pension and glorified by a privy-councillorship. He was an acute and accomplished man, practised in the world, with great self-control, yet devoted to his daughter, the only offspring of a wife whom he had lost early and loved much.

Deprived at a tender age of that parent of whom she would have become peculiarly the charge, Henrietta Temple found in the devotion of her father all that consolation of which her forlorn state was susceptible. She was not delivered over to the custody of a governess, or to the even less sympathetic supervision of relations. Mr. Temple never permitted his daughter to be separated from him; he cherished her life, and he directed her education. Resident in a city which arrogates to itself, not without justice, the title of the German Athens, his pupil availed herself of all those advantages which were offered to her by the instruction of the most skilful professors. Few persons were more accomplished than Henrietta Temple even at an early age; but her rare accomplishments were not her most remarkable characteristics. Nature, which had accorded to her that extraordinary beauty we have attempted to describe, had endowed her with great talents and a soul of sublime temper.

It was often remarked of Henrietta Temple (and the circumstance may doubtless be in some degree accounted for by the little interference and influence of women in her education) that she never was a girl. She expanded at once from a charming child into a magnificent woman. She had entered life very early, and had presided at her father's table for a year before his recall from his mission. Few women in so short a period had received so much homage; but she listened to compliments with a careless though courteous ear, and received more ardent aspirations with a smile. The men, who were puzzled, voted her cold and heartless; but men should remember that fineness of taste, as well as apathy of temperament, may account for an unsuccessful suit. Assuredly Henrietta Temple was not deficient in feeling; she entertained for her father sentiments almost of idolatry, and those more intimate or dependent acquaintances best qualified to form an opinion of her character spoke of her always as a soul of infinite tenderness.

Notwithstanding their mutual devotion to each other, there were not many points of resemblance between the characters of Mr. Temple and his daughter; she was remarkable for a frankness of demeanour and a simplicity yet strength of thought which contrasted with the artificial manners and the conventional opinions and conversation of her sire. A mind at once thoughtful and energetic permitted Henrietta Temple to form her own judgments; and an artless candour, which her father never could eradicate from her habit, generally impelled her to express them. It was indeed impossible even for him long to find fault with these ebullitions, however the diplomatist might deplore them; for Nature had so imbued the existence of this being with that indefinable charm which we call grace, that it was not in your power to behold her a moment without being enchanted. A glance, a movement, a sunny smile, a word of thrilling music, and all that was left to you was to adore. There was indeed in Henrietta Temple that rare and extraordinary combination of intellectual strength and physical softness which marks out the woman capable of exercising an irresistible influence over mankind. In the good old days she might have occasioned a siege of Troy or a battle of Actium. She was one of those women who make nations mad, and for whom a man of genius would willingly peril the empire of the world.

So at least deemed Ferdinand Armine, as he cantered through the park, talking to himself, apostrophising the woods, and shouting his passion to the winds. It was scarcely noon when he reached Ducie Bower. This was a Palladian pavilion, situated in the midst of beautiful gardens, and surrounded by green hills. The sun shone brightly, the sky was without a cloud; it appeared to him that he had never beheld a more graceful scene. It was a temple worthy of the divinity it enshrined. A façade of four Ionic columns fronted an octagon hall, adorned with statues, which led into a salon of considerable size and fine proportion. Ferdinand thought that he had never in his life entered so brilliant a chamber. The lofty walls were covered with an Indian paper of vivid fancy, and adorned with several pictures which his practised eye assured him were of great merit. The room, without being inconveniently crowded, was amply stored with furniture, every article of which bespoke a refined and luxurious taste: easy chairs of all descriptions, most inviting couches, cabinets of choice inlay, and grotesque tables covered with articles of vertu; all those charming infinite nothings, which a person of taste might some time back have easily collected during a long residence on the continent. A large lamp of Dresden china was suspended from the painted and gilded ceiling. The three tall windows opened on the gardens, and admitted a perfume so rich and various, that Ferdinand could easily believe the fair mistress, as she told him, was indeed a lover of flowers. A light bridge in the distant wood, that bounded the furthest lawn, indicated that a stream was at hand. What with the beauty of the chamber, the richness of the exterior scene, and the bright sun that painted every object with its magical colouring, and made everything appear even more fair and brilliant, Ferdinand stood for some moments quite entranced. A door opened, and Mr. Temple came forward and welcomed him with cordiality. After they had passed a half-hour in looking at the pictures and in conversation to which they gave rise, Mr. Temple, proposing an adjournment to luncheon, conducted Ferdinand into a dining-room, of which the suitable decorations wonderfully pleased his taste. A subdued tint pervaded every part of the chamber: the ceiling was painted in grey tinted frescoes of a classical and festive character, and the side table, which stood in a recess supported by four magnificent columns, was adorned with choice Etruscan vases. The air of repose and stillness which distinguished this apartment was heightened by the vast conservatory into which it led, blazing with light and beauty, groups of exotic trees, plants of radiant tint, the sound of a fountain, and gorgeous forms of tropic birds.

'How beautiful!' exclaimed Ferdinand.

"Tis pretty,' said Mr. Temple, carving a pasty, 'but we are very humble people, and cannot vie with the lords of Gothic castles.'

'It appears to me,' said Ferdinand, 'that Ducie Bower is the most exquisite place I ever beheld.'

'If you had seen it two years ago you would have thought differently,' said Mr. Temple; 'I assure you I dreaded becoming its tenant. Henrietta is entitled to all the praise, as she took upon herself the whole responsibility. There is not on the banks of the Brenta a more dingy and desolate villa than Ducie appeared when we first came; and as for the gardens, they were a perfect wilderness. She made everything. It was one vast, desolate, and neglected lawn, used as a sheep-walk when we arrived. As for the ceilings, I was almost tempted to whitewash them, and yet you see they have cleaned wonderfully; and, after all, it only required a little taste and labour. I have not laid out much money here. I built the conservatory, to be sure. Henrietta could not live without a conservatory.'

'Miss Temple is quite right,' pronounced Ferdinand. 'It is impossible to live without a conservatory.'

At this moment the heroine of their conversation entered the room, and Ferdinand turned pale. She extended to him her hand with a graceful smile; as he touched it, he trembled from head to foot.

'You were not fatigued, I hope, by your ride, Miss Temple?' at length he contrived to say.

'Not in the least! I am an experienced horsewoman. Papa and I take very long rides together.'

As for eating, with Henrietta Temple in the room, Ferdinand found that quite impossible. The moment she appeared, his appetite vanished. Anxious to speak, yet deprived of his accustomed fluency, he began to praise Ducie.

'You must see it,' said Miss Temple: 'shall we walk round the grounds?'

'My dear Henrietta,' said her father, 'I dare say Captain Armine is at this moment sufficiently tired; besides, when he moves, he will like perhaps to take his gun; you forget he is a sportsman, and that he cannot waste his morning in talking to ladies and picking flowers.'

'Indeed, sir, I assure you,' said Ferdinand, 'there is nothing I like so much as talking to ladies and picking flowers; that is to say, when the ladies have as fine taste as Miss Temple, and the flowers are as beautiful as those at Ducie.'

'Well, you shall see my conservatory, Captain Armine,' said Miss Temple, 'and you shall go and kill partridges afterwards.' So saying, she entered the conservatory, and Ferdinand followed her, leaving Mr. Temple to his pasty.

'These orange groves remind me of Palmero,' said Ferdinand.

'Ah!' said Miss Temple, 'I have never been in the sweet south.'

'You seem to me a person born to live in a Sicilian palace,' said Ferdinand, 'to wander in perfumed groves, and to glance in a moonlight warmer than this sun.'

'I see you pay compliments,' said Miss Temple, looking at him archly, and meeting a glance serious and soft.

'Believe me, not to you.'

'What do you think of this flower?' said Miss Temple, turning away rather quickly and pointing to a strange plant. 'It is the most singular thing in the world: but if it be tended by any other person than myself it withers. Is it not droll?'

'I think not,' said Ferdinand.

'I excuse you for your incredulity; no one does believe it; no one can; and yet it is quite true. Our gardener gave it up in despair. I wonder what it can be.'

'I think it must be some enchanted prince,' said Ferdinand.

'If I thought so, how I should long for a wand to emancipate him!' said Miss Temple.

'I would break your wand, if you had one,' said Ferdinand.

'Why?' said Miss Temple.

'Oh! I don't know,' said Ferdinand; 'I suppose because I believe you are sufficiently enchanting without one.'

'I am bound to consider that most excellent logic,' said Miss Temple.

'Do you admire my fountain and my birds?' she continued, after a short pause. 'After Armine, Ducie appears a little tawdry toy.'

'Ducie is Paradise,' said Ferdinand. 'I should like to pass my life in this conservatory.'

'As an enchanted prince, I suppose?' said Miss Temple.

'Exactly,' said Captain Armine; 'I would willingly this instant become a flower, if I were sure that Miss Temple would cherish my existence.'

'Cut off your tendrils and drown you with a watering-pot,' said Miss Temple; 'you really are very Sicilian in your conversation, Captain Armine.'

'Come,' said Mr. Temple, who now joined them, 'if you really should like to take a stroll round the grounds, I will order the keeper to meet us at the cottage.'

'A very good proposition,' said Miss Temple.

'But you must get a bonnet, Henrietta; I must forbid your going out uncovered.'

'No, papa, this will do,' said Miss Temple, taking a handkerchief, twisting it round her head, and tying it under her chin.

'You look like an old woman, Henrietta,' said her father, smiling.

'I shall not say what you look like, Miss Temple,' said Captain Armine, with a glance of admiration, 'lest you should think that I was this time even talking Sicilian.'

'I reward you for your forbearance with a rose,' said Miss Temple, plucking a flower. 'It is a return for your beautiful present of yesterday.'

Ferdinand pressed the gift to his lips.

They went forth; they stepped into a Paradise, where the sweetest flowers seemed grouped in every combination of the choicest forms; baskets, and vases, and beds of infinite fancy. A thousand bees and butterflies filled the air with their glancing shapes and cheerful music, and the birds from the neighbouring groves joined in the chorus of melody. The wood walks through which they now rambled admitted at intervals glimpses of the ornate landscape, and occasionally the view extended beyond the enclosed limits, and exhibited the clustering and embowered roofs of the neighbouring village, or some woody hill studded with a farmhouse, or a distant spire. As for Ferdinand, he strolled along, full of beautiful thoughts and thrilling fancies, in a dreamy state which had banished all recollection or consciousness but of the present. He was happy; positively, perfectly, supremely happy. He was happy for the first time in his life, He had no conception that life could afford such bliss as now filled his being. What a chain of miserable, tame, factitious sensations seemed the whole course of his past existence. Even the joys of yesterday were nothing to these; Armine was associated with too much of the commonplace and the gloomy to realise the ideal in which he now revelled. But now all circumstances contributed to enchant him. The novelty, the beauty of the scene, harmoniously blended with his passion. The sun seemed to him a more brilliant sun than the orb that illumined Armine; the sky more clear, more pure, more odorous. There seemed a magic sympathy in the trees, and every flower reminded him of his mistress. And then he looked around and beheld her. Was he positively awake? Was he in England? Was he in the same globe in which he had hitherto moved and acted? What was this entrancing form that moved before him? Was it indeed a woman?

O dea certè!

That voice, too, now wilder than the wildest bird, now low and hushed, yet always sweet; where was he, what did he listen to, what did he behold, what did he feel? The presence of her father alone restrained him from falling on his knees and expressing to her his adoration.

At length our friends arrived at a picturesque and ivy-grown cottage, where the keeper, with their guns and dogs, awaited Mr. Temple and his guest. Ferdinand, although a keen sportsman, beheld the spectacle with dismay. He execrated, at the same time, the existence of partridges and the invention of gunpowder. To resist his fate, however, was impossible; he took his gun and turned to bid his hostess adieu.

'I do not like to quit Paradise at all,' he said in a low voice: 'must I go?'

'Oh! certainly,' said Miss Temple. 'It will do you a great deal of good.'

Never did anyone at first shoot more wildly. In time, however, Ferdinand sufficiently rallied to recover his reputation with the keeper, who, from his first observation, began to wink his eye to his son, an attendant bush-beater, and occasionally even thrust his tongue inside his cheek, a significant gesture perfectly understood by the imp. 'For the life of me, Sam,' he afterwards profoundly observed, 'I couldn't make out this here Captain by no manner of means whatsomever. At first I thought as how he was going to put the muzzle to his shoulder. Hang me if ever I see sich a gentleman. He missed everything; and at last if he didn't hit the longest flying shots without taking aim. Hang me if ever I see sich a gentleman. He hit everything. That ere Captain puzzled me, surely.'

The party at dinner was increased by a neighbouring squire and his wife, and the rector of the parish. Ferdinand was placed at the right hand of Miss Temple. The more he beheld her the more beautiful she seemed. He detected every moment some charm before unobserved. It seemed to him that he never was in such agreeable society, though, sooth to say, the conversation was not of a very brilliant character. Mr. Temple recounted the sport of the morning to the squire, whose ears kindled at a congenial subject, and every preserve in the county was then discussed, with some episodes on poaching. The rector, an old gentleman, who had dined in old days at Armine Place, reminded Ferdinand of the agreeable circumstance, sanguine perhaps that the invitation might lead to a renewal of his acquaintance with that hospitable board. He was painfully profuse in his description of the public days of the famous Sir Ferdinand. From the service of plate to the thirty servants in livery, nothing was omitted.

'Our friend deals in Arabian tales,' whispered Ferdinand to Miss Temple; 'you can be a witness that we live quietly enough now.'

'I shall certainly never forget my visit to Armine,' replied Miss Temple; 'it was one of the agreeable days of life.'

'And that is saying a great deal, for I think your life must have abounded in agreeable days.'

'I cannot indeed lay any claim to that misery which makes many people interesting,' said Miss Temple; 'I am a very commonplace person, for I have been always happy.'

When the ladies withdrew there appeared but little inclination on the part of the squire and the rector to follow their example; and Captain Armine, therefore, soon left Mr. Temple to his fate, and escaped to the drawing-room. He glided to a seat on an ottoman, by the side of his hostess, and listened in silence to the conversation. What a conversation! At any other time, under any other circumstances, Ferdinand would have been teased and wearied with its commonplace current: all the dull detail of county tattle, in which the squire's lady was a proficient, and with which Miss Temple was too highly bred not to appear to sympathise; and yet the conversation, to Ferdinand, appeared quite charming. Every accent of Henrietta's sounded like wit; and when she bent her head in assent to her companion's obvious deductions, there was about each movement a grace so ineffable, that Ferdinand could have sat in silence and listened, entranced, for ever: and occasionally, too, she turned to Captain Armine, and appealed on some point to his knowledge or his taste. It seemed to him that he had never listened to sounds so sweetly thrilling as her voice. It was a birdlike burst of music, that well became the sparkling sunshine of her violet eyes. His late companions entered. Ferdinand rose from his seat; the windows of the salon were open; he stepped forth into the garden. He felt the necessity of being a moment alone. He proceeded a few paces beyond the ken of man, and then leaning on a statue, and burying his face in his arm, he gave way to irresistible emotion. What wild thoughts dashed through his impetuous soul at that instant, it is difficult to conjecture. Perhaps it was passion that inspired that convulsive reverie; perchance it might have been remorse. Did he abandon himself to those novel sentiments which in a few brief hours had changed all his aspirations and coloured his whole existence; or was he tortured by that dark and perplexing future, from which his imagination in vain struggled to extricate him?

He was roused from his reverie, brief but tumultuous, by the note of music, and then by the sound of a human voice. The stag detecting the huntsman's horn could not have started with more wild emotion. But one fair organ could send forth that voice. He approached, he listened; the voice of Henrietta Temple floated to him on the air, breathing with a thousand odours. In a moment he was at her side, the squire's lady was standing by her; the gentlemen, for a moment arrested from a political discussion, formed a group in a distant part of the room, the rector occasionally venturing in a practised whisper to enforce a disturbed argument. Ferdinand glided in unobserved by the fair performer. Miss Temple not only possessed a voice of rare tone and compass, but this delightful gift of nature had been cultivated with refined art. Ferdinand, himself a musician, and passionately devoted to vocal melody, listened with unexaggerated rapture.

'Oh! beautiful!' exclaimed he, as the songstress ceased.

'Captain Armine!' cried Miss Temple, looking round with a wild, bewitching smile. 'I thought you were meditating in the twilight.'

'Your voice summoned me.'

'You care for music?'

'For little else.'

'You sing?'

'I hum.'

'Try this.'

'With you?'

Ferdinand Armine was not unworthy of singing with Henrietta Temple. His mother had been his able instructress in the art even in his childhood, and his frequent residence at Naples and other parts of the south had afforded him ample opportunities of perfecting a talent thus early cultivated. But to-night the love of something beyond his art inspired the voice of Ferdinand. Singing with Henrietta Temple, he poured forth to her in safety all the passion which raged in his soul. The squire's lady looked confused; Henrietta herself grew pale; the politicians ceased even to whisper, and advanced from their corner to the instrument; and when the duet was terminated, Mr. Temple offered his sincere congratulations to his guest. Henrietta also turned with some words of commendation to Ferdinand; but the words were faint and confused, and finally requesting Captain Armine to favour them by singing alone, she rose and vacated her seat. Ferdinand took up the guitar, and accompanied himself to a Neapolitan air. It was gay and festive, a Ritornella which might summon your mistress to dance in the moonlight. And then, amid many congratulations, he offered the guitar to Miss Temple.

'No one will listen to a simple melody after anything so brilliant,' said Miss Temple, as she touched a string, and, after a slight prelude, sang these words:—

THE DESERTED.

I.

Yes, weeping is madness,
Away with this tear,
Let no sign of sadness
Betray the wild anguish I fear.
When we meet him to-night,
Be mute then my heart!
And my smile be as bright,
As if we were never to part.

II.

Girl! give me the mirror
That said I was fair;
Alas! fatal error,
This picture reveals my despair.
Smiles no longer can pass
O'er this faded brow,
And I shiver this glass,
Like his love and his fragile vow!

'The music,' said Ferdinand, full of enthusiasm, 'is——'

'Henrietta's,' replied her father.

'And the words?'

'Were found in my canary's cage,' said Henrietta Temple, rising and putting an end to the conversation.

CHAPTER VII.

In Which Captain Armine Indulges in a Reverie.

THE squire's carriage was announced, and then came his lady's shawl. How happy was Ferdinand when he recollected that he was to remain at Ducie. Remain at Ducie! Remain under the same roof as Henrietta Temple. What bliss! what ravishing bliss! All his life, and his had not been a monotonous one; it seemed that all his life could not afford a situation so adventurous and so sweet as this. Now they have gone. The squire and his lady, and the worthy rector who recollected Armine so well; they have all departed, all the adieus are uttered; after this little and unavoidable bustle, silence reigns in the salon of Ducie. Ferdinand walked to the window. The moon was up; the air was sweet and hushed; the landscape clear, though soft. Oh! what would he not have given to have strolled in that garden with Henrietta Temple, to have poured forth his whole soul to her, to have told her how wondrous fair she was, how wildly bewitching, and how he loved her, how he sighed to bind his fate with hers, and live for ever in the brilliant atmosphere of her grace and beauty.

'Good night, Captain Armine,' said Henrietta Temple.

He turned hastily round, he blushed, he grew pale. There she stood, in one hand a light, the other extended to her father's guest. He pressed her hand, he sighed, he looked confused; then suddenly letting go her hand, he walked quickly towards the door of the salon, which he opened that she might retire.

'The happiest day of my life has ended,' he muttered.

'You are so easily content then, that I think you must always be happy.'

'I fear I am not so easily content as you imagine.'

She has gone. Hours, many and long hours, must elapse before he sees her again, before he again listens to that music, watches that airy grace, and meets the bright flashing of that fascinating eye. What misery was there in this idea? How little had he seemed hitherto to prize the joy of being her companion. He cursed the hours which had been wasted away from her in the morning's sport; he blamed himself that he had not even sooner quitted the dining-room, or that he had left the salon for a moment, to commune with his own thoughts in the garden. With difficulty he restrained himself from reopening the door, to listen for the distant sound of her footsteps, or catch, perhaps, along some corridor, the fading echo of her voice. But Ferdinand was not alone; Mr. Temple still remained. That gentleman raised his face from the newspaper as Captain Armine advanced to him; and, after some observations about the day's sport, and a hope that he would repeat his trial of the manor to-morrow, proposed their retirement. Ferdinand of course assented, and in a moment he was ascending with his host the noble and Italian staircase: and he then was ushered from the vestibule into his room.

His previous visit to the chamber had been so hurried, that he had only made a general observation on its appearance. Little inclined to slumber, he now examined it more critically. In a recess was a French bed of simple furniture. On the walls, which were covered with a rustic paper, were suspended several drawings, representing views in the Saxon Switzerland. They were so bold and spirited that they arrested attention; but the quick eye of Ferdinand instantly detected the initials of the artist in the corner. They were letters that made his heart tremble, as he gazed with admiring fondness on her performances. Before a sofa, covered with a chintz of a corresponding pattern with the paper of the walls, was placed a small French table, on which were writing materials; and his toilet-table and his mantelpiece were profusely ornamented with rare flowers; on all sides were symptoms of female taste and feminine consideration.

Ferdinand carefully withdrew from his coat the flower that Henrietta had given him in the morning, and which he had worn the whole day. He kissed it, he kissed it more than once; he pressed its somewhat faded form to his lips with cautious delicacy; then tending it with the utmost care, he placed it in a vase of water, which holding in his hand, he threw himself into an easy chair, with his eyes fixed on the gift he most valued in the world.

An hour passed, and Ferdinand Armine remained fixed in the same position. But no one who beheld that beautiful and pensive countenance, and the dreamy softness of that large grey eye, could for a moment conceive that his thoughts were less sweet than the object on which they appeared to gaze. No distant recollections disturbed him now, no memory of the past, no fear of the future. The delicious present monopolised his existence. The ties of duty, the claims of domestic affection, the worldly considerations that by a cruel dispensation had seemed, as it were, to taint even his innocent and careless boyhood, even the urgent appeals of his critical and perilous situation; all, all were forgotten in one intense delirium of absorbing love.

Anon he rose from his seat, and paced his room for some minutes, with his eyes fixed on the ground. Then throwing off his clothes, and taking the flower from the vase, which he had previously placed on the table, he deposited it in his bosom. 'Beautiful, beloved flower,' exclaimed he; 'thus, thus will I win and wear your mistress!'

CHAPTER VIII.

A Strange Dream.

RESTLESS are the dreams of the lover that is young. Ferdinand Armine started awake from the agony of a terrible slumber. He had been walking in a garden with Henrietta Temple, her hand was clasped in his, her eyes fixed on the ground, as he whispered delicious words. His face was flushed, his speech panting and low. Gently he wound his vacant arm round her graceful form; she looked up, her speaking eyes met his, and their trembling lips seemed about to cling into a—
———
When lo! the splendour of the garden faded, and all seemed changed and dim; instead of the beautiful arched walks, in which a moment before they appeared to wander, it was beneath the vaulted roof of some temple that they now moved; instead of the bed of glowing flowers from which he was about to pluck an offering for her bosom, an altar rose, from the centre of which upsprang a quick and lurid tongue of fire. The dreamer gazed upon his companion, and her form was tinted with the dusky hue of the flame, and she held to her countenance a scarf, as if pressed by the unnatural heat. Great fear suddenly came over him. With haste, yet with tenderness, he himself withdrew the scarf from the face of his companion, and this movement revealed the visage of Miss Grandison.

Ferdinand Armine awoke and started up in his bed. Before him still appeared the unexpected figure. He jumped out of bed, he gazed upon the form with staring eyes and open mouth. She was there, assuredly she was there; it was Katherine, Katherine his betrothed, sad and reproachful. The figure faded before him; he advanced with outstretched hand; in his desperation he determined to clutch the escaping form: and he found in his grasp his dressing-gown, which he had thrown over the back of a chair.

'A dream, and but a dream, after all,' he muttered to himself; 'and yet a strange one.'

His brow was heated; he opened the casement. It was still night; the moon had vanished, but the stars were still shining. He recalled with an effort the scene with which he had become acquainted yesterday for the first time. Before him, serene and still, rose the bowers of Ducie. And their mistress? That angelic form whose hand he had clasped in his dream, was not then merely a shadow. She breathed, she lived, and under the same roof. Henrietta Temple was at this moment under the same roof as himself: and what were her slumbers? Were they wild as his own, or sweet and innocent as herself? Did his form flit over her closed vision at this charmed hour, as hers had visited his? Had it been scared away by an apparition as awful? Bore anyone to her the same relation as Katherine Grandison to him? A fearful surmise, that had occurred to him now for the first time, and which it seemed could never again quit his brain. The stars faded away, the breath of morn was abroad, the chant of birds arose. Exhausted in body and in mind, Ferdinand Armine flung himself upon his bed, and soon was lost in slumbers undisturbed as the tomb.

CHAPTER IX.

Which I Hope May Prove as Agreeable to the Reader as to Our
Hero.

FERDINAND'S servant, whom he had despatched the previous evening to Armine, returned early with his master's letters; one from his 'mother, and one from Miss Grandison.

They were all to arrive at the Place on the day after the morrow. Ferdinand opened these epistles with a trembling hand. The sight of Katherine's, his Katherine's, handwriting was almost as terrible as his dream. It recalled to him, with a dreadful reality, his actual situation, which he had driven from his thoughts. He had quitted his family, his family who were so devoted to him, and whom he so loved, happy, nay, triumphant, a pledged and rejoicing bridegroom. What had occurred during the last eight-and-forty hours seemed completely to have changed all his feelings, all his wishes, all his views, all his hopes! He had in that interval met a single human being, a woman, a girl, a young and innocent girl; he had looked upon that girl and listened to her voice, and his soul was changed as the earth by the sunrise. As lying in his bed he read these letters, and mused over their contents, and all the thoughts that they suggested, the strangeness of life, the mystery of human nature, were painfully impressed upon him. His melancholy father, his fond and confiding mother, the devoted Glastonbury, all the mortifying circumstances of his illustrious race, rose in painful succession before him. Nor could he forget his own wretched follies and that fatal visit to Bath, of which the consequences clanked upon his memory like degrading and disgraceful fetters. The burden of existence seemed intolerable. That domestic love which had so solaced his existence, recalled now only the most painful associations. In the wildness of his thoughts he wished himself alone in the world, to struggle with his fate and mould his fortunes. He felt himself a slave and a sacrifice. He cursed Armine, his ancient house, and his broken fortunes. He felt that death was preferable to life without Henrietta Temple. But even supposing that he could extricate himself from his rash engagement; even admitting that all worldly considerations might be thrown aside, and the pride of his father, and his mother's love, and Glastonbury's pure hopes, might all be outraged; what chance, what hope was there of obtaining his great object? What was he, what was he, Ferdinand Armine, free as the air from the claims of Miss Grandison, with all sense of duty rooted out of his once sensitive bosom, and existing only for the gratification of his own wild fancies? A beggar, worse than a beggar, without a home, without the possibility of a home to offer the lady of his passion; nay, not even secure that the harsh process of the law might not instantly claim its victim, and he himself be hurried from the altar to the gaol!

Moody and melancholy, he repaired to the salon; he beheld Henrietta Temple, and the cloud left his brow, and lightness came to his heart. Never had she looked so beautiful, so fresh and bright, so like a fair flower with the dew upon its leaves. Her voice penetrated his soul; her sunny smile warmed his breast. Her father greeted him too with kindness, and inquired after his slumbers, which he assured Mr. Temple had been satisfactory.

'I find,' continued Mr. Temple, 'that the post has brought me some business to-day which, I fear, claims the morning to transact; but I hope you will not forget your promise. The keeper will be ready whenever you summon him.'

Ferdinand muttered something about trouble and intrusion, and the expected arrival of his family; but Miss Temple begged him to accept the offer, and refusal was impossible.

After breakfast Mr. Temple retired to his library, and Ferdinand found himself alone for the first time with Henrietta Temple.

She was copying a miniature of Charles the First. Ferdinand looked over her shoulder.

'A melancholy countenance!' he observed.

'It is a favourite one of mine,' she replied.

'Yet you are always gay.'

'Always.'

'I envy you, Miss Temple.'

'What, are you melancholy?'

'I have every cause.'

'Indeed, I should have thought the reverse.'

'I look upon myself as the most unfortunate of human beings,' replied Ferdinand.

He spoke so seriously, in a tone of such deep and bitter feeling, that Miss Temple could not resist looking up at her companion. His countenance was gloomy.

'You surprise me,' said Miss Temple; 'I think that few people ought to be unhappy, and I rather suspect fewer are than we imagine.'

'All I wish is,' replied he, 'that the battle of Newbury had witnessed the extinction of our family as well as our peerage.'

'A peerage, and such a peerage as yours, is a fine thing,' said Henrietta Temple, 'a very fine thing; but I would not grieve, if I were you, for that. I would sooner be an Armine without a coronet than many a brow I wot of with.'

'You misconceived a silly phrase,' rejoined Ferdinand. 'I was not thinking of the loss of our coronet, though that is only part of the system. Our family, I am sure, are fated. Birth without honour, estates without fortune, life without happiness, that is our lot.'

'As for the first,' said Miss Temple, 'the honourable are always honoured; money, in spite of what they say, I feel is not the greatest thing in the world; and as for misery, I confess I do not very readily believe in the misery of youth.'

'May you never prove it!' replied Ferdinand; 'may you never be, as I am, the victim of family profligacy and family pride!' So saying, he turned away, and, taking up a book, for a few minutes seemed wrapped in his reflections.

He suddenly resumed the conversation in a more cheerful tone. Holding a volume of Petrarch in his hand, he touched lightly, but with grace, on Italian poetry; then diverged into his travels, recounted an adventure with sprightliness, and replied to Miss Temple's lively remarks with gaiety and readiness. The morning advanced; Miss Temple closed her portfolio and visited her flowers, inviting him to follow her. Her invitation was scarcely necessary, his movements were regulated by hers; he was as faithful to her as her shadow. From the conservatory they entered the garden; Ferdinand was as fond of gardens as Miss Temple. She praised the flower-garden of Armine. He gave her some account of its principal creator. The character of Glastonbury highly interested Miss Temple. Love is confidential; it has no fear of ridicule. Ferdinand entered with freedom and yet with grace into family details, from which, at another time and to another person, he would have been the first to shrink. The imagination of Miss Temple was greatly interested by his simple, and, to her, affecting account of this ancient line living in their hereditary solitude, with all their noble pride and haughty poverty. The scene, the circumstances, were all such as please a maiden's fancy; and he, the natural hero of this singular history, seemed deficient in none of those heroic qualities which the wildest spirit of romance might require for the completion of its spell. Beautiful as his ancestors, and, she was sure, as brave, young, spirited, graceful, and accomplished, a gay and daring spirit blended with the mournful melody of his voice, and occasionally contrasted with the somewhat subdued and chastened character of his demeanour.

'Well, do not despair,' said Henrietta Temple; 'riches did not make Sir Ferdinand happy. I feel confident the house will yet flourish.'

'I have no confidence,' replied Ferdinand; 'I feel the struggle with our fate to be fruitless. Once indeed I felt like you; there was a time when I took even a fancied pride in all the follies of my grandfather. But that is past; I have lived to execrate his memory.'

'Hush! hush!'

'Yes, to execrate his memory! I repeat, to execrate his memory! His follies stand between me and my happiness.'

'Indeed, I see not that.'

'May you never! I cannot disguise from myself that I am a slave, and a wretched one, and that his career has entailed this curse of servitude upon me. But away with this! You must think me, Miss Temple, the most egotistical of human beings; and yet, to do myself justice, I never remember having spoken of myself so much before.'

'Will you walk with me?' said Miss Temple, after a moment's silence; 'you seem little inclined to avail yourself of my father's invitation to solitary sport. But I cannot stay at home, for I have visits to pay, although I fear you will consider them rather dull ones.' 'Why so?'

'My visits are to cottages.'

'I love nothing better. I used ever to be my mother's companion on such occasions.'

So, crossing the lawn, they entered a beautiful wood of considerable extent, which formed the boundary of the grounds, and, after some time passed in agreeable conversation, emerged upon a common of no ordinary extent or beauty, for it was thickly studded in some parts with lofty timber, while in others the furze and fern gave richness and variety to the vast wilderness of verdant turf, scarcely marked, except by the light hoof of Miss Temple's palfrey.

'It is not so grand as Armine Park,' said Miss Temple; 'but we are proud of our common.'

The thin grey smoke that rose in different directions was a beacon to the charitable visits of Miss Temple. It was evident that she was a visitor both habitual and beloved. Each cottage-door was familiar to her entrance. The children smiled at her approach; their mothers rose and courtesied with affectionate respect. How many names and how many wants had she to remember! yet nothing was forgotten. Some were rewarded for industry, some were admonished not to be idle; but all were treated with an engaging suavity more efficacious than gifts or punishments. The aged were solaced by her visit; the sick forgot their pains; and, as she listened with sympathising patience to long narratives of rheumatic griefs, it seemed her presence in each old chair, her tender enquiries and sanguine hopes, brought even more comfort than her plenteous promises of succour from the Bower, in the shape of arrowroot and gruel, port wine and flannel petticoats.

This scene of sweet simplicity brought back old days and old places to the memory of Ferdinand Armine. He thought of the time when he was a happy boy at his innocent home; his mother's boy, the child she so loved and looked after, when a cloud upon her brow brought a tear into his eye, and when a kiss from her lips was his most dear and desired reward. The last night he had passed at Armine, before his first departure, rose up to his recollection; all his mother's passionate fondness, all her wild fear that the day might come when her child would not love her so dearly as he did then. That time had come. But a few hours back, ay! but a few hours back, and he had sighed to be alone in the world, and had felt those domestic ties which had been the joy of his existence a burthen and a curse. A tear stole down his cheek; he stepped forth from the cottage to conceal his emotion. He seated himself on the trunk of a tree, a few paces withdrawn; he looked upon the declining sun that gilded the distant landscape with its rich yet pensive light. The scenes of the last five years flitted across his mind's eye in fleet succession; his dissipation, his vanity, his desperate folly, his hollow worldliness. Why, oh! why had he ever left his unpolluted home? Why could he not have lived and died in that sylvan paradise? Why, oh! why was it impossible to admit his beautiful companion into that sweet and serene society? Why should his love for her make his heart a rebel to his hearth? Money! horrible money! It seemed to him that the contiguous cottage and the labour of his hands, with her, were preferable to palaces and crowds of retainers without her inspiring presence. And why not screw his courage to the sticking-point, and commune in confidence with his parents? They loved him; yes, they idolised him! For him, for him alone, they sought the restoration of their house and fortunes. Why, Henrietta Temple was a treasure richer than any his ancestors had counted. Let them look on her, let them listen to her, let them breathe as he had done in her enchantment; and could they wonder, could they murmur, at his conduct? Would they not, oh! would they not, rather admire, extol it! But, then, his debts, his overwhelming debts. All the rest might be faced. His desperate engagement might be broken; his family might be reconciled to obscurity and poverty: but, ruin! what was to grapple with his impending ruin? Now his folly stung him; now the scorpion entered his soul. It was not the profligacy of his ancestor, it was not the pride of his family then, that stood between him and his love; it was his own culpable and heartless career! He covered his face with his hands; something touched him lightly; it was the parasol of Miss Temple.

'I am afraid,' she said, 'that my visits have wearied you; but you have been very kind and good.'

He rose rapidly, with a slight blush. 'Indeed,' he replied, 'I have passed a most delightful morning, and I was only regretting that life consisted of anything else but cottages and yourself.' They were late; they heard the first dinner-bell at Ducie as they re-entered the wood. 'We must hurry on,' said Miss Temple; 'dinner is the only subject on which papa is a tyrant. What a sunset! I wonder if Lady Armine will return on Saturday. When she returns, I hope you will make her call upon us, for I want to copy the pictures in your gallery.'

'If they were not heir-looms, I would give them you,' said Ferdinand; 'but, as it is, there is only one way by which I can manage it.'

'What way?' enquired Miss Temple, very innocently.

'I forget,' replied Ferdinand, with a peculiar smile. Miss Temple looked a little confused.

CHAPTER X.

Evening Stroll.

IN SPITE of his perilous situation, an indefinable sensation of happiness pervaded the soul of Ferdinand Armine, as he made his hurried toilet, and hastened to the domestic board of Ducie, where he was now the solitary guest. His eye caught Miss Temple's as he entered the room. It seemed to beam upon him with interest and kindness. His courteous and agreeable host welcomed him with polished warmth. It seemed that a feeling of intimacy was already established among them, and he fancied himself already looked upon as an habitual member of their circle. All dark thoughts were driven away. He was gay and pleasant, and duly maintained with Mr. Temple that conversation in which his host excelled. Miss Temple spoke little, but listened with evident interest to her father and Ferdinand. She seemed to delight in their society, and to be gratified by Captain Armine's evident sense of her father's agreeable qualities. When dinner was over they all rose together and repaired to the salon.

'I wish Mr. Glastonbury were here,' said Miss Temple, as Ferdinand opened the instrument. 'You must bring him some day, and then our concert will be perfect.'

Ferdinand smiled, but the name of Glastonbury made him shudder. His countenance changed at the future plans of Miss Temple. 'Some day,' indeed, when he might also take the opportunity of introducing his betrothed! But the voice of Henrietta Temple drove all care from his bosom; he abandoned himself to the intoxicating present. She sang alone; and then they sang together; and as he arranged her books, or selected her theme, a thousand instances of the interest with which she inspired him developed themselves. Once he touched her hand, and he pressed his own, unseen, to his lips.

Though the room was lit up, the windows were open and admitted the moonlight. The beautiful salon was full of fragrance and of melody; the fairest of women dazzled Ferdinand with her presence; his heart was full, his senses ravished, his hopes were high. Could there be such a demon as care in such a paradise? Could sorrow ever enter here? Was it possible that these bright halls and odorous bowers could be polluted by the miserable considerations that reigned too often supreme in his unhappy breast? An enchanted scene had suddenly risen from the earth for his delight and fascination. Could he be unhappy? Why, if all went darker even than he sometimes feared, that man had not lived in vain who had beheld Henrietta Temple! All the troubles of the world were folly here; this was fairy-land, and he some knight who had fallen from a gloomy globe upon some starry region flashing with perennial lustre.

The hours flew on; the servants brought in that light banquet whose entrance in the country seems the only method of reminding our guests that there is a morrow.

"Tis the last night,' said Ferdinand, smiling, with a sigh. 'One more song; only one more. Mr. Temple, be indulgent; it is the last night. I feel,' he added in a lower tone to Henrietta, 'I feel exactly as I did when I left Armine for the first time.'

'Because you are going to return to it? That is wilful.'

'Wilful or not, I would that I might never see it again.'

'For my part, Armine is to me the very land of romance.'

'It is strange.'

'No spot on earth ever impressed me more. It is the finest combination of art and nature and poetical associations I know; it is indeed unique.'

'I do not like to differ with you on any subject.'

'We should be dull companions, I fear, if we agreed upon everything.'

'I cannot think it.'

'Papa,' said Miss Temple, 'one little stroll upon the lawn; one little, little stroll. The moon is so bright; and autumn, this year, has brought us as yet no dew.' And as she spoke, she took up her scarf and wound it round her head. 'There,' she said, 'I look like the portrait of the Turkish page in Armine Gallery.'

There was a playful grace about Henrietta Temple, a wild and brilliant simplicity, which was the more charming because it was blended with peculiarly high breeding. No person in ordinary society was more calm, or enjoyed a more complete self-possession, yet no one in the more intimate relations of life indulged more in those little unstudied bursts of nature, which seemed almost to remind one of the playful child rather than the polished woman; and which, under such circumstances, are infinitely captivating. As for Ferdinand Armine, he looked upon the Turkish page with a countenance beaming with admiration; he wished it was Turkey wherein he then beheld her, or any other strange land, where he could have placed her on his courser, and galloped away in pursuit of a fortune wild as his soul.

Though the year was in decay, summer had lent this night to autumn, it was so soft and sweet. The moonbeam fell brightly upon Ducie Bower, and the illumined salon contrasted effectively with the natural splendour of the exterior scene. Mr. Temple reminded Henrietta of a brilliant fête which had been given at a Saxon palace, and which some circumstances of similarity recalled to his recollection. Ferdinand could not speak, but found himself unconsciously pressing Henrietta Temple's arm to his heart. The Saxon palace brought back to Miss Temple a wild melody which had been sung in the gardens on that night. She asked her father if he recollected it, and hummed the air as she made the enquiry. Her gentle murmur soon expanded into song. It was one of those wild and natural lyrics that spring up in mountainous countries, and which seem to mimic the prolonged echoes that in such regions greet the ear of the pastor and the huntsman. Oh! why did this night ever have an end!

CHAPTER XI.

A Morning Walk.

IT WAS solitude that brought despair to Ferdinand Armine. The moment he was alone his real situation thrust itself upon him; the moment he had quitted the presence of Henrietta Temple he was as a man under the influence of music when the orchestra suddenly stops. The source of all his inspiration failed him; this last night at Ducie was dreadful. Sleep was out of the question; he did not affect even the mimicry of retiring, but paced up and down his room the whole night, or flung himself, when exhausted, upon a restless sofa. Occasionally he varied these monotonous occupations, by pressing his lips to the drawings which bore her name; then relapsing into a profound reverie, he sought some solace in recalling the scenes of the morning, all her movements, every word she had uttered, every look which had illumined his soul. In vain he endeavoured to find consolation in the fond belief that he was not altogether without interest in her eyes. Even the conviction that his passion was returned, in the situation in which he was plunged, would, however flattering, be rather a source of fresh anxiety and perplexity. He took a volume from the single shelf of books that was slung against the wall; it was a volume of Corinne. The fervid eloquence of the poetess sublimated his passion; and without disturbing the tone of his excited mind, relieved in some degree its tension, by busying his imagination with other, though similar emotions. As he read, his mind became more calm and his feelings deeper, and by the time his lamp grew ghastly in the purple light of morning that now entered his chamber, his soul seemed so stilled that he closed the volume, and, though sleep was impossible, he remained nevertheless calm and absorbed.

When the first sounds assured him that some were stirring in the house, he quitted his room, and after some difficulty found a maid-servant, by whose aid he succeeded in getting into the garden. He took his way to the common where he had observed the preceding day, a fine sheet of water. The sun had not risen more than an hour; it was a fresh and ruddy morn. The cottagers were just abroad. The air of the plain invigorated him, and the singing of the birds, and all those rural sounds that rise with the husbandman, brought to his mind a wonderful degree of freshness and serenity. Occasionally he heard the gun of an early sportsman, to him at all times an animating sound; but when he had plunged into the water, and found himself struggling with that inspiring element, all sorrow seemed to leave him. His heated brow became cool and clear, his aching limbs vigorous and elastic, his jaded soul full of hope and joy. He lingered in the liquid and vivifying world, playing with the stream, for he was an expert and practised swimmer; and often, after nights of southern dissipation, had recurred to this natural bath for health and renovation. The sun had now risen far above the horizon; the village clock had long struck seven; Ferdinand was three miles from Ducie Bower. It was time to return, yet he loitered on his way, the air was so sweet and fresh, the scene so pretty, and his mind, in comparison with his recent feelings, so calm, and even happy. Just as he emerged from the woods, and entered the grounds of Ducie, he met Miss Temple. She stared, and she had cause. Ferdinand indeed presented rather an unusual figure; his head uncovered, his hair matted, and his countenance glowing with his exercise, but his figure clothed with the identical evening dress in which he had bid her a tender good night. 'Captain Armine!' exclaimed Miss Temple, 'you are an early riser, I see.'

Ferdinand looked a little confused. 'The truth is,' he replied, 'I have not risen at all. I could not sleep; why, I know not: the evening, I suppose, was too happy for so commonplace a termination; so I escaped from my room as soon as I could do so without disturbing your household; and I have been bathing, which refreshes me always more than slumber.'

'Well, I could not resign my sleep, were it only for the sake of my dreams.'

'Pleasant I trust they were. "Rosy dreams and slumbers light" are for ladies as fair as you.'

'I am grateful that I always fulfil the poet's wish; and what is more, I wake only to gather roses: see here!'

She extended to him a flower.

'I deserve it,' said Ferdinand, 'for I have not neglected your first gift;' and he offered her the rose she had given him the first day of his visit. "Tis shrivelled,' he added, 'but still very sweet, at least to me.'

'It is mine now,' said Henrietta Temple.

'Ah! you will throw it away.'

'Do you think me, then, so insensible?'

'It cannot be to you what it is to me,' replied Ferdinand.

'It is a memorial,' said Miss Temple.

'Of what, and of whom?' enquired Ferdinand.

'Of friendship and a friend.'

"Tis something to be Miss Temple's friend.'

'I am glad you think so. I believe I am very vain, but certainly I like to be——liked.'

'Then you can always gain your wish without an effort.'

'Now I think we are very good friends,' said Miss Temple, 'considering we have known each other so short a time. But then papa likes you so much.'

'I am honoured as well as gratified by the kindly dispositions of so agreeable a person as Mr. Temple. I can assure his daughter that the feeling is mutual. Your father's opinion influences you?'

'In everything. He has been so kind a father, that it would be worse than ingratitude to be less than devoted to him.'

'Mr. Temple is a very enviable person.'

'But Captain Armine knows the delight of a parent who loves him. I love my father as you love your mother.'

'I have, however, lived to feel that no person's opinion could influence me in everything; I have lived to find that even filial love, and God knows mine was powerful enough, is, after all, but a pallid moonlight beam, compared with——'

'See! my father kisses his hand to us from the window. Let us run and meet him.'

CHAPTER XII.

Containing an Ominous Incident.

THE last adieus are bidden: Ferdinand is on his road to Armine, flying from the woman whom he adores, to meet the woman to whom he is betrothed. He reined in his horse as he entered the park. As he slowly approached his home, he could not avoid feeling, that after so long an absence, he had not treated Glastonbury with the kindness and consideration he merited. While he was torturing his invention for an excuse for his conduct he observed his old tutor in the distance; and riding up and dismounting, he joined that faithful friend. Whether it be that love and falsehood are, under any circumstances, inseparable, Ferdinand Armine, whose frankness was proverbial, found himself involved in a long and confused narrative of a visit to a friend, whom he had unexpectedly met, whom he had known abroad, and to whom he was under the greatest obligations. He even affected to regret this temporary estrangement from Armine after so long a separation, and to rejoice at his escape. No names were mentioned, and the unsuspicious Glastonbury, delighted again to be his companion, inconvenienced him with no cross-examination. But this was only the commencement of the system of degrading deception which awaited him.

Willingly would Ferdinand have devoted all his time and feelings to his companion; but in vain he struggled with the absorbing passion of his soul. He dwelt in silence upon the memory of the last three days, the most eventful period of his existence. He was moody and absent, silent when he should have spoken, wandering when he should have listened, hazarding random observations instead of conversing, or breaking into hurried and inappropriate comments; so that to any worldly critic of his conduct he would have appeared at the same time both dull and excited. At length he made a desperate effort to accompany Glastonbury to the picture gallery and listen to his plans. The scene indeed was not ungrateful to him, for it was associated with the existence and the conversation of the lady of his heart: he stood entranced before the picture of the Turkish page, and lamented to Glastonbury a thousand times that there was no portrait of Henrietta Armine.

'I would sooner have a portrait of Henrietta Armine than the whole gallery together,' said Ferdinand.

Glastonbury stared.

'I wonder if there ever will be a portrait of Henrietta Armine. Come now, my dear Glastonbury,' he continued, with an air of remarkable excitement, 'let us have a wager upon it. What are the odds? Will there ever be a portrait of Henrietta Armine? I am quite fantastic to-day. You are smiling at me. Now do you know, if I had a wish certain to be gratified, it should be to add a portrait of Henrietta Armine to our gallery?'

'She died very young,' remarked Glastonbury.

'But my Henrietta Armine should not die young,' said Ferdinand. 'She should live, breathe, smile: she———'

Glastonbury looked very confused.

So strange is love, that this kind of veiled allusion to his secret passion relieved and gratified the overcharged bosom of Ferdinand. He pursued the subject with enjoyment. Anybody but Glastonbury might have thought that he had lost his senses, he laughed so loud, and talked so fast about a subject which seemed almost nonsensical; but the good Glastonbury ascribed these ebullitions to the wanton spirit of youth, and smiled out of sympathy, though he knew not why, except that his pupil appeared happy.

At length they quitted the gallery; Glastonbury resumed his labours in the hall, where he was copying an escutcheon; and after hovering a short time restlessly around his tutor, now escaping into the garden that he might muse over Henrietta Temple undisturbed, and now returning for a few minutes to his companion, lest the good Glastonbury should feel mortified by his neglect, Ferdinand broke away altogether and wandered far into the pleasaunce.

He came to the green and shady spot where he had first beheld her. There rose the cedar spreading its dark form in solitary grandeur, and holding, as it were, its state among its subject woods. It was the same scene, almost the same hour: but where was she? He waited for her form to rise, and yet it came not. He shouted Henrietta Temple, yet no fair vision blessed his expectant sight. Was it all a dream? Had he been but lying beneath these branches in a rapturous trance, and had he only woke to the shivering dulness of reality? What evidence was there of the existence of such a being as Henrietta Temple? If such a being did not exist, of what value was life? After a glimpse of Paradise, could he breathe again in this tame and frigid world? Where was Ducie? Where were its immortal bowers, those roses of supernatural fragrance, and the celestial melody of its halls? That garden, wherein he wandered and hung upon her accents; that wood, among whose shadowy boughs she glided like an antelope, that pensive twilight, on which he had gazed with such subdued emotion; that moonlight walk, when her voice floated, like Ariel's, in the purple sky: were these all phantoms? Could it be that this morn, this very morn, he had beheld Henrietta Temple, had conversed with her alone, had bidden her a soft adieu? What, was it this day that she had given him this rose?

He threw himself upon the turf, and gazed upon the flower. The flower was young and beautiful as herself, and just expanding into perfect life. To the fantastic brain of love there seemed a resemblance between this rose and her who had culled it. Its stem was tall, its countenance was brilliant, an aromatic essence pervaded its being. As he held it in his hand, a bee came hovering round its charms, eager to revel in its fragrant loveliness. More than once had Ferdinand driven the bee away, when suddenly it succeeded in alighting on the rose. Jealous of his rose, Ferdinand, in his haste, shook the flower, and the fragile head fell from the stem!

A feeling of deep melancholy came over him, with which he found it in vain to struggle, and which he could not analyse. He rose, and pressing the flower to his heart, he walked away and rejoined Glastonbury, whose task was nearly accomplished. Ferdinand seated himself upon one of the high cases which had been stowed away in the hall, folding his arms, swinging his legs, and whistling the German air which Miss Temple had sung the preceding night.

'That is a wild and pretty air,' said Glastonbury, who was devoted to music. 'I never heard it before. You travellers pick up choice things. Where did you find it?'

'I am sure I cannot tell, my dear Glastonbury; I have been asking myself the same question the whole morning. Sometimes I think I dreamt it.'

'A few more such dreams would make you a rare composer,' said Glastonbury, smiling.

'Ah! my dear Glastonbury, talking of music, I know a musician, such a musician, a musician whom I should like to introduce you to above all persons in the world.'

'You always loved music, dear Ferdinand; 'tis in the blood. You come from a musical stock on your mother's side. Is Miss Grandison musical?'

'Yes, no, that is to say, I forget: some commonplace accomplishment in the art she has, I believe; but I was not thinking of that sort of thing; I was thinking of the lady who taught me this air.'

'A lady!' said Glastonbury. 'The German ladies are highly cultivated.'

'Yes! the Germans, and the women especially, have a remarkably fine musical taste,' rejoined Ferdinand, recovering from his blunder.

'I like the Germans very much,' said Glastonbury, 'and I admire that air.'

'O! my dear Glastonbury, you should hear it sung by moonlight.'

'Indeed!' said Glastonbury.

'Yes, if you could only hear her sing it by moonlight, I venture to say, my dear Glastonbury, that you would confess that all you had ever heard, or seen, or imagined, of enchanted spirits floating in the air, and filling the atmosphere with supernatural symphonies, was realised.'

'Indeed!' said Glastonbury, 'a most accomplished performer, no doubt! Was she professional?'

'Who?' inquired Ferdinand. 'Your songstress.'

'Professional! oh! ah! yes! No! she was not a professional singer, but she was fit to be one; and that is an excellent idea, too; for I would sooner, after all, be a professional singer, and live by my art, than marry against my inclination, or not marry according to it.'

'Marry!' said Glastonbury, rather astonished; 'what, is she going to be married against her will? Poor devoted thing!'

'Devoted, indeed!' said Ferdinand; 'there is no greater curse on earth.'

Glastonbury shook his head.

'The affections should not be forced,' the old man added; 'our feelings are our own property, often our best.'

Ferdinand fell into a fit of abstraction; then, suddenly turning round, he said, 'Is it possible that I have been away from Armine only two days? Do you know it really seems to me a year!'

'You are very kind to say so, my Ferdinand,' said Glastonbury.

CHAPTER XIII.

In Which Captain Armine Finds Reason to Believe in the
Existence of Fairies.

IT IS difficult to describe the restlessness of Ferdinand Armine. His solitary dinner was an excuse for quitting Glastonbury: but to eat is as impossible as to sleep, for a man who is really in love. He took a spoonful of soup, and then jumping up from his chair, he walked up and down the room, thinking of Henrietta Temple. Then to-morrow occurred to him, and that other lady that to-morrow was to bring. He drowned the thought in a bumper of claret. Wine, mighty wine! thou best and surest consolation! What care can withstand thy inspiring influence! from what scrape canst thou not, for the moment, extricate the victim! Who can deny that our spiritual nature in some degree depends upon our corporeal condition? A man without breakfast is not a hero; a hero well fed is full of audacious invention. Everything depends upon the circulation. Let but the blood flow freely, and a man of imagination is never without resources. A fine pulse is a talisman; a charmed life; a balance at our bankers. It is good luck; it is eternity; it is wealth. Nothing can withstand us; nothing injure us; it is inexhaustible riches. So felt Ferdinand Armine, though on the verge of a moral precipice. To-morrow! did to-morrow? Did to-morrow daunt him? Not a jot. He would wrestle with to-morrow, laden as it might be with curses, and dash it to the earth. It should not be a day; he would blot it out of the calendar of time; he would effect a moral eclipse of its influence. He loved Henrietta Temple. She should be his. Who could prevent him? Was he not an Armine? Was he not the near descendant of that bold man who passed his whole life in the voluptuous indulgence of his unrestrained volition! Bravo! he willed it, and it should be done. Everything yields to determination. What a fool! what a miserable craven fool had he been to have frightened himself with the flimsy shadows of petty worldly cares! He was born to follow his own pleasure; it was supreme; it was absolute; he was a despot; he set everything and everybody at defiance; and, filling a huge tumbler to the health of the great Sir Ferdinand, he retired, glorious as an emperor.

On the whole, Ferdinand had not committed so great an indiscretion as the reader, of course shocked, might at first imagine. For the first time for some days he slept, and slept soundly. Next to wine, a renovating slumber perhaps puts us in the best humour with our destiny. Ferdinand awoke refreshed and sanguine, full of inventive life, which soon developed itself in a flow of improbable conclusions. His most rational scheme, however, appeared to consist in winning Henrietta Temple, and turning pirate, or engaging in the service of some distant and disturbed state. Why might he not free Greece, or revolutionize Spain, or conquer the Brazils? Others had embarked in these bold enterprises; men not more desperate than himself, and not better qualified for the career. Young, courageous, a warrior by profession, with a name of traditionary glory throughout the courts of Christendom, perhaps even remembered in Asia, he seemed just the individual to carve out a glorious heritage with his sword. And as for his parents, they were not in the vale of years; let them dream on in easy obscurity, and maintain themselves at Armine until he returned to redeem his hereditary domain. All that was requisite was the concurrence of his adored mistress. Perhaps, after all his foolish fears and all his petty anxiety, he might live to replace upon her brow the ancient coronet of Tewkesbury! Why not? The world is strange; nothing happens that we anticipate: when apparently stifled by the common-place, we are on the brink of stepping into the adventurous. If he married Miss Grandison, his career was closed: a most unnatural conclusion for one so young and bold. It was evident that he must marry Henrietta Temple: and then? Why then something would happen totally unexpected and unforeseen. Who could doubt it? Not he!

He rose, he mounted his horse, and galloped over to Ducie Common. Its very aspect melted his heart. He called at the cottages he had visited two days before. Without enquiring after Miss Temple, he contrived to hear a thousand circumstances relating to her which interested and charmed him. In the distance rose the woods of Ducie; he gazed upon them as if he could never withdraw his sight from their deep and silent forms. Oh, that sweet bower! Why was there any other world but Ducie? All his brave projects of war, and conquest, and imperial plunder, seemed dull and vain now. He sickened at the thought of action. He sighed to gather roses, to listen to songs sweeter than the nightingale, and wander for ever in moon-lit groves.

He turned his horse's head: slowly and sorrowfully he directed his course to Armine. Had they arrived? The stern presence of reality was too much for all his slight and glittering visions. What was he, after all? This future conqueror was a young officer on leave, obscure except in his immediate circle, with no inheritance, and very much in debt; awaited with anxiety by his affectionate parents, and a young lady whom he was about to marry for her fortune! Most impotent epilogue to a magnificent reverie!

The post arrived at Armine in the afternoon. As Ferdinand, nervous as a child returning to school, tardily regained home, he recognised the approaching postman. Hah! a letter? What was its import? The blessing of delay? or was it the herald of their instant arrival? Pale and sick at heart, he tore open the hurried lines of Katherine. The maiden aunt had stumbled while getting out of a pony phaeton, and experienced a serious accident; their visit to Armine was necessarily postponed. He read no more. The colour returned to his cheek, reinforced by his heart's liveliest blood. A thousand thoughts, a thousand wild hopes and wilder plans, came over him. Here was, at least, one interposition in his favour; others would occur. He felt fortunate. He rushed to the tower, to tell the news to Glastonbury. His tutor ascribed his agitation to the shock, and attempted to console him. In communicating the intelligence, he was obliged to finish the letter; it expressed a hope that, if their visit were postponed for more than a day or two, Katherine's dearest Ferdinand would return to Bath.

Ferdinand wandered forth into the park to enjoy his freedom. A burden had suddenly fallen from his frame; a cloud that had haunted his vision had vanished. To-day, that was so accursed, was to be marked now in his calendar with red chalk. Even Armine pleased him; its sky was brighter, its woods more vast and green. They had not arrived; they would not arrive to-morrow, that was certain; the third day, too, was a day of hope. Why! three days, three whole days of unexpected, unhoped-for freedom, it was eternity! What might not happen in three days! For three days he might fairly remain in expectation of fresh letters. It could not be anticipated, it was not even desired, that he should instantly repair to them. Come, he would forget this curse, he would be happy. The past, the future, should be nothing; he would revel in the auspicious present.

Thus communing with himself, he sauntered along, musing over Henrietta Temple, and building bright castles in the air. A man engaged with his ideas is insensible of fatigue. Ferdinand found himself at the Park gate that led to Ducie; intending only a slight stroll, he had already rambled half way to his beloved. It was a delicious afternoon: the heat of the sun had long abated; the air was sweet and just beginning to stir; not a sound was heard, except the last blow of the woodman's axe, or the occasional note of some joyous bird waking from its siesta. Ferdinand passed the gate; he entered the winding road, the road that Henrietta Temple had so admired; a beautiful green lane with banks of flowers and hedges of tall trees. He strolled along, our happy Ferdinand, indefinite of purpose, almost insensible whether he were advancing or returning home. He plucked the wild flowers, and pressed them to his lips, because she had admired them; rested on a bank, lounged on a gate, cut a stick from the hedge, traced Henrietta Temple in the road, and then turned the words into Henrietta Armine, and so—and so—and so, he, at length, stared at finding himself on Ducie Common.

Beautiful common! how he loved it! How familiar every tree and rustic roof had become to him! Could he ever forget the morning he had bathed in those fresh waters! What lake of Italy, what heroic wave of the midland ocean, could rival in his imagination that simple basin! He drew near to the woods of Ducie, glowing with the setting sun. Surely there was no twilight like the twilight of this land! The woods of Ducie are entered. He recognised the path over which she had glided; he knelt down and kissed that sacred earth. As he approached the pleasure grounds, he turned off into a side path that he might not be perceived; he caught, through a vista, a distant glimpse of the mansion. The sight of that roof wherein he had been so happy; of that roof that contained all that he cared for or thought of in this world, overcame him. He leant against a tree, and hid his face.

The twilight died away, the stars stole forth, and Ferdinand ventured in the spreading gloom of night to approach the mansion. He threw himself upon the turf, and watched the chamber where she lived. The windows were open, there were lights within the room, but the thin curtains were drawn, and concealed the inmates. Happy, happy chamber! All that was bright and fair and sweet were concentrated in those charming walls!

The curtain is withdrawn; an arm, an arm which cannot be mistaken, pulls back the drapery. Is she coming forth? No, she does not; but he sees, distinctly he sees her. She sits in an old chair that he had often praised; her head rests upon her arm, her brow seems pensive; and in her other hand she holds a volume that she scarcely appears to read. Oh! may he gaze upon her for ever! May this celestial scene, this seraphic hour, never pass away. Bright stars! do not fade; thou summer wind that playest upon his brow, perfumed by her flowers, refresh him for ever; beautiful night be for ever the canopy of a scene so sweet and still; let existence glide away in gazing on yon delicate and tender vision!

Dreams of fantastic love: the curtain closes; a ruder hand than hers has shut her from his sight! It has all vanished; the stars seem dim, the autumnal air is dank and harsh; and where he had gazed on heaven, a bat flits wild and fleet. Poor Ferdinand, unhappy Ferdinand, how dull and depressed our brave gallant has become! Was it her father who had closed the curtain? Could he himself, thought Ferdinand, have been observed?

Hark! a voice softer and sweeter than the night breaks upon the air. It is the voice of his beloved; and, indeed, with all her singular and admirable qualities, there was not anything more remarkable about Henrietta Temple than her voice. It was a rare voice; so that in speaking, and in ordinary conversation, though there was no one whose utterance was more natural and less unstudied, it forcibly affected you. She could not give you a greeting, bid you an adieu, or make a routine remark, without impressing you with her power and sweetness. It sounded like a bell, sweet and clear and thrilling; it was astonishing what influence a little word, uttered by this woman, without thought, would have upon those she addressed. Of such fine clay is man made. That beautiful voice recalled to Ferdinand all his fading visions; it renewed the spell which had recently enchanted him; it conjured up again all those sweet spirits that had a moment since hovered over him with their auspicious pinions. He could not indeed see her; her form was shrouded, but her voice reached him; a voice attuned to tenderness, even to love; a voice that ravished his ear, melted his soul, and blended with his whole existence. His heart fluttered, his pulse beat high, he sprang up, he advanced to the window! Yes! a few paces alone divide them: a single step and he will be at her side. His hand is outstretched to clutch the curtain, his———, when suddenly the music ceased. His courage vanished with its inspiration. For a moment he lingered, but his heart misgave him, and he stole back to his solitude.

What a mystery is Love! All the necessities and habits of our life sink before it. Food and sleep, that seem to divide our being as day and night divide Time, lose all their influence over the lover. He is a spiritualised being, fit only to live upon ambrosia, and slumber in an imaginary paradise. The cares of the world do not touch him; its most stirring events are to him but the dusty incidents of bygone annals. All the fortune of the world without his mistress is misery; and with her all its mischances a transient dream. Revolutions, earthquakes, the change of governments, the fall of empires, are to him but childish games, distasteful to a manly spirit. Men love in the plague, and forget the pest, though it rages about them. They bear a charmed life, and think not of destruction until it touches their idol, and then they die without a pang, like zealots for their persecuted creed. A man in love wanders in the world as a somnambulist, with eyes that seem open to those that watch him, yet in fact view nothing but their own inward fancies.

Oh! that night at Ducie, through whose long hours Ferdinand Armine, in a tumult of enraptured passion, wandered in its lawns and groves, feeding on the image of its enchanting mistress, watching the solitary light in her chamber that was to him as the pharos to a mariner in a tumultuous voyage! The morning, the grey cold morning, came at last; he had outwatched the stars, and listened to the matins of the waking birds. It was no longer possible to remain in the gardens unobserved; he regained the common.

What should he do! whither should he wend his course? To Armine? Oh! not to Armine; never could he return to Armine without the heart of Henrietta Temple. Yes! on that great venture he had now resolved; on that mighty hazard all should now be staked. Reckless of consequences, one vast object now alone sustained him. Existence without her was impossible! Ay! a day, a day, a single, a solitary day, should not elapse without his breathing to her his passion, and seeking his fate from her dark eyes.

He strolled along to the extremity of the common. It was a great table land, from whose boundary you look down on small rich valleys; and into one of these, winding his way through fields and pastures, of which the fertile soil was testified by their vigorous hedgerows, he now descended. A long, low farmhouse, with gable ends and ample porch, an antique building that in old days might have been some manorial residence, attracted his attention. Its picturesque form, its angles and twisted chimneys, its porch covered with jessamine and eglantine, its verdant homestead, and its orchard rich with ruddy fruit, its vast barns and long lines of ample stacks, produced altogether a rural picture complete and cheerful. Near it a stream, which Ferdinand followed, and which, after a devious and rapid course, emptied itself into a deep and capacious pool, touched by the early sunbeam, and grateful to the swimmer's eye. Here Ferdinand made his natural toilet; and afterwards slowly returning to the farm-house, sought an agreeable refuge from the sun in its fragrant porch.

The farmer's wife, accompanied by a pretty daughter with downcast eyes, came forth and invited him to enter. While he courteously refused her offer, he sought her hospitality. The good wife brought a table and placed it in the porch, and covered it with a napkin purer than snow. Her viands were fresh eggs, milk warm from the cow, and bread she had herself baked. Even a lover might feed on such sweet food. This happy valley and this cheerful settlement wonderfully touched the fancy of Ferdinand. The season was mild and sunny, the air scented by the flowers that rustled in the breeze, the bees soon came to rifle their sweetness, and flights of white and blue pigeons ever and anon skimmed along the sky from the neighbouring gables that were their dovecotes. Ferdinand made a salutary, if not a plenteous meal; and when the table was removed, exhausted by the fatigue and excitement of the last four-and-twenty hours, he stretched himself at full length in the porch, and fell into a gentle and dreamless slumber.

Hours elapsed before he awoke, vigorous indeed, and wonderfully refreshed; but the sun had already greatly declined. To his astonishment, as he moved, there fell from his breast a beautiful nosegay. He was charmed with this delicate attention from his hostess, or perhaps from her pretty daughter with those downcast eyes. There seemed a refinement about the gift, and the mode of its offering, which scarcely could be expected from these kind yet simple rustics. The flowers, too, were rare and choice; geraniums such as are found only in lady's bower, a cape jessamine, some musky carnations, and a rose that seemed the sister of the one that he had borne from Ducie. They were delicately bound together, too, by a bright blue riband, fastened by a gold and turquoise pin. This was most strange; this was an adventure more suitable to a Sicilian palace than an English farm-house; to the gardens of a princess than the clustered porch of his kind hostess. Ferdinand gazed at the bouquet with a glance of blended perplexity and pleasure; then he entered the farmhouse and made enquiries of his hostess, but they were fruitless. The pretty daughter with the downcast eyes was there too; but her very admiration of the gift, so genuine and unrestrained, proved, if testimony indeed were necessary, that she was not his unknown benefactor: admirer, he would have said; but Ferdinand was in love, and modest. All agreed no one, to their knowledge, had been there; and so Ferdinand, cherishing his beautiful gift, was fain to quit his new friends in as much perplexity as ever.

CHAPTER XIV.

Containing an Incident Which Is the Termination of Most
Tales, though Almost the Beginning of the Present.

IT WAS about two hours before sunset that Captain Armine summoned up courage to call at Ducie Bower. He enquired for Mr. Temple, and learned to his surprise that Mr. Temple had quitted Ducie yesterday morning for Scotland. 'And Miss Temple?' said Ferdinand. 'Is at home, Sir,' replied the servant. Ferdinand was ushered into the salon. She was not there. Our hero was very nervous; he had been bold enough in the course of his walk from the farmhouse, and indulged in a thousand imaginary conversations with his mistress; but, now that he was really about to meet her, all his fire and fancy deserted him. Everything occurred to him inauspicious to his suit; his own situation, the short time she had known him, his uncertainty of the state of her affections. How did he know she was not engaged to another? why should she not be betrothed as well as himself? This contingency had occurred to him before, and yet he had driven it from his thoughts. He began to be jealous; he began to think himself a very great fool; at any rate, he resolved not to expose himself any further. He was clearly premature; he would call to-morrow or next day: to speak to her now was certainly impossible.

The door opened; she entered, radiant as the day! What a smile! what dazzling teeth! what ravishing dimples! her eyes flashed like summer lightning; she extended to him a hand white and soft as one of those doves that had played about him in the morning. Surely never was anyone endued with such an imperial presence. So stately, so majestic, and yet withal so simply gracious; full of such airy artlessness, at one moment she seemed an empress, and then only a beautiful child; and the hand and arm that seemed fashioned to wave a sceptre, in an instant appeared only fit to fondle a gazelle, or pluck a flower.

'How do you do?' she said; and he really fancied she was going to sing. He was not yet accustomed to that marvellous voice. It broke upon the silence, like a silver bell just touched by the summer air. 'It is kind of you to come and see a lone maiden,' she continued; 'papa has deserted me, and without any preparation. I cannot endure to be separated from him, and this is almost the only time that he has refused my solicitation to accompany him. But he must travel far and quickly. My uncle has sent for him; he is very unwell, and papa is his trustee. There is business; I do not know what it is, but I dare say not very agreeable. By-the-bye, I hope Lady Armine is well?'

'My papa has deserted me,' said Ferdinand with a smile. 'They have not yet arrived, and some days may yet elapse before they reach Armine.'

'Indeed! I hope they are well.'

'Yes; they are well.'

'Did you ride here?'

'No.'

'You did not walk?'

'I hardly know how I came; I believe I walked.'

'You must be very tired; and you are standing! pray sit down; sit in that chair; you know that is your favourite chair.'

And Ferdinand seated himself in the very chair in which he had watched her the preceding night.

'This is certainly my favourite chair,' he said; 'I know no seat in the world I prefer to this.'

'Will you take some refreshment? I am sure you will; you must be very tired. Take some hock; papa always takes hock and soda water. I shall order some hock and soda water for you.' She rose and rang the bell in spite of his remonstrance.

'And have you been walking, Miss Temple?' enquired Ferdinand.

'I was thinking of strolling now,' she replied, 'but I am glad that you have called, for I wanted an excuse to be idle.'

An hour passed away, nor was the conversation on either side very brilliantly supported. Ferdinand seemed dull, but, indeed, was only moody, revolving in his mind many strange incidents and feelings, and then turning for consolation in his perplexities to the enchanting vision on which he still could gaze. Nor was Miss Temple either in her usually sparkling vein; her liveliness seemed an effort; she was more constrained, she was less fluent than before. Ferdinand, indeed, rose more than once to depart; yet still he remained. He lost his cap; he looked for his cap; and then again seated himself. Again he rose, restless and disquieted, wandered about the room, looked at a picture, plucked a flower, pulled the flower to pieces.

'Miss Temple,' he at length observed, 'I am afraid I am very stupid!'

'Because you are silent?'

'Is not that a sufficient reason?'

'Nay! I think not; I think I am rather fond of silent people myself; I cannot bear to live with a person who feels bound to talk because he is my companion. The whole day passes sometimes without papa and myself exchanging fifty words; yet I am very happy; I do not feel that we are dull:' and Miss Temple pursued her work which she had previously taken up.

'Ah! but I am not your papa; when we are very intimate with people, when they interest us, we are engaged with their feelings, we do not perpetually require their ideas. But an acquaintance, as I am, only an acquaintance, a miserable acquaintance, unless I speak or listen, I have no business to be here; unless I in some degree contribute to the amusement or the convenience of my companion, I degenerate into a bore.'

'I think you are very amusing, and you may be useful if you like, very;' and she offered him a skein of silk, which she requested him to hold.

It was a beautiful hand that was extended to him; a beautiful hand is an excellent thing in woman; it is a charm that never palls, and better than all, it is a means of fascination that never disappears. Women carry a beautiful hand with them to the grave, when a beautiful face has long ago vanished, or ceased to enchant. The expression of the hand, too, is inexhaustible; and when the eyes we may have worshipped no longer flash or sparkle, the ringlets with which we may have played are covered with a cap, or worse, a turban, and the symmetrical presence which in our sonnets has reminded us so oft of antelopes and wild gazelles, have all, all vanished, the hand, the immortal hand, defying alike time and care, still vanquishes, and still triumphs; and small, soft, and fair, by an airy attitude, a gentle pressure, or a new ring, renews with untiring grace the spell that bound our enamoured and adoring youth!

But in the present instance there were eyes as bright as the hand, locks more glossy and luxuriant than Helen's of Troy, a cheek pink as a shell, and breaking into dimples like a May morning into sunshine, and lips from which stole forth a perfume sweeter than the whole conservatory. Ferdinand sat down on a chair opposite Miss Temple, with the extended skein.

'Now this is better than doing nothing!' she said, catching his eye with a glance half-kind, half-arch. 'I suspect, Captain Armine, that your melancholy originates in idleness.'

'Ah! if I could only be employed every day in this manner!' ejaculated Ferdinand.

'Nay! not with a distaff; but you must do something. You must get into parliament.'

'You forget that I am a Catholic,' said Ferdinand.

Miss Temple slightly blushed, and talked rather quickly about her work; but her companion would not relinquish the subject.

'I hope you are not prejudiced against my faith,' said Ferdinand.

'Prejudiced! Dear Captain Armine, do not make me repent too seriously a giddy word. I feel it is wrong that matters of taste should mingle with matters of belief; but, to speak the truth, I am not quite sure that a Howard, or an Armine, who was a Protestant, like myself, would quite please my fancy so much as in their present position, which, if a little inconvenient, is very picturesque.' Ferdinand smiled. 'My great grandmother was a Protestant,' said Ferdinand, 'Margaret Armine. Do you think Margaret a pretty name?'

'Queen Margaret! yes, a fine name, I think; barring its abbreviation.'

'I wish my great grandmother's name had not been Margaret,' said Ferdinand, very seriously.

'Now, why should that respectable dame's baptism disturb your fancy?' enquired Miss Temple.

'I wish her name had been Henrietta,' replied Ferdinand. 'Henrietta Armine. You know there was a Henrietta Armine once?'

'Was there?' said Miss Temple, rising. 'Our skein is finished. You have been very good. I must go and see my flowers. Come.' And as she said this little word, she turned her fair and finely-finished neck, and looked over her shoulder at Ferdinand with an arch expression of countenance peculiar to her. That winning look, indeed, that clear, sweet voice, and that quick graceful attitude, blended into a spell which was irresistible. His heart yearned for Henrietta Temple, and rose at the bidding of her voice.

From the conservatory they stepped into the garden. It was a delicious afternoon; the sun had sunk behind the grove, and the air, which had been throughout the day somewhat oppressive, was now warm, but mild. At Ducie there was a fine old terrace facing the western hills, that bound the valley in which the Bower was situate. These hills, a ridge of moderate elevation, but of picturesque form, parted just opposite the terrace, as if on purpose to admit the setting sun, like inferior existences that had, as it were, made way before the splendour of some mighty lord or conqueror. The lofty and sloping bank which this terrace crowned was covered with rare shrubs, and occasionally a group of tall trees sprang up among them, and broke the view with an interference which was far from ungraceful, while plants, spreading forth from large marble vases, had extended over their trunks, and sometimes, in their play, had touched even their topmost branches. Between the terrace and the distant hills extended a tract of pasture-land, green and well-wooded by its rich hedgerows; not a roof was visible, though many farms and hamlets were at hand; and, in the heart of a rich and populous land, here was a region where the shepherd or the herdsman was the only evidence of human existence. It was thither, a grateful spot at such an hour, that Miss Temple and her companion directed their steps. The last beam of the sun flashed across the flaming horizon as they gained the terrace; the hills, well wooded, or presenting a bare and acute outline to the sky, rose sharply defined in form; while in another direction some more distant elevations were pervaded with a rich purple tint, touched sometimes with a rosy blaze of soft and flickering light. The whole scene, indeed, from the humble pasture-land that was soon to creep into darkness, to the proud hills whose sparkling crests were yet touched by the living beam, was bathed with lucid beauty and luminous softness, and blended with the glowing canopy of the lustrous sky. But on the terrace and the groves that rose beyond it, and on the glades and vistas into which they opened, fell the full glory of the sunset. Each moment a new shadow, now rosy, now golden, now blending in its shifting tints all the glory of the iris, fell over the rich pleasure-grounds, their groups of rare and noble trees, and their dim or glittering avenues.

The vespers of the birds were faintly dying away, the last low of the returning kine sounded over the lea, the tinkle of the sheep-bell was heard no more, the thin white moon began to gleam, and Hesperus glittered in the fading sky. It was the twilight hour!

That delicious hour that softens the heart of man, what is its magic? Not merely its beauty; it is not more beautiful than the sunrise. It is its repose. Our tumultuous passions sink with the sun, there is a fine sympathy between us and our world, and the stillness of Nature is responded to by the serenity of the soul.

At this sacred hour our hearts are pure. All worldly cares, all those vulgar anxieties and aspirations that at other seasons hover like vultures over our existence, vanish from the serene atmosphere of our susceptibility. A sense of beauty and a sentiment of love pervade our being. But if at such a moment solitude is full of joy, if, even when alone, our native sensibility suffices to entrance us with a tranquil yet thrilling bliss, how doubly sweet, how multiplied must be our fine emotions, when the most delicate influence of human sympathy combines with the power and purity of material and moral nature, and completes the exquisite and enchanting spell!

Ferdinand Armine turned from the beautiful world around him to gaze upon a countenance sweeter than the summer air, softer than the gleaming moon, brighter than the evening star. The shadowy light of purple eve fell upon the still and solemn presence of Henrietta Temple. Irresistible emotion impelled him; softly he took her gentle hand, and, bending his head, he murmured to her, 'Most beautiful, I love thee!'

As, in the oppressive stillness of some tropic night, a single drop is the refreshing harbinger of a slower that clears the heavens, so even this slight expression relieved in an instant the intensity of his over-burthened feelings, and warm, quick, and gushing flowed the words that breathed his fervid adoration. 'Yes!' he continued, 'in this fair scene, oh! let me turn to something fairer still. Beautiful, beloved Henrietta, I can repress no longer the emotions that, since I first beheld you, have vanquished my existence. I love you, I adore you; life in your society is heaven; without you I cannot live. Deem me, oh! deem me not too bold, sweet lady; I am not worthy of you, yet let me love! I am not worthy of you, but who can be? Ah! if I dared but venture to offer you my heart, if that humblest of all possessions might indeed be yours, if my adoration, if my devotion, if the consecration of my life to you, might in some degree compensate for its little worth, if I might live even but to hope——

'You do not speak. Miss Temple, Henrietta, admirable Henrietta, have I offended you? Am I indeed the victim of hopes too high and fancies too supreme? Oh! pardon me, most beautiful, I pray your pardon. Is it a crime to feel, perchance too keenly, the sense of beauty like to thine, dear lady? Ah! tell me I am forgiven; tell me indeed you do not hate me. I will be silent, I will never speak again. Yet, let me walk with you. Cease not to be my companion because I have been too bold. Pity me, pity me, dearest, dearest Henrietta. If you but knew how I have suffered, if you but knew the nights that brought no sleep, the days of fever that have been mine since first we met, if you but knew how I have fed but upon one sweet idea, one sacred image of absorbing life, since first I gazed on your transcendent form, indeed I think that you would pity, that you would pardon, that you might even——

'Tell me, is it my fault that you are beautiful! Oh! how beautiful, my wretched and exhausted soul too surely feels! Is it my fault those eyes are like the dawn, that thy sweet voice thrills through my frame, and but the slightest touch of that light hand falls like a spell on my entranced form! Ah! Henrietta, be merciful, be kind!'

He paused for a second, and yet she did not answer; but her cheek fell upon his shoulder, and the gentle pressure of her hand was more eloquent than language. That slight, sweet signal was to him as the sunrise on the misty earth. Full of hope, and joy, and confidence, he took her in his arms, sealed her cold lips with a burning kiss, and vowed to her his eternal and almighty love! He bore her to an old stone bench placed on the terrace. Still she was silent; but her hand clasped his, and her head rested on his bosom. The gleaming moon now glittered, the hills and woods were silvered by its beam, and the far meads were bathed with its clear, fair light. Not a single cloud curtained the splendour of the stars. What a rapturous soul was Ferdinand Armine's as he sat that night on the old bench, on Ducie Terrace, shrouding from the rising breeze the trembling form of Henrietta Temple! And yet it was not cold that made her shiver.

The clock of Ducie Church struck ten. She moved, saying, in a faint voice, 'We must go home, my Ferdinand!'

BOOK III.

CHAPTER I.

In Which Captain Armine Proves Himself a Complete
Tactician.

THE midnight moon flung its broad beams over the glades and avenues of Armine, as Ferdinand,
riding Miss Temple's horse, re-entered the park. His countenance was paler than the spectral
light that guided him on his way. He looked little like a pledged and triumphant lover; but in his
contracted brow and compressed lip might be read the determination of his soul. There was no
longer a contest between poverty and pride, between the maintenance or destruction of his
ancient house, between his old engagement and his present passion; that was past. Henrietta
Temple was the light in the pharos amid all his stormy fortunes; thither he directed all the
energies of his being; and to gain that port, or sink, was his unflinching resolution.

It was deep in the night before he again beheld the towers and turrets of his castle, and the ivy-
covered fragment of the old Place seemed to sleep in peace under its protecting influence. A wild
and beautiful event had happened since last he quitted those ancient walls. And what would be
its influence upon them? But it is not for the passionate lover to moralise. For him, the regrets of
the past and the chances of the future are alike lost in the ravishing and absorbing present. For a
lover that has but just secured the object of his long and tumultuous hopes is as a diver who has
just plucked a jewel from the bed of some rare sea. Panting and wild he lies upon the beach, and
the gem that he clutches is the sole idea that engrosses his existence.

Ferdinand is within his little chamber, that little chamber where his mother had bid him so
passionate a farewell. Ah! he loves another woman better than his mother now. Nay, even a
feeling of embarrassment and pain is associated with the recollection of that fond and elegant
being, whom he had recognised once as the model of all feminine perfection, and who had been
to him so gentle and so devoted. He drives his mother from his thoughts. It is of another voice
that he now muses; it is the memory of another's glance that touches his eager heart. He falls into
a reverie; the passionate past is acted again before him; in his glittering eye and the rapid play of
his features may be traced the tumult of his soul. A doubt crosses his brow. Is he indeed so
happy; is it not all a dream? He takes from his bosom the handkerchief of Henrietta Temple. He
recognises upon it her magical initials, worked in her own fine dark hair. A smile of triumphant
certainty irradiates his countenance, as he rapidly presses the memorial to his lips, and imprints
upon it a thousand kisses: and holding this cherished testimony of his felicity to his heart, sleep
at length descended upon the exhausted frame of Ferdinand Armine.

But the night that brought dreams to Ferdinand Armine brought him not visions more marvellous
and magical than his waking life. He who loves lives in an ecstatic trance. The world that
surrounds him is not the world of working man: it is fairy land. He is not of the same order as the
labouring myriads on which he seems to tread. They are to him but a swarm of humble-minded
and humble-mannered insects. For him, the human species is represented by a single individual,
and of her he makes an idol. All that is bright and rare is but invented and devised to adorn and
please her. Flowers for her were made so sweet and birds so musical. All nature seems to bear an
intimate relation to the being we adore; and as to us life would now appear intolerable, a burthen
of insupportable and wearying toil, without this transcendent sympathy, so we cannot help
fancying that were its sweet and subtle origin herself to quit this inspired scene, the universe

itself would not be unconscious of its deprivation, and somewhat of the world's lustre might be missed even by the most callous.

The morning burst as beautiful as such love. A rosy tint suffused the soft and tremulous sky, and tinted with a delicate hue the tall trees and the wide lawns, freshened with the light and vanishing dew. The air was vocal with a thousand songs; all was bright and clear, cheerful and golden. Ferdinand awoke from delicious dreams, and gazed upon the scene that responded to his own bright and glad emotions, and inhaled the balmy air, ethereal as his own soul. Love, that can illumine the dark hovel and the dismal garret, that sheds a ray of enchanting light over the close and busy city, seems to mount with a lighter and more glittering pinion in an atmosphere as brilliant as its own plumes. Fortunate the youth, the romance of whose existence is placed in a scene befitting its fair and marvellous career; fortunate the passion that is breathed in palaces, amid the ennobling creations of surrounding art, and greets the object of its fond solicitude amid perfumed gardens, and in the shade of green and silent woods! Whatever may be the harsher course of his career, however the cold world may cast its dark shadows upon his future path, he may yet consider himself thrice blessed to whom this graceful destiny has fallen, and amid the storms and troubles of after-life may look back to these hours, fair as the dawn, beautiful as the twilight, with solace and satisfaction. Disappointment may wither up his energies, oppression may bruise his spirit; but baulked, daunted, deserted, crushed, lone where once all was sympathy, gloomy where all was light, still he has not lived in vain.

Business, however, rises with the sun. The morning brings cares, and although with rebraced energies and renovated strength, then is the season that we are best qualified to struggle with the harassing brood, still Ferdinand Armine, the involved son of a ruined race, seldom rose from his couch, seldom recalled consciousness after repose, without a pang. Nor was there indeed magic withal, in the sweet spell that now bound him, to preserve him, from this black invasion. Anxiety was one of the ingredients of the charm. He might have forgotten his own broken fortunes, his audacious and sanguine spirit might have built up many a castle for the future, as brave as that of Armine; but the very inspiring recollection of Henrietta Temple, the very remembrance of the past and triumphant eve, only the more forced upon his memory the conviction that he was, at this moment, engaged also to another, and bound to be married to two women.

Something must be done; Miss Grandison might arrive this very day. It was an improbable incident, but still it might occur. While he was thus musing, his servant brought him his letters, which had arrived the preceding day, letters from his mother and Katherine, his Katherine. They brought present relief. The invalid had not amended; their movements were still uncertain. Katherine, 'his own Kate,' expressed even a faint fond wish that he would return. His resolution was taken in an instant. He decided with the prescient promptitude of one who has his dearest interests at stake. He wrote to Katherine that he would instantly fly to her, only that he daily expected his attendance would be required in town, on military business of urgent importance to their happiness. This might, this must, necessarily delay their meeting. The moment he received his summons to attend the Horse Guards, he should hurry off. In the meantime, she was to write to him here; and at all events not to quit Bath for Armine, without giving him a notice of several days. Having despatched this letter and another to his mother, Ferdinand repaired to the tower to communicate to Glastonbury the necessity of his immediate departure for London, but he also assured that good old man of his brief visit to that city. The pang of this unexpected departure was softened by the positive promise of returning in a very few days, and returning with his family.

Having made these arrangements, Ferdinand now felt that, come what might, he had at least secured for himself a certain period of unbroken bliss. He had a faithful servant, an Italian, in whose discretion he had justly unlimited confidence. To him Ferdinand intrusted the duty of bringing, each day, his letters to his retreat, which he had fixed upon should be that same picturesque farm-house, in whose friendly porch he had found the preceding day such a hospitable shelter, and where he had experienced that charming adventure which now rather delighted than perplexed him.

CHAPTER II.

A Day of Love.

MEANWHILE the beautiful Henrietta sat in her bower, her music neglected, her drawing thrown aside. Even her birds were forgotten, and her flowers untended. A soft tumult filled her frame: now rapt in reverie, she leaned her head upon her fair hand in charmed abstraction; now rising from her restless seat, she paced the chamber, and thought of his quick coming. What was this mighty revolution that a few short days, a few brief hours had occasioned? How mysterious, yet how irresistible, how overwhelming! Her father was absent, that father on whose fond idea she had alone lived; from whom the slightest separation had once been pain; and now that father claims not even her thoughts. Another, and a stranger's, image is throned in her soul. She who had moved in the world so variously, who had received so much homage and been accustomed from her childhood to all that is considered accomplished and fascinating in man, and had passed through the ordeal with a calm clear spirit; behold, she is no longer the mistress of her thoughts or feelings; she had fallen before a glance, and yielded in an instant to a burning word!

But could she blame herself? Did she repent the rapid and ravishing past? Did regret mingle with her wonder? Was there a pang of remorse, however slight, blending its sharp tooth with all her bliss? No! Her love was perfect, and her joy was full. She offered her vows to that Heaven that had accorded her happiness so supreme; she felt only unworthy of a destiny so complete. She marvelled, in the meekness and purity of her spirit, why one so gifted had been reserved for her, and what he could recognise in her imperfect and inferior qualities to devote to them the fondness of his rare existence.

Ferdinand Armine! Did there indeed ever breathe, had the wit of poet ever yet devised, a being so choice? So young, so beautiful, so lively and accomplished, so deeply and variously interesting! Was that sweet voice, indeed, only to sound in her enchanted ear, that graceful form to move only for the pleasure of her watchful eye? That quick and airy fancy but to create for her delight, and that soft, gentle heart to own no solicitude but for her will and infinite gratification? And could it be possible that he loved her, that she was indeed his pledged bride, that the accents of his adoration still echoed in her ear, and his fond embrace still clung to her mute and trembling lips! Would he always love her? Would he always be so fond? Would he be as faithful as he was now devoted? Ah! she would not lose him. That heart should never escape her. Her life should be one long vigilant device to enchain his being.

What was she five days past? Is it possible that she lived before she met him? Of what did she think, what do? Could there be pursuits without this companion, plans or feelings without this sweet friend? Life must have been a blank, vapid and dull and weary. She could not recall herself before that morning ride to Armine. How rolled away the day! How heavy must have been the hours! All that had been uttered before she listened to Ferdinand seemed without point; all that was done before he lingered at her side, aimless and without an object.

O Love! in vain they moralise; in vain they teach us thou art a delusion; in vain they dissect thine inspiring sentiment, and would mortify us into misery by its degrading analysis. The sage may announce that gratified vanity is thine aim and end; but the lover glances with contempt at his cold-blooded philosophy. Nature assures him thou art a beautiful and sublime emotion; and, he answers, canst thou deprive the sun of its heat because its ray may be decomposed; or does the diamond blaze with less splendour because thou canst analyse its effulgence?

A gentle rustling sounded at the window: Henrietta looked up, but the sight deserted her fading vision, as Ferdinand seized with softness her softer hand, and pressed it to his lips.

A moment since, and she had longed for his presence as the infant for its mother; a moment since, and she had murmured that so much of the morn had passed without his society; a moment since, and it had seemed that no time could exhaust the expression of her feelings. How she had sighed for his coming! How she had hoped that this day she might convey to him what last night she had so weakly, so imperfectly attempted! And now she sat trembling and silent, with downcast eyes and changing countenance!

'My Henrietta!' exclaimed Ferdinand, 'my beautiful Henrietta, it seemed we never should meet again, and yet I rose almost with the sun.'

'My Ferdinand,' replied Miss Temple, scarcely daring to meet his glance, 'I cannot speak; I am so happy that I cannot speak.'

'Ah! tell me, have you thought of me? Did you observe I stole your handkerchief last night? See! here it is; when I slept, I kissed it and wore it next my heart.'

'Ah! give it me,' she faintly murmured, extending her hand; and then she added, in a firmer and livelier tone, 'and did you really wear it near your heart!'

'Near thine; for thine it is, love! Sweet, you look so beautiful to-day! It seems to me you never yet looked half so fair. Those eyes are so brilliant, so very blue, so like the violet! There is nothing like your eyes!'

'Except your own.'

'You have taken away your hand. Give me back my hand, my Henrietta. I will not quit it. The whole day it shall be clasped in mine. Ah! what a hand! so soft, so very soft! There is nothing like your hand.'

'Yours is as soft, dear Ferdinand.'

'O Henrietta! I do love you so! I wish that I could tell you how I love you! As I rode home last night it seemed that I had not conveyed to you a tithe, nay, a thousandth part of what I feel.'

'You cannot love me, Ferdinand, more than I love you.'

'Say so again! Tell me very often, tell me a thousand times, how much you love me. Unless you tell me a thousand times, Henrietta, I never can believe that I am so blessed.'

They went forth into the garden. Nature, with the splendid sky and the sweet breeze, seemed to smile upon their passion. Henrietta plucked the most beautiful flowers and placed them in his breast.

'Do you remember the rose at Armine?' said Ferdinand, with a fond smile.

'Ah! who would have believed that it would have led to this?' said Henrietta, with downcast eyes.

'I am not more in love now than I was then,' said Ferdinand.

'I dare not speak of my feelings,' said Miss Temple. 'Is it possible that it can be but five days back since we first met! It seems another era.'

'I have no recollection of anything that occurred before I saw you beneath the cedar,' replied Ferdinand: 'that is the date of my existence. I saw you, and I loved. My love was at once complete; I have no confidence in any other; I have no confidence in the love that is the creature of observation, and reflection, and comparison, and calculation. Love, in my opinion, should spring from innate sympathy; it should be superior to all situations, all ties, all circumstances.'

'Such, then, we must believe is ours,' replied Henrietta, in a somewhat grave and musing tone: 'I would willingly embrace your creed. I know not why I should be ashamed of my feelings. They are natural, and they are pure. And yet I tremble. But so long as you do not think lightly of me,

Ferdinand, for whom should I care?'

'My Henrietta! my angel! my adored and beautiful! I worship you, I reverence you. Ah! my Henrietta, if you only knew how I dote upon you, you would not speak thus. Come, let us ramble in our woods.'

So saying, he withdrew her from the more public situation in which they were then placed, and entered, by a winding walk, those beautiful bowers that had given so fair and fitting a name to Ducie. Ah! that was a ramble of rich delight, as, winding his arm round her light waist, he poured into her palpitating ear all the eloquence of his passion. Each hour that they had known each other was analysed, and the feelings of each moment were compared. What sweet and thrilling confessions! Eventually it was settled, to the complete satisfaction of both, that both had fallen in love at the same time, and that they had been mutually and unceasingly thinking of each other from the first instant of their meeting.

The conversation of lovers is inexhaustible. Hour glided away after hour, as Ferdinand alternately expressed his passion and detailed the history of his past life. For the curiosity of woman, lively at all times, is never so keen, so exacting, and so interested, as in her anxiety to become acquainted with the previous career of her lover. She is jealous of all that he has done before she knew him; of every person to whom he has spoken. She will be assured a thousand times that he never loved before, yet she credits the first affirmation. She envies the mother who knew him as a child, even the nurse who may have rocked his cradle. She insists upon a minute and finished portraiture of his character and life.

Why did he not give it? More than once it was upon his lips to reveal all; more than once he was about to pour forth all his sorrows, all the entanglements of his painful situation; more than once he was about to make the full and mortifying confession, that, though his heart was hers, there existed another, who even at that moment might claim the hand that Henrietta clasped with so much tenderness. But he checked himself. He would not break the charm that surrounded him; he would not disturb the clear and brilliant stream in which his life was at this moment flowing; he had not courage to change by a worldly word the scene of celestial enchantment in which he now moved and breathed. Let us add, in some degree for his justification, that he was not altogether unmindful of the feelings of Miss Grandison. Sufficient misery remained, at all events, for her, without adding the misery of making her rival cognizant of her mortification. The deed must be done, and done promptly; but, at least, there should be no unnecessary witnesses to its harrowing achievement.

So he looked upon the radiant brow of his Henrietta, wreathed with smiles of innocent triumph, sparkling with unalloyed felicity, and beaming with unbroken devotion. Should the shade of a dark passion for a moment cloud that heaven, so bright and so serene? Should even a momentary pang of jealousy or distrust pain that pure and unsullied breast? In the midst of contending emotions, he pressed her to his heart with renewed energy, and, bending down his head, imprinted an embrace upon her blushing forehead.

They seated themselves on a bank, which, it would seem, Nature had created for the convenience of lovers. The softest moss, and the brightest flowers decked its elastic and fragrant side. A spreading beech tree shaded their heads from the sun, which now was on the decline; and occasionally its wide branches rustled with the soft breeze that passed over them in renovating and gentle gusts. The woods widened before them, and at the termination of a well-contrived avenue, they caught the roofs of the village and the tall grey tower of Ducie Church. They had wandered for hours without weariness, yet the repose was grateful, while they listened to the birds, and plucked wildflowers.

'Ah! I remember,' said Ferdinand, 'that it was not far from here, while slumbering indeed in the porch of my pretty farm-house, that the fairy of the spot dropped on my breast these beautiful flowers that I now wear. Did you not observe them, my sweet Henrietta? Do you know that I am rather mortified, that they have not made you at least a little jealous?'

'I am not jealous of fairies, dear Ferdinand.'

'And yet I half believe that you are a fairy, my Henrietta.'

'A very substantial one, I fear, my Ferdinand. Is this a compliment to my form?'

'Well, then, a sylvan nymph, much more, I assure you, to my fancy; perhaps the rosy Dryad of this fair tree; rambling in woods, and bounding over commons, scattering beautiful flowers, and dreams as bright.'

'And were your dreams bright yesterday morning?'

'I dreamed of you.'

'And when you awoke?'

'I hastened to the source of my inspiration.'

'And if you had not dreamt of me?'

'I should have come to have enquired the reason why.'

Miss Temple looked upon the ground; a blended expression of mirth and sentiment played over her features, and then looking up with a smile contending with her tearful eye, she hid her face in his breast and murmured, 'I watched him sleeping. Did he indeed dream of me?'

'Darling of my existence!' exclaimed the enraptured Ferdinand, 'exquisite, enchanting being! Why am I so happy? What have I done to deserve bliss so ineffable? But tell me, beauty, tell me how you contrived to appear and vanish without witnesses? For my enquiries were severe, and these good people must have been less artless than I imagined to have withstood them successfully.'

'I came,' said Miss Temple, 'to pay them a visit, with me not uncommon. When I entered the porch I beheld my Ferdinand asleep. I looked upon him for a moment, but I was frightened and stole away unperceived. But I left the flowers, more fortunate than your Henrietta.'

'Sweet love!'

'Never did I return home,' continued Miss Temple, 'more sad and more dispirited. A thousand times I wished that I was a flower, that I might be gathered and worn upon your heart. You smile, my Ferdinand. Indeed I feel I am very foolish, yet I know not why, I am now neither ashamed nor afraid to tell you anything. I was so miserable when I arrived home, my Ferdinand, that I went to my room and wept. And he then came! Oh! what heaven was mine! I wiped the tears from my face and came down to see him. He looked so beautiful and happy!'

'And you, sweet child, oh! who could have believed, at that moment, that a tear had escaped from those bright eyes!'

'Love makes us hypocrites, I fear, my Ferdinand; for, a moment before, I was so wearied that I was lying on my sofa quite wretched. And then, when I saw him, I pretended that I had not been out, and was just thinking of a stroll. Oh, my Ferdinand! will you pardon me?'

'It seems to me that I never loved you until this moment. Is it possible that human beings ever loved each other as we do?'

Now came the hour of twilight. While in this fond strain the lovers interchanged their hearts, the sun had sunk, the birds grown silent, and the star of evening twinkled over the tower of Ducie. The bat and the beetle warned them to return. They rose reluctantly and retraced their steps to Ducie, with hearts softer even than the melting hour.

'Must we then part?' exclaimed Ferdinand. 'Oh! must we part! How can I exist even an instant without your presence, without at least the consciousness of existing under the same roof? Oh! would I were one of your serving-men, to listen to your footstep, to obey your bell, and ever and anon to catch your voice! Oh! now I wish indeed Mr. Temple were here, and then I might be your guest.'

'My father!' exclaimed Miss Temple, in a somewhat serious tone. 'I ought to have written to him to-day! Oh! talk not of my father, speak only of yourself.'

They stood in silence as they were about to emerge upon the lawn, and then Miss Temple said, 'Dear Ferdinand, you must go; indeed you must. Press me not to enter. If you love me, now let us part. I shall retire immediately, that the morning may sooner come. God bless you, my Ferdinand. May He guard over you, and keep you for ever and ever. You weep! Indeed you must not; you so distress me. Ferdinand, be good, be kind; for my sake do not this. I love you; what can I do more? The time will come we will not part, but now we must. Good night, my Ferdinand. Nay, if you will, these lips indeed are yours. Promise me you will not remain here. Well then, when the light is out in my chamber, leave Ducie. Promise me this, and early tomorrow, earlier than you think, I will pay a visit to your cottage. Now be good, and to-morrow we will breakfast together. There now!' she added in a gay tone, 'you see woman's wit has the advantage.' And so without another word she ran away.

CHAPTER III.

Which on the Whole Is Found Very Consoling.

THE separation of lovers, even with an immediate prospect of union, involves a sentiment of deep melancholy. The reaction of our solitary emotions, after a social impulse of such peculiar excitement, very much disheartens and depresses us. Mutual passion is complete sympathy. Under such an influence there is no feeling so strong, no fancy so delicate, that it is not instantly responded to. Our heart has no secrets, though our life may. Under such an influence, each unconsciously labours to enchant the other; each struggles to maintain the reality of that ideal which has been reached in a moment of happy inspiration. Then is the season when the voice is ever soft, the eye ever bright, and every movement of the frame airy and picturesque; each accent is full of tenderness; each glance, of affection; each gesture, of grace. We live in a heaven of our own creation. All happens that can contribute to our perfect satisfaction, and can ensure our complete self-complacency. We give and we receive felicity. We adore and we are adored. Love is the May-day of the heart.

But a cloud nevertheless will dim the genial lustre of that soft and brilliant sky when we are alone; when the soft voice no longer sighs, and the bright eye no longer beams, and the form we worship no longer moves before our enraptured vision. Our happiness becomes too much the result of reflection. Our faith is not less devout, but it is not so fervent. We believe in the miracle, but we no longer witness it.

And as the light was extinguished in the chamber of Henrietta Temple, Ferdinand Armine felt for a moment as if his sun had set for ever. There seemed to be now no evidence of her existence. Would tomorrow ever come? And if it came, would the rosy hours indeed bring her in their radiant car? What if this night she died? He shuddered at this wild imagination. Yet it might be; such dire calamities had been. And now he felt his life was involved in hers, and that under such circumstances his instant death must complete the catastrophe. There was then much at stake. Had it been yet his glorious privilege that her fair cheek should have found a pillow on his heart; could he have been permitted to have rested without her door but as her guard; even if the same roof at any distance had screened both their heads; such dark conceptions would not perhaps have risen up to torture him; but as it was, they haunted him like evil spirits as he took his lonely way over the common to gain his new abode.

Ah! the morning came, and such a morn! Bright as his love! Ferdinand had passed a dreamy night, and when he woke he could not at first recognise the locality. It was not Armine. Could it be Ducie? As he stretched his limbs and rubbed his eyes, he might be excused for a moment fancying that all the happiness of yesterday was indeed a vision. He was, in truth, sorely perplexed as he looked around the neat but humble chamber, and caught the first beam of the sun struggling through a casement shadowed by the jessamine. But on his heart there rested a curl of dark and flowing hair, and held together by that very turquoise of which he fancied he had been dreaming. Happy, happy Ferdinand! Why shouldst thou have cares? And may not the course even of thy true love run smooth?

He recks not of the future. What is the future to one so blessed? The sun is up, the lark is singing, the sky is bluer than the love-jewel at his heart. She will be here soon. No gloomy images disturb him now. Cheerfulness is the dowry of the dawn.

Will she indeed be here? Will Henrietta Temple indeed come to visit him? Will that consummate being before whom, but a few days back, he stood entranced; to whose mind the very idea of his existence had not then even occurred; will she be here anon to visit him? to visit her beloved! What has he done to be so happy? What fairy has touched him and his dark fortunes with her wand? What talisman does he grasp to call up such bright adventures of existence? He does not err. He is an enchanted being; a spell indeed pervades his frame; he moves in truth in a world of marvels and miracles. For what fairy has a wand like love, what talisman can achieve the deeds of passion?

He quitted the rustic porch, and strolled up the lane that led to Ducie. He started at a sound: it was but the spring of a wandering bird. Then the murmur of a distant wheel turned him pale; and he stopped and leant on a neighbouring gate with a panting heart. Was she at hand? There is not a moment when the heart palpitates with such delicate suspense as when a lover awaits his mistress in the spring days of his passion. Man watching the sun rise from a mountain awaits not an incident to him more beautiful, more genial, and more impressive. With her presence it would seem that both light and heat fall at the same time upon his heart: his emotions are warm and sunny, that a moment ago seemed dim and frigid; a thrilling sense of joy pervades his frame; the air is sweeter, and his ears seem to echo with the music of a thousand birds.

The sound of the approaching wheel became more audible; it drew near, nearer; but lost the delicacy that distance lent it. Alas! it did not propel the car of a fairy, or the chariot of a heroine, but a cart, whose taxed springs bowed beneath the portly form of an honest yeoman who gave Captain Armine a cheerful good-morrow as he jogged by, and flanked his jolly whip with unmerciful dexterity. The loudness of the unexpected salute, the crack of the echoing thong, shook the fine nerves of a fanciful lover, and Ferdinand looked so confused, that if the honest yeoman had only stopped to observe him, the passenger might have really been excused for mistaking him for a poacher, at the least, by his guilty countenance.

This little worldly interruption broke the wings of Ferdinand's soaring fancy. He fell to earth. Doubt came over him whether Henrietta would indeed come. He was disappointed, and so he became distrustful. He strolled on, however, in the direction of Ducie, yet slowly, as there was more than one road, and to miss each other would have been mortifying.

His quick eye was in every quarter; his watchful ear listened in every direction: still she was not seen, and not a sound was heard except the hum of day. He became nervous, agitated, and began to conjure up a crowd of unfortunate incidents. Perhaps she was ill; that was very bad. Perhaps her father had suddenly returned. Was that worse? Perhaps something strange had happened. Perhaps———

Why! why does his face turn so pale, and why is his step so suddenly arrested? Ah! Ferdinand Armine, is not thy conscience clear? That pang was sharp. No, no, it is impossible; clearly, absolutely impossible; this is weak indeed. See! he smiles! He smiles at his weakness. He waves his arm as if in contempt. He casts away, with defiance, his idle apprehensions. His step is more assured, and the colour returns to his cheek. And yet her father must return. Was he prepared for that occurrence? This was a searching question. It induced a long, dark train of harassing recollections. He stopped to ponder. In what a web of circumstances was he now involved! Howsoever he might act, self-extrication appeared impossible. Perfect candour to Miss Temple might be the destruction of her love; even modified to her father, would certainly produce his banishment from Ducie. As the betrothed of Miss Grandison, Miss Temple would abjure him; as the lover of Miss Temple, under any circumstances, Mr. Temple would reject him. In what light would he appear to Henrietta were he to dare to reveal the truth? Would she not look upon him as the unresisting libertine of the hour, engaging in levity her heart as he had already trifled with another's? For that absorbing and overwhelming passion, pure, primitive, and profound, to which she now responded with an enthusiasm as fresh, as ardent, and as immaculate, she would only recognise the fleeting fancy of a vain and worldly spirit, eager to add another triumph to a long list of conquests, and proud of another evidence of his irresistible influence. What security was there for her that she too should not in turn be forgotten for another? that another eye should not shine brighter than hers, and another voice sound to his ear with a sweeter tone?

Oh, no! he dared not disturb and sully the bright flow of his present existence; he shrank from the fatal word that would dissolve the spell that enchanted them, and introduce all the calculating cares of a harsh world into the thoughtless Eden in which they now wandered. And, for her father, even if the sad engagement with Miss Grandison did not exist, with what front could Ferdinand solicit the hand of his daughter? What prospect could he hold out of worldly prosperity to the anxious consideration of a parent? Was he himself independent? Was he not worse than a beggar? Could he refer Mr. Temple to Sir Ratcliffe? Alas! it would be an insult to both! In the meantime, every hour Mr. Temple might return, or something reach the ear of Henrietta fatal to all his aspirations. Armine with all its cares, Bath with all its hopes; his melancholy father, his fond and sanguine mother, the tender-hearted Katherine, the devoted Glastonbury, all rose up before him, and crowded on his tortured imagination. In the agony of his mind he wished himself alone in the world: he sighed for some earthquake to swallow up Armine and all its fatal fortunes; and as for those parents, so affectionate and virtuous, and to whom he had hitherto been so dutiful and devoted, he turned from their idea with a sensation of weariness, almost of dislike.

He sat down on the trunk of a tree and buried his face in his hands. His reverie had lasted some time, when a gentle sound disturbed him. He looked up; it was Henrietta. She had driven over the common in her pony-chair and unattended. She was but a few steps from him; and as he looked up, he caught her fond smile. He sprang from his seat; he was at her side in an instant; his heart beat so tumultuously that he could not speak; all dark thoughts were forgotten; he seized with a trembling touch her extended hand, and gazed upon her with a glance of ecstasy. For, indeed, she looked so beautiful that it seemed to him he had never before done justice to her surpassing loveliness. There was a bloom upon her cheek, as upon some choice and delicate fruit; her violet eyes sparkled like gems; while the dimples played and quivered on her cheeks, as you may sometimes watch the sunbeam on the pure surface of fair water. Her countenance, indeed, was wreathed with smiles. She seemed the happiest thing on earth; the very personification of a poetic spring; lively, and fresh, and innocent; sparkling, and sweet, and soft. When he beheld her, Ferdinand was reminded of some gay bird, or airy antelope; she looked so bright and joyous!

'He is to get in,' said Henrietta with a smile, and drive her to their cottage. Have I not managed well to come alone? We shall have such a charming drive to-day.'

'You are so beautiful!' murmured Ferdinand.

'I am content if you but think so. You did not hear me approach? What were you doing? Plunged in meditation? Now tell me truly, were you thinking of her?'

'Indeed, I have no other thought. Oh, my Henrietta! you are so beautiful to-day. I cannot talk of anything but your beauty.'

'And how did you sleep? Are you comfortable? I have brought you some flowers to make your room look pretty.'

They soon reached the farm-house. The good-wife seemed a little surprised when she observed her guest driving Miss Temple, but far more pleased. Henrietta ran into the house to see the children, spoke some kind words to the little maiden, and asked if their guest had breakfasted. Then, turning to Ferdinand, she said, 'Have you forgotten that you are to give me a breakfast? It shall be in the porch. Is it not sweet and pretty? See, here are your flowers, and I have brought you some fruit.'

The breakfast was arranged. 'But you do not play your part, sweet Henrietta,' he said; 'I cannot breakfast alone.'

She affected to share his repast, that he might partake of it; but, in truth, she only busied herself in arranging the flowers. Yet she conducted herself with so much dexterity, that Ferdinand had an opportunity of gratifying his appetite, without being placed in a position, awkward at all times, insufferable for a lover, that of eating in the presence of others who do not join you in the occupation.

'Now,' she suddenly said, sitting by his side, and placing a rose in his dress, 'I have a little plan today, which I think will be quite delightful. You shall drive me to Armine.'

Ferdinand started. He thought of Glastonbury.

His miserable situation recurred to him. This was the bitter drop in the cup; yes! in the very plenitude of his rare felicity he expressed a pang. His confusion was not unobserved by Miss Temple; for she was very quick in her perception; but she could not comprehend it. It did not rest on her mind, particularly when Ferdinand assented to her proposition, but added, 'I forgot that Armine is more interesting to you than to me. All my associations with Armine are painful. Ducie is my delight.'

'Ah! my romance is at Armine; yours at Ducie. What we live among, we do not always value. And yet I love my home,' she added, in a somewhat subdued, even serious tone; 'all my associations with Ducie are sweet and pleasant. Will they always be so?'

She hit upon a key to which the passing thoughts of Ferdinand too completely responded, but he restrained the mood of his mind. As she grew grave, he affected cheerfulness. 'My Henrietta must always be happy,' he said, 'at least, if her Ferdinand's love can make her so.'

She did not reply, but she pressed his hand. Then, after a moment's silence, she said, 'My Ferdinand must not be low-spirited about dear Armine. I have confidence in our destiny; I see a happy, a very happy future.'

Who could resist so fair a prophet? Not the sanguine mind of the enamoured Ferdinand Armine. He drank inspiration from her smiles, and dwelt with delight on the tender accents of her animating sympathy. 'I never shall be low-spirited with you,' he replied; 'you are my good genius. O Henrietta! what heaven it is to be together!'

'I bless you for these words. We will not go to Armine to-day. Let us walk. And to speak the truth, for I am not ashamed of saying anything to you, it would be hardly discreet, perhaps, to be driving about the country in this guise. And yet,' she added, after a moment's hesitation, 'what care I for what people say? O Ferdinand! I think only of you!'

That was a delicious ramble which these young and enamoured creatures took that sunny morn! The air was sweet, the earth was beautiful, and yet they were insensible to everything but their mutual love. Inexhaustible is the converse of fond hearts! A simple story, too, and yet there are so many ways of telling it!

'How strange that we should have ever met!' said Henrietta Temple.

'Indeed, I think it most natural,' said Ferdinand; 'I will believe it the fulfilment of a happy destiny. For all that I have sighed for now I meet, and more, much more than my imagination could ever hope for.'

'Only think of that morning drive,' resumed Henrietta, 'such a little time ago, and yet it seems an age! Let us believe in destiny, dear Ferdinand, or you must think of me, I fear, that which I would not wish.'

'My own Henrietta, I can think of you only as the noblest and the sweetest of beings. My love is ever equalled by my gratitude!'

'My Ferdinand, I had read of such feelings, but did not believe in them. I did not believe, at least, that they were reserved for me. And yet I have met many persons, and seen something more, much more than falls to the lot of women of my age. Believe me, indeed, my eye has hitherto been undazzled, and my heart untouched.' He pressed her hand.

'And then,' she resumed, 'in a moment; but it seemed not like common life. That beautiful wilderness, that ruinous castle! As I gazed around, I felt not as is my custom. I felt as if some fate were impending, as if my life and lot were bound up, as it were, with that strange and silent scene. And then he came forward, and I beheld him, so unlike all other men, so beautiful, so pensive! O Ferdinand! pardon me for loving you!' and she gently turned her head, and hid her face on his breast.

'Darling Henrietta,' lowly breathed the enraptured lover, 'best, and sweetest, and loveliest of women, your Ferdinand, at that moment, was not less moved than you were. Speechless and pale I had watched my Henrietta, and I felt that I beheld the being to whom I must dedicate my existence.'

'I shall never forget the moment when I stood before the portrait of Sir Ferdinand. Do you know my heart was prophetic; I wanted not that confirmation of a strange conjecture. I felt that you must be an Armine. I had heard so much of your grandfather, so much of your family. I loved them for their glory, and for their lordly sorrows.'

'Ah! my Henrietta, 'tis that alone which galls me. It is bitter to introduce my bride to our house of cares.'

'You shall never think it so,' she replied with animation. 'I will prove a true Armine. Happier in the honour of that name, than in the most rich possessions! You do not know me yet. Your wife shall not disgrace you or your lineage. I have a spirit worthy of you, Ferdinand; at least, I dare to hope so. I can break, but I will not bend. We will wrestle together with all our cares; and my Ferdinand, animated by his Henrietta, shall restore the house.'

'Alas! my noble-minded girl, I fear a severe trial awaits us. I can offer you only love.'

'Is there anything else in this world?'

'But, to bear you from a roof of luxury, where you have been cherished from your cradle, with all that ministers to the delicate delights of woman, to—oh! my Henrietta, you know not the disheartening and depressing burthen of domestic cares.' His voice faltered as he recalled his melancholy father; and the disappointment, perhaps the destruction, that his passion was preparing for his roof.

'There shall be no cares; I will endure everything; I will animate all. I have energy; indeed I have, my Ferdinand. I have, young as I may be, I have often inspirited, often urged on my father. Sometimes, he says, that had it not been for me, he would not have been what he is. He is my father, the best and kindest parent that ever loved his child; yet, what are fathers to you, my Ferdinand? and, if I could assist him, what may I not do for——'

'Alas! my Henrietta, we have no theatre for action. You forget our creed.'

'It was the great Sir Ferdinand's. He made a theatre.'

'My Henrietta is ambitious,' said Ferdinand, smiling.

'Dearest, I would be content, nay! that is a weak phrase, I would, if the choice were in my power now to select a life most grateful to my views and feelings, choose some delightful solitude, even as Armine, and pass existence with no other aim but to delight you. But we were speaking of other circumstances. Such happiness, it is said, is not for us. And I wished to show you that I have a spirit that can struggle with adversity, and a soul prescient of overwhelming it.'

'You have a spirit I reverence, and a soul I worship, nor is there a happier being in the world this moment than Ferdinand Armine. With such a woman as you every fate must be a triumph. You have touched upon a chord of my heart that has sounded before, though in solitude. It was but the wind that played on it before; but now that tone rings with a purpose. This is glorious sympathy. Let us leave Armine to its fate. I have a sword, and it shall go hard if I do not carve out a destiny worthy even of Henrietta Temple.'

CHAPTER IV.

Henrietta Visits Armine, Which Leads to a Rather
Perplexing Encounter.

THE communion of this day, of the spirit of which the conversation just noticed may convey an intimation, produced an inspiriting effect on the mind of Ferdinand. Love is inspiration; it encourages to great deeds, and develops the creative faculty of our nature. Few great men have flourished who, were they candid, would not acknowledge the vast advantages they have experienced in the earlier years of their career from the spirit and sympathy of woman. It is woman whose prescient admiration strings the lyre of the desponding poet whose genius is afterwards to be recognised by his race, and which often embalms the memory of the gentle mistress whose kindness solaced him in less glorious hours. How many an official portfolio would never have been carried, had it not been for her sanguine spirit and assiduous love! How many a depressed and despairing advocate has clutched the Great Seal, and taken his precedence before princes, borne onward by the breeze of her inspiring hope, and illumined by the sunshine of her prophetic smile! A female friend, amiable, clever, and devoted, is a possession more valuable than parks and palaces; and, without such a muse, few men can succeed in life, none be content.

The plans and aspirations of Henrietta had relieved Ferdinand from a depressing burthen. Inspired by her creative sympathy, a new scene opened to him, adorned by a magnificent perspective. His sanguine imagination sought refuge in a triumphant future. That love for which he had hitherto schooled his mind to sacrifice every worldly advantage appeared suddenly to be transformed into the very source of earthly success. Henrietta Temple was to be the fountain, not only of his bliss, but of his prosperity. In the revel of his audacious fancy he seemed, as it were, by a beautiful retribution, to be already rewarded for having devoted, with such unhesitating readiness, his heart upon the altar of disinterested affection. Lying on his cottage-couch, he indulged in dazzling visions; he wandered in strange lands with his beautiful companion, and offered at her feet the quick rewards of his unparalleled achievements.

Recurring to his immediate situation, he resolved to lose no time in bringing his affairs to a crisis. He was even working himself up to his instant departure, solaced by the certainty of his immediate return, when the arrival of his servant announced to him that Glastonbury had quitted Armine on one of those antiquarian rambles to which he was accustomed. Gratified that it was now in his power to comply with the wish of Henrietta to visit his home, and perhaps, in truth, not very much mortified that so reasonable an excuse had arisen for the postponement of his intended departure, Ferdinand instantly rose, and as speedily as possible took his way to Ducie. He found Henrietta in the garden. He had arrived, perhaps, earlier than he was expected; yet what joy to see him! And when he himself proposed an excursion to Armine, her grateful smile melted his very heart. Indeed, Ferdinand this morning was so gay and light-hearted, that his excessive merriment might almost have been as suspicious as his passing gloom the previous day. Not less tender and fond than before, his sportive fancy indulged in infinite expressions of playful humour and delicate pranks of love. When he first recognised her gathering a nosegay, too, for him, himself unobserved, he stole behind her on tiptoe, and suddenly clasping her delicate waist, and raising her gently in the air, 'Well, lady-bird,' he exclaimed, 'I, too, will pluck a flower!'

Ah! when she turned round her beautiful face, full of charming confusion, and uttered a faint cry of fond astonishment, as she caught his bright glance, what happiness was Ferdinand Armine's, as he felt this enchanting creature was his, and pressed to his bosom her noble and throbbing form!

'Perhaps this time next year, we may be travelling on mules,' said Ferdinand, as he flourished his whip, and the little pony trotted along. Henrietta smiled. 'And then,' continued he, 'we shall remember our pony-chair that we turn up our noses at now. Donna Henrietta, jogged to death over dull vegas, and picking her way across rocky sierras, will be a very different person from Miss Temple, of Ducie Bower. I hope you will not be very irritable, my child; and pray vent your spleen upon your muleteer, and not upon your husband.'

'Now, Ferdinand, how can you be so ridiculous?'

'Oh! I have no doubt I shall have to bear all the blame. "You brought me here," it will be: "Ungrateful man, is this your love? not even post-horses!"'

'As for that,' said Henrietta, 'perhaps we shall have to walk. I can fancy ourselves, you with an Andalusian jacket, a long gun, and, I fear, a cigar; and I with all the baggage.'

'Children and all,' added Ferdinand.

Miss Temple looked somewhat demure, turned away her face a little, but said nothing.

'But what think you of Vienna, sweetest?' enquired Ferdinand in a more serious tone; 'upon my honour, I think we might do great things there. A regiment and a chamberlainship at the least!'

'In mountains or in cities I shall be alike content, provided you be my companion,' replied Miss Temple.

Ferdinand let go the reins, and dropped his whip. 'My Henrietta,' he exclaimed, looking in her face, 'what an angel you are!'

This visit to Armine was so delightful to Miss Temple; she experienced so much gratification in wandering about the park and over the old castle, and gazing on Glastonbury's tower, and wondering when she should see him, and talking to her Ferdinand about every member of his family, that Captain Armine, unable to withstand the irresistible current, postponed from day to day his decisive visit to Bath, and, confident in the future, would not permit his soul to be the least daunted by any possible conjuncture of ill fortune. A week, a whole happy week glided away, and spent almost entirely at Armine. Their presence there was scarcely noticed by the single female servant who remained; and, if her curiosity had been excited, she possessed no power of communicating it into Somersetshire. Besides, she was unaware that her young master was nominally in London. Sometimes an hour was snatched by Henrietta from roaming in the pleasaunce, and interchanging vows of mutual love and admiration, to the picture-gallery, where she had already commenced a miniature copy of the portrait of the great Sir Ferdinand. As the sun set they departed in their little equipage. Ferdinand wrapped his Henrietta in his fur cloak, for the autumn dews began to rise, and, thus protected, the journey of ten miles was ever found too short. It is the habit of lovers, however innocent their passion, to grow every day less discreet; for every day their almost constant companionship becomes more a necessity. Miss Temple had almost unconsciously contrived at first that Captain Armine, in the absence of her father, should not be observed too often at Ducie; but now Ferdinand drove her home every evening, and drank tea at the Bower, and the evening closed with music and song. Each night he crossed over the common to his farmhouse more fondly and devotedly in love.

One morning at Armine, Henrietta being alone in the gallery busied with her drawing, Ferdinand having left her for a moment to execute some slight commission for her, she heard some one enter, and, looking up to catch his glance of love, she beheld a venerable man, of a mild and benignant appearance, and dressed in black, standing, as if a little surprised, at some distance. Herself not less confused, she nevertheless bowed, and the gentleman advanced with hesitation, and with a faint blush returned her salute, and apologised for his intrusion. 'He thought Captain Armine might be there.'

'He was here but this moment,' replied Miss Temple; 'and doubtless will instantly return.' Then she turned to her drawing with a trembling hand.

'I perceive, madam,' said the gentleman, advancing and speaking in a soft and engaging tone, while looking at her labour with a mingled air of diffidence and admiration, 'that you are a fine artist.'

'My wish to excel may have assisted my performance,' replied Miss Temple.

'You are copying the portrait of a very extraordinary personage,' said the stranger.

'Do you think that it is like Captain Armine?' enquired Miss Temple with some hesitation.

'It is always so considered,' replied the stranger. Henrietta's hand faltered; she looked at the door of the gallery, then at the portrait; never was she yet so anxious for the reappearance of Ferdinand. There was a silence which she was compelled to break, for the stranger was both mute and motionless, and scarcely more assured than herself.

'Captain Armine will be here immediately, I have no doubt.'

The stranger bowed. 'If I might presume to criticise so finished a performance,' he remarked, 'I should say that you had conveyed, madam, a more youthful character than the original presents.' Henrietta did not venture to confess that such was her intention. She looked again at the door, mixed some colour, and then cleared it immediately off her palette. 'What a beautiful gallery is this!' she exclaimed, as she changed her brush, which was, however, without a fault.

'It is worthy of Armine,' said the stranger.

'Indeed there is no place so interesting,' said Miss Temple.

'It pleases me to hear it praised,' said the stranger.

'You are well acquainted with it?' enquired Miss Temple.

'I have the happiness to live here,' said the stranger.

'I am not then mistaken in believing that I speak to Mr. Glastonbury.'

'Indeed, madam, that is my name,' replied the gentleman; 'I fancy we have often heard of each other. This a most unexpected meeting, madam, but for that reason not less delightful. I have myself just returned from a ramble of some days, and entered the gallery little aware that the family had arrived. You met, I suppose, my Ferdinand on the road. Ah! you wonder, perhaps, at my familiar expression, madam. He has been my Ferdinand so many years, that I cannot easily school myself no longer to style him so. But I am aware that there are now other claims————'

'My dearest Glastonbury,' exclaimed Ferdinand Armine, starting as he re-entered the gallery, and truly in as great a fright as a man could well be, who perhaps, but a few hours ago, was to conquer in Spain or Germany. At the same time, pale and eager, and talking with excited rapidity, he embraced his tutor, and scrutinised the countenance of Henrietta to ascertain whether his fatal secret had been discovered.

That countenance was fond, and, if not calm, not more confused than the unexpected appearance under the circumstances might account for. 'You have often heard me mention Mr. Glastonbury,' he said, addressing himself to Henrietta. 'Let me now have the pleasure of making you acquainted. My oldest, my best friend, my second father; an admirable artist, too, I can assure you. He is qualified to decide even upon your skill. And when did you arrive, my dearest friend? and where have you been? Our old haunts? Many sketches? What abbey have you explored, what antique treasures have you discovered? I have such a fine addition for your herbal! The Barbary cactus, just what you wanted; I found it in my volume of Shelley; and beautifully dried, beautifully; it will quite charm you. What do you think of this drawing? Is it not beautiful? quite the character, is it not?' Ferdinand paused for lack of breath.

'I was just observing as you entered,' said Glastonbury, very quietly, 'to Miss————'

'I have several letters for you,' said Ferdinand, interrupting him, and trembling from head to foot lest he might say Miss Grandison. 'Do you know you are just the person I wanted to see? How fortunate that you should just arrive! I was annoyed to find you were away. I cannot tell you how much I was annoyed!'

'Your dear parents?' enquired Glastonbury.

'Are quite well,' said Ferdinand, 'perfectly well. They will be so glad to see you, so very glad. They do so long to see you, my dearest Glastonbury. You cannot imagine how they long to see you.'

'I shall find them within, think you?' enquired Glastonbury.

'Oh! they are not here,' said Ferdinand; 'they have not yet arrived. I expect them every day. Every day I expect them. I have prepared everything for them, everything. What a wonderful autumn it has been!'

And Glastonbury fell into the lure and talked about the weather, for he was learned in the seasons, and prophesied by many circumstances a hard winter. While he was thus conversing, Ferdinand extracted from Henrietta that Glastonbury had not been in the gallery more than a very few minutes; and he felt assured that nothing fatal had transpired. All this time Ferdinand was reviewing his painful situation with desperate rapidity and prescience. All that he aspired to now was that Henrietta should quit Armine in as happy ignorance as she had arrived: as for Glastonbury, Ferdinand cared not what he might suspect, or ultimately discover. These were future evils that subsided into insignificance compared with any discovery on the part of Miss Temple.

Comparatively composed, Ferdinand now suggested to Henrietta to quit her drawing, which indeed was so advanced that it might be finished at Ducie; and, never leaving her side, and watching every look, and hanging on every accent of his old tutor, he even ventured to suggest that they should visit the tower. The proposal, he thought, might lull any suspicion that might have been excited on the part of Miss Temple. Glastonbury expressed his gratification at the suggestion, and they quitted the gallery, and entered the avenue of beech trees.

'I have heard so much of your tower, Mr. Glastonbury,' said Miss Temple, 'I am sensible, I assure you, of the honour of being admitted.'

The extreme delicacy that was a characteristic of Glastonbury preserved Ferdinand Armine from the dreaded danger. It never for an instant entered Glastonbury's mind that Henrietta was not Miss Grandi-He thought it a little extraordinary, indeed, that she should arrive at Armine only in the company of Ferdinand; but much might be allowed to plighted lovers; besides, there might be some female companion, some aunt or cousin, for aught he knew, at the Place. It was only his parents that Ferdinand had said had not yet arrived. At all events, he felt at this moment that Ferdinand, perhaps, even because he was alone with his intended bride, had no desire that any formal introduction or congratulations should take place; and only pleased that the intended wife of his pupil should be one so beautiful, so gifted, and so gracious, one apparently so worthy in every way of his choice and her lot, Glastonbury relapsed into his accustomed ease and simplicity, and exerted himself to amuse the young lady with whom he had become so unexpectedly acquainted, and with whom, in all probability, it was his destiny in future to be so intimate. As for Henrietta, nothing had occurred in any way to give rise to the slightest suspicion in her mind. The agitation of Ferdinand at this unexpected meeting between his tutor and his betrothed was in every respect natural. Their engagement, as she knew, was at present a secret to all; and although, under such circumstances, she herself at first was disposed not to feel very much at her ease, still she was so well acquainted with Mr. Glastonbury from report, and he was so unlike the common characters of the censorious world, that she was, from the first, far less annoyed than she otherwise would have been, and soon regained her usual composure, and was even gratified and amused with the adventure.

A load, however, fell from the heart of Ferdinand, when he and his beloved bade Glastonbury a good afternoon. This accidental and almost fatal interview terribly reminded him of his difficult and dangerous position; it seemed the commencement of a series of misconceptions, mortifications, and misfortunes, which it was absolutely necessary to prevent by instantly arresting them with the utmost energy and decision. It was bitter to quit Armine and all his joys, but in truth the arrival of his family was very doubtful: and, until the confession of his real situation was made, every day might bring some disastrous discovery. Some ominous clouds in the horizon formed a capital excuse for hurrying Henrietta off to Ducie. They quitted Armine at an unusually early hour. As they drove along, Ferdinand revolved in his mind the adventure of the morning, and endeavoured to stimulate himself to the exertion of instantly repairing to Bath. But he had not courage to confide his purpose to Henrietta. When, however, they arrived at Ducie, they were welcomed with intelligence which rendered the decision, on his part, absolutely necessary. But we will reserve this for the next chapter.

CHAPTER V.

Which Contains Something Very Unexpected.

MISS TEMPLE had run up stairs to take off her bonnet; Ferdinand stood before the wood fire in the salon. Its clear, fragrant flame was agreeable after the cloudy sky of their somewhat chill drive. He was musing over the charms of his Henrietta, and longing for her reappearance, when she entered; but her entrance filled him with alarm. She was pale, her lips nearly as white as her forehead. An expression of dread was impressed on her agitated countenance. Ere he could speak she held forth her hand to his extended grasp. It was cold, it trembled.

'Good God! you are ill!' he exclaimed. 'No!' she faintly murmured, 'not ill.' And then she paused, as if stifled, leaning down her head with eyes fixed upon the ground.

The conscience of Ferdinand pricked him. Had she heard————

But he was reassured by her accents of kindness. 'Pardon me, dearest,' she said; 'I am agitated; I shall soon be better.'

He held her hand with firmness while she leant upon his shoulder. After a few minutes of harrowing silence, she said in a smothered voice, 'Papa returns to-morrow.'

Ferdinand turned as pale as she; the blood fled to his heart, his frame trembled, his knees tottered, his passive hand scarcely retained hers; he could not speak. All the possible results of this return flashed across his mind, and presented themselves in terrible array to his alarmed imagination. He could not meet Mr. Temple; that was out of the question. Some explanation must immediately and inevitably ensue, and that must precipitate the fatal discovery. The great object was to prevent any communication between Mr. Temple and Sir Ratcliffe before Ferdinand had broken his situation to his father. How he now wished he had not postponed his departure for Bath! Had he only quitted Armine when first convinced of the hard necessity, the harrowing future would now have been the past, the impending scenes, however dreadful, would have ensued; perhaps he might have been at Ducie at this moment, with a clear conscience and a frank purpose, and with no difficulties to overcome but those which must necessarily arise from Mr. Temple's natural consideration for the welfare of his child. These, however difficult to combat, seemed light in comparison with the perplexities of his involved situation. Ferdinand bore Henrietta to a seat, and hung over her in agitated silence, which she ascribed only to his sympathy for her distress, but which, in truth, was rather to be attributed to his own uncertain purpose, and to the confusion of an invention which he now ransacked for desperate expedients. While he was thus revolving in his mind the course which he must now pursue, he sat down on the ottoman on which her feet rested, and pressed her hand to his lips while he summoned to his aid all the resources of his imagination. It at length appeared to him that the only mode by which he could now gain time, and secure himself from dangerous explanations, was to involve Henrietta in a secret engagement. There was great difficulty, he was aware, in accomplishing this purpose. Miss Temple was devoted to her father; and though for a moment led away, by the omnipotent influence of an irresistible passion, to enter into a compact without the sanction of her parent, her present agitation too clearly indicated her keen sense that she had not conducted herself towards him in her accustomed spirit of unswerving and immaculate duty; that, if not absolutely indelicate, her behaviour must appear to him very inconsiderate, very rash, perhaps even unfeeling. Unfeeling! What, to that father, that fond and widowed father, of whom she was the only and cherished child! All his goodness, all his unceasing care, all his anxiety, his ready sympathy, his watchfulness for her amusement, her comfort, her happiness, his vigilance in her hours of sickness, his pride in her beauty, her accomplishments, her affection, the smiles and tears of long, long years, all passed before her, till at last she released herself with a quick movement from the hold of Ferdinand, and, clasping her hands together, burst into a sigh so bitter, so profound, so full of anguish, that Ferdinand started from his seat.

'Henrietta!' he exclaimed, 'my beloved Henrietta!'

'Leave me,' she replied, in a tone almost of sternness.

He rose and walked up and down the room, overpowered by contending emotions. The severity of her voice, that voice that hitherto had fallen upon his ear like the warble of a summer bird, filled him with consternation. The idea of having offended her, of having seriously offended her, of being to her, to Henrietta, to Henrietta, that divinity to whom his idolatrous fancy clung with such rapturous devotion, in whose very smiles and accents it is no exaggeration to say he lived and had his being, the idea of being to her, even for a transient moment, an object of repugnance, seemed something too terrible for thought, too intolerable for existence. All his troubles, all his cares, all his impending sorrows, vanished into thin air, compared with this unforeseen and sudden visitation. Oh! what was future evil, what was tomorrow, pregnant as it might be with misery, compared with the quick agony of the instant? So long as she smiled, every difficulty appeared surmountable; so long as he could listen to her accents of tenderness, there was no dispensation with which he could not struggle. Come what may, throned in the palace of her heart, he was a sovereign who might defy the world in arms; but, thrust from that great seat, he was a fugitive without a hope, an aim, a desire; dull, timid, exhausted, broken-hearted!

And she had bid him leave her. Leave her! Henrietta Temple had bid him leave her! Did he live? Was this the same world in which a few hours back he breathed, and blessed his God for breathing? What had happened? What strange event, what miracle had occurred, to work this awful, this portentous change? Why, if she had known all, if she had suddenly shared that sharp and perpetual woe ever gnawing at his own secret heart, even amid his joys; if he had revealed to her, if anyone had betrayed to her his distressing secret, could she have said more? Why, it was to shun this, it was to spare himself this horrible catastrophe, that he had involved himself in his agonising, his inextricable difficulties. Inextricable they must be now; for where, now, was the inspiration that before was to animate him to such great exploits? How could he struggle any longer with his fate? How could he now carve out a destiny? All that remained for him now was to die; and, in the madness of his sensations, death seemed to him the most desirable consummation.

The temper of a lover is exquisitely sensitive. Mortified and miserable, at any other time Ferdinand, in a fit of harassed love, might have instantly quitted the presence of a mistress who had treated him with such unexpected and such undeserved harshness. But the thought of the morrow, the mournful conviction that this was the last opportunity for their undisturbed communion, the recollection that, at all events, their temporary separation was impending; all these considerations had checked his first impulse. Besides, it must not be concealed that more than once it occurred to him that it was utterly impossible to permit Henrietta to meet her father in her present mood. With her determined spirit and strong emotions, and her difficulty of concealing her feelings; smarting, too, under the consciousness of having parted with Ferdinand in anger, and of having treated him with injustice; and, therefore, doubly anxious to bring affairs to a crisis, a scene in all probability would instantly ensue; and Ferdinand recoiled at present from the consequences of any explanations.

Unhappy Ferdinand! It seemed to him that he had never known misery before. He wrung his hands in despair; his mind seemed to desert him. Suddenly he stopped; he looked at Henrietta; her face was still pale, her eyes fixed upon the decaying embers of the fire, her attitude unchanged. Either she was unconscious of his presence, or she did not choose to recognise it. What were her thoughts?

Still of her father? Perhaps she contrasted that fond and faithful friend of her existence, to whom she owed such an incalculable debt of gratitude, with the acquaintance of the hour, to whom, in a moment of insanity, she had pledged the love that could alone repay it. Perhaps, in the spirit of self-torment, she conjured up against this too successful stranger all the menacing spectres of suspicion, distrust, and deceit; recalled to her recollection the too just and too frequent tales of man's impurity and ingratitude; and tortured herself by her own apparition, the merited victim of his harshness, his neglect, or his desertion. And when she had at the same time both shocked and alarmed her fancy by these distressful and degrading images, exhausted by these imaginary vexations, and eager for consolation in her dark despondency, she may have recurred to the yet innocent cause of her sorrow and apprehension, and perhaps accused herself of cruelty and injustice for visiting on his head the mere consequences of her own fitful and morbid temper. She may have recalled his unvarying tenderness, his unceasing admiration; she may have recollected those impassioned accents that thrilled her heart, those glances of rapturous affection that fixed her eye with fascination. She may have conjured up that form over which of late she had mused in a trance of love, that form bright with so much beauty, beaming with so many graces, adorned with so much intelligence, and hallowed by every romantic association that could melt the heart or mould the spirit of woman; she may have conjured up this form, that was the god of her idolatry, and rushed again to the altar in an ecstasy of devotion.

The shades of evening were fast descending, the curtains of the chamber were not closed, the blaze of the fire had died away. The flickering light fell upon the solemn countenance of Henrietta Temple, now buried in the shade, now transiently illumined by the fitful flame.

On a sudden he advanced, with a step too light even to be heard, knelt at her side, and, not venturing to touch her hand, pressed his lips to her arm, and with streaming eyes, and in a tone of plaintive tenderness, murmured, 'What have I done?'

She turned, her eyes met his, a wild expression of fear, surprise, delight, played over her countenance; then, bursting into tears, she threw her arms round his neck, and hid her face upon his breast.

He did not disturb this effusion of her suppressed emotions. His throbbing heart responded to her tumultuous soul. At length, when the strength of her passionate affections had somewhat decreased, when the convulsive sobs had subsided into gentle sighs, and ever and anon he felt the pressure of her sweet lips sealing her remorseful love and her charming repentance upon his bosom, he dared to say, 'Oh! my Henrietta, you did not doubt your Ferdinand?'

'Dearest Ferdinand, you are too good, too kind, too faultless, and I am very wicked.'

Taking her hand and covering it with kisses, he said in a distinct, but very low voice, 'Now tell me, why were you unhappy?'

'Papa,' sighed Henrietta, 'dearest papa, that the day should come when I should grieve to meet him!'

'And why should my darling grieve?' said Ferdinand.

'I know not; I ask myself, what have I done? what have I to fear? It is no crime to love; it may be a misfortune; God knows that I have almost felt to-night that such it was. But no, I never will believe it can be either wrong or unhappy to love you.'

'Bless you, for such sweet words,' replied Ferdinand. 'If my heart can make you happy, felicity shall be your lot.'

'It is my lot. I am happy, quite happy, and grateful for my happiness.'

'And your father-our father, let me call him [she pressed his hand when he said this]—he will be happy too?'

'So I would hope.'

'If the fulfilment of my duty can content him,' continued Ferdinand, 'Mr. Temple shall not repent his son-in-law.'

'Oh! do not call him Mr. Temple; call him father. I love to hear you call him father.'

'Then what alarms my child?'

'I hardly know,' said Henrietta in a hesitating tone. 'I think—I think it is the suddenness of all this. He has gone, he comes again; he went, he returns; and all has happened. So short a time, too, Ferdinand. It is a life to us; to him, I fear,' and she hid her face, 'it is only———a fortnight.'

'We have seen more of each other, and known more of each other, in this fortnight, than we might have in an acquaintance which had continued a life.'

'That's true, that's very true. We feel this, Ferdinand, because we know it. But papa will not feel like us: we cannot expect him to feel like us. He does not know my Ferdinand as I know him. Papa, too, though the dearest, kindest, fondest father that ever lived, though he has no thought but for my happiness and lives only for his daughter, papa naturally is not so young as we are. He is, too, what is called a man of the world. He has seen a great deal; he has formed his opinions of men and life. We cannot expect that he will change them in your, I mean in our favour. Men of the world are of the world, worldly. I do not think they are always right; I do not myself believe in their infallibility. There is no person more clever and more judicious than papa. No person is more considerate. But there are characters so rare, that men of the world do not admit them into their general calculations, and such is yours, Ferdinand.'

Here Ferdinand seemed plunged in thought, but he pressed her hand, though he said nothing.

'He will think we have known each other too short a time,' continued Miss Temple. 'He will be mortified, perhaps alarmed, when I inform him I am no longer his.'

'Then do not inform him,' said Ferdinand.

She started.

'Let me inform him,' continued Ferdinand, giving another turn to his meaning, and watching her countenance with an unfaltering eye.

'Dearest Ferdinand, always prepared to bear every burthen!' exclaimed Miss Temple. 'How generous and good you are! No, it would be better for me to speak first to my father. My soul, I will never have a secret from you, and you, I am sure, will never have one from your Henrietta. This is the truth; I do not repent the past, I glory in it; I am yours, and I am proud to be yours. Were the past to be again acted, I would not falter. But I cannot conceal from myself that, so far as my father is concerned, I have not conducted myself towards him with frankness, with respect, or with kindness. There is no fault in loving you. Even were he to regret, he could not blame such an occurrence: but he will regret, he will blame, he has a right both to regret and blame, my doing more than love you—my engagement—without his advice, his sanction, his knowledge, or even his suspicion!'

'You take too refined a view of our situation,' replied Ferdinand. 'Why should you not spare your father the pain of such a communication, if painful it would be? What has passed is between ourselves, and ought to be between ourselves. If I request his permission to offer you my hand, and he yields his consent, is not that ceremony enough?'

'I have never concealed anything from papa,' said Henrietta, 'but I will be guided by you.'

'Leave, then, all to me,' said Ferdinand; 'be guided but by the judgment of your own Ferdinand, my Henrietta, and believe me all will go right. I will break this intelligence to your father. So we will settle it?' he continued enquiringly.

'It shall be so.'

'Then arises the question,' said Ferdinand, 'when it would be most advisable for me to make the communication. Now your father, Henrietta, who is a man of the world, will of course expect that, when I do make it, I shall be prepared to speak definitely to him upon all matters of business. He will think, otherwise, that I am trifling with him. To go and request of a man like your father, a shrewd, experienced man of the world like Mr. Temple, permission to marry his daughter, without showing to him that I am prepared with the means of maintaining a family, is little short of madness. He would be offended with me, he would be prejudiced against me. I must, therefore, settle something first with Sir Ratcliffe.

Much, you know, unfortunately, I cannot offer your father; but still, sweet love, there must at least be an appearance of providence and management. We must not disgust your father with our union.'

'Oh! how can he be disgusted?'

'Dear one! This, then, is what I propose; that, as to-morrow we must comparatively be separated, I should take advantage of the next few days, and get to Bath, and bring affairs to some arrangement. Until my return I would advise you to say nothing to your father.'

'How can I live under the same roof with him, under such circumstances?' exclaimed Miss Temple; 'how can I meet his eye, how can I speak to him with the consciousness of a secret engagement, with the recollection that, all the time he is lavishing his affection upon me, my heart is yearning for another, and that, while he is laying plans of future companionship, I am meditating, perhaps, an eternal separation!'

'Sweet Henrietta, listen to me one moment. Suppose I had quitted you last night for Bath, merely for this purpose, as indeed we had once thought of, and that your father had arrived at Ducie before I had returned to make my communication: would you style your silence, under such circumstances, a secret engagement? No, no, dear love; this is an abuse of terms. It would be a delicate consideration for a parent's feelings.'

'O Ferdinand! would we were united, and had no cares!'

'You would not consider our projected union a secret engagement, if, after passing to-morrow with your father, you expected me on the next day to communicate to him our position. Is it any more a secret engagement because six or seven days are to elapse before this communication takes place, instead of one? My Henrietta is indeed fighting with shadows!'

'Ferdinand, I cannot reason like you; but I feel unhappy when I think of this.'

'Dearest Henrietta! feel only that you are loved. Think, darling, the day will come when we shall smile at all these cares. All will flow smoothly yet, and we shall all yet live at Armine, Mr. Temple and all.'

'Papa likes you so much too, Ferdinand, I should be miserable if you offended him.'

'Which I certainly should do if I were not to speak to Sir Ratcliffe first.'

'Do you, indeed, think so?'

'Indeed I am certain.'

'But cannot you write to Sir Ratcliffe, Ferdinand? Must you really go? Must we, indeed, be separated? I cannot believe it; it is inconceivable; it is impossible; I cannot endure it.'

'It is, indeed, terrible,' said Ferdinand. 'This consideration alone reconciles me to the necessity: I know my father well; his only answer to a communication of this kind would be an immediate summons to his side. Now, is it not better that this meeting should take place when we must necessarily be much less together than before, than at a later period, when we may, perhaps, be constant companions with the sanction of our parents?'

'O Ferdinand! you reason, I only feel.'

Such an observation from one's mistress is rather a reproach than a compliment. It was made, in the present instance, to a man whose principal characteristic was, perhaps, a too dangerous susceptibility; a man of profound and violent passions, yet of a most sweet and tender temper; capable of deep reflection, yet ever acting from the impulse of sentiment, and ready at all times to sacrifice every consideration to his heart. The prospect of separation from Henrietta, for however short a period, was absolute agony to him; he found difficulty in conceiving existence without the influence of her perpetual presence: their parting even for the night was felt by him as an onerous deprivation. The only process, indeed, that could at present prepare and console him for the impending sorrow would have been the frank indulgence of the feelings which it called forth. Yet behold him, behold this unhappy victim of circumstances, forced to deceive, even for her happiness, the being whom he idolised; compelled, at this hour of anguish, to bridle his heart, lest he should lose for a fatal instant his command over his head; and, while he was himself conscious that not in the wide world, perhaps, existed a man who was sacrificing more for his mistress, obliged to endure, even from her lips, a remark which seemed to impute to him a deficiency of feeling. And yet it was too much; he covered his eyes with his hand, and said, in a low and broken voice, 'Alas! my Henrietta, if you knew all, you would not say this!'

'My Ferdinand,' she exclaimed, touched by that tender and melancholy tone, 'why, what is this? you weep! What have I said, what done? Dearest Ferdinand, do not do this.' And she threw herself on her knees before him, and looked up into his face with scrutinising affection.

He bent down his head, and pressed his lips to her forehead. 'O Henrietta!' he exclaimed, 'we have been so happy!'

'And shall be so, my own. Doubt not my word, all will go right. I am so sorry, I am so miserable, that I made you unhappy to-night. I shall think of it when you are gone. I shall remember how naughty I was. It was so wicked, so very, very wicked; and he was so good.'

'Gone! what a dreadful word! And shall we not be together to-morrow, Henrietta? Oh! what a morrow! Think of me, dearest. Do not let me for a moment escape from your memory.'

'Tell me exactly your road; let me know exactly where you will be at every hour; write to me on the road; if it be only a line, only a little word; only his dear name; only Ferdinand!'

'And how shall I write to you? Shall I direct to you here?'

Henrietta looked perplexed. 'Papa opens the bag every morning, and every morning you must write, or I shall die. Ferdinand, what is to be done'?'

'I will direct to you at the post-office. You must send for your letters.'

'I tremble. Believe me, it will be noticed. It will look so—so—so—clandestine.'

'I will direct them to your maid. She must be our confidante.'

'Ferdinand!'

"Tis only for a week.'

'O Ferdinand! Love teaches us strange things.'

'My darling, believe me, it is wise and well. Think how desolate we should be without constant correspondence. As for myself, I shall write to you every hour, and, unless I hear from you as often, I shall believe only in evil!'

'Let it be as you wish. God knows my heart is pure. I pretend no longer to regulate my destiny. I am yours, Ferdinand. Be you responsible for all that affects my honour or my heart.'

'A precious trust, my Henrietta, and dearer to me than all the glory of my ancestors.'

The clock sounded eleven. Miss Temple rose. 'It is so late, and we in darkness here! What will they think? Ferdinand, sweetest, rouse the fire. I ring the bell. Lights will come, and then———'
Her voice faltered.

'And then———' echoed Ferdinand. He took up his guitar, but he could not command his voice.

''Tis your guitar,' said Henrietta; 'I am happy that it is left behind.'

The servant entered with lights, drew the curtains, renewed the fire, arranged the room, and withdrew.

'Little knows he our misery,' said Henrietta. 'It seemed strange, when I felt my own mind, that there could be anything so calm and mechanical in the world.'

Ferdinand was silent. He felt that the hour of departure had indeed arrived, yet he had not courage to move. Henrietta, too, did not speak. She reclined on the sofa, as it were, exhausted, and placed her handkerchief over her face. Ferdinand leant over the fire. He was nearly tempted to give up his project, confess all to his father by letter, and await his decision. Then he conjured up the dreadful scenes at Bath, and then he remembered that, at all events, tomorrow he must not appear at Ducie. 'Henrietta!' he at length said.

'A minute, Ferdinand, yet a minute,' she exclaimed in an excited tone; 'do not speak, I am preparing myself.'

He remained in his leaning posture; and in a few moments Miss Temple rose and said, 'Now, Ferdinand, I am ready.' He looked round. Her countenance was quite pale, but fixed and calm. 'Let us embrace,' she said, 'but let us say nothing.'

He pressed her to his arms. She trembled. He imprinted a thousand kisses on her cold lips; she received them with no return. Then she said in a low voice, 'Let me leave the room first;' and, giving him one kiss upon his forehead, Henrietta Temple disappeared.

When Ferdinand with a sinking heart and a staggering step quitted Ducie, he found the night so dark that it was with extreme difficulty he traced, or rather groped, his way through the grove. The absolute necessity of watching every step he took in some degree diverted his mind from his painful meditations. The atmosphere of the wood was so close, that he congratulated himself when he had gained its skirts; but just as he was about to emerge upon the common, and was looking forward to the light of some cottage as his guide in this gloomy wilderness, a flash of lightning that seemed to cut the sky in twain, and to descend like a flight of fiery steps from the highest heavens to the lowest earth, revealed to him for a moment the whole broad bosom of the common, and showed to him that nature to-night was as disordered and perturbed as his own heart. A clap of thunder, that might have been the herald of Doomsday, woke the cattle from their slumbers. They began to moan and low to the rising wind, and cluster under the trees, that sent forth with their wailing branches sounds scarcely less dolorous and wild. Avoiding the woods, and striking into the most open part of the country, Ferdinand watched the progress of the tempest.

For the wind had now risen to such a height that the leaves and branches of the trees were carried about in vast whirls and eddies, while the waters of the lake, where in serener hours Ferdinand was accustomed to bathe, were lifted out of their bed, and inundated the neighbouring settlements. Lights were now seen moving in the cottages, and then the forked lightning, pouring down at the same time from opposite quarters of the sky, exposed with an awful distinctness, and a fearful splendour, the wide-spreading scene of danger and devastation.

Now descended the rain in such overwhelming torrents, that it was as if a waterspout had burst, and Ferdinand gasped for breath beneath its oppressive power; while the blaze of the variegated lightning, the crash of the thunder, and the roar of the wind, all simultaneously in movement, indicated the fulness of the storm. Succeeded then that strange lull that occurs in the heart of a tempest, when the unruly and disordered elements pause, as it were, for breath, and seem to concentrate their energies for an increased and final explosion. It came at last; and the very earth seemed to rock in the passage of the hurricane.

Exposed to all the awful chances of the storm, one solitary being alone beheld them without terror. The mind of Ferdinand Armine grew calm, as nature became more disturbed. He moralised amid the whirlwind. He contrasted the present tumult and distraction with the sweet and beautiful serenity which the same scene had presented when, a short time back, he first beheld it. His love, too, had commenced in stillness and in sunshine; was it, also, to end in storm and in destruction?

BOOK IV.

CHAPTER I.

Which Contains a Love-Letter.

LET us pause. We have endeavoured to trace, in the preceding portion of this history, the development of that passion which is at once the principle and end of our existence; that passion compared to whose delights all the other gratifications of our nature—wealth, and power, and fame, sink into insignificance; and which, nevertheless, by the ineffable beneficence of our Creator, is open to his creatures of all conditions, qualities, and climes. Whatever be the lot of man, however unfortunate, however oppressed, if he only love and be loved, he must strike a balance in favour of existence; for love can illumine the dark roof of poverty, and can lighten the fetters of the slave.

But, if the most miserable position of humanity be tolerable with its support, so also the most splendid situations of our life are wearisome without its inspiration. The golden palace requires a mistress as magnificent; and the fairest garden, besides the song of birds and the breath of flowers, calls for the sigh of sympathy. It is at the foot of woman that we lay the laurels that without her smile would never have been gained: it is her image that strings the lyre of the poet, that animates our voice in the blaze of eloquent faction, and guides our brain in the august toils of stately councils.

But this passion, so charming in its nature, so equal in its dispensation, so universal in its influence, never assumes a power so vast, or exerts an authority so captivating, as when it is experienced for the first time. Then it is truly irresistible and enchanting, fascinating and despotic; and, whatever may be the harsher feelings that life may develop, there is no one, however callous or constrained he may have become, whose brow will not grow pensive at the memory of first love.

The magic of first love is our ignorance that it can ever end. It is the dark conviction that feelings the most ardent may yet grow cold, and that emotions the most constant and confirmed are, nevertheless, liable to change, that taints the feebler spell of our later passions, though they may spring from a heart that has lost little of its original freshness, and be offered to one infinitely more worthy of the devotion than was our first idol. To gaze upon a face, and to believe that for ever we must behold it with the same adoration; that those eyes, in whose light we live, will for ever meet ours with mutual glances of rapture and devotedness; to be conscious that all conversation with others sounds vapid and spiritless, compared with the endless expression of our affection; to feel our heart rise at the favoured voice; and to believe that life must hereafter consist of a ramble through the world, pressing but one fond hand, and leaning but upon one faithful breast; oh! must this sweet credulity indeed be dissipated? Is there no hope for them so full of hope? no pity for them so abounding with love?

And can it be possible that the hour can ever arrive when the former votaries of a mutual passion so exquisite and engrossing can meet each other with indifference, almost with unconsciousness, and recall with an effort their vanished scenes of felicity, that quick yet profound sympathy, that ready yet boundless confidence, all that charming abandonment of self, and that vigilant and prescient fondness that anticipates all our wants and all our wishes? It makes the heart ache but to picture such vicissitudes to the imagination. They are images full of distress, and misery, and gloom. The knowledge that such changes can occur flits over the mind like the thought of death, obscuring all our gay fancies with its bat-like wing, and tainting the healthy atmosphere of our happiness with its venomous expirations. It is not so much ruined cities that were once the capital glories of the world, or mouldering temples breathing with oracles no more believed, or arches of triumph which have forgotten the heroic name they were piled up to celebrate, that fill the mind with half so mournful an expression of the instability of human fortunes, as these sad spectacles of exhausted affections, and, as it were, traditionary fragments of expired passion. The morning, which broke sweet, and soft, and clear, brought Ferdinand, with its first glimmer, a letter from Henrietta.

Henrietta to Ferdinand.

Mine own! I have not lain down the whole night. What a terrible, what an awful night! To think that he was in the heart of that fearful storm! What did, what could you do? How I longed to be with you! And I could only watch the tempest from my window, and strain my eyes at every flash of lightning, in the vain hope that it might reveal him! Is he well, is he unhurt? Until my messenger return I can imagine only evil. How often I was on the point of sending out the household, and yet I thought it must be useless, and might displease him! I knew not what to do. I beat about my chamber like a silly bird in a cage. Tell me the truth, my Ferdinand; conceal nothing. Do not think of moving to-day. If you feel the least unwell, send immediately for advice. Write to me one line, only one line, to tell me you are well. I shall be in despair until I hear from you. Do not keep the messenger an instant. He is on my pony. He promises to return in a very, very short time. I pray for you, as I prayed for you the whole long night, that seemed as if it would never end. God bless you, my Ferdinand! Write only one word to your own Henrietta.

Ferdinand to Henrietta.

Sweetest, dearest Henrietta!

I am quite well, and love you, if that could be, more than ever. Darling, to send to see after her Ferdinand! A wet jacket, and I experienced no greater evil, does not frighten me. The storm was magnificent; I would not have missed it for the world. But I regret it now, because my Henrietta did not sleep. Sweetest love, let me come on to you! Your page is inexorable. He will not let me write another line. God bless you, my Henrietta, my beloved, my matchless Henrietta! Words cannot tell you how I love you, how I dote upon you, my darling. Thy Ferdinand.

Henrietta to Ferdinand.

No! you must not come here. It would be unwise, it would be silly. We could only be together a moment, and, though a moment with you is heaven, I cannot endure again the agony of parting. O Ferdinand! what has that separation not cost me! Pangs that I could not conceive any human misery could occasion. My Ferdinand, may we some day be happy! It seems to me now that happiness can never come again. And yet I ought to be grateful that he was uninjured last night. I dared not confess to you before what evils I anticipated. Do you know I was so foolish that I thought every flash of lightning must descend on your head. I dare not now own how foolish I was. God be praised that he is well. But is he sure that he is quite well? If you have the slightest cold, dearest, do not move. Postpone that journey on which all our hopes are fixed. Colds bring fever. But you laugh at me; you are a man and a soldier; you laugh at a woman's caution.

Ohl my Ferdinand, I am so selfish that I should not care if you were ill, if I might only be your nurse. What happiness, what exquisite happiness, would that be!

Do not be angry with your Henrietta, but I am nervous about concealing our engagement from papa. What I have promised I will perform, fear not that; I will never deceive you, no, not even for your fancied benefit; but I feel the burthen of this secrecy more than I can express, more than I wish to express. I do not like to say anything that can annoy you, especially at this moment, when I feel from my own heart how you must require all the support and solace of unbroken fondness. I have such confidence in your judgment, my Ferdinand, that I feel convinced you have acted wisely; but come back as soon as you can. I know it must be more than a week; I know that that prospect was only held out by your affection. Days must elapse before you can reach Bath; and I know, Ferdinand, I know your office is more difficult than you will confess. But come back, my own, as soon as you can, and write to me at the post-office, as you settled. If you are well, as you say, leave the farm directly. The consciousness that you are so near makes me restless. Remember, in a few hours papa will be here. I wish to meet him with as much calmness as I can command.

Ferdinand, I must bid you adieu! My tears are too evident. See, they fall upon the page. Think of me always. Never let your Henrietta be absent from your thoughts. If you knew how desolate this house is! Your guitar is on the sofa; a ghost of departed joy!

Farewell, Ferdinand! I cannot write, I cannot restrain my tears. I know not what to do. I almost wish papa would return, though I dread to see him. I feel the desolation of this house, I am so accustomed to see you here!

Heaven be with you, and guard over you, and cherish you, and bless you. Think always of me. Would that this pen could express the depth and devotion of my feelings!

Henrietta.

CHAPTER II.

Which, Supposing the Reader Is Interested in the
Correspondence, Pursues It.

DEAREST! A thousand, thousand thanks, a thousand, thousand blessings, for your letter from Armine, dear, dear Armine, where some day we shall be so happy! It was such a darling letter, so long, so kind, and so clear. How could you for a moment fancy that your Henrietta would not be able to decipher that dear, dear handwriting! Always cross, dearest: your handwriting is so beautiful that I never shall find the slightest difficulty in making it out, if your letters were crossed a thousand times. Besides, to tell the truth, I should rather like to experience a little difficulty in reading your letters, for I read them so often, over and over again, till I get them by heart, and it is such a delight every now and then to find out some new expression that escaped me in the first fever of perusal; and then it is sure to be some darling word, fonder than all the rest!

Oh! my Ferdinand, how shall I express to you my love? It seems to me now that I never loved you until this separation, that I have never been half grateful enough to you for all your goodness. It makes me weep to remember all the soft things you have said, all the kind things you have done for me, and to think that I have not conveyed to you at the time a tithe of my sense of all your gentle kindness. You are so gentle, Ferdinand! I think that is the greatest charm of your character. My gentle, gentle love! so unlike all other persons that I have met with! Your voice is so sweet, your manner so tender, I am sure you have the kindest heart that ever existed: and then it is a daring spirit, too, and that I love!

Be of good cheer, my Ferdinand, all will go well. I am full of hope, and would be of joy, if you were here, and yet I am joyful, too, when I think of all your love. I can sit for hours and recall the past, it is so sweet. When I received your dear letter from Armine yesterday, and knew indeed that you had gone, I went and walked in our woods, and sat down on the very bank we loved so, and read your letter over and over again; and then I thought of all you had said. It is so strange; I think I could repeat every word you have uttered since we first knew each other. The morning that began so miserably wore away before I dreamed it could be noon.

Papa arrived about an hour before dinner. So kind and good! And why should he not be? I was ashamed of myself afterwards for seeming surprised that he was the same as ever. He asked me if your family had returned to Armine. I said that you had expected them daily. Then he asked me if I had seen you. I said very often, but that you had now gone to Bath, as their return had been prevented by the illness of a relative. Did I right in this? I looked as unconcerned as I could when I spoke of you, but my heart throbbed, oh! how it throbbed! I hope, however, I did not change colour; I think not; for I had schooled myself for this conversation. I knew it must ensue. Believe me, Ferdinand, papa really likes you, and is prepared to love you. He spoke of you in a tone of genuine kindness. I gave him your message about the shooting at Armine; that you regretted his unexpected departure had prevented you from speaking before, but that it was at his entire command, only that, after Ducie, all you could hope was, that the extent of the land might make up for the thinness of the game. He was greatly pleased. Adieu! All good angels guard over you. I will write every day to the post-office, Bath. Think of me very much. Your own faithful Henrietta.

Letter II.

Henrietta to Ferdinand.

O Ferdinand, what heaven it is to think of you, and to read your letters! This morning brought me two; the one from London, and the few lines you wrote me as the mail stopped on the road. Do you know, you will think me very ungrateful, but those dear few lines, I believe I must confess, I prefer them even to your beautiful long letter. It was so kind, so tender, so sweetly considerate, so like my Ferdinand, to snatch the few minutes that should have been given to rest and food to write to his Henrietta. I love you for it a thousand times more than ever! I hope you are really well: I hope you tell me truth. This is a great fatigue, even for you. It is worse than our mules that we once talked of. Does he recollect? Oh! what joyous spirits my Ferdinand was in that happy day! I love him when he laughs, and yet I think he won my heart with those pensive eyes of his! Papa is most kind, and suspects nothing. Yesterday I mentioned you first. I took up your guitar, and said to whom it belonged. I thought it more natural not to be silent about you. Besides, dearest, papa really likes you, and I am sure will love you very much when he knows all, and it is such a pleasure to me to hear you praised and spoken of with kindness by those I love. I have, of course, little to say about myself. I visit my birds, tend my flowers, and pay particular attention to all those I remember that you admired or touched. Sometimes I whisper to them, and tell them that you will soon return, for, indeed, they seem to miss you, and to droop their heads like their poor mistress. Oh! my Ferdinand, shall we ever again meet? Shall I, indeed, ever again listen to that sweet voice, and will it tell me again that it loves me with the very selfsame accents that ring even now in my fascinated ear?

O Ferdinand! this love is a fever, a fever of health. I cannot sleep; I can scarcely countenance my father at his meals. I am wild and restless; but I am happy, happy in the consciousness of your fond devotion. To-morrow I purpose visiting our farm-house. I think papa will shoot to-morrow. My heart will throb, I fancy, when I see our porch. God bless my own love; the idol of his fond and happy

Henrietta.

Letter III.

Henrietta to Ferdinand.

Dearest! No letter since the few lines on the road, but I suppose it was impossible. To-morrow will bring me one, I suppose, from Bath. I know not why I tremble when I write that word. All is well here, papa most kind, the same as ever. He went a little on your land to-day, a very little, but it pleased me. He has killed an Armine hare! Oh! what a morning have I spent; so happy, so sorrowful, so full of tears and smiles! I hardly know whether I laughed or wept most. That dear, dear farm-house! And then they all talked of you. How they do love my Ferdinand! But so must everyone. The poor woman has lost her heart to you, I suspect, and I am half inclined to be a little jealous. She did so praise you! So kind, so gentle, giving such little trouble, and, as I fear, so much too generous! Exactly like my Ferdinand; but, really, this was unnecessary. Pardon me, love, but I am learning prudence.

Do you know, I went into your room? I contrived to ascend alone; the good woman followed me, but I was there alone a moment, and, and, and, what do you think I did? I pressed my lips to your pillow. I could not help it; when I thought that his dear head had rested there so often and so lately, I could not refrain from pressing my lips to that favoured resting-place, and I am afraid I shed a tear besides.

When mine own love receives this he will be at Bath. How I pray that you may find all your family well and happy! I hope they will love me. I already love them, and dear, dear Armine. I shall never have courage to go there again until your return. It is night, and I am writing this in my own room. Perhaps the hour may have its influence, but I feel depressed. Oh, that I were at your side! This house is so desolate without you. Everything reminds me of the past. My Ferdinand, how can I express to you what I feel—the affection, the love, the rapture, the passionate joy, with which your image inspires me? I will not be miserable, I will be grateful to Heaven that I am loved by one so rare and gifted. Your portrait is before me; I call it yours; it is so like! 'Tis a great consolation. My heart is with you. Think of me as I think of you. Awake or asleep my thoughts are alike yours, and now I am going to pray for you. Thine own Henrietta.

Letter IX.

My best beloved! The week is long past, but you say nothing of returning. Oh! my Ferdinand, your Henrietta is not happy. I read your dear letters over and over again. They ought to make me happy. I feel in the consciousness of your affection that I ought to be the happiest person in the world, and yet, I know not why, I am very depressed. You say that all is going well; but why do you not enter into detail? There are difficulties; I am prepared for them. Believe me, my Ferdinand, that your Henrietta can endure as well as enjoy. Your father, he frowns upon our affection? Tell me, tell me all, only do not leave me in suspense. I am entitled to your confidence, Ferdinand. It makes me hate myself to think that I do not share your cares as well as your delights. I am jealous of your sorrows, Ferdinand, if I may not share them.

Do not let your brow be clouded when you read this. I could kill myself if I thought I could increase your difficulties. I love you; God knows how I love you. I will be patient; and yet, my Ferdinand, I feel wretched when I think that all is concealed from papa, and my lips are sealed until you give me permission to open them.

Pray write to me, and tell me really how affairs are. Be not afraid to tell your Henrietta everything. There is no misery so long as we love; so long as your heart is mine, there is nothing which I cannot face, nothing which, I am persuaded, we cannot overcome. God bless you, Ferdinand. Words cannot express my love. Henrietta.

Letter X.

Mine own! I wrote to you yesterday a letter of complaints. I am so sorry, for your dear letter has come to-day, and it is so kind, so fond, so affectionate, that it makes me miserable that I should occasion you even a shade of annoyance. Dearest, how I long to prove my love! There is nothing that I would not do, nothing that I would not endure, to convince you of my devotion! I will do all that you wish. I will be calm, I will be patient, I will try to be content. You say that you are sure all will go right; but you tell me nothing. What said your dear father? your mother? Be not afraid to speak.

You bid me tell you all that I am doing. Oh! my Ferdinand, life is a blank without you. I have seen no one, I have spoken to no one, save papa. He is very kind, and yet somehow or other I dread to be with him. This house seems so desolate, so very desolate. It seems a deserted place since your departure, a spot that some good genius has quitted, and all the glory has gone. I never care for my birds or flowers now. They have lost their music and their sweetness. And the woods, I cannot walk in them, and the garden reminds me only of the happy past. I have never been to the farm-house again. I could not go now, dearest Ferdinand; it would only make me weep. I think only of the morning, for it brings me your letters. I feed upon them, I live upon them. They are my only joy and solace, and yet——— but no complaints to-day, no complaints, dearest Ferdinand; let me only express my devoted love. Oh! that my weak pen could express a tithe of my fond devotion. Ferdinand, I love you with all my heart, and all my soul, and all my spirit's strength. I have no thought but for you, I exist only on your idea. Write, write; tell me that you love me, tell me that you are unchanged. It is so long since I heard that voice, so long since I beheld that fond, soft eye! Pity me, my Ferdinand. This is captivity. A thousand, thousand loves. Your devoted

Henrietta.

Letter XI.

Ferdinand, dearest Ferdinand, the post to-day has brought me no letter. I cannot credit my senses. I think the postmaster must have thought me mad. No letter! I could not believe his denial. I was annoyed, too, at the expression of his countenance. This mode of correspondence, Ferdinand, I wish not to murmur, but when I consented to this clandestine method of communication, it was for a few days, a few, few days, and then——- But I cannot write. I am quite overwhelmed. Oh! will to-morrow ever come?

Henrietta.

Letter XII.

Dearest Ferdinand, I wish to be calm. Your letter occasions me very serious uneasiness. I quarrel not with its tone of affection. It is fond, very fond, and there were moments when I could have melted over such expressions; but, Ferdinand, it is not candid. Why are we separated? For a purpose. Is that purpose effected? Were I to judge only from your letters, I should even suppose that you had not spoken to your father; but that is, of course, impossible. Your father disapproves of our union. I feel it; I know it; I was even prepared for it. Come, then, and speak to my father. It is due to me not to leave him any more in the dark; it will be better, believe me, for yourself, that he should share our confidence. Papa is not a rich man, but he loves his daughter. Let us make him our friend. Ah! why did I ever conceal anything from one so kind and good? In this moment of desolation, I feel, I keenly feel, my folly, my wickedness. I have no one to speak to, no one to console me. This constant struggle to conceal my feelings will kill me. It was painful when all was joy, but now, O Ferdinand! I can endure this life no longer. My brain is weak, my spirit perplexed and broken. I will not say if you love; but, Ferdinand, if you pity me, write, and write definitely, to your unhappy

Henrietta.

Letter XVIII.

You tell me that, in compliance with my wishes, you will write definitely. You tell me that circumstances have occurred, since your arrival at Bath, of a very perplexing and annoying nature, and that they retard that settlement with your father that you had projected and partly arranged; that it is impossible to enter into detail in letters; and assuring me of your love, you add that you have been anxious to preserve me from sharing your anxiety. O Ferdinand! what anxiety can you withhold like that you have occasioned me? Dearest, dearest Ferdinand, I will, I must still believe that you are faultless; but, believe me, a want of candour in our situation, and, I believe, in every situation, is a want of common sense. Never conceal anything from your

Henrietta.

I now take it for granted that your father has forbidden our union; indeed this is the only conclusion that I can draw from your letter. Ferdinand, I can bear this, even this. Sustained by your affection, I will trust to time, to events, to the kindness of my friends, and to that overruling Providence, which will not desert affections so pure as ours, to bring about sooner or later some happier result. Confident in your love, I can live in solitude, and devote myself to your memory, I——

O Ferdinand! kneel to your father, kneel to your kind mother; tell them all, tell them how I love you, how I will love them; tell them your Henrietta will have no thought but for their happiness; tell them she will be as dutiful to them as she is devoted to you. Ask not for our union, ask them only to permit you to cherish our acquaintance. Let them return to Armine; let them cultivate our friendship; let them know papa; let them know me; let them know me as I am, with all my faults, I trust not worldly, not selfish, not quite insignificant, not quite unprepared to act the part that awaits a member of their family, either in its splendour or its proud humility; and, if not worthy of their son (as who can be?), yet conscious, deeply conscious of the value and blessing of his affection, and prepared to prove it by the devotion of my being. Do this, my Ferdinand, and happiness will yet come.

But, my gentle love, on whatever course you may decide, remember your Henrietta. I do not reproach you; never will I reproach you; but remember the situation in which you have placed me. All my happy life I have never had a secret from my father; and now I am involved in a private engagement and a clandestine correspondence. Be just to him; be just to your Henrietta! Return, I beseech you on my knees; return instantly to Ducie; reveal everything. He will be kind and gracious; he will be our best friend; in his hand and bosom we shall find solace and support. God bless you, Ferdinand! All will yet go well, mine own, own love. I smile amid my tears when I think that we shall so soon meet. Oh! what misery can there be in this world if we may but share it together?

Thy fond, thy faithful, thy devoted
Henrietta.

CHAPTER III.

Containing the Arrival at Ducie of a Distinguished Guest.

IT WAS about three weeks after Ferdinand Armine had quitted Ducie that Mr. Temple entered the breakfast-room one morning, with an open note in his hand, and told Henrietta to prepare for visitors, as her old friend, Lady Bellair, had written to apprise him of her intention to rest the night at Ducie, on her way to the North.

'She brings with her also the most charming woman in the world,' added Mr. Temple, with a smile.

'I have little doubt Lady Bellair deems her companion so at present,' said Miss Temple, 'whoever she may be; but, at any rate, I shall be glad to see her ladyship, who is certainly one of the most amusing women in the world.'

This announcement of the speedy arrival of Lady Bellair made some bustle in the household of Ducie Bower; for her ladyship was in every respect a memorable character, and the butler who had remembered her visits to Mr. Temple before his residence at Ducie, very much interested the curiosity of his fellow-servants by his intimations of her ladyship's eccentricities.

'You will have to take care of the parrot, Mary,' said the butler; 'and you, Susan, must look after the page. We shall all be well cross-examined as to the state of the establishment; and so I advise you to be prepared. Her ladyship is a rum one, and that's the truth.'

In due course of time, a handsome travelling chariot, emblazoned with a viscount's coronet, and carrying on the seat behind a portly man-servant and a lady's maid, arrived at Ducie. They immediately descended, and assisted the assembled household of the Bower to disembark the contents of the chariot; but Mr. Temple and his daughter were too well acquainted with Lady Bellair's character to appear at this critical moment. First came forth a stately dame, of ample proportions and exceedingly magnificent attire, being dressed in the extreme of gorgeous fashion, and who, after being landed on the marble steps, was for some moments absorbed in the fluttering arrangement of her plumage; smoothing her maroon pelisse, shaking the golden riband of her emerald bonnet, and adjusting the glittering pelerine of point device, that shaded the fall of her broad but well-formed shoulders. In one hand the stately dame lightly swung a bag that was worthy of holding the Great Seal itself, so rich and so elaborate were its materials and embroidery; and in the other she at length took a glass which was suspended from her neck by a chain-cable of gold, and glanced with a flashing eye, as dark as her ebon curls and as brilliant as her well-rouged cheek, at the surrounding scene.

The green parrot, in its sparkling cage, followed next, and then came forth the prettiest, liveliest, smallest, best-dressed, and, stranger than all, oldest little lady in the world. Lady Bellair was of childlike stature, and quite erect, though ninety years of age; the tasteful simplicity of her costume, her little plain white silk bonnet, her grey silk dress, her apron, her grey mittens, and her Cinderella shoes, all admirably contrasted with the vast and flaunting splendour of her companion, not less than her ladyship's small yet exquisitely proportioned form, her highly-finished extremities, and her keen sarcastic grey eye. The expression of her countenance now, however, was somewhat serious. An arrival was an important moment that required all her practised circumspection; there was so much to arrange, so much to remember, and so much to observe.

The portly serving-man had advanced, and, taking his little mistress in his arms, as he would a child, had planted her on the steps. And then her ladyship's clear, shrill, and now rather fretful voice was heard.

'Here! where's the butler? I don't want you, stupid [addressing her own servant], but the butler of the house, Mister's butler; what is his name, Mr. Twoshoes' butler? I cannot remember names. Oh! you are there, are you? I don't want you. How is your master? How is your charming lady? Where is the parrot? I don't want it. Where's the lady? Why don't you answer? Why do you stare so? Miss Temple! no! not Miss Temple! The lady, my lady, my charming friend, Mrs. Floyd! To be sure so; why did not you say so before? But she has got two names. Why don't you say both names? My dear,' continued Lady Bellair, addressing her travelling companion, 'I don't know your name. Tell all these good people your name; your two names! I like people with two names. Tell them, my dear, tell them; tell them your name, Mrs. Thingabob, or whatever it is, Mrs. Thingabob Twoshoes.'

Mrs. Montgomery Floyd, though rather annoyed by this appeal, still contrived to comply with the request in the most dignified manner; and all the servants bowed to Mrs. Montgomery Floyd. To the great satisfaction of this stately dame, Lady Bellair, after scanning everything and everybody with the utmost scrutiny, indicated some intention of entering, when suddenly she turned round:

'Man, there's something wanting. I had three things to take charge of. The parrot and my charming friend; that is only two. There is a third. What is it? You don't know! Here, you man, who are you? Mr. Temple's servant. I knew your master when he was not as high as that cage. What do you think of that?' continued her ladyship, with a triumphant smile. 'What do you laugh at, sir? Did you ever see a woman ninety years old before? That I would wager you have not. What do I want? I want something. Why do you tease me by not remembering what I want? Now, I knew a gentleman who made his fortune by once remembering what a very great man wanted. But then the great man was a minister of state. I dare say if I were a minister of state, instead of an old woman ninety years of age, you would contrive somehow or other to find out what I wanted. Never mind, never mind. Come, my charming friend, let me take your arm. Now I will introduce you to the prettiest, the dearest, the most innocent and charming lady in the world. She is my greatest favourite. She is always my favourite. You are my favourite, too; but you are only my favourite for the moment. I always have two favourites: one for the moment, and one that I never change, and that is my sweet Henrietta Temple. You see I can remember her name, though I couldn't yours. But you are a good creature, a dear good soul, though you live in a bad set, my dear, a very bad set indeed; vulgar people, my dear; they may be rich, but they have no ton. This is a fine place. Stop, stop,' Lady Bellair exclaimed, stamping her little foot and shaking her little arm, 'Don't drive away; I remember what it was. Gregory! run, Gregory! It is the page! There was no room for him behind, and I told him to lie under the seat. Poor dear boy! He must be smothered. I hope he is not dead. Oh! there he is. Has Miss Temple got a page? Does her page wear a feather? My page has not got a feather, but he shall have one, because he was not smothered. Here! woman, who are you? The housemaid. I thought so. I always know a housemaid. You shall take care of my page. Take him at once, and give him some milk and water; and, page, be very good, and never leave this good young woman, unless I send for you. And, woman, good young woman, perhaps you may find an old feather of Miss Temple's page. Give it to this good little boy, because he was not smothered.'

CHAPTER IV.

Containing Some Account of the Viscountess Dowager
Bellair.

THE Viscountess Dowager Bellair was the last remaining link between the two centuries. Herself born of a noble family, and distinguished both for her beauty and her wit, she had reigned for a quarter of a century the favourite subject of Sir Joshua; had flirted with Lord Carlisle, and chatted with Dr. Johnson. But the most remarkable quality of her ladyship's destiny was her preservation. Time, that had rolled on nearly a century since her birth, had spared alike her physical and mental powers. She was almost as active in body, and quite as lively in mind, as when seventy years before she skipped in Marylebone Gardens, or puzzled the gentlemen of the Tuesday Night Club at Mrs. Cornely's masquerades. These wonderful seventy years indeed had passed to Lady Bellair like one of those very masked balls in which she had formerly sparkled; she had lived in a perpetual crowd of strange and brilliant characters. All that had been famous for beauty, rank, fashion, wit, genius, had been gathered round her throne; and at this very hour a fresh and admiring generation, distinguished for these qualities, cheerfully acknowledged her supremacy, and paid to her their homage. The heroes and heroines of her youth, her middle life, even of her old age, had vanished; brilliant orators, profound statesmen, inspired bards, ripe scholars, illustrious warriors; beauties whose dazzling charms had turned the world mad; choice spirits, whose flying words or whose fanciful manners made every saloon smile or wonder—all had disappeared. She had witnessed revolutions in every country in the world; she remembered Brighton a fishing-town, and Manchester a village; she had shared the pomp of nabobs and the profusion of loan-mongers; she had stimulated the early ambition of Charles Fox, and had sympathised with the last aspirations of George Canning; she had been the confidant of the loves alike of Byron and Alfieri; had worn mourning for General Wolfe, and given a festival to the Duke of Wellington; had laughed with George Selwyn, and smiled at Lord Alvanley; had known the first macaroni and the last dandy; remembered the Gunnings, and introduced the Sheridans! But she herself was unchanged; still restless for novelty, still eager for amusement; still anxiously watching the entrance on the stage of some new stream of characters, and indefatigable in attracting the notice of everyone whose talents might contribute to her entertainment, or whose attention might gratify her vanity. And, really, when one recollected Lady Bel-lair's long career, and witnessed at the same time her diminutive form and her unrivalled vitality, he might almost be tempted to believe, that if not absolutely immortal, it was at least her strange destiny not so much vulgarly to die, as to grow like the heroine of the fairy tale, each year smaller and smaller,

'Fine by degrees, and beautifully less,'

until her ladyship might at length subside into airy nothingness, and so rather vanish than expire. It was the fashion to say that her ladyship had no heart; in most instances an unmeaning phrase; in her case certainly an unjust one. Ninety years of experience had assuredly not been thrown away on a mind of remarkable acuteness; but Lady Bellair's feelings were still quick and warm, and could be even profound. Her fancy was so lively, that her attention was soon engaged; her taste so refined, that her affection was not so easily obtained. Hence she acquired a character for caprice, because she repented at leisure those first impressions which with her were irresistible;

for, in truth, Lady Bellair, though she had nearly completed her century, and had passed her whole life in the most artificial circles, was the very creature of impulse. Her first homage she always declared was paid to talent, her second to beauty, her third to blood. The favoured individual who might combine these three splendid qualifications, was, with Lady Bellair, a nymph, or a demi-god. As for mere wealth, she really despised it, though she liked her favourites to be rich.

Her knowledge of human nature, which was considerable, her acquaintance with human weaknesses, which was unrivalled, were not thrown away upon Lady Bellair. Her ladyship's perception of character was fine and quick, and nothing delighted her so much as making a person a tool. Capable, where her heart was touched, of the finest sympathy and the most generous actions, where her feelings were not engaged she experienced no compunction in turning her companions to account, or, indeed, sometimes in honouring them with her intimacy for that purpose. But if you had the skill to detect her plots, and the courage to make her aware of your consciousness of them, you never displeased her, and often gained her friendship. For Lady Bellair had a fine taste for humour, and when she chose to be candid, an indulgence which was not rare with her, she could dissect her own character and conduct with equal spirit and impartiality. In her own instance it cannot be denied that she comprised the three great qualifications she so much prized: for she was very witty; had blood in her veins, to use her own expression; and was the prettiest woman in the world, for her years. For the rest, though no person was more highly bred, she could be very impertinent; but if you treated her with servility, she absolutely loathed you.

Lady Bellair, after the London season, always spent two or three months at Bath, and then proceeded to her great grandson's, the present viscount's, seat in the North, where she remained until London was again attractive. Part of her domestic diplomacy was employed each year, during her Bath visit, in discovering some old friend, or making some new acquaintance, who would bear her in safety, and save her harmless from all expenses and dangers of the road, to Northumberland; and she displayed often in these arrangements talents which Talleyrand might have envied. During the present season, Mrs. Montgomery Floyd, the widow of a rich East Indian, whose intention it was to proceed to her estate in Scotland at the end of the autumn, had been presented to Lady Bellair by a friend well acquainted with her ladyship's desired arrangements. What an invaluable acquaintance at such a moment for Lady Bellair! Mrs. Montgomery Floyd, very rich and very anxious to be fashionable, was intoxicated with the flattering condescension and anticipated companionship of Lady Bellair. At first Lady Bellair had quietly suggested that they should travel together to Northumberland. Mrs. Montgomery Floyd was enchanted with the proposal. Then Lady Bellair regretted that her servant was very ill, and that she must send her to town immediately in her own carriage; and then Mrs. Montgomery Floyd insisted, in spite of the offers of Lady Bellair, that her ladyship should take a seat in her carriage, and would not for an instant hear of Lady Bellair defraying, under such circumstances, any portion of the expense. Lady Bellair held out to the dazzled vision of Mrs. Montgomery Floyd a brilliant perspective of the noble lords and wealthy squires whose splendid seats, under the auspices of Lady Bellair, they were to make their resting-places during their progress; and in time Lady Bellair, who had a particular fancy for her own carriage, proposed that her servants should travel in that of Mrs. Montgomery Floyd. Mrs. Montgomery Floyd smiled a too willing assent. It ended by Mrs. Montgomery Floyd's servants travelling to Lord Bellair's, where their mistress was to meet them, in that lady's own carriage, and Lady Bellair travelling in her own chariot with her own servants, and Mrs. Montgomery Floyd defraying the expenditure of both expeditions.

CHAPTER V.

In Which Lady Bellair Gives Some Account of Some of Her Friends.

LADY BELLAIR really loved Henrietta Temple. She was her prime and her permanent favourite, and she was always lamenting that Henrietta would not come and stay with her in London, and marry a duke. Lady Bellair was a great matchmaker. When, therefore, she was welcomed by the fair mistress of Ducie Bower, Lady Bellair was as genuine as she was profuse in her kind phrases. 'My sweet, sweet young friend,' she said, as Henrietta bowed her head and offered her lips to the little old lady, 'it is something to have such a friend as you. What old woman has such a sweet friend as I have! Now let me look at you. It does my heart good to see you. I feel younger. You are handsomer than ever, I declare you are. Why will you not come and stay with me, and let me find you a husband? There is the Duke of Derandale, he is in love with you already; for I do nothing but talk of you. No, you should not marry him, he is not good enough. He is not good enough. He is not refined. I love a duke, but I love a duke that is refined more. You shall marry Lord Fitzwarrene.

He is my favourite; he is worthy of you. You laugh; I love to see you laugh. You are so fresh and innocent! There is your worthy father talking to my friend Mrs. Twoshoes; a very good creature, my love, a very worthy soul, but no ton; I hate French words, but what other can I use? And she will wear gold chains, which I detest. You never wear gold chains, I am sure. The Duke of —would not have me, so I came to you,' continued her ladyship, returning the salutation of Mr. Temple. 'Don't ask me if I am tired; I am never tired. There is nothing I hate so much as being asked whether I am well; I am always well. There, I have brought you a charming friend; give her your arm; and you shall give me yours,' said the old lady, smiling, to Henrietta. 'We make a good contrast; I like a good contrast, but not an ugly one. I cannot bear anything that is ugly; unless it is a very ugly man indeed, who is a genius and very fashionable. I liked Wilkes, and I liked Curran; but they were famous, the best company in the world. When I was as young as you, Lady Lavington and I always hunted in couples, because she was tall, and I was called the Queen of the Fairies. Pretty women, my sweet child, should never be alone. Not that I was very pretty, but I was always with pretty women, and at last the men began to think that I was pretty too.'

'A superbly pretty place,' simpered the magnificent Mrs. Montgomery Floyd to Mr. Temple, 'and of all the sweetly pretty persons I ever met, I assure you I think Miss Temple the most charming. Such a favourite too with Lady Bellair! You know she calls Miss Temple her real favourite,' added the lady, with a playful smile.

The ladies were ushered to their apartments by Henrietta, for the hour of dinner was at hand, and Mrs. Montgomery Floyd indicated some anxiety not to be hurried in her toilet. Indeed, when she reappeared, it might have been matter of marvel how she could have effected such a complete transformation in so short a period. Except a train, she was splendid enough for a birthday at St. James's, and wore so many brilliants that she glittered like a chandelier. However, as Lady Bellair loved a contrast, this was perhaps not unfortunate; for certainly her ladyship, in her simple costume which had only been altered by the substitution of a cap that should have been immortalised by Mieris or Gerard Douw, afforded one not a little startling to her sumptuous fellow-traveller.

'Your dinner is very good,' said Lady Bellair to Mr. Temple. 'I eat very little and very plainly, but I hate a bad dinner; it dissatisfies everybody else, and they are all dull. The best dinners now are a new man's; I forget his name; the man who is so very rich. You never heard of him, and she (pointing with her fork to Mrs. Montgomery) knows nobody. What is his name? Gregory, what is the name of the gentleman I dine with so often? the gentleman I send to when I have no other engagement, and he always gives me a dinner, but who never dines with me. He is only rich, and I hate people who are only rich; but I must ask him next year. I ask him to my evening parties, mind; I don't care about them; but I will not have stupid people, who are only rich, at my dinners. Gregory, what is his name?'

'Mr. Million de Stockville, my lady.'

'Yes, that is the man, good Gregory. You have no deer, have you?' enquired her ladyship of Mr. Temple. 'I thought not. I wish you had deer. You should send a haunch in my name to Mr. Million de Stockville, and that would be as good as a dinner to him. If your neighbour, the duke, had received me, I should have sent it from thence. I will tell you what I will do; I will write a note from this place to the duke, and get him to do it for me. He will do anything for me. He loves me, the duke, and I love him; but his wife hates me.'

'And you have had a gay season in town this year, Lady Bellair?' enquired Miss Temple. 'My dear, I always have a gay season.' 'What happiness!' softly exclaimed Mrs. Montgomery Floyd. 'I think nothing is more delightful than gaiety.'

'And how is our friend Mr. Bonmot this year?' said Mr. Temple.

'My dear, Bonmot is growing very old. He tells the same stories over again, and therefore I never see him. I cannot bear wits that have run to seed: I cannot ask Bonmot to my dinners, and I told him the reason why; but I said I was at home every morning from two till six, and that he might come then, for he does not go out to evening parties, and he is huffy, and so we have quarrelled.'

'Poor Mr. Bonmot,' said Miss Temple.

'My dear, there is the most wonderful man in the world, I forget his name, but everybody is mad to have him. He is quite the fashion. I have him to my parties instead of Bonmot, and it is much better. Everybody has Bonmot; but my man is new, and I love something new. Lady Frederick Berrington brought him to me. Do you know Lady Frederick Berrington? Oh! I forgot, poor dear, you are buried alive in the country; I must introduce you to Lady Frederick. She is charming, she will taste you, she will be your friend; and you cannot have a better friend, my dear, for she is very pretty, very witty, and has got blood in her veins. I won't introduce you to Lady Frederick,' continued Lady Bellair to. Mrs. Montgomery Floyd; 'she is not in your way. I shall introduce you to Lady Splash and Dashaway; she is to be your friend.'

Mrs. Montgomery Floyd seemed consoled by the splendid future of being the friend of Lady Splash and Dashaway, and easily to endure, with such a compensation, the somewhat annoying remarks of her noble patroness.

'But as for Bonmot,' continued Lady Bellair, 'I will have nothing to do with him. General Faneville, he is a dear good man, and gives me dinners. I love dinners: I never dine at home, except when I have company. General Faneville not only gives me dinners, but lets me always choose my own party. And he said to me the other day, "Now, Lady Bellair, fix your day, and name your party." I said directly, "General, anybody but Bonmot." You know Bonmot is his particular friend.'

'But surely that is cruel,' said Henrietta Temple, smiling.

'I am cruel,' said Lady Bellair, 'when I hate a person I am very cruel, and I hate Bonmot. Mr. Fox wrote me a copy of verses once, and called me "cruel fair;" but I was not cruel to him, for I dearly loved Charles Fox; and I love you, and I love your father. The first party your father ever was at, was at my house. There, what do you think of that? And I love my grandchildren; I call them all my grand-children. I think great-grandchildren sounds silly; I am so happy that they have married so well. My dear Selina is a countess; you shall be a countess, too,' added Lady Bellair, laughing. 'I must see you a countess before I die. Mrs. Grenville is not a countess, and is rather poor; but they will be rich some day; and Grenville is a good name: it sounds well. That is a great thing. I hate a name that does not sound well.'

CHAPTER VI.

Containing a Conversation Not Quite so Amusing as the Last.

IN THE evening Henrietta amused her guests with music. Mrs. Montgomery Floyd was enthusiastically fond of music, and very proud of her intimate friendship with Pasta. 'Oh! you know her, do you?' 'Very well; you shall bring her to my house. She shall sing at all my parties; I love music at my evenings, but I never pay for it, never. If she will not come in the evening, I will try to ask her to dinner, once at least. I do not like singers and tumblers at dinner, but she is very fashionable, and young men like her; and what I want at my dinners are young men, young men of very great fashion. I rather want young men at my dinners. I have some; Lord Languid always comes to me, and he is very fine, you know, very fine indeed. He goes to very few places, but he always comes to me.' Mrs. Montgomery Floyd quitted the piano, and seated herself by Mr. Temple. Mr. Temple was gallant, and Mrs. Montgomery Floyd anxious to obtain the notice of a gentleman whom Lady Bellair had assured her was of the first ton. Her ladyship herself beckoned Henrietta Temple to join her on the sofa, and, taking her hand very affectionately, explained to her all the tactics by which she intended to bring-about a match between her and Lord Fitzwarrene, very much regretting, at the same time, that her dear grandson, Lord Bellair, was married; for he, after all, was the only person worthy of her. 'He would taste you, my dear; he would understand you. Dear Bellair! he is so very handsome, and so very witty. Why did he go and marry? And yet I love his wife. Do you know her? Oh! she is charming: so very pretty, so very witty, and such good blood in her veins. I made the match. Why were you not in England? If you had only come to England a year sooner, you should have married Bellair. How provoking!'

'But, really, dear Lady Bellair, your grandson is very happy. What more can you wish?'

'Well, my dear, it shall be Lord Fitzwarrene, then. I shall give a series of parties this year, and ask Lord Fitzwarrene to every one. Not that it is very easy to get him, my child. There is nobody so difficult as Lord Fitzwarrene. That is quite right. Men should always be difficult. I cannot bear men who come and dine with you when you want them.'

'What a charming place is Ducie!' sighed Mrs. Montgomery Floyd to Mr. Temple. 'The country is so delightful.'

'But you would not like to live in the country only,' said Mr. Temple.

'Ah! you do not know me!' sighed the sentimental Mrs. Montgomery Floyd. 'If you only knew how I love flowers! I wish you could but see my conservatory in Park-lane!'

'And how did you find Bath this year, Lady Bellair?' enquired Miss Temple.

'Oh! my dear, I met a charming man there, I forget his name, but the most distinguished person I ever met; so very handsome, so very witty, and with blood in his veins, only I forget his name, and it is a very good name, too. My dear,' addressing herself to Mrs. Montgomery Floyd, 'tell me the name of my favourite.'

Mrs. Montgomery Floyd looked a little puzzled: 'My great favourite!' exclaimed the irritated Lady Bellair, rapping her fan against the sofa. 'Oh! why do you not remember names! I love people who remember names. My favourite, my Bath favourite. What is his name? He is to dine with me in town. What is the name of my Bath favourite who is certainly to dine with me in town?'

'Do you mean Captain Armine?' enquired Mrs. Montgomery Floyd. Miss Temple turned pale.
'That is the man,' said Lady Bellair. 'Oh! such a charming man. You shall marry him, my dear;
you shall not marry Lord Fitzwarrene.'

'But you forget he is going to be married,' said Mrs. Montgomery Floyd.

Miss Temple tried to rise, but she could not. She held down her head. She felt the fever in her
cheek. 'Is our engagement, then, so notorious?' she thought to herself.

'Ah! yes, I forgot he was going to be married,' said Lady Bellair. 'Well, then, it must be Lord
Fitzwarrene. Besides, Captain Armine is not rich, but he has got a very fine place though, and I
will go and stop there some day. And, besides, he is over head-and-ears in debt, so they say.
However, he is going to marry a very rich woman, and so all will be right. I like old families in
decay to get round again.'

Henrietta dreaded that her father should observe her confusion; she had recourse to every art to
prevent it. 'Dear Ferdinand,' she thought to herself, 'thy very rich wife will bring thee, I fear, but
a poor dower. Ah! would he were here!'

'Whom is Captain Armine going to marry?' enquired Mr. Temple.

'Oh! a very proper person,' said Lady Bellair. 'I forget her name. Miss Twoshoes, or something.
What is her name, my dear?'

'You mean Miss Grandison, madam?' responded Mrs. Montgomery Floyd.

'To be sure, Miss Grandison, the great heiress. The only one left of the Grandisons. I knew her
grandfather. He was my son's schoolfellow.'

'Captain Armine is a near neighbour of ours,' said Mr. Temple.

'Oh! you know him,' said Lady Bellair. 'Is not he charming?'

'Are you certain he is going to be married to Miss Grandison?' enquired Mr. Temple.

'Oh! there is no doubt in the world,' said Mrs. Montgomery Floyd. 'Everything is quite settled.
My most particular friend, Lady Julia Harteville, is to be one of the bridesmaids. I have seen all
the presents. Both the families are at Bath at this very moment. I saw the happy pair together
every day. They are related, you know. It is an excellent match, for the Armines have great
estates, mortgaged to the very last acre. I have heard that Sir Ratcliffe Armine has not a thousand
a year he can call his own. We are all so pleased,' added Mrs. Montgomery Floyd, as if she were
quite one of the family. 'Is it not delightful?'

'They are to be married next month,' said Lady Bellair. 'I did not quite make the match, but I did
something. I love the Grandisons, because Lord Grandison was my son's friend fifty years ago.'

'I never knew a person so pleased as Lady Armine is,' continued Mrs. Montgomery Floyd. 'The
truth is, Captain Armine has been wild, very wild indeed; a little of a roue; but then such a fine
young man, so very handsome, so truly distinguished, as Lady Bellair says, what could you
expect? But he has sown his wild oats now. They have been engaged these six months; ever
since he came from abroad. He has been at Bath all the time, except for a fortnight or so, when
he went to his Place to make the necessary preparations. We all so missed him. Captain Armine
was quite the life of Bath I am almost ashamed to repeat what was said of him,' added Mrs.
Montgomery Floyd, blushing through her rouge; 'but they said every woman was in love with
him.'

'Fortunate man!' said Mr. Temple, bowing, but with a grave expression.

'And he says, he is only going to marry because he is wearied of conquests,' continued Mrs.
Montgomery Floyd; 'how impertinent, is it not? But Captain Armine says such things! He is
quite a privileged person at Bath!'

Miss Temple rose and left the room. When the hour of general retirement had arrived, she had not returned. Her maid brought a message that her mistress was not very well, and offered her excuses for not again descending.

CHAPTER VII.

In Which Mr. Temple Pays a Visit to His Daughter's
Chamber.

HENRIETTA, when she quitted the room, never stopped until she had gained her own chamber. She had no light but a straggling moonbeam revealed sufficient.

She threw herself upon her bed, choked with emotion. She was incapable of thought; a chaos of wild images flitted over her brain. Thus had she remained, perchance an hour, with scarcely self-consciousness, when her servant entered with a light to arrange her chamber, and nearly shrieked when, on turning round, she beheld her mistress.

This intrusion impressed upon Miss Temple the absolute necessity of some exertion, if only to preserve herself at this moment from renewed interruptions. She remembered where she was, she called back with an effort some recollection of her guests, and she sent that message to her father which we have already noticed. Then she was again alone. How she wished at that moment that she might ever be alone; that the form and shape of human being should no more cross her vision; that she might remain in this dark chamber until she died! There was no more joy for her; her sun was set, the lustre of her life was gone; the lute had lost its tone, the flower its perfume, the bird its airy wing. What a fleet, as well as fatal, tragedy! How swift upon her improvidence had come her heart-breaking pang! There was an end of faith, for he was faithless; there was an end of love, for love had betrayed her; there was an end of beauty, for beauty had been her bane. All that hitherto made life delightful, all the fine emotions, all the bright hopes, and the rare accomplishments of our nature, were dark delusions now, cruel mockeries, and false and cheating phantoms! What humiliation! what despair! And he had seemed so true, so pure, so fond, so gifted! What! could it be, could it be that a few short weeks back this man had knelt to her, had adored her? And she had hung upon his accents, and lived in the light of his enraptured eyes, and pledged to him her heart, dedicated to him her life, devoted to him all her innocent and passionate affections, worshipped him as an idol! Why, what was life that it could bring upon its swift wing such dark, such agonising vicissitudes as these? It was not life; it was frenzy!

Some one knocked gently at her door. She did not answer, she feigned sleep. Yet the door opened, she felt, though her eyes were shut and her back turned, that there was a light in the room. A tender step approached her bed. It could be but one person, that person whom she had herself deceived. She knew it was her father.

Mr. Temple seated himself by her bedside; he bent his head and pressed his lips upon her forehead. In her desolation some one still loved her. She could not resist the impulse; she held forth her hand without opening her eyes, her father held it clasped in his.

'Henrietta,' he at length said, in a tone of peculiar sweetness.

'Oh! do not speak, my father. Do not speak. You alone have cause to reproach me. Spare me; spare your child.'

'I came to console, not to reproach,' said Mr. Temple. 'But if it please you, I will not speak; let me, however, remain.'

'Father, we must speak. It relieves me even to confess my indiscretion, my fatal folly. Father, I feel, yet why, I know not, I feel that you know all!'

'I know much, my Henrietta, but I do not know all.'

'And if you knew all, you would not hate me?'

'Hate you, my Henrietta! These are strange words to use to a father; to a father, I would add, like me. No one can love you, Henrietta, as your father loves you; yet speak to me not merely as a father; speak to me as your earliest, your best, your fondest, your most faithful friend.'

She pressed his hand, but answer, that she could not.

'Henrietta, dearest, dearest Henrietta, answer me one question.'

'I tremble, sir.'

'Then we will speak to-morrow.'

'Oh! no, to-night. To-morrow may never come. There is no night for me; I cannot sleep. I should go mad if it were not for you. I will speak; I will answer any questions. My conscience is quite clear except to you; no one, no power on earth or heaven, can reproach me, except my father.'

'He never will. But, dearest, tell me; summon up your courage to meet my question. Are you engaged to this person?'

'I was.'

'Positively engaged?'

'Long ere this I had supposed we should have claimed your sanction. He left me only to speak to his father.'

'This may be the idle tattle of women?'

'No, no,' said Henrietta, in a voice of deep melancholy; 'my fears had foreseen this dark reality. This week has been a week of terror to me; and yet I hoped, and hoped, and hoped. Oh! what a fool have I been.'

'I know this person was your constant companion in my absence; that you have corresponded with him. Has he written very recently?'

'Within two days.'

'And his letters?'

'Have been of late most vague. Oh! my father, indeed, indeed I have not conducted myself so ill as you perhaps imagine. I shrunk from this secret engagement; I opposed by every argument in my power, this clandestine correspondence; but it was only for a week, a single week; and reasons, plausible and specious reasons, were plentiful. Alas! alas! all is explained now. All that was strange, mysterious, perplexed in his views and conduct, and which, when it crossed my mind, I dismissed with contempt,—all is now too clear.'

'Henrietta, he is unworthy of you.'

'Hush! hush! dear father. An hour ago I loved him. Spare him, if you only wish to spare me.'

'Cling to my heart, my child. A father's love has comfort. Is it not so?'

'I feel it is; I feel calmer since you came and we have spoken. I never can be happy again; my spirit is quite broken. And yet, I feel I have a heart now, which I thought I had not before you came. Dear, dear father,' she said, rising and putting her arms round Mr. Temple's neck and leaning on his bosom, and speaking in a sweet yet very mournful voice, 'henceforth your happiness shall be mine. I will not disgrace you; you shall not see me grieve; I will atone, I will endeavour to atone, for my great sins, for sins they were towards you.'

'My child, the time will come when we shall remember this bitterness only as a lesson. But I know the human heart too well to endeavour to stem your sorrow now; I only came to soothe it. My blessing is upon you, my child. Let us talk no more. Henrietta, I will send your maid to you. Try to sleep; try to compose yourself.'

'These people—to-morrow—what shall I do?'

'Leave all to me. Keep your chamber until they have gone. You need appear no more.'

'Oh! that no human being might again see me!'

'Hush! that is not a wise wish. Be calm; we shall yet be happy. To-morrow we will talk; and so good night, my child; good night, my own Henrietta.'

Mr. Temple left the room. He bade the maid go to her mistress, in as calm a tone as if indeed her complaint had been only a headache; and then he entered his own apartment. Over the mantel-piece was a portrait of his daughter, gay and smiling as the spring; the room was adorned with her drawings. He drew the chair near the fire, and gazed for some time abstracted upon the flame, and then hid his weeping countenance in his hands. He sobbed convulsively.

CHAPTER VIII.

In Which Glastonbury Is Very Much Astonished.

IT WAS a gusty autumnal night; Glastonbury sat alone in his tower; every now and then the wind, amid a chorus of groaning branches and hissing rain, dashed against his window; then its power seemed gradually lulled, and perfect stillness succeeded, until a low moan was heard again in the distance, which gradually swelled into storm. The countenance of the good old man was not so serene as usual. Occasionally his thoughts seemed to wander from the folio opened before him, and he fell into fits of reverie which impressed upon his visage an expression rather of anxiety than study.

The old man looked up to the portrait of the unhappy Lady Armine, and heaved a deep sigh. Were his thoughts of her or of her child? He closed his book, he replaced it upon its shelf, and, taking from a cabinet an ancient crucifix of carved ivory, he bent down before the image of his Redeemer.

Even while he was buried in his devotions, praying perchance for the soul of that sinning yet sainted lady whose memory was never absent from his thoughts, or the prosperity of that family to whom he had dedicated his faithful life, the noise of ascending footsteps was heard in the sudden stillness, and immediately a loud knocking at the door of his outer chamber.

Surprised at this unaccustomed interruption, Glastonbury rose, and enquired the object of his yet unseen visitor; but, on hearing a well-known voice, the door was instantly unbarred, and Ferdinand Armine, pale as a ghost and deluged to the skin, appeared before him. Glastonbury ushered his guest into his cell, replenished the fire, retrimmed the lamp, and placed Ferdinand in his own easy seat.

'You are wet; I fear thoroughly?'

'It matters not,' said Captain Armine, in a hollow voice.

'From Bath?' enquired Glastonbury.

But his companion did not reply. At length he said, in a voice of utter wretchedness, 'Glastonbury, you see before you the most miserable of human beings.'

The good father started.

'Yes!' continued Ferdinand; 'this is the end of all your care, all your affection, all your hopes, all your sacrifices. It is over; our house is fated; my life draws to an end.'

'Speak, my Ferdinand,' said Glastonbury, for his pupil seemed to have relapsed into moody silence, 'speak to your friend and father. Disburden your mind of the weight that presses on it. Life is never without hope, and, while this remains,' pointing to the crucifix, 'never without consolation.'

'I cannot speak; I know not what to say. My brain sinks under the effort. It is a wild, a complicated tale; it relates to feelings with which you cannot sympathise, thoughts that you cannot share. O Glastonbury! there is no hope; there is no solace.'

'Calm yourself, my Ferdinand; not merely as your friend, but as a priest of our holy church, I call upon you to speak to me. Even to me, the humblest of its ministers, is given a power that can sustain the falling and make whole the broken in spirit. Speak, and speak fearlessly; nor shrink from exposing the very inmost recesses of your breast; for I can sympathise with your passions, be they even as wild as I believe them.'

Ferdinand turned his eyes from the fire on which he was gazing, and shot a scrutinising glance at his kind confessor, but the countenance of Glastonbury was placid, though serious.

'You remember,' Ferdinand at length murmured, 'that we met, we met unexpectedly, some six weeks back.'

'I have not forgotten it,' replied Glastonbury.

'There was a lady,' Ferdinand continued in a hesitating tone.

'Whom I mistook for Miss Grandison,' observed Glastonbury, 'but who, it turned out, bore another name.'

'You know it?'

'I know all; for her father has been here.'

'Where are they?' exclaimed Ferdinand eagerly, starting from his seat and seizing the hand of Glastonbury. 'Only tell me where they are, only tell me where Henrietta is, and you will save me, Glastonbury. You will restore me to life, to hope, to heaven.'

'I cannot,' said Glastonbury, shaking his head. 'It is more than ten days ago that I saw this lady's father for a few brief and painful moments; for what purpose your conscience may inform you. From the unexpected interview between ourselves in the gallery, my consequent misconception, and the conversation which it occasioned, I was not so unprepared for this interview with him as I otherwise might have been. Believe me, Ferdinand, I was as tender to your conduct as was consistent with my duty to my God and to my neighbour.'

'You betrayed me, then,' said Ferdinand.

'Ferdinand!' said Glastonbury reproachfully, 'I trust that I am free from deceit of any kind. In the present instance I had not even to communicate anything. Your own conduct had excited suspicion; some visitors from Bath to this gentleman and his family had revealed everything; and, in deference to the claims of an innocent lady, I could not refuse to confirm what was no secret to the world in general, what was already known to them in particular, what was not even doubted, and alas! not dubitable.'

'Oh! my father, pardon me, pardon me; pardon the only disrespectful expression that ever escaped the lips of your Ferdinand towards you; most humbly do I ask your forgiveness. But if you knew all———God!

God! my heart is breaking! You have seen her, Glastonbury; you have seen her. Was there ever on earth a being like her? So beautiful, so highly-gifted, with a heart as fresh, as fragrant as the dawn of Eden; and that heart mine; and all lost, all gone and lost! Oh! why am I alive?' He threw himself back in his chair, and covered his face and wept.

'I would that deed or labour of mine could restore you both to peace,' said Glastonbury, with streaming eyes.

'So innocent, so truly virtuous!' continued Ferdinand. 'It seemed to me I never knew what virtue was till I knew her. So frank, so generous! I think I see her now, with that dear smile of hers that never more may welcome me!'

'My child, I know not what to say; I know not what advice to give; I know not what even to wish. Your situation is so complicated, so mysterious, that it passes my comprehension. There are others whose claims, whose feelings should be considered. You are not, of course, married?'

Ferdinand shook his head.

'Does Miss Grandison know all?'

'Nothing.'

'Your family?'

Ferdinand shook his head again.

'What do you yourself wish? What object are you aiming at? What game have you yourself been playing? I speak not in harshness; but I really do not understand what you have been about. If you have your grandfather's passions, you have his brain too. I did not ever suppose that you were "infirm of purpose."'

'I have only one wish, only one object. Since I first saw Henrietta, my heart and resolution have never for an instant faltered; and if I do not now succeed in them I am determined not to live.'

'The God of all goodness have mercy on this distracted house!' exclaimed Glastonbury, as he piously lifted his hands to heaven.

'You went to Bath to communicate this great change to your father,' he continued. 'Why did you not? Painful as the explanation must be to Miss Grandison, the injustice of your conduct towards her is aggravated by delay.'

'There were reasons,' said Ferdinand, 'reasons which I never intended anyone to know; but now I have no secrets. Dear Glastonbury, even amid all this overwhelming misery, my cheek burns when I confess to you that I have, and have had for years, private cares of my own of no slight nature.'

'Debts?' enquired Glastonbury.

'Debts,' replied Ferdinand, 'and considerable ones.'

'Poor child!' exclaimed Glastonbury. 'And this drove you to the marriage?'

'To that every worldly consideration impelled me: my heart was free then; in fact, I did not know I had a heart; and I thought the marriage would make all happy. But now, so far as I am myself concerned, oh! I would sooner be the commonest peasant in this county, with Henrietta Temple for the partner of my life, than live at Armine with all the splendour of my ancestors.'

'Honour be to them; they were great men,' exclaimed Glastonbury.

'I am their victim,' replied Ferdinand. 'I owe my ancestors nothing, nay, worse than nothing; I owe them———'

'Hush! hush!' said Glastonbury. 'If only for my sake, Ferdinand, be silent.'

'For yours, then, not for theirs.'

'But why did you remain at Bath?' enquired Glastonbury.

'I had not been there more than a day or two, when my principal creditor came down from town and menaced me. He had a power of attorney from an usurer at Malta, and talked of applying to the Horse Guards. The report that I was going to marry an heiress had kept these fellows quiet, but the delay and my absence from Bath had excited his suspicion. Instead, therefore, of coming to an immediate explanation with Katherine, brought about as I had intended by my coldness and neglect, I was obliged to be constantly seen with her in public, to prevent myself from being arrested. Yet I wrote to Ducie daily. I had confidence in my energy and skill. I thought that Henrietta might be for a moment annoyed or suspicious; I thought, however, she would be supported by the fervour of my love. I anticipated no other evil. Who could have supposed that these infernal visitors would have come at such a moment to this retired spot?'

'And now, is all known now?' enquired Glastonbury.

'Nothing,' replied Ferdinand; 'the difficulty of my position was so great that I was about to cut the knot, by quitting Bath and leaving a letter addressed to Katherine, confessing all. But the sudden silence of Henrietta drove me mad. Day after day elapsed; two, three, four, five, six days, and I heard nothing. The moon was bright; the mail was just going off. I yielded to an irresistible impulse. I bid adieu to no one. I jumped in. I was in London only ten minutes. I dashed to Ducie. It was deserted. An old woman told me the family had gone, had utterly departed; she knew not where, but she thought for foreign parts. I sank down; I tottered to a seat in that hall where I had been so happy. Then it flashed across my mind that I might discover their course and pursue them. I hurried to the nearest posting town. I found out their route. I lost it for ever at the next stage. The clue was gone; it was market-day, and in a great city, where horses are changed every minute, there is so much confusion that my enquiries were utterly baffled. And here I am, Mr. Glastonbury,' added Ferdinand, with a kind of mad smile. 'I have travelled four days, I have not slept a wink, I have tasted no food; but I have drunk, I have drunk well. Here I am, and I have half a mind to set fire to that accursed pile called Armine Castle for my funeral pyre.'

'Ferdinand, you are not well,' said Mr. Glastonbury, grasping his hand. 'You need rest. You must retire; indeed you must. I must be obeyed. My bed is yours.'

'No! let me go to my own room,' murmured Ferdinand, in a faint voice. 'That room where my mother said the day would come—oh! what did my mother say? Would there were only mother's love, and then I should not be here or thus.'

'I pray you, my child, rest here.'

'No! let us to the Place, for an hour; I shall not sleep more than an hour. I am off again directly the storm is over. If it had not been for this cursed rain I should have caught them. And yet, perhaps, they are in countries where there is no rain. Ah! who would believe what happens in this world? Not I, for one. Now, give me your arm. Good Glastonbury! you are always the same. You seem to me the only thing in the world that is unchanged.'

Glastonbury, with an air of great tenderness and anxiety, led his former pupil down the stairs. The weather was more calm. There were some dark blue rifts in the black sky which revealed a star or two. Ferdinand said nothing in their progress to the Place except once, when he looked up to the sky, and said, as it were to himself, 'She loved the stars.'

Glastonbury had some difficulty in rousing the man and his wife, who were the inmates of the Place; but it was not very late, and, fortunately, they had not retired for the night. Lights were brought into Lady Armine's drawing-room. Glastonbury led Ferdinand to a sofa, on which he rather permitted others to place him than seated himself. He took no notice of anything that was going on, but remained with his eyes open, gazing feebly with a rather vacant air.

Then the good Glastonbury looked to the arrangement of his sleeping-room, drawing the curtains, seeing that the bed was well aired and warmed, and himself adding blocks to the wood fire which soon kindled. Nor did he forget to prepare, with the aid of the good woman, some hot potion that might soothe and comfort his stricken and exhausted charge, who in this moment of distress and desolation had come, as it were, and thrown himself on the bosom of his earliest friend. When all was arranged Glastonbury descended to Ferdinand, whom he found in exactly the same position as that in which he left him. He offered no resistance to the invitation of Glastonbury to retire to his chamber. He neither moved nor spoke, and yet seemed aware of all they were doing. Glastonbury and the stout serving-man bore him to his chamber, relieved him from his wet garments, and placed him in his earliest bed. When Glastonbury bade him good night, Ferdinand faintly pressed his hand, but did not speak; and it was remarkable, that while he passively submitted to their undressing him, and seemed incapable of affording them the slightest aid, yet he thrust forth his hand to guard a lock of dark hair that was placed next to his heart.

CHAPTER IX.

In Which Glastonbury Finds That a Serene Temper Does Not
Always Bring a Serene Life.

THOSE quiet slumbers, that the regular life and innocent heart of the good Glastonbury
generally ensured, were sadly broken this night, as he lay awake meditating over the distracted
fortunes of the of Armine house. They seemed now to be most turbulent and clouded; and that
brilliant and happy future, in which of late he had so fondly indulged, offered nothing but gloom
and disquietude. Nor was it the menaced disruption of those ties whose consummation was to
restore the greatness and splendour of the family, and all the pain and disappointment and
mortification and misery that must be its consequence, that alone made him sorrowful.
Glastonbury had a reverence for that passion which sheds such a lustre over existence, and is the
pure and prolific source of much of our better conduct; the time had been when he, too, had
loved, and with a religious sanctity worthy of his character and office; he had been for a long life
the silent and hopeless votary of a passion almost ideal, yet happy, though 'he never told his
love;' and, indeed, although the unconscious mistress of his affections had been long removed
from that world where his fidelity was almost her only comfort, that passion had not waned, and
the feelings that had been inspired by her presence were now cherished by her memory. His
tender and romantic nature, which his venerable grey hairs had neither dulled nor hardened,
made him deeply sympathise with his unhappy pupil; the radiant image of Henrietta Temple, too,
vividly impressed on his memory as it was, rose up before him; he recollected his joy that the
chosen partner of his Ferdinand's bosom should be worthy of her destiny; he thought of this fair
creature, perchance in solitude and sickness, a prey to the most mortifying and miserable
emotions, with all her fine and generous feelings thrown back upon herself; deeming herself
deceived, deserted, outraged, where she had looked for nothing but fidelity, and fondness, and
support; losing all confidence in the world and the world's ways; but recently so lively with
expectation and airy with enjoyment, and now aimless, hopeless, wretched, perhaps broken-
hearted. The tears trickled down the pale cheek of Glastonbury as he revolved in his mind these
mournful thoughts; and almost unconsciously he wrung his hands as he felt his utter want of
power to remedy these sad and piteous circumstances. Yet he was not absolutely hopeless. There
was ever open to the pious Glastonbury one perennial source of trust and consolation. This was a
fountain that was ever fresh and sweet, and he took refuge from the world's harsh courses and
exhausting cares in its salutary flow and its refreshing shade, when, kneeling before his crucifix,
he commended the unhappy Ferdinand and his family to the superintending care of a merciful
Omnipotence.

The morning brought fresh anxieties. Glastonbury was at the Place at an early hour, and found
Ferdinand in a high state of fever. He had not slept an instant, was very excited, talked of
departing immediately, and rambled in his discourse. Glastonbury blamed himself for having left
him a moment, and resolved to do so no more. He endeavoured to soothe him; assured him that if
he would be calm all would yet go well; that they would consult together what was best to be
done; and that he would make enquiries after the Temple family. In the meantime he despatched
the servant for the most eminent physician of the county; but as hours must necessarily elapse
before his arrival, the difficulty of keeping Ferdinand still was very great. Talk he would, and of

nothing but Henrietta. It was really agonising to listen to his frantic appeals to Glastonbury to exert himself to discover her abode; yet Glastonbury never left his side; and with promises, expressions of confidence, and the sway of an affected calmness, for in truth dear Glastonbury was scarcely less agitated than his patient, Ferdinand was prevented from rising, and the physician at length arrived.

After examining Ferdinand, with whom he remained a very short space, this gentleman invited Glastonbury to descend, and they left the patient in charge of a servant.

'This is a bad case,' said the physician.

'Almighty God preserve him!' exclaimed the agitated Glastonbury. 'Tell me the worst!'

'Where are Sir Ratcliffe and Lady Armine?'

'At Bath.'

'They must be sent for instantly.'

'Is there any hope?'

'There is hope; that is all. I shall now bleed him copiously, and then blister; but I can do little. We must trust to nature. I am afraid of the brain. I cannot account for his state by his getting wet or his rapid travelling. Has he anything on his mind?'

'Much,' said Glastonbury.

The physician shook his head.

'It is a precious life!' said Glastonbury, seizing his arm. 'My dear doctor, you must not leave us.'

They returned to the bedchamber.

'Captain Armine,' said the physician, taking his hand and seating himself on the bed, 'you have a bad cold and some fever; I think you should lose a little blood.'

'Can I leave Armine to-day, if I am bled?' enquired Ferdinand, eagerly, 'for go I must!'

'I would not move to-day,' said the physician.

'I must, indeed I must. Mr. Glastonbury will tell you I must.'

'If you set off early to-morrow you will get over as much ground in four-and-twenty hours as if you went this evening,' said the physician, fixing the bandage on the arm as he spoke, and nodding to Mr. Glastonbury to prepare the basin.

'To-morrow morning?' said Ferdinand.

'Yes, to-morrow,' said the physician, opening his lancet.

'Are you sure that I shall be able to set off tomorrow?' said Ferdinand.

'Quite,' said the physician, opening the vein.

The dark blood flowed sullenly; the physician exchanged an anxious glance with Glastonbury; at length the arm was bandaged up, a composing draught, with which the physician had been prepared, given to his patient, and the doctor and Glastonbury withdrew. The former now left Armine for three hours, and Glastonbury prepared himself for his painful office of communicating to the parents the imminent danger of their only child.

Never had a more difficult task devolved upon an individual than that which now fell to the lot of the good Glastonbury, in conducting the affairs of a family labouring under such remarkable misconceptions as to the position and views of its various members. It immediately occurred to him, that it was highly probable that Miss Grandison, at such a crisis, would choose to accompany the parents of her intended husband. What incident, under the present circumstances, could be more awkward and more painful? Yet how to prevent its occurrence? How crude to communicate the real state of such affairs at any time by letter! How impossible at the moment he was preparing the parents for the alarming, perhaps fatal illness of their child, to enter on such subjects at all, much more when the very revelation, at a moment which required all their energy and promptitude, would only be occasioning at Bath scenes scarcely less distracting and disastrous than those occurring at Armine. It was clearly impossible to enter into any details at present; and yet Glastonbury, while he penned the sorrowful lines, and softened the sad communication with his sympathy, added a somewhat sly postscript, wherein he impressed upon Lady Armine the advisability, for various reasons, that she should only be accompanied by her husband.

CHAPTER X.

In Which Ferdinand Armine Is Much Concerned.

THE contingency which Glastonbury feared, surely happened; Miss Grandison insisted upon immediately rushing to her Ferdinand; and as the maiden aunt was still an invalid, and was incapable of enduring the fatigues of a rapid and anxious journey, she was left behind. Within a few hours of the receipt of Glastonbury's letter, Sir Ratcliffe and Lady Armine, and their niece, were on their way. They found letters from Glastonbury in London, which made them travel to Armine even through the night.

In spite of all his remedies, the brain fever which the physician foresaw had occurred; and when his family arrived, the life of Ferdinand was not only in danger but desperate. It was impossible that even the parents could see their child, and no one was allowed to enter his chamber but his nurse, the physician, and occasionally Glastonbury; for this name, with others less familiar to the household, sounded so often on the frenzied lips of the sufferer, that it was recommended that Glastonbury should often be at his bedside. Yet he must leave it, to receive the wretched Sir Ratcliffe and his wife and their disconsolate companion. Never was so much unhappiness congregated together under one roof; and yet, perhaps Glastonbury, though the only one who retained the least command over himself, was, with his sad secret, the most woe-begone of the tribe.

As for Lady Armine, she sat without the door of her son's chamber the whole day and night, clasping a crucifix in her hands, and absorbed in silent prayer. Sir Ratcliffe remained below prostrate. The unhappy Katherine in vain offered the consolation she herself so needed; and would have wandered about that Armine of which she had heard so much, and where she was to have been so happy, a forlorn and solitary being, had it not been for the attentions of the considerate Glastonbury, who embraced every opportunity of being her companion. His patience, his heavenly resignation, his pious hope, his vigilant care, his spiritual consolation, occasionally even the gleams of agreeable converse with which he attempted to divert her mind, consoled and maintained her. How often did she look at his benignant countenance, and not wonder that the Armines were so attached to this engaging and devoted friend?

For three days did the unhappy family expect in terrible anticipation that each moment would witness the last event in the life of their son. His distracted voice caught too often the vigilant and agonised ear of his mother; yet she gave no evidence of the pang, except by clasping her crucifix with increased energy. She had promised the physician that she would command herself, that no sound should escape her lips, and she rigidly fulfilled the contract on which she was permitted to remain.

On the eve of the fourth day Ferdinand, who had never yet closed his eyes, but who had become during the last twelve hours somewhat more composed, fell into a slumber. The physician lightly dropped the hand which he had scarcely ever quitted, and, stealing out of the room, beckoned, his finger pressed to his lips, to Lady Armine to follow him. Assured by the symbol that the worst had not yet happened, she followed the physician to the end of the gallery, and he then told her that immediate danger was past.

'And now, my dear madam,' said the physician to her, 'you must breathe some fresh air. Oblige me by descending.'

Lady Armine no longer refused; she repaired with a slow step to Sir Ratcliffe; she leant upon her husband's breast as she murmured to him her hopes. They went forth together. Katherine and Glastonbury were in the garden. The appearance of Lady Armine gave them hopes. There was a faint smile on her face which needed not words to explain it. Katherine sprang forward, and threw her arms round her aunt's neck.

'He may be saved! he may be saved,' whispered the mother; for in this hushed house of impending death they had lost almost the power as well as the habit, of speaking in any other tone.

'He sleeps,' said the physician; 'all present danger is past.'

'It is too great joy,' murmured Katherine; and Glastonbury advanced and caught in his arms her insensible form.

CHAPTER XI.

In Which Ferdinand Begins to Be a Little Troublesome.

FROM the moment of this happy slumber Ferdinand continued to improve. Each day the bulletin was more favourable, until his progress, though slow, was declared certain, and even relapse was no longer apprehended. But his physician would not allow him to see any one of his family. It was at night, and during his slumbers, that Lady Armine stole into his room to gaze upon her beloved child; and, if he moved in the slightest degree, faithful to her promise and the injunction of the physician, she instantly glided behind his curtain, or a large Indian screen which she had placed there purposely. Often, indeed, did she remain in this fond lurking-place, silent and trembling, when her child was even awake, listening to every breath, and envying the nurse that might gaze on him undisturbed; nor would she allow any sustenance that he was ordered to be prepared by any but her own fair, fond hands; and she brought it herself even to his door. For Ferdinand himself, though his replies to the physician sufficiently attested the healthy calmness of his mind, he indeed otherwise never spoke, but lay on his bed without repining, and seemingly plunged in mild and pensive abstraction. At length, one morning he enquired for Glastonbury, who, with the sanction of the physician, immediately attended him.

When he met the eye of that faithful friend he tried to extend his hand. It was so wan that Glastonbury trembled while he touched it.

'I have given you much trouble,' he said, in a faint voice.

'I think only of the happiness of your recovery,' said Glastonbury.

'Yes, I am recovered,' murmured Ferdinand; 'it was not my wish.'

'Oh! be grateful to God for this great mercy, my Ferdinand.'

'You have heard nothing?' enquired Ferdinand.

Glastonbury shook his head.

'Fear not to speak; I can struggle no more. I am resigned. I am very much changed.'

'You will be happy, dear Ferdinand,' said Glastonbury, to whom this mood gave hopes.

'Never,' he said, in a more energetic tone; 'never.'

'There are so many that love you,' said Glastonbury, leading his thoughts to his family.

'Love!' exclaimed Ferdinand, with a sigh, and in a tone almost reproachful.

'Your dear mother,' said Glastonbury.

'Yes! my dear mother,' replied Ferdinand, musingly. Then in a quicker tone, 'Does she know of my illness? Did you write to them?'

'She knows of it.'

'She will be coming, then. I dread her coming. I can bear to see no one. You, dear Glastonbury, you; it is a consolation to see you, because you have seen,' and here his voice faltered, 'you have seen—her.'

'My Ferdinand, think only of your health; and happiness, believe me, will yet be yours.'

'If you could only find out where she is,' continued Ferdinand, 'and go to her. Yes! my dear Glastonbury, good, dear, Glastonbury, go to her,' he added in an imploring tone; 'she would believe you; everyone believes you. I cannot go; I am powerless; and if I went, alas! she would not believe me.'

'It is my wish to do everything you desire,' said Glastonbury, 'I should be content to be ever labouring for your happiness. But I can do nothing unless you are calm.'

'I am calm; I will be calm; I will act entirely as you wish; only I beseech you see her.'

'On that head let us at present say no more,' replied Glastonbury, who feared that excitement might lead to relapse; yet anxious to soothe him, he added, 'Trust in my humble services ever, and in the bounty of a merciful Providence.'

'I have had frightful dreams,' said Ferdinand. 'I thought I was in a farm-house; everything was so clear, so vivid. Night after night she seemed to me sitting on this bed. I touched her; her hand was in mine; it was so burning hot! Once, oh! once, once I thought she had forgiven me!'

'Hush! hush! hush!'

'No more: we will speak of her no more. When comes my mother?'

'You may see her to-morrow, or the day after.'

'Ah! Glastonbury, she is here.'

'She is.'

'Is she alone?'

'Your father is with her.'

'My mother and my father. It is well.' Then, after a minute's pause, he added with some earnestness, 'Do not deceive me, Glastonbury; see what deceit has brought me to. Are you sure that they are quite alone?'

'There are none here but your dearest friends; none whose presence should give you the slightest care.'

'There is one,' said Ferdinand.

'Dear Ferdinand, let me now leave you, or sit by your side in silence. To-morrow you will see your mother.'

'To-morrow! Ah! to-morrow. Once to me tomorrow was brighter even than to-day.' He turned his back and spoke no more. Glastonbury glided out of the room.

CHAPTER XII.

Containing the Intimation of a Somewhat Mysterious Adventure.

IT WAS absolutely necessary that Lady Armine's interview with her son be confined merely to observations about his health. Any allusion to the past might not only produce a relapse of his fever, but occasion explanations, at all times most painful, but at the present full of difficulty and danger. It was therefore with feelings of no common anxiety that Glastonbury prepared the mother for this first visit to her son, and impressed upon her the absolute necessity of not making any allusion at present to Miss Grandison, and especially to her presence in the house. He even made for this purpose a sort of half-confidant of the physician, who, in truth, had heard enough during the fever to excite his suspicions; but this is a class of men essentially discreet, and it is well, for few are the family secrets ultimately concealed from them.

The interview occurred without any disagreeable results. The next day, Ferdinand saw his father for a few minutes. In a short time, Lady Armine was established as nurse to her son; Sir Ratcliffe, easy in mind, amused himself with his sports; and Glastonbury devoted himself to Miss Grandison. The intimacy, indeed, between the tutor of Ferdinand and his intended bride became daily more complete, and Glastonbury was almost her inseparable companion. She found him a very interesting one. He was the most agreeable guide amid all the haunts of Armine and its neighbourhood, and drove her delightfully in Lady Armine's pony phaeton. He could share, too, all her pursuits, and open to her many new ones. Though time had stolen something of its force from the voice of Adrian Glastonbury, it still was wondrous sweet; his musical accomplishments were complete; and he could guide the pencil or prepare the herbal, and indite fair stanzas in his fine Italian handwriting in a lady's album. All his collections, too, were at Miss Grandison's service. She handled with rising curiosity his medals, copied his choice drawings, and even began to study heraldry. His interesting conversation, his mild and benignant manners, his captivating simplicity, and the elegant purity of his mind, secured her confidence and won her heart. She loved him as a father, and he soon exercised over her an influence almost irresistible.

Every morning as soon as he awoke, every evening before he composed himself again for the night's repose, Ferdinand sent for Glastonbury, and always saw him alone. At first he requested his mother to leave the room, but Lady Armine, who attributed these regular visits to a spiritual cause, scarcely needed the expression of this desire. His first questions to Glastonbury were ever the same. 'Had he heard anything? Were there any letters? He thought there might be a letter, was he sure? Had he sent to Bath; to London, for his letters?' When he was answered in the negative, he usually dwelt no more upon the subject. One morning he said to Glastonbury, 'I know Katherine is in the house.'

'Miss Grandison is here,' replied Glastonbury.

'Why don't they mention her? Is all known?'

'Nothing is known,' said Glastonbury.

'Why don't they mention her, then? Are you sure all is not known?'

'At my suggestion, her name has not been mentioned. I was unaware how you might receive the intelligence; but the true cause of my suggestion is still a secret.'

'I must see her,' said Ferdinand, 'I must speak to her.'

'You can see her when you please,' replied Glastonbury; 'but I would not speak upon the great subject at present.'

'But she is existing all this time under a delusion. Every day makes my conduct to her more infamous.'

'Miss Grandison is a wise and most admirable young lady,' said Glastonbury. 'I love her from the bottom of my heart; I would recommend no conduct that could injure her, assuredly none that can disgrace you.'

'Dear Glastonbury, what shall I do?'

'Be silent; the time will come when you may speak. At present, however anxious she may be to see you, there are plausible reasons for your not meeting. Be patient, my Ferdinand.'

'Good Glastonbury, good, dear Glastonbury, I am too quick and fretful. Pardon me, dear friend. You know not what I feel. Thank God, you do not; but my heart is broken.'

When Glastonbury returned to the library, he found Sir Ratcliffe playing with his dogs, and Miss Grandison copying a drawing.

'How is Ferdinand?' enquired the father.

'He mends daily,' replied Glastonbury. 'If only May-day were at hand instead of Christmas, he would soon be himself again; but I dread the winter.'

'And yet the sun shines.' said Miss Grandison.

Glastonbury went to the window and looked at the sky. 'I think, my dear lady, we might almost venture upon our promised excursion to the Abbey today. Such a day as this may not quickly be repeated. We might take our sketch-book.'

'It would be delightful,' said Miss Grandison; 'but before I go, I must pick some flowers for Ferdinand.' So saying, she sprang from her seat, and ran out into the garden.

'Kate is a sweet creature,' said Sir Ratcliffe to Glastonbury. 'Ah! my dear Glastonbury, you know not what happiness I experience in the thought that she will soon be my daughter.'

Glastonbury could not refrain from sighing. He took up the pencil and touched her drawing.

'Do you know, dear Glastonbury,' resumed Sir Ratcliffe, 'I had little hope in our late visitation. I cannot say I had prepared myself for the worst, but I anticipated it. We have had so much unhappiness in our family, that I could not persuade myself that the cup was not going to be dashed from our lips.'

'God is merciful,' said Glastonbury.

'You are his minister, dear Glastonbury, and a worthy one. I know not what we should have done without you in this awful trial; but, indeed, what could I have done throughout life without you?'

'Let us hope that everything is for the best,' said Glastonbury.

'And his mother, his poor mother, what would have become of her? She never could have survived his loss. As for myself, I would have quitted England for ever, and gone into a monastery.'

'Let us only remember that he lives,' said Glastonbury.

'And that we shall soon all be happy,' said Sir Ratcliffe, in a more animated tone. 'The future is, indeed, full of solace. But we must take care of him; he is too rapid in his movements. He has my father's blood in him, that is clear. I never could well make out why he left Bath so suddenly, and rushed down in so strange a manner to this place.'

'Youth is impetuous,' said Glastonbury.

'It was lucky you were here, Glastonbury.'

'I thank God that I was,' said Glastonbury, earnestly; then checking himself, he added, 'that I have been of any use.'

'You are always of use. What should we do without you? I should long ago have sunk. Ah! Glastonbury, God in his mercy sent you to us.'

'See here,' said Katherine, entering, her fair cheek glowing with animation, 'only dahlias, but they will look pretty, and enliven his room. Oh! that I might write him a little word, and tell him I am here! Do not you think I might, Mr. Glastonbury?'

'He will know that you are here to-day,' said Glastonbury. 'To-morrow———'

'Ah! you always postpone it,' said Miss Grandison, in a tone half playful, half reproachful; 'and yet it is selfish to murmur. It is for his good that I bear this bereavement, and that thought should console me. Heigho!'

Sir Ratcliffe stepped forward and kissed his niece. Glastonbury was busied on the drawing: he turned away his face.

Sir Ratcliffe took up his gun. 'God bless you, dear Kate,' he said; 'a pleasant drive and a choice sketch. We shall meet at dinner.'

'At dinner, dear uncle; and better sport than yesterday.'

'Ha! ha!' said Sir Ratcliffe. 'But Armine is not like Grandison. If I were in the old preserves, you should have no cause to jeer at my sportsmanship.'

Miss Grandison's good wishes were prophetic: Sir Ratcliffe found excellent sport, and returned home very late, and in capital spirits. It was the dinner-hour, and yet Katherine and Glastonbury had not returned. He was rather surprised. The shades of evening were fast descending, and the distant lawns of Armine were already invisible; the low moan of the rising wind might be just distinguished; and the coming night promised to be raw and cloudy, perhaps tempestuous. Sir Ratcliffe stood before the crackling fire in the dining-room, otherwise in darkness, but the flame threw a bright yet glancing light upon the Snyders, so that the figures seemed really to move in the shifting shades, the eye of the infuriate boar almost to emit sparks of rage, and there wanted but the shouts of the huntsmen and the panting of the dogs to complete the tumult of the chase. Just as Sir Ratcliffe was anticipating some mischance to his absent friends, and was about to steal upon tip-toe to Lady Armine, who was with Ferdinand, to consult her, the practised ear of a man who lived much in the air caught the distant sound of wheels, and he went out to welcome them.

'Why, you are late,' said Sir Ratcliffe, as the phaeton approached the house. 'All right, I hope?' He stepped forward to assist Miss Grandison. The darkness of the evening prevented him from observing her swollen eyes and agitated countenance. She sprang out of the carriage in silence, and immediately ran up into her room. As for Glastonbury, he only observed it was very cold, and entered the house with Sir Ratcliffe.

'This fire is hearty,' said Glastonbury, warming himself before it: 'you have had good sport, I hope? We are not to wait dinner for Miss Grandison, Sir Ratcliffe. She will not come down this evening; she is not very well.'

'Not very well: ah! the cold, I fear. You have been imprudent in staying so late. I must run and tell Lady Armine.'

'Oblige me, I pray, by not doing so,' said Glastonbury; 'Miss Grandison most particularly requested that she should not be disturbed.'

It was with some difficulty that Glastonbury could contrive that Miss Grandison's wishes should be complied with; but at length he succeeded in getting Sir Ratcliffe to sit down to dinner, and affecting a cheerfulness which was far from his spirit, the hour of ten at length arrived, and Glastonbury, before retiring to his tower, paid his evening visit to Ferdinand.

CHAPTER XIII.

In Which the Family Perplexities Rather Increase
than Diminish.

IF EVER there were a man who deserved a serene and happy life it was Adrian Glastonbury. He had pursued a long career without injuring or offending a human being; his character and conduct were alike spotless; he was void of guile; he had never told a falsehood, never been entangled in the slightest deceit; he was easy in his circumstances; he had no relations to prey upon his purse or his feelings; and, though alone in the world, was blessed with such a sweet and benignant temper, gifted with so many resources, and adorned with so many accomplishments, that he appeared to be always employed, amused, and contented. And yet, by a strange contrariety of events, it appeared that this excellent person was now placed in a situation which is generally the consequence of impetuous passions not very scrupulous in obtaining their ends. That breast, which heretofore would have shrunk from being analysed only from the refined modesty of its nature, had now become the depository of terrible secrets: the day could scarcely pass over without finding him in a position which rendered equivocation on his part almost a necessity, while all the anxieties inseparable from pecuniary embarrassments were forced upon his attention, and his feelings were racked from sympathy with individuals who were bound to him by no other tie, but to whose welfare he felt himself engaged to sacrifice all his pursuits, and devote all his time and labour. And yet he did not murmur, although he had scarcely hope to animate him. In whatever light he viewed coming events, they appeared ominous only of evil. All that he aimed at now was to soothe and support, and it was his unshaken confidence in Providence that alone forbade him to despair.

When he repaired to the Place in the morning he found everything in confusion. Miss Grandison was very unwell; and Lady Armine, frightened by the recent danger from which they had escaped, very alarmed. She could no longer conceal from Ferdinand that his Katherine was here, and perhaps Lady Armine was somewhat surprised at the calmness with which her son received the intelligence. But Miss Grandison was not only very unwell but very obstinate. She would not leave her room, but insisted that no medical advice should be called in. Lady Armine protested, supplicated, adjured; Miss Grandison appealed to Mr. Glastonbury; and Glastonbury, who was somewhat of a physician, was called in, and was obliged to assure Lady Armine that Miss Grandison was only suffering from a cold and only required repose. A warm friendship subsisted between Lady Armine and her niece. She had always been Katherine's favourite aunt, and during the past year there had been urgent reasons why Lady Armine should have cherished this predisposition in her favour. Lady Armine was a fascinating person, and all her powers had been employed to obtain an influence over the heiress. They had been quite successful. Miss Grandison looked forward almost with as much pleasure to being Lady Armine's daughter as her son's bride. The intended mother-in-law was in turn as warmhearted as her niece was engaging; and eventually Lady Armine loved Katherine for herself alone.

In a few days, however, Miss Grandison announced that she was quite recovered, and Lady Armine again devoted her unbroken attention to her son, who was now about to rise for the first time from his bed. But although Miss Grandison was no longer an invalid, it is quite certain that if the attention of the other members of the family had not been so entirely engrossed, a very great change in her behaviour could not have escaped their notice. Her flowers and drawings seemed to have lost their relish; her gaiety to have deserted her. She passed a great portion of the morning in her room; and although it was announced to her that Ferdinand was aware of her being an inmate of the Place, and that in a day or two they might meet, she scarcely evinced, at this prospect of resuming his society, so much gratification as might have been expected; and though she daily took care that his chamber should still be provided with flowers, it might have been remarked that the note she had been so anxious to send him was never written. But how much, under the commonest course of circumstances, happens in all domestic circles that is never observed or never remarked till the observation is too late!

At length the day arrived when Lady Armine invited her niece to visit her son. Miss Grandison expressed her readiness to accompany her aunt, but took an opportunity of requesting Glastonbury to join them; and all three proceeded to the chamber of the invalid.

The white curtain of the room was drawn; but though the light was softened, the apartment was by no means obscure. Ferdinand was sitting in an easy-chair, supported by pillows. A black handkerchief was just twined round his forehead, for his head had been shaved, except a few curls on the side and front, which looked stark and lustreless. He was so thin and pale, and his eyes and cheeks were so wan and hollow, that it was scarcely credible that in so short a space of time a man could have become such a wreck. When he saw Katherine he involuntarily dropped his eyes, but extended his hand to her with some effort of earnestness. She was almost as pale as he, but she took his hand. It was so light and cold, it felt so much like death, that the tears stole down her cheek.

'You hardly know me, Katherine,' said Ferdinand, feebly. 'This is good of you to visit a sick man.'

Miss Grandison could not reply, and Lady Armine made an observation to break the awkward pause.

'And how do you like Armine?' said Ferdinand. 'I wish I could be your guide. But Glastonbury is so kind!'

A hundred times Miss Grandison tried to reply, to speak, to make the commonest observation, but it was in vain. She grew paler every moment; her lips moved, but they sent forth no sound.

'Kate is not well,' said Lady Armine. 'She has been very unwell. This visit,' she added in a whisper to Ferdinand, 'is a little too much for her.'

Ferdinand sighed.

'Mother,' he at length said, 'you must ask Katherine to come and sit here with you; if indeed she will not feel the imprisonment.'

Miss Grandison turned in her chair, and hid her face with her handkerchief.

'My sweet child,' said Lady Armine, rising and kissing her, 'this is too much for you. You really must restrain yourself. Ferdinand will soon be himself again; he will indeed.'

Miss Grandison sobbed aloud. Glastonbury was much distressed, but Ferdinand avoided catching his eye; and yet, at last, Ferdinand said with an effort, and in a very kind voice, 'Dear Kate, come and sit by me.'

Miss Grandison went into hysterics; Ferdinand sprang from his chair and seized her hand; Lady Armine tried to restrain her son; Glastonbury held the agitated Katherine.

'For God's sake, Ferdinand, be calm,' exclaimed Lady Armine. 'This is most unfortunate. Dear, dear Katherine, but she has such a heart! All the women have in our family, and none of the men, 'tis so odd. Mr. Glastonbury, water if you please, that glass of water; sal volatile; where is the sal volatile? My own, own Katherine, pray, pray restrain yourself! Ferdinand is here; remember,

Ferdinand is here, and he will soon be well; soon quite well. Believe me, he is already quite another thing. There, drink that, darling, drink that. You are better now?'

'I am so foolish,' said Miss Grandison, in a mournful voice. 'I never can pardon myself for this. Let me go.'

Glastonbury bore her out of the room; Lady Armine turned to her son. He was lying back in his chair, his hands covering his eyes. The mother stole gently to him, and wiped tenderly his brow, on which hung the light drops of perspiration, occasioned by his recent exertion.

'We have done too much, my own dear Ferdinand. Yet who could have expected that dear girl would have been so affected? Glastonbury was indeed right in preventing you so long from meeting. And yet it is a blessing to see that she has so fond a heart. You are fortunate, my Ferdinand: you will indeed be happy with her.'

Ferdinand groaned.

'I shall never be happy,' he murmured.

'Never happy, my Ferdinand! Oh! you must not be so low-spirited. Think how much better you are; think, my Ferdinand, what a change there is for the better. You will soon be well, dearest, and then, my love, you know you cannot help being happy.'

'Mother,' said Ferdinand, 'you are deceived; you are all deceived: I—I————'

'No! Ferdinand, indeed we are not. I am confident, and I praise God for it, that you are getting better every day. But you have done too much, that is the truth. I will leave you now, love, and send the nurse, for my presence excites you. Try to sleep, love.' And Lady Armine rang the bell, and quitted the room.

CHAPTER XIV.

In Which Some Light Is Thrown upon Some Circumstances Which
Were Before Rather Mysterious.

LADY ARMINE now proposed that the family should meet in Ferdinand's room after dinner;
but Glastonbury, whose opinion on most subjects generally prevailed, scarcely approved of this
suggestion. It was therefore but once acted upon during the week that followed the scene
described in our last chapter, and on that evening Miss Grandison had so severe a headache, that
it was quite impossible for her to join the circle. At length, however, Ferdinand made his
appearance below, and established himself in the library: it now, therefore, became absolutely
necessary that Miss Grandison should steel her nerves to the altered state of her betrothed, which
had at first apparently so much affected her sensibility, and, by the united influence of habit and
Mr. Glastonbury, it is astonishing what progress she made. She even at last could so command
her feelings, that she apparently greatly contributed to his amusement. She joined in the family
concerts, once even read to him.

Every morning, too, she brought him a flower, and often offered him her arm. And yet Ferdinand
could not resist observing a great difference in her behaviour towards him since he had last
quitted her at Bath. Far from conducting herself, as he had nervously apprehended, as if her
claim to be his companion were irresistible, her carriage, on the contrary, indicated the most
retiring disposition; she annoyed him with no expressions of fondness, and listened to the kind
words which he occasionally urged himself to bestow upon her with a sentiment of grave regard
and placid silence, which almost filled him with astonishment.

One morning, the weather being clear and fine, Ferdinand insisted that his mother, who had as
yet scarcely quitted his side, should drive out with Sir Ratcliffe; and, as he would take no refusal,
Lady Armine agreed to comply. The carriage was ordered, was at the door; and as Lady Armine
bade him adieu, Ferdinand rose from his seat and took the arm of Miss Grandison, who seemed
on the point of retiring; for Glastonbury remained, and therefore Ferdinand was not without a
companion.

'I will see you go off,' said Ferdinand.

'Adieu!' said Lady Armine. 'Take care of him, dear Kate,' and the phaeton was soon out of sight.

'It is more like May than January,' said Ferdinand to his cousin. 'I fancy I should like to walk a
little.'

'Shall I send for Mr. Glastonbury?' said Katherine.

'Not if my arm be not too heavy for you,' said Ferdinand. So they walked slowly on, perhaps
some fifty yards, until they arrived at a garden-seat, very near the rose-tree whose flowers
Henrietta Temple so much admired. It had no flowers now, but seemed as desolate as their
unhappy loves.

'A moment's rest,' said Ferdinand, and sighed. 'Dear Kate, I wish to speak to you.'

Miss Grandison turned pale.

'I have something on my mind, Katherine, of which I would endeavour to relieve myself.'

Miss Grandison did not reply, but she trembled. 'It concerns you, Katherine.'

Still she was silent, and expressed no astonishment at this strange address.

'If I were anything now but an object of pity, a miserable and broken-hearted man,' continued

Ferdinand, 'I might shrink from this communication; I might delegate to another this office, humiliating as it then might be to me, painful as it must, under any circumstances, be to you. But,' and here his voice faltered, 'but I am far beyond the power of any mortification now. The world and the world's ways touch me no more. There is a duty to fulfil; I will fulfil it. I have offended against you, my sweet and gentle cousin; grievously, bitterly, infamously offended.'

'No, no, no!' murmured Miss Grandison.

'Katherine, I am unworthy of you; I have deceived you. It is neither for your honour nor your happiness that these ties which our friends anticipate should occur between us. But, Katherine, you are avenged.'

'Oh! I want no vengeance!' muttered Miss Grandison, her face pale as marble, her eyes convulsively closed. 'Cease, cease, Ferdinand; this conversation is madness; you will be ill again.'

'No, Katherine, I am calm. Fear not for me. There is much to tell; it must be told, if only that you should not believe that I was a systematic villain, or that my feelings were engaged to another when I breathed to you those vows.'

'Oh! anything but that; speak of anything but that!'

Ferdinand took her hand.

'Katherine, listen to me. I honour you, my gentle cousin, I admire, I esteem you; I could die content if I could but see you happy. With your charms and virtues I thought that we might be happy. My intentions were as sincere as my belief in our future felicity. Oh! no, dear Katherine, I could not trifle with so pure and gentle a bosom.'

'Have I accused you, Ferdinand?'

'But you will when you know all.'

'I do know all,' said Miss Grandison, in a hollow voice.

Her hand fell from the weak and trembling grasp of her cousin.

'You do know all,' he at length exclaimed. 'And can you, knowing all, live under the same roof with me? Can you see me? Can you listen to me? Is not my voice torture to you? Do you not hate and despise me?'

'It is not my nature to hate anything; least of all could I hate you.'

'And could you, knowing all, still minister to my wants and watch my sad necessities? This gentle arm of yours; could you, knowing all, let me lean upon it this morning? O Katherine! a happy lot be yours, for you deserve one!'

'Ferdinand, I have acted as duty, religion, and it may be, some other considerations prompted me. My feelings have not been so much considered that they need now be analysed.'

'Reproach me, Katherine, I deserve your reproaches.'

'Mine may not be the only reproaches that you have deserved, Ferdinand; but permit me to remark, from me you have received none. I pity you, I sincerely pity you.'

'Glastonbury has told you?' said Ferdinand.

'That communication is among the other good offices we owe him,' replied Miss Grandison.

'He told you?' said Ferdinand enquiringly.

'All that it was necessary I should know for your honour, or, as some might think, for my own happiness; no more, I would listen to no more. I had no idle curiosity to gratify. It is enough that your heart is another's; I seek not, I wish not, to know that person's name.'

'I cannot mention it,' said Ferdinand; 'but there is no secret from you. Glastonbury may—should tell all.'

'Amid the wretched she is not the least miserable,' said Miss Grandison.

'O Katherine!' said Ferdinand, after a moment's pause, 'tell me that you do not hate me; tell me that you pardon me; tell me that you think me more mad than wicked!'

'Ferdinand,' said Miss Grandison, 'I think we are both unfortunate.'

'I am without hope,' said Ferdinand; 'but you, Katherine, your life must still be bright and fair.'

'I can never be happy, Ferdinand, if you are not. I am alone in the world. Your family are my only relations; I cling to them. Your mother is my mother; I love her with the passion of a child. I looked upon our union only as the seal of that domestic feeling that had long bound us all. My happiness now entirely depends upon your family; theirs I feel is staked upon you. It is the conviction of the total desolation that must occur if our estrangement be suddenly made known to them, and you, who are so impetuous, decide upon any rash course, in consequence, that has induced me to sustain the painful part that I now uphold. This is the reason that I would not reproach you, Ferdinand, that I would not quarrel with you, that I would not desert them in this hour of their affliction.'

'Katherine, beloved Katherine!' exclaimed the distracted Ferdinand, 'why did we ever part?'

'No! Ferdinand, let us not deceive ourselves. For me, that separation, however fruitful at the present moment in mortification and unhappiness, must not be considered altogether an event of unmingled misfortune. In my opinion, Ferdinand, it is better to be despised for a moment than to be neglected for a life.'

'Despised! Katherine, for God's sake, spare me; for God's sake, do not use such language! Despised! Katherine, at this moment I declare most solemnly all that I feel is, how thoroughly, how infamously unworthy I am of you! Dearest Katherine, we cannot recall the past, we cannot amend it; but let me assure you that at this very hour there is no being on earth I more esteem, more reverence than yourself.'

'It is well, Ferdinand. I would not willingly believe that your feelings towards me were otherwise than kind and generous. But let us understand each other. I shall remain at present under this roof. Do not misapprehend my views. I seek not to recall your affections. The past has proved to me that we are completely unfitted for each other. I have not those dazzling qualities that could enchain a fiery brain like yours. I know myself; I know you; and there is nothing that would fill me with more terror now than our anticipated union. And now, after this frank conversation, let our future intercourse be cordial and unembarrassed; let us remember we are kinsfolk. The feelings between us should by nature be amiable: no incident has occurred to disturb them, for I have not injured or offended you; and as for your conduct towards me, from the bottom of my heart I pardon and forget it.'

'Katherine,' said Ferdinand, with streaming eyes, 'kindest, most generous of women! My heart is too moved, my spirit too broken, to express what I feel. We are kinsfolk; let us be more. You say my mother is your mother. Let me assert the privilege of that admission. Let me be a brother to you; you shall find me, if I live, a faithful one.'

CHAPTER XV.

Which Leaves Affairs in General in a Scarcely More
Satisfactory Position than the Former One.

FERDINAND felt much calmer in his mind after this conversation with his cousin. Her affectionate attention to him now, instead of filling him as it did before with remorse, was really a source of consolation, if that be not too strong a phrase to describe the state of one so thoroughly wretched as Captain Armine; for his terrible illness and impending death had not in the slightest degree allayed or affected his profound passion for Henrietta Temple. Her image unceasingly engaged his thoughts; he still clung to the wild idea that she might yet be his. But his health improved so slowly, that there was faint hope of his speedily taking any steps to induce such a result. All his enquiries after her, and Glastonbury, at his suggestion, had not been idle, were quite fruitless. He made no doubt that she had quitted England. What might not happen, far away from him, and believing herself betrayed and deserted? Often when he brooded over these terrible contingencies, he regretted his recovery.

Yet his family, thanks to the considerate conduct of his admirable cousin, were still contented and happy. His slow convalescence was now their only source of anxiety. They regretted the unfavourable season of the year; they looked forward with hope to the genial influence of the coming spring. That was to cure all their cares; and yet they might well suspect, when they watched his ever pensive, and often suffering countenance, that there were deeper causes than physical debility and bodily pain to account for that moody and woe-begone expression. Alas! how changed from that Ferdinand Armine, so full of hope, and courage, and youth, and beauty, that had burst on their enraptured vision on his return from Malta. Where was that gaiety now that made all eyes sparkle, that vivacious spirit that kindled energy in every bosom? How miserable to see him crawling about with a wretched stick, with his thin, pale face, and tottering limbs, and scarcely any other pursuit than to creep about the pleasaunce, where, when the day was fair, his servant would place a camp-stool opposite the cedar tree where he had first beheld Henrietta Temple; and there he would sit, until the unkind winter breeze would make him shiver, gazing on vacancy; yet peopled to his mind's eye with beautiful and fearful apparitions.

And it is love, it is the most delightful of human passions, that can bring about such misery! Why will its true course never run smooth? Is there a spell over our heart, that its finest emotions should lead only to despair? When Ferdinand Armine, in his reveries, dwelt upon the past; when he recalled the hour that he had first seen her, her first glance, the first sound of her voice, his visit to Ducie, all the passionate scenes to which it led, those sweet wanderings through its enchanted bowers, those bright mornings, so full of expectation that was never baulked, those soft eyes, so redolent of tenderness that could never cease; when from the bright, and glowing, and gentle scenes his memory conjured up, and all the transport and the thrill that surrounded them like an atmosphere of love, he turned to his shattered and broken-hearted self, the rigid heaven above, and what seemed to his perhaps unwise and ungrateful spirit, the mechanical sympathy and common-place affection of his companions, it was as if he had wakened from some too vivid and too glorious dream, or as if he had fallen from some brighter and more favoured planet upon our cold, dull earth.

And yet it would seem the roof of Armine Place protected a family that might yield to few in the beauty and engaging qualities of its inmates, their happy accomplishments, their kind and cordial hearts. And all were devoted to him. It was on him alone the noble spirit of his father dwelt still with pride and joy: it was to soothe and gratify him that his charming mother exerted all her graceful care and all her engaging gifts. It was for him, and his sake, the generous heart of his cousin had submitted to mortification without a murmur, or indulged her unhappiness only in solitude; and it was for him that Glastonbury exercised a devotion that might alone induce a man to think with complacency both of his species and himself. But the heart, the heart, the jealous and despotic heart! It rejects all substitutes, it spurns all compromise, and it will have its purpose or it will break.

BOOK V.

CHAPTER I.

Containing the Appearance on Our Stage of a New and
Important Character.

THE Marquis of Montfort was the grandson of that nobleman who had been Glastonbury's
earliest patron. The old duke had been dead some years; his son had succeeded to his title, and
Digby, that youth whom the reader may recollect was about the same age as Ferdinand Armine,
and was his companion during the happy week in London which preceded his first military visit
to the Mediterranean, now bore the second title of the family.

The young marquis was an excellent specimen of a class inferior in talents, intelligence, and
accomplishments, in public spirit and in private virtues, to none in the world, the English
nobility. His complete education had been carefully conducted; and although his religious creed,
for it will be remembered he was a Catholic, had deprived him of the advantage of matriculating
at an English university, the zeal of an able and learned tutor, and the resources of a German
Alma Mater, had afforded every opportunity for the development of his considerable talents.
Nature had lavished upon him other gifts besides his distinguished intelligence and his amiable
temper: his personal beauty was remarkable, and his natural grace was not less evident than his
many acquired accomplishments.

On quitting the University of Bonn, Lord Montfort had passed several years on the continent of
Europe, and had visited and resided at most of its courts and capitals, an admired and cherished
guest; for, debarred at the period of our story from occupying the seat of his ancestors in the
senate, his native country offered no very urgent claims upon his presence. He had ultimately
fixed upon Rome as his principal residence, for he was devoted to the arts, and in his palace were
collected some of the rarest specimens of ancient and modern invention.

At Pisa, Lord Montfort had made the acquaintance of Mr. Temple, who was residing in that city
for the benefit of his daughter's health, who, it was feared by her physicians, was in a decline. I
say the acquaintance of Mr. Temple; for Lord Montfort was aware of the existence of his
daughter only by the occasional mention of her name, as Miss Temple was never seen. The
agreeable manners, varied information, and accomplished mind of Mr. Temple, had attracted and
won the attention of the young nobleman, who shrank in general from the travelling English, and
all their arrogant ignorance. Mr. Temple was in turn equally pleased with a companion alike
refined, amiable, and enlightened; and their acquaintance would have ripened into intimacy, had
not the illness of Henrietta and her repugnance to see a third person, and the unwillingness of her
father that she should be alone, offered in some degree a bar to its cultivation.

Yet Henrietta was glad that her father had found a friend and was amused, and impressed upon
him not to think of her, but to accept Lord Montfort's invitations to his villa. But Mr. Temple
invariably declined them.

'I am always uneasy when I am away from you, dearest,' said Mr. Temple; 'I wish you would go
about a little. Believe me, it is not for myself that I make the suggestion, but I am sure you would
derive benefit from the exertion. I wish you would go with me and see Lord Montfort's villa.
There would be no one there but himself. He would not in the least annoy you, he is so quiet; and
he and I could stroll about and look at the busts and talk to each other. You would hardly know
he was present, he is such a very quiet person.'

Henrietta shook her head; and Mr. Temple could not urge the request.

Fate, however, had decided that Lord Montfort and Henrietta Temple should become acquainted. She had more than once expressed a wish to see the Campo Santo; it was almost the only wish that she had expressed since she left England. Her father, pleased to find that anything could interest her, was in the habit of reminding her of this desire, and suggesting that she should gratify it. But there was ever an excuse for procrastination. When the hour of exertion came, she would say, with a faint smile, 'Not to-day, dearest papa;' and then, arranging her shawl, as if even in this soft clime she shivered, composed herself upon that sofa which now she scarcely ever quitted.

And this was Henrietta Temple! That gay and glorious being, so full of graceful power and beautiful energy, that seemed born for a throne, and to command a nation of adoring subjects! What are those political revolutions, whose strange and mighty vicissitudes we are ever dilating on, compared with the moral mutations that are passing daily under our own eye; uprooting the hearts of families, shattering to pieces domestic circles, scattering to the winds the plans and prospects of a generation, and blasting as with a mildew the ripening harvest of long cherished affection!

'It is here that I would be buried,' said Henrietta Temple.

They were standing, the father and the daughter, in the Campo Santo. She had been gayer that morning; her father had seized a happy moment, and she had gone forth, to visit the dead. That vast and cloistered cemetery was silent and undisturbed; not a human being was there, save themselves and the keeper. The sun shone brightly on the austere and ancient frescoes, and Henrietta stood opposite that beautiful sarcophagus, that seemed prepared and fitting to receive her destined ashes.

'It is here that I would be buried,' said she.

Her father almost unconsciously turned his head to gaze upon the countenance of his daughter, to see if there were indeed reason that she should talk of death. That countenance was changed since the moment we first feebly attempted to picture it. That flashing eye had lost something of its brilliancy, that superb form something of its roundness and its stag-like state; the crimson glory of that mantling cheek had faded like the fading eve; and yet it might be thought, it might be suffering, perhaps, the anticipation of approaching death, and as it were the imaginary contact with a serener existence, but certainly there was a more spiritual expression diffused over the whole appearance of Henrietta Temple, and which by many might be preferred even to that more lively and glowing beauty which, in her happier hours, made her the very queen of flowers and sunshine.

'It is strange, dear papa,' she continued, 'that my first visit should be to a cemetery.'

At this moment their attention was attracted by the sound of the distant gates of the cemetery opening, and several persons soon entered. This party consisted of some of the authorities of the city and some porters, bearing on a slab of verd antique a magnificent cinerary vase, that was about to be placed in the Campo. In reply to his enquiries, Mr. Temple learned that the vase had been recently excavated in Catania, and that it had been purchased and presented to the Campo by the Marquis of Montfort. Henrietta would have hurried her father away, but with all her haste they had not reached the gates before Lord Montfort appeared.

Mr. Temple found it impossible, although Henrietta pressed his arm in token of disapprobation, not to present Lord Montfort to his daughter. He then admired his lordship's urn, and then his lordship requested that he might have the pleasure of showing it to them himself. They turned; Lord Montfort explained to them its rarity, and pointed out to them its beauty. His voice was soft and low, his manner simple but rather reserved. While he paid that deference to Henrietta which her sex demanded, he addressed himself chiefly to her father. She was not half so much annoyed as she had imagined; she agreed with her father that he was a very quiet man; she was even a little interested by his conversation, which was refined and elegant; and she was pleased that he did not seem to require her to play any part in the discourse, but appeared quite content in being her father's friend. Lord Montfort seemed to be attached to her father, and to appreciate him. And this was always a recommendation to Henrietta Temple.

The cinerary urn led to a little controversy between Mr. Temple and his friend; and Lord Montfort wished that Mr. Temple would some day call on him at his house in the Lung' Arno, and he would show him some specimens which he thought might influence his opinion. 'I hardly dare to ask you to come now,' said his lordship, looking at Miss Temple; 'and yet Miss Temple might like to rest.'

It was evident to Henrietta that her father would be pleased to go, and yet that he was about to refuse for her sake. She could not bear that he should be deprived of so much and such refined amusement, and be doomed to an uninteresting morning at home, merely to gratify her humour. She tried to speak, but could not at first command her voice; at length she expressed her wish that Mr. Temple should avail himself of the invitation. Lord Montfort bowed lowly, Mr. Temple seemed gratified, and they all turned together and quitted the cemetery.

As they walked along to the house, conversation did not flag. Lord Montfort expressed his admiration of Pisa. 'Silence and art are two great charms,' said his lordship.

At length they arrived at his palace. A venerable Italian received them. They passed through a vast hall, in which were statues, ascended a magnificent double staircase, and entered a range of saloons. One of them was furnished with more attention to comfort than an Italian cares for, and herein was the cabinet of urns and vases his lordship had mentioned.

'This is little more than a barrack,' said Lord Montfort; 'but I can find a sofa for Miss Temple.' So saying, he arranged with great care the cushions of the couch, and, when she seated herself, placed a footstool near her. 'I wish you would allow me some day to welcome you at Rome,' said the young marquis. 'It is there that I indeed reside.'

Lord Montfort and Mr. Temple examined the contents of the cabinet. There was one vase which Mr. Temple greatly admired for the elegance of its form. His host immediately brought it and placed it on a small pedestal near Miss Temple. Yet he scarcely addressed himself to her, and Henrietta experienced none of that troublesome attention from which, in the present state of her health and mind, she shrank. While Mr. Temple was interested with his pursuit, Lord Montfort went to a small cabinet opposite, and brought forth a curious casket of antique gems. 'Perhaps,' he said, placing it by Miss Temple, 'the contents of this casket might amuse you;' and he walked away to her father.

In the course of an hour a servant brought in some fruits and wine.

'The grapes are from my villa,' said Lord Montfort. 'I ventured to order them, because I have heard their salutary effects have been marvellous. Besides, at this season, even in Italy they are rare. At least \ you cannot accuse me of prescribing a disagreeable remedy,' he added with a slight smile, as he handed a plate to Miss Temple. She moved to receive them. Her cushions slipped from behind her, Lord Montfort immediately arranged them with skill and care. He was so kind that she really wished to thank him; but before she could utter a word he was again conversing with her father.

At length Mr. Temple indicated his intention to retire, and spoke to his daughter.

'This has been a great exertion for you, Henrietta,' he said; 'this has indeed been a busy day.'

'I am not wearied; and we have been much pleased.' It was the firmest tone in which she had spoken for a long time. There was something in her manner which recalled to Mr. Temple her vanished animation. The affectionate father looked for a moment happy. The sweet music of these simple words dwelt on his ear.

He went forward and assisted Henrietta to rise. She closed the casket with care, and delivered it herself to her considerate host. Mr. Temple bade him adieu; Henrietta bowed, and nearly extended her hand. Lord Montfort attended them to the gate; a carriage was waiting there.

'Ah! we have kept your lordship at home,' said Mr. Temple.

'I took the liberty of ordering the carriage for Miss Temple,' he replied. 'I feel a little responsible for her kind exertion to-day.'

CHAPTER II.

In Which Lord Montfort Contrives That Miss Temple Should be
Left Alone.

AND how do you like my friend, Henrietta?' said Mr. Temple, as they drove home.

'I like your friend much, papa. He is quite as quiet as you said; he is almost the only person I have seen since I quitted England who has not jarred my nerves. I felt quite sorry that I had so long prevented you both from cultivating each other's acquaintance. He does not interfere with me in the least.'

'I wish I had asked him to look in upon us in the evening,' said Mr. Temple, rather enquiringly.

'Not to-day,' said Henrietta. 'Another day, dearest papa.'

The next day Lord Montfort sent a note to Mr. Temple, to enquire after his daughter, and to impress upon him the importance of her eating his grapes. His servant left a basket. The rest of the note was about cinerary urns. Mr. Temple, while he thanked him, assured him of the pleasure it would give both his daughter and himself to see him in the evening.

This was the first invitation to his house that Mr. Temple had ventured to give him, though they had now known each other some time.

In the evening Lord Montfort appeared. Henrietta was lying on her sofa, and her father would not let her rise. Lord Montfort had brought Mr. Temple some English journals, which he had received from Leghorn. The gentlemen talked a little on foreign politics; and discussed the character of several of the most celebrated foreign ministers. Lord Montfort gave an account of his visit to Prince Esterhazy. Henrietta was amused. German politics and society led to German literature. Lord Montfort, on this subject, seemed completely informed. Henrietta could not refrain from joining in a conversation for which she was fully qualified. She happened to deplore her want of books. Lord Montfort had a library; but it was at Rome: no matter; it seemed that he thought nothing of sending to Rome. He made a note very quietly of some books that Henrietta expressed a wish to see, and begged that Mr. Temple would send the memorandum to his servant.

'But surely to-morrow will do,' said Mr. Temple. 'Rome is too far to send to this evening.'

'That is an additional reason for instant departure,' said his lordship calmly.

Mr. Temple summoned a servant.

'Send this note to my house,' said his lordship. 'My courier will bring us the books in four days,' he added, turning to Miss Temple. 'I am sorry you should have to wait, but at Pisa I really have nothing.'

From this day Lord Montfort passed every evening at Mr. Temple's house. His arrival never disturbed Miss Temple; she remained on the sofa. If she spoke to him he was always ready to converse with her, yet he never obtruded his society. He seemed perfectly contented with the company of her father. Yet with all this calmness and reserve, there was no air of affected indifference, no intolerable nonchalance; he was always attentive, always considerate, often kind. However apparently engaged with her father, it seemed that his vigilance anticipated all her wants. If she moved, he was at her side; if she required anything, it would appear that he read her thoughts, for it was always offered. She found her sofa arranged as if by magic. And if a shawl were for a moment missing, Lord Montfort always knew where it had been placed. In the meantime, every morning brought something for the amusement of Mr. Temple and his daughter; books, prints, drawings, newspapers, journals of all countries, and caricatures from Paris and London, were mingled with engravings of Henrietta's favourite Campo Santo.

One evening Mr. Temple and his guest were speaking of a celebrated Professor of the University. Lord Montfort described his extraordinary acquirements and discoveries, and his rare simplicity. He was one of those eccentric geniuses that are sometimes found in decayed cities with ancient institutions of learning. Henrietta was interested in his description. Almost without thought she expressed a wish to see him.

'He shall come to-morrow,' said Lord Montfort, 'if you please. Believe me,' he added, in a tone of great kindness, 'that if you could prevail upon yourself to cultivate Italian society a little, it would repay you.'

The professor was brought. Miss Temple was much entertained. In a few days he came again, and introduced a friend scarcely less distinguished. The society was so easy, that even Henrietta found it no burthen. She remained upon her sofa; the gentlemen drank their coffee and conversed. One morning Lord Montfort had prevailed upon her to visit the studio of a celebrated sculptor. The artist was full of enthusiasm for his pursuit, and showed them with pride his great work, a Diana that might have made one envy Endymion. The sculptor declared it was the perfect resemblance of Miss Temple, and appealed to her father. Mr. Temple could not deny the striking likeness. Miss Temple smiled; she looked almost herself again; even the reserved Lord Montfort was in raptures.

'Oh! it is very like,' said his lordship. 'Yes! now it is exactly like. Miss Temple does not often smile; but now one would believe she really was the model.'

They were bidding the sculptor farewell.

'Do you like him?' whispered Lord Montfort of Miss Temple.

'Extremely; he is full of ideas.'

'Shall I ask him to come to you this evening?'

'Yes, do!'

And so it turned out that in time Henrietta found herself the centre of a little circle of eminent and accomplished men. Her health improved as she brooded less over her sorrows. It gratified her to witness the pleasure of her father. She was not always on her sofa now. Lord Montfort had sent her an English chair, which suited her delightfully.

They even began to take drives with him in the country an hour or so before sunset. The country around Pisa is rich as well as picturesque; and their companion always contrived that there should be an object in their brief excursions. He spoke, too, the dialect of the country; and they paid, under his auspices, a visit to a Tuscan farmer. All this was agreeable; even Henrietta was persuaded that it was better than staying at home. The variety of pleasing objects diverted her mind in spite of herself. She had some duties to perform in this world yet remaining. There was her father: her father who had been so devoted to her, who had never uttered a single reproach to her for all her faults and follies, and who, in her hour of tribulation, had clung to her with such fidelity. Was it not some source of satisfaction to see him again comparatively happy? How selfish for her to mar this graceful and innocent enjoyment! She exerted herself to contribute to the amusement of her father and his kind friend, as well as to share it. The colour returned a little to her cheek; sometimes she burst for a moment into something like her old gaiety; and though these ebullitions were often followed by a gloom and moodiness, against which she found it in vain to contend, still, on the whole, the change for the better was decided, and Mr. Temple yet hoped that in time his sight might again be blessed and his life illustrated by his own brilliant

Henrietta.

CHAPTER III.

In Which Mr. Temple and His Daughter, with Their New
Friend, Make an Unexpected Excursion.

ONE delicious morning, remarkable even in the south, Lord Montfort called upon them in his carriage, and proposed a little excursion. Mr. Temple looked at his daughter, and was charmed that Henrietta consented. She rose from her seat, indeed, with unwonted animation, and the three friends had soon quitted the city and entered its agreeable environs.

'It was wise to pass the winter in Italy,' said Lord Montfort, 'but to see Tuscany in perfection I should choose the autumn. I know nothing more picturesque than the carts laden with grapes, and drawn by milk-white steers.'

They drove gaily along at the foot of green hills, crowned ever and anon by a convent or a beautiful stone-pine. The landscape attracted the admiration of Miss Temple. A palladian villa rose from the bosom of a gentle elevation, crowned with these picturesque trees. A broad terrace of marble extended in front of the villa, on which were ranged orange trees. On either side spread an olive-grove. The sky was without a cloud, and deeply blue; bright beams of the sun illuminated the building. The road had wound so curiously into this last branch of the Apennines, that the party found themselves in a circus of hills, clothed with Spanish chestnuts and olive trees, from which there was apparently no outlet. A soft breeze, which it was evident had passed over the wild flowers of the mountains, refreshed and charmed their senses.

'Could you believe we were only two hours' drive from a city?' said Lord Montfort.

'Indeed,' said Henrietta, 'if there be peace in this world, one would think that the dweller in that beautiful villa enjoyed it.'

'He has little to disturb him,' said Lord Montfort: 'thanks to his destiny and his temper.'

'I believe we make our miseries,' said Henrietta, with a sigh. 'After all, nature always offers us consolation. But who lives here?'

'I sometimes steal to this spot,' replied his lordship.

'Oh! this, then, is your villa? Ah! you have surprised us!'

'I only aimed to amuse you.'

'You are very kind, Lord Montfort,' said Mr. Temple; 'and we owe you much.'

They stopped, they ascended the terrace, they entered the villa. A few rooms only were furnished, but their appearance indicated the taste and pursuits of its occupier. Busts and books were scattered about; a table was covered with the implements of art; and the principal apartment opened into an English garden.

'This is one of my native tastes,' said Lord Montfort, 'that will, I think, never desert me.'

The memory of Henrietta was recalled to the flowers of Ducie and of Armine. Amid all the sweets and sunshine she looked sad. She walked away from her companions; she seated herself on the terrace; her eyes were suffused with tears. Lord Montfort took the arm of Mr. Temple, and led him away to a bust of Germanicus.

'Let me show it to Henrietta,' said Mr. Temple; 'I must fetch her.'

Lord Montfort laid his hand gently on his companion. The emotion of Henrietta had not escaped his quick eye.

'Miss Temple has made a great exertion,' he said. 'Do not think me pedantic, but I am something of a physician. I have long perceived that, although Miss Temple should be amused, she must sometimes be left alone.'

Mr. Temple looked at his companion, but the countenance of Lord Montfort was inscrutable. His lordship offered him a medal and then opened a portfolio of Marc Antonios.

'These are very rare,' said Lord Montfort; 'I bring them into the country with me, for really at Rome there is no time to study them. By-the-bye, I have a plan,' continued his lordship, in a somewhat hesitating tone; 'I wish I could induce you and Miss Temple to visit me at Rome.'

Mr. Temple shrugged his shoulders, and sighed.

'I feel confident that a residence at Rome would benefit Miss Temple,' said his lordship, in a voice a little less calm than usual. 'There is much to see, and I would take care that she should see it in a manner which would not exhaust her. It is the most delightful climate, too, at this period. The sun shines here to-day, but the air of these hills at this season is sometimes treacherous. A calm life, with a variety of objects, is what she requires. Pisa is calm, but for her it is too dull. Believe me, there is something in the blended refinement and interest of Rome that she would find exceedingly beneficial. She would see no one but ourselves; society shall be at her command if she desire it.'

'My dear lord,' said Mr. Temple, 'I thank you from the bottom of my heart for all your considerate sympathy; but I cannot flatter myself that Henrietta could avail herself of your really friendly offer. My daughter is a great invalid. She————'

But here Miss Temple joined them.

'We have a relic of a delicate temple here,' said Lord Montfort, directing her gaze to another window. 'You see it now to advantage; the columns glitter in the sun. There, perhaps, was worshipped some wood-nymph, or some river-god.'

The first classic ruin that she had yet beheld attracted the attention of Miss Temple. It was not far, and she acceded to the proposition of Lord Montfort to visit it. That little ramble was delightful. The novelty and the beauty of the object greatly interested her. It was charming also to view it under the auspices of a guide so full of information and feeling.

'Ah!' said Lord Montfort, 'if I might only be your cicerone at Rome!'

'What say you, Henrietta?' said Mr. Temple, with a smile. 'Shall we go to Rome?'

The proposition did not alarm Miss Temple as much as her father anticipated. Lord Montfort pressed the suggestion with delicacy; he hinted at some expedients by which the journey might be rendered not very laborious. But as she did not reply, his lordship did not press the subject; sufficiently pleased, perhaps, that she had not met it with an immediate and decided negative. When they returned to the villa they found a collation prepared for them worthy of so elegant an abode. In his capacity of a host, Lord Montfort departed a little from that placid and even constrained demeanour which generally characterised him. His manner was gay and flowing; and he poured out a goblet of Monte Pulciano and presented it to Miss Temple.

'You must pour a libation,' he said, 'to the nymph of the fane.'

CHAPTER IV.

Showing That It Is the First Step That Is Ever the Most Difficult.

ABOUT a week after this visit to the villa, Mr. Temple and his daughter were absolutely induced to accompany Lord Montfort to Rome. It is impossible to do justice to the tender solicitude with which he made all the arrangements for the journey. Wherever they halted they found preparations for their reception; and so admirably had everything been concerted, that Miss Temple at length found herself in the Eternal City with almost as little fatigue as she had reached the Tuscan villa.

The palace of Lord Montfort was in the most distinguished quarter of the city, and situate in the midst of vast gardens full of walls of laurel, arches of ilex, and fountains of lions. They arrived at twilight, and the shadowy hour lent even additional space to the huge halls and galleries. Yet in the suite of rooms intended for Mr. Temple and his daughter, every source of comfort seemed to have been collected. The marble floors were covered with Indian mats and carpets, the windows were well secured from the air which might have proved fatal to an invalid, while every species of chair and couch, and sofa, courted the languid or capricious form of Miss Temple, and she was even favoured with an English stove, and guarded by an Indian screen. The apartments were supplied with every book which it could have been supposed might amuse her; there were guitars of the city and of Florence, and even an English piano; a library of the choicest music; and all the materials of art. The air of elegance and cheerful comfort that pervaded these apartments, so unusual in this land, the bright blaze of the fire, evert the pleasant wax-lights, all combined to deprive the moment of that feeling of gloom and exhaustion which attends an arrival at a strange place at a late hour, and Henrietta looked around her, and almost fancied she was once more at Ducie. Lord Montfort introduced his fellow-travellers to their apartments, presented to them the servant who was to assume the management of their little household, and then reminding them of their mutual promises that they were to be entirely their own masters, and not trouble themselves about him any more than if they were at Pisa, he shook them both by the hand, and bade them good-night.

It must be confessed that the acquaintance of Lord Montfort had afforded consolation to Henrietta Temple. It was impossible to be insensible to the sympathy and solicitude of one so highly gifted and so very amiable. Nor should it be denied that this homage, from one of his distinguished rank, was entirely without its charm. To find ourselves, when deceived and deserted, unexpectedly an object of regard and consideration, will bring balm to most bosoms; but to attract in such a situation the friendship of an individual whose deferential notice under any circumstances must be flattering, and to be admired by one whom all admire, these are accidents of fortune which few could venture to despise. And Henrietta had now few opportunities to brood over the past; a stream of beautiful and sublime objects passed unceasingly before her vision. Her lively and refined taste, and her highly cultured mind, could not refrain from responding to these glorious spectacles. She saw before her all that she had long read of, all that she had long mused over. Her mind became each day more serene and harmonious as she gazed on these ideal creations, and dwelt on their beautiful repose. Her companion, too, exerted every art to prevent these amusements from degenerating into fatiguing expeditions. The Vatican was open to Lord Montfort when it was open to none others. Short visits, but numerous ones, was his system. Sometimes they entered merely to see a statue or a picture they were reading or conversing about the preceding eve; and then they repaired to some modern studio, where their entrance always made the sculptor's eyes sparkle. At dinner there was always some distinguished guest whom Henrietta wished to see; and as she thoroughly understood the language, and spoke it with fluency and grace, she was tempted to enter into conversations, where all seemed delighted that she played her part. Sometimes, indeed, Henrietta would fly to her chamber to sigh, but suddenly the palace resounded with tones of the finest harmony, or the human voice, with its most felicitous skill, stole upon her from the distant galleries. Although Lord Montfort was not himself a musician, and his voice could not pour forth those fatal sounds that had ravished her soul from the lips of Ferdinand Armine, he was well acquainted with the magic of music; and while he hated a formal concert, the most eminent performers were often at hand in his palace, to contribute at the fitting moment to the delight of his guests. Who could withstand the soft influence of a life so elegant and serene, or refuse to yield up the spirit to its gentle excitement and its mild distraction? The colour returned to Henrietta's cheek and the lustre to her languid eye: her form regained its airy spring of health; the sunshine of her smile burst forth once more.

It would have been impossible for an indifferent person not to perceive that Lord Montfort witnessed these changes with feelings of no slight emotion. Perhaps he prided himself upon his skill as a physician, but he certainly watched the apparent convalescence of his friend's daughter with zealous interest. And yet Henrietta herself was not aware that Lord Montfort's demeanour to her differed in any degree from what it was at Pisa. She had never been alone with him in her life; she certainly spoke more to him than she used, but then, she spoke more to everybody; and Lord Montfort certainly seemed to think of nothing but her pleasure and convenience and comfort; but he did and said everything so quietly, that all this kindness and solicitude appeared to be the habitual impulse of his generous nature. He certainly was more intimate, much more intimate, than during the first week of their acquaintance, but scarcely more kind; for she remembered he had arranged her sofa the very first day they met, though he did not even remain to receive her thanks.

One day a discussion rose about Italian society between Mr. Temple and his host. His lordship was a great admirer of the domestic character and private life of the Italians. He maintained that there was no existing people who more completely fulfilled the social duties than this much scandalised nation, respecting whom so many silly prejudices are entertained by the English, whose travelling fellow-countrymen, by-the-bye, seldom enter into any society but that tainted circle that must exist in all capitals.

'You have no idea,' he said, turning to Henrietta, 'what amiable and accomplished people are the better order of Italians. I wish you would let me light up this dark house some night, and give you an Italian party.'

'I should like it very much,' said Mr. Temple.

Whenever Henrietta did not enter her negative Lord Montfort always implied her assent, and it was resolved that the Italian party should be given.

All the best families in Rome were present, and not a single English person. There were some perhaps, whom Lord Montfort might have wished to invite, but Miss Temple had chanced to express a wish that no English might be there, and he instantly acted upon her suggestion. The palace was magnificently illuminated. Henrietta had scarcely seen before its splendid treasures of art. Lord Montfort, in answer to her curiosity, had always playfully depreciated them, and said that they must be left for rainy days. The most splendid pictures and long rows of graceful or solemn statues were suddenly revealed to her; rooms and galleries were opened that had never been observed before; on all sides cabinets of vases, groups of imperial busts, rare bronzes, and vivid masses of tesselated pavement. Over all these choice and beautiful objects a clear yet soft light was diffused, and Henrietta never recollected a spectacle more complete and effective.

These rooms and galleries were soon filled with guests, and Henrietta could not be insensible to the graceful and engaging dignity with which Lord Montfort received the Roman world of fashion. That constraint which at first she had attributed to reserve, but which of late she had ascribed to modesty, now entirely quitted him. Frank, yet always dignified, smiling, apt, and ever felicitous, it seemed that he had a pleasing word for every ear, and a particular smile for every face. She stood at some distance leaning on her father's arm, and watching him. Suddenly he turned and looked around. It was they whom he wished to catch. He came up to Henrietta and said, 'I wish to introduce you to the Princess————.

She is an old lady, but of the first distinction here. I would not ask this favour of you unless I thought you would be pleased.'

Henrietta could not refuse his request. Lord Montfort presented her and her father to the princess, the most agreeable and important person in Rome; and having now provided for their immediate amusement, he had time to attend to his guests in general. An admirable concert now, in some degree, hushed the general conversation. The voices of the most beautiful women in Rome echoed in those apartments. When the music ceased, the guests wandered about the galleries, and at length the principal saloons were filled with dancers. Lord Montfort approached Miss Temple. 'There is one room in the palace you have never yet visited,' he said, 'my tribune; 'tis open to-night for the first time.'

Henrietta accepted his proffered arm. 'And how do you like the princess?' he said, as they walked along. 'It is agreeable to live in a country where your guests amuse themselves.'

At the end of the principal gallery, Henrietta perceived an open door which admitted them into a small octagon chamber, of Ionic architecture. The walls were not hung with pictures, and one work of art alone solicited their attention. Elevated on a pedestal of porphyry, surrounded by a rail of bronze arrows of the lightest workmanship, was that statue of Diana which they had so much admired at Pisa. The cheek, by an ancient process, the secret of which has been recently regained at Rome, was tinted with a delicate glow.

'Do you approve of it?' said Lord Montfort to the admiring Henrietta. 'Ah, dearest Miss Temple,' he continued, 'it is my happiness that the rose has also returned to a fairer cheek than this.'

CHAPTER V.

Which Contains Some Rather Painful Explanations.

THE reader will not perhaps be much surprised that the Marquis of Montfort soon became the declared admirer of Miss Temple. He made the important declaration after a very different fashion from the unhappy Ferdinand Armine: he made it to the lady's father. Long persuaded that Miss Temple's illness had its origin in the mind, and believing that in that case the indisposition of the young lady had probably arisen, from one cause or another, in the disappointment of her affections, Lord Montfort resolved to spare her feelings, unprepared, the pain of a personal appeal. The beauty, the talent, the engaging disposition, and the languid melancholy of Miss Temple, had excited his admiration and pity, and had finally won a heart capable of deep affections, but gifted with great self-control. He did not conceal from Mr. Temple the conviction that impelled him to the course which he had thought proper to pursue, and this delicate conduct relieved Mr. Temple greatly from the unavoidable embarrassment of his position. Mr. Temple contented himself with communicating to Lord Montfort that his daughter had indeed entered into an engagement with one who was not worthy of her affections, and that the moment her father had been convinced of the character of the individual, he had quitted England with his daughter. He expressed his unqualified approbation of the overture of Lord Montfort, to whom he was indeed sincerely attached, and which gratified all those worldly feelings from which Mr. Temple was naturally not exempt. In such an alliance Mr. Temple recognised the only mode by which his daughter's complete recovery could be secured. Lord Montfort in himself offered everything which it would seem that the reasonable fancy of woman could desire. He was young, handsome, amiable, accomplished, sincere, and exceedingly clever; while, at the same time, as Mr. Temple was well aware, his great position would insure that reasonable gratification of vanity from which none are free, which is a fertile source of happiness, and which would, at all times, subdue any bitter recollections which might occasionally arise to cloud the retrospect of his daughter.

It was Mr. Temple, who, exerting all the arts of his abandoned profession, now indulging in intimations and now in panegyric, conveying to his daughter, with admirable skill, how much the intimate acquaintance with Lord Montfort contributed to his happiness, gradually fanning the feeling of gratitude to so kind a friend, which already had been excited in his daughter's heart, into one of zealous regard, and finally seizing his opportunity with practised felicity, it was Mr. Temple who had at length ventured to communicate to his daughter the overture which had been confided to him.

Henrietta shook her head.

'I have too great a regard for Lord Montfort to accede to his wishes,' said Miss Temple. 'He deserves something better than a bruised spirit, if not a broken heart.'

'But, my dearest Henrietta, you really take a wrong, an impracticable view of affairs. Lord Montfort must be the best judge of what will contribute to his own happiness.'

'Lord Montfort is acting under a delusion,' replied Miss Temple. 'If he knew all that had occurred he would shrink from blending his life with mine.'

'Lord Montfort knows everything,' said the father, 'that is, everything he should know.'

'Indeed!' said Miss Temple. 'I wonder he does not look upon me with contempt; at the least, with pity.'

'He loves you, Henrietta,' said her father.

'Ah! love, love, love! name not love to me. No, Lord Montfort cannot love me. It is not love that he feels.'

'You have gained his heart, and he offers you his hand. Are not these proofs of love?'

'Generous, good young man!' exclaimed Henrietta; 'I respect, I admire him; I might have loved him. But it is too late.'

'My beloved daughter, oh! do not say so! For my sake, do not say so,' exclaimed Mr. Temple. 'I have no wish, I have had no wish, my child, but for your happiness. Lean upon your father, listen to him, be guided by his advice. Lord Montfort possesses every quality which can contribute to the happiness of woman. A man so rarely gifted I never met. There is not a woman in the world, however exalted her rank, however admirable her beauty, however gifted her being, who might not feel happy and honoured in the homage of such a man. Believe me, my dearest daughter, that this is an union which must lead to happiness. Indeed, were it to occur, I could die content. I should have no more cares, no more hopes. All would then have happened that the most sanguine parent, even with such a child as you, could wish or imagine. We should be so happy! For his sake, for my sake, for all our sakes, dearest Henrietta, grant his wish. Believe me, believe me, he is indeed worthy of you.'

'I am not worthy of him,' said Henrietta, in a melancholy voice.

'Ah, Henrietta, who is like you!' exclaimed the fond and excited father.

At this moment a servant announced that Lord Montfort would, with their permission, wait upon them. Henrietta seemed plunged in thought. Suddenly she said, 'I cannot rest until this is settled. Papa, leave me with him a few moments alone.' Mr. Temple retired.

A faint blush rose to the cheek of her visitor when he perceived that Miss Temple was alone. He seated himself at her side, but he was unusually constrained.

'My dear Lord Montfort,' said Miss Temple,' calmly, 'I have to speak upon a painful subject, but I have undergone so much suffering, that I shall not shrink from this. Papa has informed me this morning that you have been pleased to pay me the highest compliment that a man can pay a woman. I wish to thank you for it. I wish to acknowledge it in terms the strongest and the warmest I can use. I am sensible of the honour, the high honour that you have intended me. It is indeed an honour of which any woman might be proud. You have offered me a heart of which I know the worth. No one can appreciate the value of your character better than myself. I do justice, full justice, to your virtues, your accomplishments, your commanding talents, and your generous soul. Except my father, there is no one who holds so high a place in my affection as yourself. You have been my kind and true friend; and a kind and true friendship, faithful and sincere, I return you. More than friends we never can be, for I have no heart to give.'

'Ah, dearest Miss Temple,' said Lord Montfort, agitated, 'I ask nothing but that friendship; but let me enjoy it in your constant society; let the world recognise my right to be your consoler.'

'You deserve a better and a brighter fate. I should not be your friend if I could enter into such an engagement.'

'The only aim of my life is to make you happy,' said Lord Montfort.

'I am sure that I ought to be happy with such a friend,' said Henrietta Temple, 'and I am happy. How different is the world to me from what it was before I knew you! Ah, why will you disturb this life of consolation? Why will you call me back to recollections that I would fain banish? Why———'

'Dearest Miss Temple,' said Lord Montfort, 'do not reproach me! You make me wretched.

Remember, dear lady, that I have not sought this conversation; that if I were presumptuous in my plans and hopes, I at least took precautions that I should be the only sufferer by their nonfulfilment.'

'Best and most generous of men! I would not for the world be unkind to you. Pardon my distracted words. But you know all? Has papa told you all? It is my wish.'

'It is not mine,' replied Lord Montfort; 'I wish not to penetrate your sorrows, but only to soothe them.'

'Oh, if we had but met earlier,' said Henrietta Temple; 'if we had but known each other a year ago! when I was, not worthy of you, but more worthy of you. But now, with health shattered, the lightness of my spirit vanished, the freshness of my feelings gone, no, my kind friend, my dear and gentle friend! my affection for you is too sincere to accede to your request; and a year hence Lord Montfort will thank me for my denial.'

'I scarcely dare to speak,' said Lord Montfort, in a low tone, as if suppressing his emotion, 'if I were to express my feelings, I might agitate you. I will not then venture to reply to what you have urged; to tell you I think you the most beautiful and engaging being that ever breathed; or how I dote upon your pensive spirit, and can sit for hours together gazing on the language of those dark eyes. O Miss Temple, to me you never could have been more beautiful, more fascinating. Alas! I may not even breathe my love; I am unfortunate. And yet, sweet lady, pardon this agitation I have occasioned you; try to love me yet; endure at least my presence; and let me continue to cherish that intimacy that has thrown over my existence a charm so inexpressible.' So saying, he ventured to take her hand, and pressed it with devotion to his lips.

CHAPTER VI.

Which Contains an Event Not Less Important Than the One
Which Concluded Our Second Book.

LORD MONTFORT was scarcely disheartened by this interview with Miss Temple. His lordship was a devout believer in the influence of time. It was unnatural to suppose that one so young and so gifted as Henrietta could ultimately maintain that her career was terminated because her affections had been disappointed by an intimacy which was confessedly of so recent an origin as the fatal one in question. Lord Montfort differed from most men in this respect, that the consciousness of this intimacy did not cost him even a pang. He preferred indeed to gain the heart of a woman like Miss Temple, who, without having in the least degree forfeited the innate purity of her nature and the native freshness of her feelings, had yet learnt in some degree to penetrate the mystery of the passions, to one so untutored in the world's ways, that she might have bestowed upon him a heart less experienced indeed, but not more innocent. He was convinced that the affection of Henrietta, if once obtained, might be relied on, and that the painful past would only make her more finely appreciate his high-minded devotion, and amid all the dazzling characters and seducing spectacles of the world, cling to him with a firmer gratitude and a more faithful fondness. And yet Lord Montfort was a man of deep emotions, and of a very fastidious taste. He was a man of as romantic a temperament as Ferdinand Armine; but with Lord Montfort, life was the romance of reason; with Ferdinand, the romance of imagination. The first was keenly alive to all the imperfections of our nature, but he also gave that nature credit for all its excellencies. He observed finely, he calculated nicely, and his result was generally happiness. Ferdinand, on the contrary, neither observed nor calculated. His imagination created fantasies, and his impetuous passions struggled to realise them.

Although Lord Montfort carefully abstained from pursuing the subject which nevertheless engrossed his thoughts, he had a vigilant and skilful ally in Mr. Temple. That gentleman lost no opportunity of pleading his lordship's cause, while he appeared only to advocate his own; and this was the most skilful mode of controlling the judgment of his daughter.

Henrietta Temple, the most affectionate and dutiful of children, left to reflect, sometimes asked herself whether she were justified, from what she endeavoured to believe was a mere morbid feeling, in not accomplishing the happiness of that parent who loved her so well? There had been no concealment of her situation, or of her sentiments. There had been no deception as to the past. Lord Montfort knew all. She told him that she could bestow only a broken spirit. Lord Montfort aspired only to console it. She was young. It was not probable that the death which she had once sighed for would be accorded to her. Was she always to lead this life? Was her father to pass the still long career which probably awaited him in ministering to the wearisome caprices of a querulous invalid? This was a sad return for all his goodness: a gloomy catastrophe to all his bright hopes. And if she could ever consent to blend her life with another's, what individual could offer pretensions which might ensure her tranquillity, or even happiness, equal to those proffered by Lord Montfort? Ah! who was equal to him? so amiable, so generous, so interesting! It was in such a mood of mind that Henrietta would sometimes turn with a glance of tenderness and gratitude to that being who seemed to breathe only for her solace and gratification. If it be agonising to be deserted, there is at least consolation in being cherished. And who cherished her?

One whom all admired; one to gain whose admiration, or even attention, every woman sighed. What was she before she knew Montfort? If she had not known Montfort, what would she have been even at this present? She recalled the hours of anguish, the long days of bitter mortification, the dull, the wearisome, the cheerless, hopeless, uneventful hours that were her lot when lying on her solitary sofa at Pisa, brooding over the romance of Armine and all its passion; the catastrophe of Ducie, and all its baseness. And now there was not a moment without kindness, without sympathy, without considerate attention and innocent amusement. If she were querulous, no one murmured; if she were capricious, everyone yielded to her fancies; but if she smiled, everyone was happy. Dear, noble Montfort, thine was the magic that had worked this change! And for whom were all these choice exertions made? For one whom another had trifled with, deserted, betrayed! And Montfort knew it. He dedicated his life to the consolation of a despised woman. Leaning on the arm of Lord Montfort, Henrietta Temple might meet the eye of Ferdinand Armine and his rich bride, at least without feeling herself an object of pity!

Time had flown. The Italian spring, with all its splendour, illumined the glittering palaces and purple shores of Naples. Lord Montfort and his friends were returning from Capua in his galley. Miss Temple was seated between her father and their host. The Ausonian clime, the beautiful scene, the sweet society, had all combined to produce a day of exquisite enjoyment. Henrietta Temple could not refrain from expressing her delight. Her eye sparkled like the star of eve that glittered over the glowing mountains; her cheek was as radiant as the sunset.

'Ah! what a happy day this has been!' she exclaimed.

The gentle pressure of her hand reminded her of the delight her exclamation had afforded one of her companions. With a trembling heart Lord Montfort leant back in the galley; and yet, ere the morning sun had flung its flaming beams over the city, Henrietta Temple was his betrothed.

BOOK VI.

CHAPTER I.

Which Contains a Remarkable Change of Fortune.

ALTHOUGH Lord Montfort was now the received and recognised admirer of Miss Temple, their intended union was not immediate. Henrietta was herself averse from such an arrangement, but it was not necessary for her to urge this somewhat ungracious desire, as Lord Montfort was anxious that she should be introduced to his family before their marriage, and that the ceremony should be performed in his native country. Their return to England, therefore, was now meditated. The event was hastened by an extraordinary occurrence.

Good fortune in this world, they say, is seldom single. Mr. Temple at this moment was perfectly content with his destiny. Easy in his own circumstances, with his daughter's future prosperity about to be provided for by an union with the heir to one of the richest peerages in the kingdom, he had nothing to desire. His daughter was happy, he entertained the greatest esteem and affection for his future son-in-law, and the world went well with him in every respect.

It was in this fulness of happiness that destiny, with its usual wild caprice, resolved 'to gild refined gold and paint the lily;' and it was determined that Mr. Temple should wake one morning among the wealthiest commoners of England.

There happened to be an old baronet, a great humourist, without any very near relations, who had been a godson of Mr. Temple's grandfather. He had never invited or encouraged any intimacy or connection with the Temple family, but had always throughout life kept himself aloof from any acquaintance with them. Mr. Temple indeed had only seen him once, but certainly under rather advantageous circumstances. It was when Mr. Temple was minister at the German Court, to which we have alluded, that Sir Temple Devereux was a visitor at the capital at which Mr. Temple was Resident. The minister had shown him some civilities, which was his duty; and Henrietta had appeared to please him. But he had not remained long at this place; and refused at the time to be more than their ordinary guest; and had never, by any letter, message, or other mode of communication, conveyed to them the slightest idea that the hospitable minister and his charming daughter had dwelt a moment on his memory. And yet Sir Temple Devereux had now departed from the world, where it had apparently been the principal object of his career to avoid ever making a friend, and had left the whole of his large fortune to the Right Honourable Pelham Temple, by this bequest proprietor of one of the finest estates in the county of York, and a very considerable personal property, the accumulated savings of a large rental and a long life.

This was a great event. Mr. Temple had the most profound respect for property. It was impossible for the late baronet to have left his estate to an individual who could more thoroughly appreciate its possession. Even personal property was not without its charms; but a large landed estate, and a large landed estate in the county of York, and that large landed estate flanked by a good round sum of Three per Cent. Consols duly recorded in the Rotunda of Threadneedle Street,—it was a combination of wealth, power, consideration, and convenience which exactly hit the ideal of Mr. Temple, and to the fascination of which perhaps the taste of few men would be insensible. Mr. Temple being a man of family, had none of the awkward embarrassments of a parvenu to contend with. 'It was the luckiest thing in the world,' he would say, 'that poor Sir Temple was my grandfather's godson, not only because in all probability it obtained us his fortune, but because he bore the name of Temple: we shall settle down in Yorkshire scarcely as strangers, we shall not be looked upon as a new family, and in a little time the whole affair will be considered rather one of inheritance than bequest. But, after all, what is it to me! It is only for your sake, Digby, that I rejoice. I think it will please your family. I will settle everything immediately on Henrietta. They shall have the gratification of knowing that their son is about to marry the richest heiress in England.'

The richest heiress in England! Henrietta Temple the richest heiress in England! Ah! how many feelings with that thought arise! Strange to say, the announcement of this extraordinary event brought less joy than might have been supposed to the heiress herself.

It was in her chamber and alone, that Henrietta Temple mused over this freak of destiny. It was in vain to conceal it, her thoughts recurred to Ferdinand. They might have been so happy! Why was he not true? And perhaps he had sacrificed himself to his family, perhaps even personal distress had driven him to the fatal deed. Her kind feminine fancy conjured up every possible extenuation of his dire offence. She grew very sad. She could not believe that he was false at Ducie; oh, no! she never could believe it! He must have been sincere, and if sincere, oh! what a heart was lost there! What would she not have given to have been the means of saving him from all his sorrows! She recalled his occasional melancholy, his desponding words, and how the gloom left his brow and his eye brightened when she fondly prophesied that she would restore the house. She might restore it now; and now he was another's, and she, what was she? A slave like him. No longer her own mistress, at the only moment she had the power to save him. Say what they like, there is a pang in balked affection, for which no wealth, power, or place, watchful indulgence, or sedulous kindness, can compensate. Ah! the heart, the heart!

CHAPTER II.

In Which the Reader Is Again Introduced to Captain
Armine, during His Visit to London.

MISS GRANDISON had resolved upon taking a house in London for the season, and had obtained a promise from her uncle and aunt to be her guests. Lady Armine's sister was to join them from Bath. As for Ferdinand, the spring had gradually restored him to health, but not to his former frame of mind. He remained moody and indolent, incapable of exertion, and a prey to the darkest humours; circumstances, however, occurred which rendered some energy on his part absolutely necessary. His creditors grew importunate, and the arrangement of his affairs or departure from his native land was an alternative now inevitable. The month of April, which witnessed the arrival of the Temples and Lord Montfort in England, welcomed also to London Miss Grandison and her guests. A few weeks after, Ferdinand, who had evaded the journey with his family, and who would not on any account become a guest of his cousin, settled himself down at a quiet hotel in the vicinity of Grosvenor-square; but not quite alone, for almost at the last hour Glastonbury had requested permission to accompany him, and Ferdinand, who duly valued the society of the only person with whom he could converse about his broken fortunes and his blighted hopes without reserve, acceded to his wish with the greatest satisfaction.

A sudden residence in a vast metropolis, after a life of rural seclusion, has without doubt a very peculiar effect upon the mind. The immense population, the multiplicity of objects, the important interests hourly impressed upon the intelligence, the continually occurring events, the noise, the bustle, the general and widely-spread excitement, all combine to make us keenly sensible of our individual insignificance; and those absorbing passions that in our solitude, fed by our imagination, have assumed such gigantic and substantial shapes, rapidly subside, by an almost imperceptible process, into less colossal proportions, and seem invested, as it were, with a more shadowy aspect. As Ferdinand Armine jostled his way through the crowded streets of London, urged on by his own harassing and inexorable affairs, and conscious of the impending peril of his career, while power and wealth dazzled his eyes in all directions, he began to look back upon the passionate past with feelings of less keen sensation than heretofore, and almost to regret that a fatal destiny or his impetuous soul had entailed upon him so much anxiety, and prompted him to reject the glittering cup of fortune that had been proffered to him so opportunely. He sighed for enjoyment and repose; the memory of his recent sufferings made him shrink from that reckless indulgence of the passions, of which the consequences had been so severe.

It was in this mood, exhausted by a visit to his lawyer, that he stepped into a military club and took up a newspaper. Caring little for politics, his eye wandered over, uninterested, its pugnacious leading articles and tedious parliamentary reports; and he was about to throw it down when a paragraph caught his notice which instantly engrossed all his attention. It was in the 'Morning Post' that he thus read:

'The Marquis of Montfort, the eldest son of the Duke of————, whose return to England we recently noticed, has resided for several years in Italy. His lordship is considered one of the most accomplished noblemen of the day, and was celebrated at Rome for his patronage of the arts. Lord Montfort will shortly be united to the beautiful Miss Temple, the only daughter of the Right Honourable Pelham Temple. Miss Temple is esteemed one of the richest heiresses in England, as she will doubtless inherit the whole of the immense fortune to which her father so unexpectedly acceded. Mr. Temple is a widower, and has no son. Mr. Temple was formerly our minister at several of the German Courts, where he was distinguished by his abilities and his hospitality to his travelling countrymen. It is said that the rent-roll of the Yorkshire estates of the late Sir Temple Devereux is not less than 15,000L. per annum. The personal property is also very considerable. We understand that Mr. Temple has purchased the mansion of the Duke of ———, in Grosvenor-square. Lord Montfort accompanied Mr. Temple and his amiable daughter to this country.'

What a wild and fiery chaos was the mind of Ferdinand Armine when he read this paragraph. The wonders it revealed succeeded each other with such rapidity that for some time he was deprived of the power of reflection. Henrietta Temple in England! Henrietta Temple one of the greatest heiresses in the country! Henrietta Temple about to be immediately married to another! His Henrietta Temple, the Henrietta Temple whom he adored, and by whom he had been worshipped! The Henrietta Temple whose beautiful lock of hair was at this very moment on his heart! The Henrietta Temple for whom he had forfeited fortune, family, power, almost life!

O Woman, Woman! Put not thy trust in woman! And yet, could he reproach her? Did she not believe herself trifled with by him, outraged, deceived, deluded, deserted? And did she, could she love another? Was there another to whom she had poured forth her heart as to him, and all that beautiful flow of fascinating and unrivalled emotion? Was there another to whom she had pledged her pure and passionate soul? Ah, no! he would not, he could not believe it. Light and false Henrietta could never be. She had been seen, she had been admired, she had been loved: who that saw her would not admire and love? and he was the victim of her pique, perhaps of her despair.

But she was not yet married. They were, according to these lines, to be soon united. It appeared they had travelled together; that thought gave him a pang. Could he not see her? Could he not explain all? Could he not prove that his heart had ever been true and fond? Could he not tell her all that had happened, all that he had suffered, all the madness of his misery; and could she resist that voice whose accents had once been her joy, that glance which had once filled her heart with rapture? And when she found that Ferdinand, her own Ferdinand, had indeed never deceived her, was worthy of her choice affection, and suffering even at this moment for her sweet sake, what were all the cold-blooded ties in which she had since involved herself? She was his by an older and more ardent bond. Should he not claim his right? Could she deny it?

Claim what? The hand of an heiress. Should it be said that an Armine came crouching for lucre, where he ought to have commanded for love? Never! Whatever she might think, his conduct had been faultless to her. It was not for Henrietta to complain. She was not the victim, if one indeed there might chance to be. He had loved her, she had returned his passion; for her sake he had made the greatest of sacrifices, forfeited a splendid inheritance, and a fond and faithful heart. When he had thought of her before, pining perhaps in some foreign solitude, he had never ceased reproaching himself for his conduct, and had accused himself of deception and cruelty; but now, in this moment of her flush prosperity, 'esteemed one of the richest heiresses in England' (he ground his teeth as he recalled that phrase), and the affianced bride of a great noble (his old companion, Lord Montfort, too; what a strange thing is life!), proud, smiling, and prosperous, while he was alone, with a broken heart and worse than desperate fortunes, and all for her sake, his soul became bitter: he reproached her with want of feeling; he pictured her as void of genuine sensibility; he dilated on her indifference since they had parted; her silence, so strange, now no longer inexplicable; the total want of interest she had exhibited as to his career; he sneered at the lightness of her temperament; he cursed her caprice; he denounced her infernal treachery; in the distorted phantom of his agonised imagination she became to him even an object of hatred. Poor Ferdinand Armine! it was the first time he had experienced the maddening pangs of jealousy.

Yet how he had loved this woman! How he had doated on her! And now they might have been so happy! There is nothing that depresses a man so much as the conviction of bad fortune. There seemed, in this sudden return, great wealth, and impending marriage of Henrietta Temple, such a combination, so far as Ferdinand Armine was concerned, of vexatious circumstances; it would appear that he had been so near perfect happiness and missed it, that he felt quite weary of existence, and seriously meditated depriving himself of it.

It so happened that he had promised this day to dine at his cousin's; for Glastonbury, who was usually his companion, had accepted an invitation this day to dine with the noble widow of his old patron. Ferdinand, however, found himself quite incapable of entering into any society, and he hurried to his hotel to send a note of excuse to Brook-street. As he arrived, Glastonbury was just about to step into a hackney-coach, so that Ferdinand had no opportunity of communicating his sorrows to his friend, even had he been inclined.

CHAPTER III.

In Which Glastonbury Meets the Very Last Person in the
World He Expected, and the Strange Consequences.

WHEN Glastonbury arrived at the mansion of the good old duchess, he found nobody in the drawing-room but a young man of distinguished appearance, whose person was unknown to him, but who nevertheless greeted him with remarkable cordiality. The good Glastonbury returned, with some confusion, his warm salutation.

'It is many years since we last met, Mr. Glastonbury,' said the young man. 'I am not surprised you have forgotten me. I am Digby; perhaps you recollect me?'

'My dear child! My dear lord! You have indeed changed! You are a man, and I am a very old one.' 'Nay! my dear sir, I observe little change. Believe me, I have often recalled your image in my long absence, and I find now that my memory has not deceived me.'

Glastonbury and his companion fell into some conversation about the latter's travels, and residence at Rome, in the midst of which their hostess entered.

'I have asked you, my dear sir, to meet our family circle,' said her Grace, 'for I do not think I can well ask you to meet any who love you better. It is long since you have seen Digby.'

'Mr. Glastonbury did not recognise me, grandmamma,' said Lord Montfort.

'These sweet children have all grown out of your sight, Mr. Glastonbury,' said the duchess; 'but they are very good. And as for Digby, I really think he comes to see his poor grandmother every day.'

The duke and duchess, and two young daughters, were now announced.

'I was so sorry that I was not at home when you called, Glastonbury,' said his Grace; 'but I thought I should soon hear of you at grandmamma's.'

'And, dear Mr. Glastonbury, why did you not come up and see me?' said the younger duchess.

'And, dear Mr. Glastonbury, do you remember me?' said one beautiful daughter.

'And me, Mr. Glastonbury, me? I am Isabella.'

Blushing, smiling, bowing, constrained from the novelty of his situation, and yet every now and then quite at ease when his ear recalled a familiar voice, dear Mr. Glastonbury was gratified and happy. The duke took him aside, and they were soon engaged in conversation.

'How is Henrietta to-day, Digby?' enquired Isabella.

'I left her an hour ago; we have been riding, and expected to meet you all. She will be here immediately.'

There was a knock, and soon the drawing-room door opened, and Miss Temple was announced.

'I must make papa's apologies,' said Henrietta, advancing and embracing the old duchess. 'I hope he may get here in the evening: but he bade me remind your Grace that your kind invitation was only provisionally accepted.'

'He is quite right,' said the old lady; 'and indeed I hardly expected him, for he told me there was a public dinner which he was obliged to attend. I am sure that our dinner is a very private one indeed,' continued the old lady with a smile. 'It is really a family party, though there is one member of the family here whom you do not know, my dear Miss Temple, and whom, I am sure, you will love as much as all of us do. Digby, where is———'

At this moment dinner was announced. Lord Montfort offered his arm to Henrietta. 'There, lead the way,' said the old lady; 'the girls must beau themselves, for I have no young men to-day for them. I suppose man and wife must be parted, so I must take my son's arm; Mr. Glastonbury, you will hand down the duchess.' But before Glastonbury's name was mentioned Henrietta was half-way down stairs.

The duke and his son presided at the dinner. Henrietta sat on one side of Lord Montfort, his mother on the other. Glastonbury sat on the right hand of the duke, and opposite their hostess; the two young ladies in the middle. All the guests had been seated without Glastonbury and Henrietta recognising each other; and, as he sat on the same side of the table as Miss Temple, it was not until Lord Montfort asked Mr. Glastonbury to take wine with him, that Henrietta heard a name that might well indeed turn her pale.

Glastonbury! It never entered into her head at the moment that it was the Mr. Glastonbury whom she had known. Glastonbury! what a name! What dreadful associations did it not induce! She looked forward, she caught the well-remembered visage; she sunk back in her chair. But Henrietta Temple had a strong mind; this was surely an occasion to prove it. Mr. Glastonbury's attention was not attracted to her: he knew, indeed, that there was a lady at the table, called Henrietta, but he was engrossed with his neighbours, and his eye never caught the daughter of Mr. Temple. It was not until the ladies rose to retire that Mr. Glastonbury beheld that form which he had not forgotten, and looked upon a lady whose name was associated in his memory with the most disastrous and mournful moments of his life. Miss Temple followed the duchess out of the room, and Glastonbury, perplexed and agitated, resumed his seat.

But Henrietta was the prey of emotions far more acute and distracting. It seemed to her that she had really been unacquainted with the state of her heart until this sudden apparition of Glastonbury. How his image recalled the past! She had schooled herself to consider it all a dream; now it lived before her. Here was one of the principal performers in that fatal tragedy of Armine. Glastonbury in the house, under the same roof as she? Where was Ferdinand? There was one at hand who could tell her. Was he married? She had enjoyed no opportunity of ascertaining it since her return: she had not dared to ask. Of course he was married; but was he happy? And Glastonbury, who, if he did not know all, knew so much. How strange it must be to Glastonbury to meet her! Dear Glastonbury! She had not forgotten the days when she so fondly listened to Ferdinand's charming narratives of all his amiable and simple life! Dear, dear Glastonbury, whom she was so to love! And she met him now, and did not speak to him, or looked upon him as a stranger; and he—he would, perhaps, look upon her with pity, certainly with pain. O Life! what a heart-breaking thing is life! And our affections, our sweet and pure affections, fountains of such joy and solace, that nourish all things, and make the most barren and rigid soil teem with life and beauty, oh! why do we disturb the flow of their sweet waters, and pollute their immaculate and salutary source! Ferdinand, Ferdinand Armine, why were you false?

The door opened. Mr. Glastonbury entered, followed by the duke and his son. Henrietta was sitting in an easy chair, one of Lord Montfort's sisters, seated on an ottoman at her side, held her hand. Henrietta's eye met Glastonbury's; she bowed to him.

'How your hand trembles, Henrietta!' said the young lady.

Glastonbury approached her with a hesitating step. He blushed faintly, he looked exceedingly perplexed. At length he reached her, and stood before her, and said nothing.

'You have forgotten me, Mr. Glastonbury,' said Henrietta; for it was absolutely necessary that some one should break the awkward silence, and she pointed to a chair at her side.

'That would indeed be impossible,' said Glastonbury.

'Oh, you knew Mr. Glastonbury before,' said the young lady. 'Grandmamma, only think, Henrietta knew Mr. Glastonbury before.'

'We were neighbours in Nottinghamshire,' said Henrietta, in a quick tone.

'Isabella,' said her sister, who was seated at the piano, 'the harp awaits you.' Isabella rose, Lord Montfort was approaching Henrietta, when the old duchess called to him.

Henrietta and Glastonbury were alone.

'This is a strange meeting, Mr. Glastonbury,' said Henrietta.

What could poor Glastonbury say? Something he murmured, but not very much to the purpose.

'Have you been in Nottinghamshire lately?' said Henrietta.

'I left it about ten days back with———,' and here Glastonbury stopped, 'with a friend,' he concluded.

'I trust all your friends are well,' said Henrietta, in a tremulous voice.

'No; yes; that is,' said Glastonbury, 'something better than they were.'

'I am sorry that my father is not here,' said Miss Temple; 'he has a lively remembrance of all your kindness.'

'Kindness, I fear,' said Glastonbury, in a melancholy tone, 'that was most unfortunate.'

'We do not deem it so, sir,' was the reply.

'My dear young lady,' said Glastonbury, but his voice faltered as he added, 'we have had great unhappiness.'

'I regret it,' said Henrietta. 'You had a marriage, I believe, expected in your family?'

'It has not occurred,' said Glastonbury.

'Indeed!'

'Alas! madam,' said her companion, 'if I might venture indeed to speak of one whom I will not name, and yet———'

'Pray speak, sir,' said Miss Temple, in a kind, yet hushed voice.

'The child of our affections, madam, is not what he was. God, in His infinite mercy, has visited him with great afflictions.'

'You speak of Captain Armine, sir?'

'I speak indeed of my broken-hearted Ferdinand; I would I could say yours. O Miss Temple, he is a wreck.' 'Yes! yes!' said Henrietta in a low tone.

'What he has endured,' continued Glastonbury, 'passes all description of mine. His life has indeed been spared, but under circumstances that almost make me regret he lives.'

'He has not married!' muttered Henrietta.

'He came to Ducie to claim his bride, and she was gone,' said Glastonbury; 'his mind sunk under the terrible bereavement. For weeks he was a maniac; and, though Providence spared him again to us, and his mind, thanks to God, is again whole, he is the victim of a profound melancholy, that seems to defy alike medical skill and worldly vicissitude.'

'Digby, Digby!' exclaimed Isabella, who was at the harp, 'Henrietta is fainting.' Lord Montfort rushed forward just in time to seize her cold hand.

'The room is too hot,' said one sister.

'The coffee is too strong,' said the other.

'Air,' said the young duchess.

Lord Montfort carried Henrietta into a distant room. There was a balcony opening into a garden. He seated her on a bench, and never quitted her side, but contrived to prevent anyone approaching her. The women clustered together.

'Sweet creature!' said the old duchess, 'she often makes me tremble; she has but just recovered,

Mr. Glastonbury, from a long and terrible illness.'

'Indeed!' said Glastonbury.

'Poor dear Digby,' continued her grace, 'this will quite upset him again. He was in such spirits about her health the other day.'

'Lord Montfort?' enquired Glastonbury.

'Our Digby. You know that he is to be married to Henrietta next month.'

'Holy Virgin!' muttered Glastonbury; and, seizing advantage of the confusion, he effected his escape.

CHAPTER IV.

In Which Mr. Glastonbury Informs Captain Armine of His
Meeting with Miss Temple.

IT WAS still an early hour when Mr. Glastonbury arrived at his hotel. He understood, however, that Captain Armine had already returned and retired. Glastonbury knocked gently at his door, and was invited to enter. The good man was pale and agitated. Ferdinand was already in bed. Glastonbury took a chair, and seated himself by his side.

'My dear friend, what is the matter?' said Ferdinand.

'I have seen her, I have seen her!' said Glastonbury.

'Henrietta! seen Henrietta?' enquired Ferdinand.

Glastonbury nodded assent, but with a most rueful expression of countenance.

'What has happened? what did she say?' asked Ferdinand in a quick voice.

'You are two innocent lambs,' said Glastonbury, rubbing his hands.

'Speak, speak, my Glastonbury.'

'I wish that my death could make you both happy,' said Glastonbury; 'but I fear that would do you no good.'

'Is there any hope?' said Ferdinand. 'None!' said Glastonbury. 'Prepare yourself, my dear child, for the worst.'

'Is she married?' enquired Ferdinand.

'No; but she is going to be.'

'I know it,' said Ferdinand.

Glastonbury stared.

'You know it? what! to Digby?'

'Digby, or whatever his name may be; damn him!'

'Hush! hush!' said Glastonbury.

'May all the curses————'

'God forbid,' said Glastonbury, interrupting him.

'Unfeeling, fickle, false, treacherous————'

'She is an angel,' said Glastonbury, 'a very angel. She has fainted, and nearly in my arms.'

'Fainted! nearly in your arms! Oh, tell me all, tell me all, Glastonbury,' exclaimed Ferdinand, starting up in his bed with an eager voice and sparkling eyes. 'Does she love me?'

'I fear so,' said Glastonbury. 'Fear!'

'Oh, how I pity her poor innocent heart!' said Glastonbury.

'When I told her of all your sufferings————'

'Did you tell her? What then?'

'And she herself has barely recovered from a long and terrible illness.'

'My own Henrietta! Now I could die happy,' said Ferdinand.

'I thought it would break your heart,' said Glastonbury.

'It is the only happy moment I have known for months,' said Ferdinand.

'I was so overwhelmed that I lost my presence of mind,' said Glastonbury. 'I really never meant to tell you anything. I do not know how I came into your room.'

'Dear, dear Glastonbury, I am myself again.'

'Only think!' said Glastonbury; 'I never was so unhappy in my life.'

'I have endured for the last four hours the tortures of the damned,' said Ferdinand, 'to think that she was going to be married, to be married to another; that she was happy, proud, prosperous, totally regardless of me, perhaps utterly forgetful of the past; and that I was dying like a dog in this cursed caravanserai! O Glastonbury! nothing that I have ever endured has been equal to the hell of this day. And now you have come and made me comparatively happy. I shall get up directly.'

Glastonbury looked quite astonished; he could not comprehend how his fatal intelligence could have produced effects so directly contrary from those he had anticipated. However, in answer to Ferdinand's reiterated enquiries, he contrived to give a detailed account of everything that had occurred, and Ferdinand's running commentary continued to be one of constant self-congratulation.

'There is, however, one misfortune,' said Ferdinand, 'with which you are unacquainted, my dear friend.'

'Indeed!' said Glastonbury, 'I thought I knew enough.'

'Alas! she has become a great heiress!'

'Is that it?' said Glastonbury.

'There is the blow,' said Ferdinand. 'Were it not for that, by the soul of my grandfather, I would tear her from the arms of this stripling.'

'Stripling!' said Glastonbury. 'I never saw a truer nobleman in my life.'

'Ah!' exclaimed Ferdinand.

'Nay, second scarcely to yourself! I could not believe my eyes,' continued Glastonbury. 'He was but a child when I saw him last; but so were you, Ferdinand. Believe me, he is no ordinary rival.'

'Good-looking?'

'Altogether of a most princely presence. I have rarely met a personage so highly accomplished, or who more quickly impressed you with his moral and intellectual excellence.'

'And they are positively engaged?'

'To be married next month,' replied Glastonbury.

'O Glastonbury! why do I live?' exclaimed Ferdinand; 'why did I recover?'

'My dear child, but just now you were comparatively happy.'

'Happy! You cannot mean to insult me. Happy! Oh, is there in this world a thing so deplorable as I am!'

'I thought I did wrong to say anything,' said Glastonbury, speaking as it were to himself.

Ferdinand made no observation. He turned himself in his bed, with his face averted from Glastonbury.

'Good night,' said Glastonbury, after remaining some time in silence.

'Good night,' said Ferdinand, in a faint and mournful tone.

CHAPTER V.

Which, on the Whole, Is Perhaps as Remarkable a chapter as
Any in the Work.

WRETCHED as he was, the harsh business of life could not be neglected; Captain Armine was obliged to be in Lincoln's Inn by ten o'clock the next morning. It was on his return from his lawyer, as he was about to cross Berkeley-square, that a carriage suddenly stopped in the middle of the road, and a female hand apparently beckoned to him from the window. He was at first very doubtful whether he were indeed the person to whom the signal was addressed, but as on looking around there was not a single human being in sight, he at length slowly approached the equipage, from which a white handkerchief now waved with considerable agitation. Somewhat perplexed by this incident, the mystery was, however, immediately explained by the voice of Lady Bellair. 'You wicked man,' said her little ladyship, in a great rage. 'Oh! how I hate you! I could cut you up into minced meat; that I could. Here I have been giving parties every night, all for you too. And you have been in town, and never called on me. Tell me your name. How is your wife? Oh! you are not married. You should marry; I hate a ci-devant jeune homme. However, you can wait a little. Here, James, Thomas, Peter, what is your name, open the door and let him in. There get in, get in; I have a great deal to say to you.' And Ferdinand found that it was absolutely necessary to comply.

'Now, where shall we go?' said her ladyship; 'I have got till two o'clock. I make it a rule to be at home every day from two till six, to receive my friends. You must come and call upon me. You may come every day if you like. Do not leave your card. I hate people who leave cards. I never see them; I order all to be burnt. I cannot bear people who leave bits of paper at my house. Do you want to go anywhere? You do not! Why do not you? How is your worthy father, Sir Peter? Is his name Sir Peter or Sir Paul? Well, never mind, you know whom I mean. And your charming mother, my favourite friend? She is charming; she is quite one of my favourites. And were not you to marry? Tell me, why have you not? Miss—Miss—you know whom I mean, whose grandfather was my son's friend. In town, are they? Where do they live? Brook-street! I will go and call upon them. There, pull the string, and tell him where they live.'

And so, in a few minutes, Lady Bellair's carriage stopped opposite the house of Miss Grandison. 'Are they early risers?' said her ladyship; 'I get up every morning at six. I dare say they will not receive me; but do you show yourself, and then they cannot refuse.'

In consequence of this diplomatic movement Lady Bellair effected an entrance. Leaning on the arm of Ferdinand, her ladyship was ushered into the morning-room, where she found Lady Armine and Katherine.

'My dear lady, how do you do? And my sweet miss! Oh! your eyes are so bright, that it quite makes me young to look upon them! I quite love you, that I do. Your grandfather and my poor son were bosom friends. And, my dear lady, where have you been all this time? Here have I been giving parties every night, and all for you; all for my Bath friends; telling everybody about you; talking of nothing else; everybody longing to see you; and you have never been near me. My dinner-parties are over; I shall not give any more dinners until June. But I have three evenings yet; to-night, you must come to me to-night, and Thursday, and Saturday; you must come on all three nights. Oh! why did you not call upon me? I should have asked you to dinner. I would have asked you to meet Lord Colonnade and Lady Ionia! They would have just suited you; they would have tasted you! But I tell you what I will do; I will come and dine with you some day. Now, when will you have me? Let me see, when am I. free?' So saying, her ladyship opened a little red book, which was her inseparable companion in London. 'All this week I am ticketed; Monday, the Derricourts, dull, but then he is a duke. Tuesday I dine with Bonmot; we have made it up; he gives me a dinner. Wednesday, Wednesday, where is Wednesday? General Faneville, my own party. Thursday, the Maxburys, bad dinner, but good company. Friday, Waring Cutts, a famous house for eating; but that is not in my way; however, I must go, for he sends me pines. And Saturday, I dine off a rabbit, by myself, at one o'clock, to go and see my dear darling Lady St. Julians at Richmond. So it cannot be this or next week. I will send you a note; I will tell you to-night. And now I must go, for it is five minutes to two, I am always at home from two till six; I receive my friends; you may come every day, and you must come to see my new squirrel; my darling, funny little grandson gave it me. And, my dear miss, where is that wicked Lady Grandison? Do you ever see her, or are you enemies? She has got the estate, has not she? She never calls upon me. Tell her she is one of my greatest favourites. Oh! why does not she come? I should have asked her to dinner; and now all my dinners are over till June. Tell me where she lives, and I will call upon her to-morrow.'

So saying, and bidding them all farewell very cordially, her ladyship took Ferdinand's arm and retired.

Captain Armine returned to his mother and cousin, and sat an hour with them, until their carriage was announced. Just as he was going away, he observed Lady Bellair's little red book, which she had left behind.

'Poor Lady Bellair, what will she do?' said Miss Grandison; 'we must take it to her immediately.'

'I will leave it,' said Ferdinand, 'I shall pass her house.'

Bellair House was the prettiest mansion in May Fair. It was a long building, in the Italian style, situate in the midst of gardens, which, though not very extensive, were laid out with so much art and taste, that it was very difficult to believe that you were in a great city. The house was furnished and adorned with all that taste for which Lady Bellair was distinguished. All the reception rooms were on the ground floor, and were all connected. Ferdinand, who remembered Lady Bellair's injunctions not to leave cards, attracted by the spot, and not knowing what to do with himself, determined to pay her ladyship a visit, and was ushered into an octagon library, lined with well-laden dwarf cases of brilliant volumes, crowned with no lack of marble busts, bronzes, and Etruscan vases. On each side opened a magnificent saloon, furnished in that classic style which the late accomplished and ingenious Mr. Hope first rendered popular in this country. The wings, projecting far into the gardens, comprised respectively a dining-room and a conservatory of considerable dimensions. Isolated in the midst of the gardens was a long building, called the summer-room, lined with Indian matting, and screened on one side from the air merely by Venetian blinds. The walls of this chamber were almost entirely covered with caricatures, and prints of the country seats of Lady Bellair's friends, all of which she took care to visit. Here also were her parrots, and some birds of a sweeter voice, a monkey, and the famous squirrel.

Lady Bellair was seated in a chair, the back of which was much higher than her head; at her side was a little table with writing materials, on which also was placed a magnificent bell, by Benvenuto Cellini, with which her ladyship summoned her page, who, in the meantime, loitered in the hall.

'You have brought me my book!' she exclaimed, as Ferdinand entered with the mystical volume.

'Give it me, give it me. Here I cannot tell Mrs. Fancourt what day I can dine with her. I am engaged all this week and all next, and I am to dine with your dear family when I like. But Mrs. Fancourt must choose her day, because they will keep. You do not know this gentleman,' she said, turning to Mrs. Fan-court. 'Well, I shall not introduce you; he will not suit you; he is a fine gentleman, and only dines with dukes.'

Mrs. Fancourt consequently looked very anxious for an introduction.

'General Faneville,' Lady Bellair continued, to a gentleman on her left, 'what day do I dine with you? Wednesday. Is our party full? You must make room for him; he is my greatest favourite. All the ladies are in love with him.'

General Faneville expressed his deep sense of the high honour; Ferdinand protested he was engaged on Wednesday; Mrs. Fancourt looked very disappointed that she had thus lost another opportunity of learning the name of so distinguished a personage.

There was another knock. Mrs. Fancourt departed. Lady Maxbury, and her daughter, Lady Selina, were announced.

'Have you got him?' asked Lady Bellair, very eagerly, as her new visitors entered.

'He has promised most positively,' answered Lady Maxbury.

'Dear, good creature!' exclaimed Lady Bellair, 'you are the dearest creature that I know. And you are charming,' she continued, addressing herself to Lady Selina; 'if I were a man, I would marry you directly. There now, he (turning to Ferdinand) cannot marry you, because he is married already; but he should, if he were not. And how will he come?' enquired Lady Bellair.

'He will find his way,' said Lady Maxbury.

'And I am not to pay anything?' enquired Lady Bellair.

'Not anything,' said Lady Maxbury.

'I cannot bear paying,' said Lady Bellair. 'But will he dance, and will he bring his bows and arrows? Lord Dorfield protests 'tis nothing without the bows and arrows.'

'What, the New Zealand chief, Lady Bellair?' enquired the general.

'Have you seen him?' enquired Lady Bellair, eagerly.

'Not yet,' replied the gentleman.

'Well, then, you will see him to-night,' said Lady Bellair, with an air of triumph. 'He is coming to me to-night.'

Ferdinand rose, and was about to depart.

'You must not go without seeing my squirrel,' said her ladyship, 'that my dear funny grandson gave me: he is such a funny boy. You must see it, you must see it,' added her ladyship, in a peremptory tone. 'There, go out of that door, and you will find your way to my summer-room, and there you will find my squirrel.'

The restless Ferdinand was content to quit the library, even with the stipulation of first visiting the squirrel. He walked through a saloon, entered the conservatory, emerged into the garden, and at length found himself in the long summer-room. At the end of the room a lady was seated, looking over a book of prints; as she heard a footstep she raised her eyes, and Ferdinand beheld Henrietta Temple.

He was speechless; he felt rooted to the ground; all power of thought and motion alike deserted him.

There he stood, confounded and aghast. Nor indeed was his companion less disturbed. She remained with her eyes fixed on Ferdinand with an expression of fear, astonishment, and distress impressed upon her features. At length Ferdinand in some degree rallied, and he followed the first impulse of his mind, when mind indeed returned to him: he moved to retire.

He had retraced half his steps, when a voice, if human voice indeed it were that sent forth tones so full of choking anguish, pronounced his name.

'Captain Armine!' said the voice.

How he trembled, yet mechanically obedient to his first impulse, he still proceeded to the door.

'Ferdinand!' said the voice.

He stopped, he turned, she waved her hand wildly, and then leaning her arm on the table, buried her face in it. Ferdinand walked to the table at which she was sitting; she heard his footstep near her, yet she neither looked up nor spoke. At length he said, in a still yet clear voice, 'I am here.'

'I have seen Mr. Glastonbury,' she muttered.

'I know it,' he replied.

'Your illness has distressed me,' she said, after a slight pause, her face still concealed, and speaking in a hushed tone. Ferdinand made no reply, and there was another pause, which Miss Temple broke.

'I would that we were at least friends,' she said. The tears came into Ferdinand's eyes when she said this, for her tone, though low, was now sweet. It touched his heart.

'Our mutual feelings now are of little consequence,' he replied.

She sighed, but made no reply. At length Ferdinand said, 'Farewell, Miss Temple.'

She started, she looked up, her mournful countenance harrowed his heart. He knew not what to do; what to say. He could not bear her glance; he in his turn averted his eyes.

'Our misery is—has been great,' she said in a firmer tone, 'but was it of my making?'

'The miserable can bear reproaches; do not spare me. My situation, however, proves my sincerity. I have erred certainly,' said Ferdinand; 'I could not believe that you could have doubted me. It was a mistake,' he added, in a tone of great bitterness.

Miss Temple again covered her face as she said, 'I cannot recall the past: I wish not to dwell on it. I desire only to express to you the interest I take in your welfare, my hope that you may yet be happy. Yes! you can be happy, Ferdinand; Ferdinand, for my sake you will be happy.'

'O Henrietta, if Henrietta I indeed may call you, this is worse than that death I curse myself for having escaped.'

'No, Ferdinand, say not that. Exert yourself, only exert yourself, bear up against irresistible fate. Your cousin, everyone says she is so amiable; surely———'

'Farewell, madam, I thank you for your counsel.'

'No, Ferdinand, you shall not go, you shall not go in anger. Pardon me, pity me, I spoke for your sake, I spoke for the best.'

'I, at least, will never be false,' said Ferdinand with energy. 'It shall not be said of me that I broke vows consecrated by the finest emotions of our nature. No, no, I have had my dream; it was but a dream: but while I live, I will live upon its sweet memory.'

'Ah! Ferdinand, why were you not frank; why did you conceal your situation from me?'

'No explanation of mine can change our respective situations,' said Ferdinand; 'I content myself therefore by saying that it was not Miss Temple who had occasion to criticise my conduct.'

'You are bitter.'

'The lady whom I injured, pardoned me. She is the most generous, the most amiable of her sex; if only in gratitude for all her surpassing goodness, I would never affect to offer her a heart which never can be hers. Katherine is indeed more than woman. Amid my many and almost unparalleled sorrows, one of my keenest pangs is the recollection that I should have clouded the life, even for a moment, of that admirable person. Alas! alas! that in all my misery the only woman who sympathises with my wretchedness is the woman I have injured. And so delicate as well as so generous! She would not even enquire the name of the individual who had occasioned our mutual desolation.'

'Would that she knew all,' murmured Henrietta; 'would that I knew her.'

'Your acquaintance could not influence affairs. My very affection for my cousin, the complete appreciation which I now possess of her character, before so little estimated and so feebly comprehended by me, is the very circumstance that, with my feelings, would prevent our union. She may, I am confident she will, yet be happy. I can never make her so. Our engagement in old days was rather the result of family arrangements than of any sympathy. I love her far better now than I did then, and yet she is the very last person in the world that I would marry. I trust, I believe, that my conduct, if it have clouded for a moment her life, will not ultimately, will not long obscure it; and she has every charm and virtue and accident of fortune to attract the admiration and attention of the most favoured. Her feelings towards me at any time could have been but mild and calm. It is a mere abuse of terms to style such sentiments love. But,' added he sarcastically, 'this is too delicate a subject for me to dilate on to Miss Temple.'

'For God's sake, do not be so bitter!' she exclaimed; and then she added, in a voice half of anguish, half of tenderness, 'Let me never be taunted by those lips! O Ferdinand, why cannot we be friends?'

'Because we are more than friends. To me such a word from your lips is mere mockery. Let us never meet. That alone remains for us. Little did I suppose that we ever should have met again. I go nowhere, I enter no single house; my visit here this morning was one of those whimsical vagaries which cannot be counted on. This old lady indeed seems, somehow or other, connected with our destiny. I believe I am greatly indebted to her.'

The page entered the room. 'Miss Temple,' said the lad, 'my lady bid me say the duchess and Lord Montfort were here.'

Ferdinand started, and darting, almost unconsciously, a glance of fierce reproach at the miserable Henrietta, he rushed out of the room and made his escape from Bellair House without re-entering the library.

CHAPTER VI.

Containing an Evening Assembly at Bellair House.

SEATED on an ottoman in the octagon library, occasionally throwing a glance at her illuminated and crowded saloons, or beckoning, with a fan almost as long as herself, to a distant guest, Lady Bellair received the world on the evening of the day that had witnessed the strange rencontre between Henrietta Temple and Ferdinand Armine. Her page, who stood at the library-door in a new fancy dress, received the announcement of the company from the other servants, and himself communicated the information to his mistress.

'Mr. Million de Stockville, my lady,' said the page.

'Hem!' said her ladyship, rather gruffly, as, with no very amiable expression of countenance, she bowed, with her haughtiest dignity, to a rather common-looking personage in a gorgeously-embroidered waistcoat.

'Lady Ionia Colonnade, my lady.' Lady Bellair bestowed a smiling nod on this fair and classic dame, and even indicated, by a movement of her fan, that she might take a seat on her ottoman.

'Sir Ratcliffe and Lady Armine, my lady, and Miss Grandison.'

'Dear, good people!' exclaimed Lady Bellair, 'how late you are! and where is your wicked son? There, go into the next room, go, go, and see the wonderful man. Lady Ionia, you must know Lady Armine; she is like you; she is one of my favourites. Now then, there all of you go together. I will not have anybody stay here except my niece. This is my niece,' Lady Bellair added, pointing to a young lady seated by her side; 'I give this party for her.' 'General Faneville, my lady.' 'You are very late,' said Lady Bellair. 'I dined at Lord Rochfort's,' said the general bowing. 'Rochfort's! Oh! where are they? where are the Rochforts? they ought to be here. I must, I will see them. Do you think Lady Rochfort wants a nursery governess? Because I have a charming person who would just suit her. Go and find her out, General, and enquire; and if she do not want one, find out some one who does. Ask Lady Maxbury. There, go, go.'

'Mr. and Miss Temple, my lady.'

'Oh, my darling!' said Lady Bellair, 'my real darling! sit by me. I sent Lady Ionia away, because I determined to keep this place for you. I give this party entirely in your honour, so you ought to sit here. You are a good man,' she continued, addressing Mr. Temple; 'but I can't love you so well as your daughter.'

'I should be too fortunate,' said Mr. Temple, smiling.

'I knew you when you ate pap,' said Lady Bellair, laughing.

'Mrs. Montgomery Floyd, my lady.'

Lady Bellair assumed her coldest and haughtiest glance. Mrs. Montgomery appeared more gorgeous than ever. The splendour of her sweeping train almost required a page to support it; she held a bouquet which might have served for the centre-piece of a dinner-table. A slender youth, rather distinguished in appearance, simply dressed, with a rose-bud just twisted into his black coat, but whose person distilled odours whose essence might have exhausted a conservatory, lounged at her side.

'May I have the honour to present to your ladyship Lord Catchimwhocan?' breathed forth Mrs. Montgomery, exulting in her companion, perhaps in her conquest.

Lady Bellair gave a short and ungracious nod. Mrs. Montgomery recognised Mr. and Miss

Temple. 'There, go, go,' said Lady Bellair, interrupting her, 'nobody must stop here; go and see the wonderful man in the next room.'

'Lady Bellair is so strange,' whimpered Mrs. Montgomery, in an apologetical whisper to Miss Temple, and she moved away, covering her retreat by the graceful person of Lord Catchimwhocan.

'Some Irish guardsman, I suppose,' said Lady Bellair. 'I never heard of him; I hate guardsmen.'

'Rather a distinguished-looking man, I think,' said Mr. Temple.

'Do you think so?' said Lady Bellair, who was always influenced by the last word. 'I will ask him for Thursday and Saturday. I think I must have known his grandfather. I must tell him not to go about with that horrid woman. She is so very fine, and she uses musk; she puts me in mind of the Queen of Sheba,' said the little lady, laughing, 'all precious stones and frankincense. I quite hate her.'

'I thought she was quite one of your favourites, Lady Bellair?' said Henrietta Temple rather maliciously.

'A Bath favourite, my dear; a Bath favourite. I wear my old bonnets at Bath, and use my new friends; but in town I have old friends and new dresses.'

'Lady Frederick Berrington, my lady.' 'Oh! my dear Lady Frederick, now I will give you a treat. I will introduce you to my sweet, sweet friend, whom I am always talking to you of. You deserve to know her; you will taste her; there, sit down, sit by her, and talk to her, and make love to her.'

'Lady Womandeville, my lady.'

'Ah! she will do for the lord; she loves a lord. My dear lady, you come so late, and yet I am always so glad to see you. I have such a charming friend for you, the handsomest, most fashionable, witty person, quite captivating, and his grandfather was one of my dearest friends. What is his name? what is his name? Lord Catchimwhocan. Mind, I introduce you to him, and ask him to your house very often.'

Lady Womandeville smiled, expressed her delight, and moved on.

Lord Montfort, who had arrived before the Temples, approached the ottoman.

'Is the duchess here?' enquired Henrietta, as she shook hands with him.

'And Isabella,' he replied. Henrietta rose, and taking his arm, bid adieu to Lady Bellair.

'God bless you,' said her ladyship, with great emphasis. 'I will not have you speak to that odious Mrs. Floyd, mind.'

When Lord Montfort and Henrietta succeeded in discovering the duchess, she was in the conservatory, which was gaily illuminated with coloured lamps among the shrubs. Her Grace was conversing with cordiality with a lady of very prepossessing appearance, in whom the traces of a beauty once distinguished were indeed still considerable, and her companion, an extremely pretty person, in the very bloom of girlhood. Lord Montfort and Henrietta were immediately introduced to these ladies, as Lady Armine and Miss Grandison. After the scene of the morning, it was not easy to deprive Miss Temple of her equanimity; after that shock, no incident connected with the Armine family could be surprising; she was even desirous of becoming acquainted with Miss Grandison, and she congratulated herself upon the opportunity which had so speedily offered itself to gratify her wishes. The duchess was perfectly delighted with Lady Armine, whose manners were fascinating; between the families there was some connection of blood, and Lady Armine, too, had always retained a lively sense of the old duke's services to her son. Henrietta had even to listen to enquiries made after Ferdinand, and she learnt that he was slowly recovering from an almost fatal illness, that he could not endure the fatigues of society, and that he was even living at an hotel for the sake of quiet. Henrietta watched the countenance of Katherine, as Lady Armine gave this information. It was serious, but not disturbed. Her Grace did not separate from her new friends the whole of the evening, and they parted with a mutually expressed wish that they might speedily and often meet. The duchess pronounced Lady Armine the most charming person she had ever met; while, on the other hand, Miss Grandison was warm in her admiration of Henrietta Temple and Lord Montfort, whom she thought quite worthy even of so rare a prize.

CHAPTER VII.

Containing a Very Important Communication.

BETWEEN the unexpected meeting with Captain Armine in the morning and the evening assembly at Bellair House, a communication had been made by Miss Temple to Lord Montfort, which ought not to be quite unnoticed. She had returned home with his mother and himself, and her silence and depression had not escaped him. Soon after their arrival they were left alone, and then Henrietta said, 'Digby, I wish to speak to you!'

'My own!' said Lord Montfort, as he seated himself by her on the sofa, and took her hand. Miss Temple was calm; but he would have been a light observer who had not detected her suppressed agitation.

'Dearest Digby,' she continued, 'you are so generous and so kind, that I ought to feel no reluctance in speaking to you upon this subject; and yet it pains me very much.' She hesitated.

'I can only express my sympathy with any sorrow of yours, Henrietta,' said Lord Montfort. 'Speak to me as you always do, with that frankness which so much delights me.'

'Let your thoughts recur to the most painful incident of my life, then,' said Henrietta.

'If you require it,' said Lord Montfort, in a serious tone.

'It is not my fault, dearest Digby, that a single circumstance connected with that unhappy event should be unknown to you. I wished originally that you should know all. I have a thousand times since regretted that your consideration for my feelings should ever have occasioned an imperfect confidence between us; and something has occurred to-day which makes me lament it bitterly.'

'No, no, dearest Henrietta; you feel too keenly,' said Lord Montfort.

'Indeed, Digby, it is so,' said Henrietta very mournfully.

'Speak, then, dearest Henrietta.'

'It is necessary that you should know the name of that person who once exercised an influence over my feelings, which I never affected to disguise to you.'

'Is it indeed necessary?' enquired Lord Montfort.

'It is for my happiness,' replied Henrietta.

'Then, indeed, I am anxious to learn it.'

'He is in this country,' said Henrietta, 'he is in this town; he may be in the same room with you to-morrow; he has been in the same room with me even this day.'

'Indeed!' said Lord Montfort.

'He bears a name not unknown to you,' said Henrietta, 'a name, too, that I must teach myself to mention, and yet———'

Lord Montfort rose and took a pencil and a sheet of paper from the table, 'Write it,' he said in a kind tone.

Henrietta took the pencil, and wrote,

'Armine.'

'The son of Sir Ratcliffe?' said Lord Montfort.

'The same,' replied Henrietta.

'You heard then of him last night?' enquired her companion.

'Even so; of that, too, I was about to speak.'

'I am aware of the connection of Mr. Glastonbury with the Armine family,' said Lord Montfort, quietly.

There was a dead pause. At length Lord Montfort said, 'Is there anything you wish me to do?'

'Much,' said Henrietta. 'Dearest Digby,' she continued, after a moment's hesitation, 'do not misinterpret me; my heart, if such a heart be worth possessing, is yours. I can never forget who solaced me in my misery; I can never forget all your delicate tenderness, Digby. Would that I could make a return to you more worthy of all your goodness; but if the grateful devotion of my life can repay you, you shall be satisfied.'

He took her hand and pressed it to his lips. 'It is of you, and of your happiness that I can alone think,' he murmured.

'Now let me tell you all,' said Henrietta, with desperate firmness. 'I have done this person great injustice.'

'Hah!' said Lord Montfort.

'It cuts me to the heart,' said Henrietta.

'You have then misconceived his conduct?' enquired Lord Montfort.

'Utterly.'

'It is indeed a terrible situation for you,' said Lord Montfort; 'for all of us,' he added, in a lower tone.

'No, Digby; not for all of us; not even for myself; for if you are happy I will be. But for him, yes! I will not conceal it from you, I feel for him.'

'Your destiny is in your own hands, Henrietta.'

'No, no, Digby; do not say so,' exclaimed Miss Temple, very earnestly; 'do not speak in that tone of sacrifice. There is no need of sacrifice; there shall be none. I will not, I do not falter. Be you firm. Do not desert me in this moment of trial. It is for support I speak; it is for consolation. We are bound together by ties the purest, the holiest. Who shall sever them? No! Digby, we will be happy; but I am interested in the destiny of this unhappy person. You, you can assist me in rendering it more serene; in making him, perhaps, not less happy than ourselves.'

'I would spare no labour,' said Lord Montfort.

'Oh, that you would not!' exclaimed Miss Temple. 'You are so good, so noble! You would sympathise even with him. What other man in your situation would?'

'What can be done?'

'Listen: he was engaged to his cousin even on that fatal day when we first met; a lady with every charm and advantage that one would think could make a man happy; young, noble, and beautiful; of a most amiable and generous disposition, as her subsequent conduct has proved; and of great wealth.'

'Miss Grandison?' said Lord Montfort.

'Yes: his parents looked forward to their union with delight, not altogether unmixed with anxiety. The Armines, with all their princely possessions, are greatly embarrassed from the conduct of the last head of their house. Ferdinand himself has, I grieve to say, inherited too much of his grandfather's imprudent spirit; his affairs, I fear, are terribly involved. When I knew him, papa was, as you are aware, a poor man. This marriage would have cured all; my Digby, I wish it to take place.'

'How can we effect it?' asked Lord Montfort.

'Become his friend, dear Digby. I always think you can do anything. Yes! my only trust is in you. Oh! my Digby, make us all happy.'

Lord Montfort rose and walked up and down the room, apparently in profound meditation. At length he said, 'Rest assured, Henrietta, that to secure your happiness nothing shall ever be wanting on my part. I will see Mr. Glastonbury on this subject. At present, dearest, let us think of lighter things.'

CHAPTER VIII.

Which Is Rather Strange.

IT WAS on the morning after the assembly at Bellair House that Ferdinand was roused from his welcome slumbers, for he had passed an almost sleepless night, by his servant bringing him a note, and telling him that it had been left by a lady in a carriage. He opened it, and read as follows:—

'Silly, silly Captain Armine! why did you not come to my Vauxhall last night? I wanted to present you to the fairest damsel in the world, who has a great fortune too; but that you don't care about. When are you going to be married? Miss Grandison looked charming, but disconsolate without her knight. Your mother is an angel, and the Duchess of——is quite in love with her. Your father, too, is a worthy man. I love your family very much. Come and call upon poor old doting bedridden H. B., who is at home every day from two to six to receive her friends. Has charming Lady Armine got a page? I have one that would just suit her. He teases my poor squirrel so that I am obliged to turn him away; but he is a real treasure. That fine lady, Mrs. Montgomery Floyd, would give her ears for him; but I love your mother much more, and so she shall have him. He shall come to her to-night. All the world takes tea with H. B. on Thursday and Saturday.'

'One o'clock!' said Ferdinand. 'I may as well get up and call in Brook-street, and save my mother from this threatened infliction. Heigho! Day after day, and each more miserable than the other. How will this end?'

When Ferdinand arrived in Brook-street, he went up stairs without being announced, and found in the drawing-room, besides his mother and Katherine, the duchess, Lord Montfort, and Henrietta Temple.

The young ladies were in their riding-habits. Henrietta appeared before him, the same Henrietta whom he had met, for the first time, in the pleasaunce at Armine. Retreat was impossible. Her Grace received Ferdinand cordially, and reminded him of old days. Henrietta bowed, but she was sitting at some distance with Miss Grandison, looking at some work. Her occupation covered her confusion. Lord Montfort came forward with extended hand.

'I have the pleasure of meeting an old friend,' said his lordship.

Ferdinand just touched his lordship's finger, and bowed rather stiffly; then, turning to his mother, he gave her Lady Bellair's note. 'It concerns you more than myself,' he observed.

'You were not at Lady Bellair's last night, Captain Armine,' said her Grace.

'I never go anywhere,' was the answer.

'He has been a great invalid,' said Lady Armine.

'Where is Glastonbury, Ferdinand?' said Lady Armine. 'He never comes near us.'

'He goes every day to the British Museum.'

'I wish he would take me,' said Katherine. 'I have never been there. Have you?' she enquired, turning to Henrietta.

'I am ashamed to say never,' replied Henrietta. 'It seems to me that London is the only city of which I know nothing.'

'Ferdinand,' said Katherine, 'I wish you would go with us to the Museum some day. Miss Temple would like to go. You know Miss Temple,' she added, as if she of course supposed he had not that pleasure.

Ferdinand bowed; Lord Montfort came forward, and turned the conversation to Egyptian antiquities. When a quarter of an hour had passed, Ferdinand thought that he might now withdraw.

'Do you dine at home, Katherine, to-day?' he enquired.

Miss Grandison looked at Miss Temple; the young ladies whispered.

'Ferdinand,' said Katherine, 'what are you going to do?'

'Nothing particular.'

'We are going to ride, and Miss Temple wishes you would come with us.'

'I should be very happy, but I have some business to attend to.'

'Dear Ferdinand, that is what you always say. You really appear to me to be the most busy person in the world.'

'Pray come, Captain Armine,' said Lord Montfort.

'Thank you; it is really not in my power.' His hat was in his hand; he was begging her Grace to bear his compliments to the duke, when Henrietta rose from her seat, and, coming up to him, said, 'Do, Captain Armine, come with us; I ask you as a favour.'

That voice! Oh! it came o'er his ear 'like the sweet south;' it unmanned him quite. He scarcely knew where he was. He trembled from head to foot. His colour deserted him, and the unlucky hat fell to the floor; and yet she stood before him, awaiting his reply, calm, quite calm, serious, apparently a little anxious. The duchess was in earnest conversation with his mother. Lord Montfort had walked up to Miss Grandison, and was engaged in arranging a pattern for her. Ferdinand and Henrietta were quite unobserved. He looked up; he caught her eye; and then he whispered, 'This is hardly fair.'

She stretched forth her hand, took his hat, and laid it on the table; then, turning to Katherine, she said, in a tone which seemed to admit no doubt, 'Captain Armine will ride with us;' and she seated herself by Lady Armine.

The expedition was a little delayed by Ferdinand having to send for his horse; the others had, in the meantime, arrived. Yet this half-hour, by some contrivance, did at length disappear. Lord Montfort continued talking to Miss Grandison. Henrietta remained seated by Lady Armine. Ferdinand revolved a great question in, his mind, and it was this: Was Lord Montfort aware of the intimate acquaintance between himself and Miss Temple? And what was the moving principle of her present conduct? He conjured up a thousand reasons, but none satisfied him. His curiosity was excited, and, instead of regretting his extracted promise to join the cavalcade, he rejoiced that an opportunity was thus afforded him of perhaps solving a problem in the secret of which he now began to feel extremely interested.

And yet in truth when Ferdinand found himself really mounted, and riding by the side of Henrietta Temple once more, for Lord Montfort was very impartial in his attentions to his fair companions, and Ferdinand continually found himself next to Henrietta, he really began to think the world was bewitched, and was almost sceptical whether he was or was not Ferdinand Armine. The identity of his companion too was so complete: Henrietta Temple in her riding-habit was the very image most keenly impressed upon his memory. He looked at her and stared at her with a face of curious perplexity. She did not, indeed, speak much; the conversation was always general, and chiefly maintained by Lord Montfort, who, though usually silent and reserved, made on this occasion successful efforts to be amusing. His attention to Ferdinand too was remarkable; it was impossible to resist such genuine and unaffected kindness. It smote Ferdinand's heart that he had received his lordship's first advances so ungraciously. Compunction rendered him now doubly courteous; he was even once or twice almost gay.

The day was as fine as a clear sky, a warm sun, and a western breeze could render it. Tempted by so much enjoyment, their ride was long. It was late, much later than they expected, when they returned home by the green lanes of pretty Willesden, and the Park was quite empty when they emerged from the Edgware-road into Oxford-street.

'Now the best thing we can all do is to dine in St. James'-square,' said Lord Montfort. 'It is ten minutes past eight. We shall just be in time, and then we can send messages to Grosvenor-square and Brook-street. What say you, Armine? You will come, of course?'

'Thank you, if you would excuse me.'

'No, no; why excuse you?' said Lord Montfort: 'I think it shabby to desert us now, after all our adventures.'

'Really you are very kind, but I never dine out.'

'Dine out! What a phrase! You will not meet a human being; perhaps not even my father. If you will not come, it will spoil everything.'

'I cannot dine in a frock,' said Ferdinand.

'I shall,' said Lord Montfort, 'and these ladies must dine in their habits, I suspect.'

'Oh! certainly, certainly,' said the ladies.

'Do come, Ferdinand,' said Katherine.

'I ask you as a favour,' said Henrietta, turning to him and speaking in a low voice.

'Well,' said Ferdinand, with a sigh.

'That is well,' said Montfort; 'now let us trot through the Park, and the groom can call in Grosvenor-square and Brook-street, and gallop after us. This is amusing, is it not?'

CHAPTER IX.

Which Is on the Whole Almost as Perplexing as the Preceding
One.

WHEN Ferdinand found himself dining in St. James'-square, in the very same room where he had passed so many gay hours during that boyish month of glee which preceded his first joining his regiment, and then looked opposite him and saw Henrietta Temple, it seemed to him that, by some magical process or other, his life was acting over again, and the order of the scenes and characters had, by some strange mismanagement, got confused. Yet he yielded himself up to the excitement which had so unexpectedly influenced him; he was inflamed by a species of wild delight which he could not understand, nor stop to analyse; and when the duchess retired with the young ladies to their secret conclave in the drawing-room, she said, 'I like Captain Armine very much; he is so full of spirit and imagination. When we met him this morning, do you know, I thought him rather stiff and fine. I regretted the bright boyish flow that I so well recollected, but I see I was mistaken.'

'Ferdinand is much changed,' said Miss Grandison. 'He was once the most brilliant person, I think, that ever lived: almost too brilliant; everybody by him seemed so tame. But since his illness he has quite changed. I have scarcely heard him speak or seen him smile these six months. There is not in the whole world a person so wretchedly altered. He is quite a wreck. I do not know what is the matter with him to-day. He seemed once almost himself.'

'He indulged his feelings too much, perhaps,' said Henrietta; 'he lived, perhaps, too much alone, after so severe an illness.'

'Oh, no! it is not that,' said Miss Grandison, 'it is not exactly that. Poor Ferdinand! he is to be pitied. I fear he will never be happy again.'

'Miss Grandison should hardly say that,' said the duchess, 'if report speaks truly.'

Katherine was about to reply, but checked herself.

Henrietta rose from her seat rather suddenly, and asked Katherine to touch the piano.

The duchess took up the 'Morning Post.'

'Poor Ferdinand! he used to sing once so beautifully, too!' said Katherine to Miss Temple, in a hushed voice. 'He never sings now.'

'You must make him,' said Henrietta.

Miss Grandison shook her head.

'You have influence with him; you should exert it,' said Henrietta.

'I neither have, nor desire to have, influence with him,' said Miss Grandison. 'Dearest Miss Temple, the world is in error with respect to myself and my cousin; and yet I ought not to say to you what I have not thought proper to confess even to my aunt.'

Henrietta leant over and kissed her forehead. 'Say what you like, dearest Miss Grandison; you speak to a friend, who loves you, and will respect your secret.'

The gentlemen at this moment entered the room, and interrupted this interesting conversation.

'You must not quit the instrument, Miss Grandison,' said Lord Montfort, seating himself by her side. Ferdinand fell into conversation with the duchess; and Miss Temple was the amiable victim of his Grace's passion for écarté.

'Captain Armine is a most agreeable person,' said Lord Montfort.

Miss Grandison rather stared. 'We were just speaking of Ferdinand,' she replied, 'and I was lamenting his sad change.'

'Severe illness, illness so severe as his, must for the moment change anyone; we shall soon see him himself again.'

'Never,' said Miss Grandison mournfully.

'You must inspire him,' said Lord Montfort. 'I perceive you have great influence with him.'

'I give Lord Montfort credit for much acuter perception than that,' said Miss Grandison.

Their eyes met: even Lord Montfort's dark vision shrank before the searching glance of Miss Grandison. It conveyed to him that his purpose was not undiscovered.

'But you can exert influence, if you please,' said Lord Montfort.

'But it may not please me,' said Miss Grandison.

At this moment Mr. Glastonbury was announced. He had a general invitation, and was frequently in the habit of paying an evening visit when the family were disengaged. When he found Ferdinand, Henrietta, and Katherine, all assembled together, and in so strange a garb, his perplexity was wondrous. The tone of comparative ease, too, with which Miss Temple addressed him, completed his confusion. He began to suspect that some critical explanation had taken place. He looked around for information.

'We have all been riding,' said Lord Montfort.

'So I perceive,' said Glastonbury.

'And as we were too late for dinner, took refuge here,' continued his lordship.

'I observe it,' said Glastonbury.

'Miss Grandison is an admirable musician, sir.'

'She is an admirable lady in every respect,' said Glastonbury.

'Perhaps you will join her in some canzonette; I am so stupid as not to be able to sing. I wish I could induce Captain Armine.'

'He has left off singing,' said Glastonbury, mournfully. 'But Miss Temple?' added Glastonbury, bowing to that lady.

'Miss Temple has left off singing, too,' said Lord Montfort, quietly.

'Come, Mr. Glastonbury,' said the duchess, 'time was when you and I have sung together. Let us try to shame these young folks.' So saying, her Grace seated herself at the piano, and the gratified Glastonbury summoned all his energies to accompany her.

Lord Montfort seated himself by Ferdinand. 'You have been severely ill, I am sorry to hear.'

'Yes; I have been rather shaken.'

'This spring will bring you round.'

'So everyone tells me. I cannot say I feel its beneficial influence.'

'You should,' said Lord Montfort. 'At our age we ought to rally quickly.'

'Yes! Time is the great physician. I cannot say I have much more faith in him than in the spring.'

'Well, then, there is Hope; what think you of that?'

'I have no great faith,' said Ferdinand, affecting to smile.

'Believe, then, in optimism,' said Henrietta Temple, without taking her eyes off the cards. 'Whatever is, is best.'

'That is not my creed, Miss Temple,' said Ferdinand, and he rose and was about to retire.

'Must you go? Let us all do something to-morrow!' said Lord Montfort, interchanging a glance with Henrietta. 'The British Museum; Miss Grandison wishes to go to the British Museum. Pray come with us.'

'You are very good, but————'

'Well! I will write you a little note in the morning and tell you our plans,' said Lord Montfort. 'I hope you will not desert us.'

Ferdinand bowed and retired: he avoided catching the eye of Henrietta.

The carriages of Miss Temple and Miss Grandison were soon announced, and, fatigued with their riding-dresses, these ladies did not long remain.

'To-day has been a day of trial,' said Henrietta, as she was about to bid Lord Montfort farewell. 'What do you think of affairs? I saw you speaking to Katherine. What do you think?'

'I think Ferdinand Armine is a formidable rival. Do you know, I am rather jealous?'

'Digby! can you be ungenerous?'

'My sweet Henrietta, pardon my levity. I spoke in the merest playfulness. Nay,' he continued, for she seemed really hurt, 'say good night very sweetly.'

'Is there any hope?' said Henrietta.

'All's well that ends well,' said Lord Montfort, smiling; 'God bless you.'

Glastonbury was about to retire, when Lord Montfort returned and asked him to come up to his lordship's own apartments, as he wished to show him a curious antique carving.

'You seemed rather surprised at the guests you found here to-night,' said Lord Montfort when they were alone.

Glastonbury looked a little confused. 'It was certainly a curious meeting, all things considered,' continued Lord Montfort: 'Henrietta has never concealed anything of the past from me, but I have always wished to spare her details. I told her this morning I should speak to you upon the subject, and that is the reason why I have asked you here.'

'It is a painful history,' said Glastonbury.

'As painful to me as anyone,' said his lordship; 'nevertheless, it must be told. When did you first meet Miss Temple?'

'I shall never forget it,' said Glastonbury, sighing and moving very uneasily in his chair. 'I took her for Miss Grandison.' And Glastonbury now entered into a complete history of everything that had occurred.

'It is a strange, a wonderful story,' said Lord Montfort, 'and you communicated everything to Miss Grandison?'

'Everything but the name of her rival. To that she would not listen. It was not just, she said, to one so unfortunate and so unhappy.'

'She seems an admirable person, that Miss Grandison,' said Lord Montfort.

'She is indeed as near an angel as anything earthly can be,' said Glastonbury.

'Then it is still a secret to the parents?'

'Thus she would have it,' said Glastonbury. 'She clings to them, who love her indeed as a daughter; and she shrank from the desolation that was preparing for them.'

'Poor girl!' said Lord Montfort, 'and poor Armine! By heavens, I pity him from the bottom of my heart.'

'If you had seen him as I have,' said Glastonbury, 'wilder than the wildest Bedlamite! It was an awful sight.'

'Ah! the heart, the heart,' said Lord Montfort: 'it is a delicate organ, Mr. Glastonbury. And think you his father and mother suspect nothing?'

'I know not what they think,' said Glastonbury, 'but they must soon know all.' And he seemed to shudder at the thought.

'Why must they?' asked Lord Montfort.

Glastonbury stared.

'Is there no hope of softening and subduing all their sorrows?' said Lord Montfort; 'cannot we again bring together these young and parted spirits?'

'It is my only hope,' said Glastonbury, 'and yet I sometimes deem it a forlorn one.'

'It is the sole desire of Henrietta,' said Lord Montfort; 'cannot you assist us? Will you enter into this conspiracy of affection with us?'

'I want no spur to such a righteous work,' said Glastonbury, 'but I cannot conceal from myself the extreme difficulty. Ferdinand is the most impetuous of human beings. His passions are a whirlwind; his volition more violent than becomes a suffering mortal.'

'You think, then, there is no difficulty but with him?'

'I know not what to say,' said Glastonbury; 'calm as appears the temperament of Miss Grandison, she has heroic qualities. Oh! what have I not seen that admirable young lady endure! Alas! my Digby, my dear lord, few passages of this terrible story are engraven on my memory more deeply than the day when I revealed to her the fatal secret. Yet, and chiefly for her sake, it was my duty.'

'It was at Armine?'

'At Armine. I seized an opportunity when we were alone together, and without fear of being disturbed. We had gone to view an old abbey in the neighbourhood. We were seated among its ruins, when I took her hand and endeavoured to prepare her for the fatal intelligence, "All is not right with Ferdinand," she immediately said; "there is some mystery. I have long suspected it." She listened to my recital, softened as much as I could for her sake, in silence. Yet her paleness I never can forget. She looked like a saint in a niche. When I had finished, she whispered me to leave her for some short time, and I walked away, out of sight indeed, but so near that she might easily summon me. I stood alone until it was twilight, in a state of mournful suspense that I recall even now with anguish. At last I heard my name sounded, in a low yet distinct voice, and I looked round and she was there. She had been weeping. I took her hand and pressed it, and led her to the carriage. When I approached our unhappy home, she begged me to make her excuses to the family, and for two or three days we saw her no more. At length she sent for me, and told me she had been revolving all these sad circumstances in her mind, and she felt for others more even than for herself; that she forgave Ferdinand, and pitied him, and would act towards him as a sister; that her heart was distracted with the thoughts of the unhappy young lady, whose name she would never know, but that if by her assistance I could effect their union, means should not be wanting, though their source must be concealed; that for the sake of her aunt, to whom she is indeed passionately attached, she would keep the secret, until it could no longer be maintained; and that in the meantime it was to be hoped that health might be restored to her cousin, and Providence in some way interfere in favour of this unhappy family.'

'Angelic creature!' said Lord Montfort. 'So young, too; I think so beautiful. Good God! with such a heart what could Armine desire?'

'Alas!' said Glastonbury, and he shook his head. 'You know not the love of Ferdinand Armine for Henrietta Temple. It is a wild and fearful thing; it passeth human comprehension.'

Lord Montfort leant back in his chair, and covered his face with his hands. After some minutes he looked up, and said in his usual placid tone, and with an' unruffled brow, 'Will you take anything before you go, Mr. Glastonbury?'

CHAPTER X.

In Which Captain Armine Increases His Knowledge of the
Value of Money, and Also Becomes Aware of the Advantage of
an Acquaintance Who Burns Coals.

FERDINAND returned to his hotel in no very good humour, revolving in his mind Miss Temple's advice about optimism. What could she mean? Was there really a conspiracy to make him marry his cousin, and was Miss Temple one of the conspirators? He could scarcely believe this, and yet it was the most probable, deduction from all that had been said and done. He had lived to witness such strange occurrences, that no event ought now to astonish him. Only to think that he had been sitting quietly in a drawing-room with Henrietta Temple, and she avowedly engaged to be married to another person, who was present; and that he, Ferdinand Armine, should be the selected companion of their morning ride, and be calmly invited to contribute to their daily amusement by his social presence! What next? If this were not an insult, a gross, flagrant, and unendurable outrage, he was totally at a loss to comprehend what was meant by offended pride. Optimism, indeed! He felt far more inclined to embrace the faith of the Manichee! And what a fool was he to have submitted to such a despicable, such a degrading situation! What infinite weakness not to be able to resist her influence, the influence of a woman who had betrayed him! Yes! betrayed him. He had for some period reconciled his mind to entertain the idea of Henrietta's treachery to him. Softened by time, atoned for by long suffering, extenuated by the constant sincerity of his purpose, his original imprudence, to use his own phrase in describing his misconduct, had gradually ceased to figure as a valid and sufficient cause for her behaviour to him. When he recollected how he had loved this woman, what he had sacrificed for her, and what misery he had in consequence entailed upon himself and all those dear to him; when he contrasted his present perilous situation with her triumphant prosperity, and remembered that while he had devoted himself to a love which proved false, she who had deserted him was, by a caprice of fortune, absolutely rewarded for her fickleness; he was enraged, he was disgusted, he despised himself for having been her slave; he began even to hate her. Terrible moment when we first dare to view with feelings of repugnance the being that our soul has long idolised! It is the most awful of revelations. We start back in horror, as if in the act of profanation.

Other annoyances, however, of a less ethereal character, awaited our hero on his return to his hotel. There he found a letter from his lawyer, informing him that he could no longer parry the determination of one of Captain Armine's principal creditors to arrest him instantly for a considerable sum. Poor Ferdinand, mortified and harassed, with his heart and spirit alike broken, could scarcely refrain from a groan. However, some step must be taken. He drove Henrietta from his thoughts, and, endeavouring to rally some of his old energy, revolved in his mind what desperate expedient yet remained.

His sleep was broken by dreams of bailiffs, and a vague idea of Henrietta Temple triumphing in his misery; but he rose early, wrote a diplomatic note to his menacing creditor, which he felt confident must gain him time, and then, making a careful toilet, for when a man is going to try to borrow money it is wise to look prosperous, he took his way to a quarter of the town where lived a gentleman with whose brother he had had some previous dealings at Malta, and whose acquaintance he had made in England in reference to them.

It was in that gloomy quarter called Golden-square, the murky repose of which strikes so mysteriously on the senses after the glittering bustle of the adjoining Regent-street, that Captain Armine stopped before a noble yet now dingy mansion, that in old and happier days might probably have been inhabited by his grandfather, or some of his gay friends. A brass plate on the door informed the world that here resided Messrs. Morris and Levison, following the not very ambitious calling of coal merchants. But if all the pursuers of that somewhat humble trade could manage to deal in coals with the same dexterity as Messrs. Morris and Levison, what very great coal merchants they would be!

The ponderous portal obeyed the signal of the bell, and apparently opened without any human means; and Captain Armine, proceeding down a dark yet capacious passage, opened a door, which invited him by an inscription on ground glass that assured him he was entering the counting-house. Here several clerks, ensconced within lofty walls of the darkest and dullest mahogany, were busily employed; yet one advanced to an aperture in this fortification and accepted the card which the visitor offered him. The clerk surveyed the ticket with a peculiar glance; and then, begging the visitor to be seated, disappeared. He was not long absent, but soon invited Ferdinand to follow him. Captain Armine was ushered up a noble staircase, and into a saloon that once was splendid. The ceiling was richly carved, and there still might be detected the remains of its once gorgeous embellishment in the faint forms of faded deities and the traces of murky gilding. The walls of this apartment were crowded with pictures, arranged, however, with little regard to taste, effect, or style. A sprawling copy of Titian's Venus flanked a somewhat prim peeress by Hoppner; a landscape that smacked of Gainsborough was the companion of a dauby moonlight, that must have figured in the last exhibition; and insipid Roman matrons by Hamilton, and stiff English heroes by Northcote, contrasted with a vast quantity of second-rate delineations of the orgies of Dutch boors and portraits of favourite racers and fancy dogs. The room was crowded with ugly furniture of all kinds, very solid, and chiefly of mahogany; among which were not less than three escritoires, to say nothing of the huge horsehair sofas. A sideboard of Babylonian proportions was crowned by three massive and enormous silver salvers, and immense branch candlesticks of the same precious metal, and a china punch-bowl which might have suited the dwarf in Brobdignag. The floor was covered with a faded Turkey carpet. But amid all this solid splendour there were certain intimations of feminine elegance in the veil of finely-cut pink paper which covered the nakedness of the empty but highly-polished fire-place, and in the hand-screens, which were profusely ornamented with ribbon of the same hue, and one of which afforded a most accurate if not picturesque view of Margate, while the other glowed with a huge wreath of cabbage-roses and jonquils.

Ferdinand was not long alone, and Mr. Levison, the proprietor of all this splendour, entered. He was a short, stout man, with a grave but handsome countenance, a little bald, but nevertheless with an elaborateness of raiment which might better have become a younger man. He wore a plum-colored frock coat of the finest cloth; his green velvet waistcoat was guarded by a gold chain, which would have been the envy of a new town council; an immense opal gleamed on the breast of his embroidered shirt; and his fingers were covered with very fine rings.

'Your sarvant, Captin,' said Mr. Levison, and he placed a chair for his guest.

'How are you, Levison?' responded our hero in an easy voice. 'Any news?'

Mr. Levison shrugged his shoulders, as he murmured, 'Times is very bad, Captin.'

'Oh! I dare say,' said Ferdinand; 'I wish they were as well with me as with you. By Jove, Levison, you must be making an immense fortune.'

Mr. Levison shook his head, as he groaned out, 'I work hard, Captin; but times is terrible.'

'Fiddlededee! Come! I want you to assist me a little, old fellow. No humbug between us.'

'Oh!' groaned Mr. Levison, 'you could not come at a worse time; I don't know what money is.'

'Of course. However, the fact is, money I must have; and so, old fellow, we are old friends, and you must get it.'

'What do you want, Captin?' slowly spoke Mr. Levison, with an expression of misery.

'Oh! I want rather a tolerable sum, and that is the truth; but I only want it for a moment.'

'It is not the time, 'tis the money,' said Mr. Levison. 'You know me and my pardner, Captin, are always anxious to do what we can to sarve you.'

'Well, now you can do me a real service, and, by Jove, you shall never repent it. To the point; I must have 1,500L.'

'One thousand five hundred pounds!' exclaimed Mr. Levison. "Tayn't in the country.'

'Humbug! It must be found. What is the use of all this stuff with me? I want 1,500L., and you must give it me.'

'I tell you what it is, Captin,' said Mr. Levison, leaning over the back of a chair, and speaking with callous composure; 'I tell you what it is, me and my pardner are very willing always to assist you; but we want to know when the marriage is to come off, and that's the truth.'

'Damn the marriage,' said Captain Armine, rather staggered.

'There it is, though,' said Mr. Levison, very quietly. 'You know, Captin, there is the arrears on that 'ere annuity, three years next Michaelmas. I think it's Michaelmas; let me see.' So saying, Mr. Levison opened an escritoire, and brought forward an awful-looking volume, and, consulting the terrible index, turned to the fatal name of Armine. 'Yes! three years next Michaelmas, Captin.'

'Well, you will be paid,' said Ferdinand.

'We hope so,' said Mr. Levison; 'but it is a long figure.'

'Well, but you get capital interest?'

'Pish!' said Mr. Levison; 'ten per cent.! Why! it is giving away the money. Why! that's the raw, Captin. With this here new bill annuities is nothink. Me and my pardner don't do no annuities now. It's giving money away; and all this here money locked up; and all to sarve you.'

'Well; you will not help me,' said Ferdinand, rising.

'Do you raly want fifteen hundred?' asked Mr. Levison.

'By Jove, I do.'

'Well now, Captin, when is this marriage to come off?'

'Have I not told you a thousand times, and Morris too, that my cousin is not to marry until one year has passed since my grandfather's death? It is barely a year. But of course, at this moment, of all others, I cannot afford to be short.'

'Very true, Captin; and we are the men to sarve you, if we could. But we cannot. Never was such times for money; there is no seeing it. However, we will do what we can. Things is going very bad at Malta, and that's the truth. There's that young Catchimwhocan, we are in with him wery deep; and now he has left the Fusiliers and got into Parliament, he don't care this for us. If he would only pay us, you should have the money; so help me, you should.'

'But he won't pay you,' said Ferdinand. 'What can you do?'

'Why, I have a friend,' said Mr. Levison, 'who I know has got three hundred pound at his bankers, and he might lend it us; but we shall have to pay for it.'

'I suppose so,' said Ferdinand. 'Well, three hundred.'

'I have not got a shilling myself,' said Mr. Levison. 'Young Touchemup left us in the lurch yesterday for 750L., so help me, and never gave us no notice. Now, you are a gentleman, Captin; you never pay, but you always give us notice.'

Ferdinand could not help smiling at Mr. Levison's idea of a gentleman.

'Well, what else can you do?'

'Why, there is two hundred coming in to-morrow,' said Mr. Levison; 'I can depend on that.'

'Well, that is five.'

'And you want fifteen hundred,' said Mr. Levison. 'Well, me and my pardner always like to sarve you, and it is very awkward certainly for you to want money at this moment. But if you want to buy jewels, I can get you any credit you like, you know.'

'We will talk of that by and by,' said Ferdinand.

'Fifteen hundred pound!' ejaculated Mr. Levison. 'Well, I suppose we must make it 700L. somehow or other, and you must take the rest in coals.'

'Oh, by Jove, Levison, that is too bad.'

'I don't see no other way,' said Mr. Levison, rather doggedly.

'But, damn it, my good fellow, my dear Levison, what the deuce am I to do with 800L. worth of coals?'

'Lord! My dear Captin, 800L. worth of coals is a mere nothink. With your connection, you will get rid of them in a morning. All you have got to do, you know, is to give your friends an order on us, and we will let you have cash at a little discount.'

'Then you can let me have the cash now at a little discount, or even a great; I cannot get rid of 800L. worth of coals.'

'Why, 'tayn't four hundred chaldron, Captin,' rejoined Mr. Levison. 'Three or four friends would do the thing. Why, Baron Squash takes ten thousand chaldron of us every year; but he has such a knack, he gits the Clubs to take them.'

'Baron Squash, indeed! Do you know whom you are talking to, Mr. Levison? Do you think that I am going to turn into a coal merchant? your working partner, by Jove! No, sir; give me the 700L., without the coals, and charge what interest you please.' 'We could not do it, Captin. 'Tayn't our way.' 'I ask you once more, Mr. Levison, will you let me have the money, or will you not?'

'Now, Captin, don't be so high and mighty! 'Tayn't the way to do business. Me and my pardner wish to sarve you; we does indeed. And if a hundred pound will be of any use to you, you shall have it on your acceptance; and we won't be curious about any name that draws; we won't indeed.'

'Well, Mr. Levison,' said Ferdinand, rising, 'I see we can do nothing to-day. The hundred pounds would be of no use to me. I will think over your proposition. Good morning to you.'

'Ah, do!' said Mr. Levison, bowing and opening the door, 'do, Captin; we wish to sarve you, we does indeed. See how we behave about that arrears. Think of the coals; now do. Now for a bargin; come! Come, Captin, I dare say now you could get us the business of the Junior Sarvice Club; and then you shall have the seven hundred on your acceptance for three months, at two shillings in the pound; come!'

CHAPTER XI.

In Which Captain Armine Unexpectedly Resumes His
Acquaintance with Lord Catchimwhocan, Who Introduces Him
to Mr. Bond Sharpe.

FERDINAND quitted his kind friend Mr. Levison in no very amiable mood; but just as he was leaving the house, a cabriolet, beautifully painted, of a brilliant green colour picked out with a somewhat cream-coloured white, and drawn by a showy Holstein horse of tawny tint, with a flowing and milk-white tail and mane, and caparisoned in harness almost as precious as Mr. Levison's sideboard, dashed up to the door.

'Armine, by Jove!' exclaimed the driver, with great cordiality.

'Ah! Catch, is it you?' said Ferdinand. 'What! have you been here?' said Lord Catchimwhocan. 'At the old work, eh? Is "me and my pardner" troublesome? for your countenance is not very radiant.'

'By Jove, old fellow!' said Ferdinand, in a depressed tone, 'I am in a scrape, and also in a rage. Nothing is to be done here.'

'Never mind,' said his lordship; 'keep up your spirits, jump into my cab, and we will see how we can carry on the war. I am only going to speak one word to "me and my pardner."'

So saying, his lordship skipped into the house as gay as a lark, although he had a bill for a good round sum about to be dishonoured in the course of a few hours.

'Well, my dear Armine,' he resumed, when he reappeared and took the reins; 'now as I drive along, tell me all about it; for if there be a man in the world whom I should like to "sarve," it is thyself, my noble Ferdinand.'

With this encouragement, Captain Armine was not long in pouring his cares into a congenial bosom.

'I know the man to "sarve" you,' said Catchimwhocan.

'The fact is, these fellows here are regular old-fashioned humbugs. The only idea they have is money, money. They have no enlightened notions. I will introduce you to a regular trump; and if he does not do our business, I am much mistaken. Courage, old fellow! How do you like this start?'

'Deuced neat. By-the-bye, Catch, my boy, you are going it rather, I see.'

'To be sure. I have always told you there is a certain system in affairs which ever prevents men being floored. No fellow is ever dished who has any connection. What man that ever had his run was really ever fairly put hors de combat, unless he was some one who ought never to have entered the arena, blazing away without any set, making himself a damned fool and everybody his enemy. So long as a man bustles about and is in a good set, something always turns up. I got into Parliament, you see; and you, you are going to be married.'

All this time the cabriolet was dashing down Regent-street, twisting through the Quadrant, whirling along Pall Mall, until it finally entered Cleveland-row, and stopped before a newly painted, newly pointed, and exceedingly compact mansion, the long brass knocker of whose dark green door sounded beneath the practised touch of his lordship's tiger. Even the tawny Holstein horse, with the white flowing mane, seemed conscious of the locality, and stopped before the accustomed resting-place in the most natural manner imaginable. A tall serving-man, well-powdered, and in a dark and well-appointed livery, immediately appeared.

'At home?' enquired Lord Catchimwhocan, with a peculiarly confidential expression.

'To you, my lord,' responded the attendant.

'Jump out, Armine,' said his lordship; and they entered the house.

'Alone?' said his lordship.

'Not alone,' said the servant, ushering the friends into the dining-room, 'but he shall have your lordship's card immediately. There are several gentlemen waiting in the third drawing-room; so I have shown your lordship in here, and shall take care that he sees your lordship before anyone.'

'That's a devilish good fellow,' said Lord Catchimwhocan, putting his hand into his waistcoat pocket to give him a sovereign; but not finding one, he added, 'I shall remember you.'

The dining-room into which they were shown was at the back of the house, and looked into agreeable gardens. The apartment was in some little confusion at this moment, for their host gave a dinner to-day, and his dinners were famous. The table was arranged for eight guests; its appointments indicated refined taste. A candelabrum of Dresden china was the centre piece; there was a whole service of the same material, even to the handles of the knives and forks; and the choice variety of glass attracted Ferdinand's notice. The room was lofty and spacious; it was simply and soberly furnished; not an object which could distract the taste or disturb the digestion. But the sideboard, which filled a recess at the end of the apartment, presented a crowded group of gold plate that might have become a palace; magnificent shields, tall vases, ancient tankards, goblets of carved ivory set in precious metal, and cups of old ruby glass mounted on pedestals, glittering with gems. This accidental display certainly offered an amusing contrast to the perpetual splendour of Mr. Levison's buffet; and Ferdinand was wondering whether it would turn out that there was as marked a difference between the two owners, when his companion and himself were summoned to the presence of Mr. Bond Sharpe.

They ascended a staircase perfumed with flowers, and on each landing-place was a classic tripod or pedestal crowned with a bust. And then they were ushered into a drawing-room of Parisian elegance; buhl cabinets, marqueterie tables, hangings of the choicest damask suspended from burnished cornices of old carving. The chairs had been rifled from a Venetian palace; the couches were part of the spoils of the French revolution. There were glass screens in golden frames, and a clock that represented the death of Hector, the chariot wheel of Achilles conveniently telling the hour. A round table of mosaic, mounted on a golden pedestal, was nearly covered with papers; and from an easy-chair, supported by air cushions, half rose to welcome them Mr. Bond Sharpe. He was a man not many years the senior of Captain Armine and his friend; of elegant appearance, pale, pensive, and prepossessing. Deep thought was impressed upon his clear and protruding brow, and the expression of his grey sunken eyes, which were delicately arched, was singularly searching. His figure was slight but compact. His dress was plain, but a model in its fashion. He was habited entirely in black, and his only ornament were his studs, which were turquoise and of great size: but there never were such boots, so brilliant and so small!

He welcomed Lord Catchimwhocan in a voice scarcely above a whisper, and received Captain Armine in a manner alike graceful and dignified.

'My dear Sharpe,' said his lordship, 'I am going to introduce to you my most particular friend, and an old brother officer. This is Captain Armine, the only son of Sir Ratcliffe, and the heir of Armine Castle. He is going to be married very soon to his cousin, Miss Grandison, the greatest heiress in England.'

'Hush, hush,' said Ferdinand, shrinking under this false representation, and Mr. Sharpe with considerate delicacy endeavoured to check his lordship.

'Well, never mind, I will say nothing about that,' continued Lord Catchimwhocan. 'The long and the short of it is this, that my friend Armine is hard up, and we must carry on the war till we get into winter quarters. You are just the man for him, and by Jove, my dear Sharpe, if you wish sensibly to oblige me, who I am sure am one of your warmest friends, you will do everything for Armine that human energy can possibly effect.'

'What is the present difficulty that you have?' enquired Mr. Sharpe of our hero, in a calm whisper.

'Why, the present difficulty that he has,' said Lord Catchimwhocan, 'is that he wants 1,500L.'

'I suppose you have raised money, Captain Armine?' said Mr. Sharpe.

'In every way,' said Captain Armine.

'Of course,' said Mr. Sharpe, 'at your time of life one naturally does. And I suppose you are bothered for this 1,500L.'

'I am threatened with immediate arrest, and arrest in execution.'

'Who is the party?'

'Why, I fear an unmanageable one, even by you. It is a house at Malta.'

'Mr. Bolus, I suppose?'

'Exactly.'

'I thought so.'

'Well, what can be done?' said Lord Catchimwhocan.

'Oh! there is no difficulty,' said Mr. Sharpe quietly. 'Captain Armine can have any money he likes.'

'I shall be happy,' said Captain Armine, 'to pay any consideration you think fit.'

'Oh! my dear sir, I cannot think of that. Money is a drug now. I shall be happy to accommodate you without giving you any trouble. You can have the 1,500L., if you please, this moment.'

'Really, you are very generous,' said Ferdinand, much surprised, 'but I feel I am not entitled to such favours. What security can I give you?'

'I lend the money to you. I want no security. You can repay me when you like. Give me your note of hand.' So saying, Mr. Sharpe opened a drawer, and taking out his cheque-book drew a draft for the 1,500L. 'I believe I have a stamp in the house,' he continued, looking about. 'Yes, here is one. If you will fill this up, Captain Armine, the affair may be concluded at once.'

'Upon my honour, Mr. Sharpe,' said Ferdinand, very confused, 'I do not like to appear insensible to this extraordinary kindness, but really I came here by the merest accident, and without any intention of soliciting or receiving such favours. And my kind friend here has given you much too glowing an account of my resources. It is very probable I shall occasion you great inconvenience.'

'Really, Captain Armine,' said Mr. Sharpe with a slight smile, 'if we were talking of a sum of any importance, why, one might be a little more punctilious, but for such a bagatelle we have already wasted too much time in its discussion. I am happy to serve you.'

Ferdinand stared, remembering Mr. Levison and the coals. Mr. Sharpe himself drew up the note, and presented it to Ferdinand, who signed it and pocketed the draft.

'I have several gentlemen waiting,' said Mr. Bond Sharpe; 'I am sorry I cannot take this opportunity of cultivating your acquaintance, Captain Armine, but I should esteem it a great honour if you would dine with me to-day. Your friend Lord Catchimwhocan favours me with his company, and you might meet a person or two who would amuse you.'

'I really shall be very happy,' said Ferdinand.

And Mr. Bond Sharpe again slightly rose and bowed them out of the room.

'Well, is not he a trump?' said Lord Catchimwhocan, when they were once more in the cab.

'I am so astonished,' said Ferdinand, 'that I cannot speak. Who in the name of fortune is this great man?'

'A genius,' said Lord Catchimwhocan. 'Don't you think he is a deuced good-looking fellow?'

'The best-looking fellow I ever saw,' said the grateful Ferdinand.

'And capital manners?'

'Most distinguished.'

'Neatest dressed man in town!'

'Exquisite taste!'

'What a house!'

'Capital!'

'Did you ever see such furniture? It beats your rooms at Malta.'

'I never saw anything more complete in my life.'

'What plate!' 'Miraculous!' 'And, believe me, we shall have the best dinner in town.'

'Well, he has given me an appetite,' said Ferdinand. 'But who is he?'

'Why, by business he is what is called a conveyancer; that is to say, he is a lawyer by inspiration.'

'He is a wonderful man,' said Ferdinand. 'He must be very rich.'

'Yes; Sharpe must be worth his quarter of a million. And he has made it in such a deuced short time!'

'Why, he is not much older than we are!'

'Ten years ago that man was a prizefighter,' said Lord Catchimwhocan.

'A prizefighter!' exclaimed Ferdinand.

'Yes; and licked everybody. But he was too great a genius for the ring, and took to the turf.'

'Ah!'

'Then he set up a hell.'

'Hum!'

'And then he turned it into a subscription-house.'

'Hoh!'

'He keeps his hell still, but it works itself now. In the mean time he is the first usurer in the world, and will be in the next Parliament.'

'But if he lends money on the terms he accommodates me, he will hardly increase his fortune.'

'Oh! he can do the thing when he likes. He took a fancy to you. The fact is, my dear fellow, Sharpe is very rich and wants to get into society. He likes to oblige young men of distinction, and can afford to risk a few thousands now and then. By dining with him to-day you have quite repaid him for his loan. Besides, the fellow has a great soul; and, though born on a dung-hill, nature intended him for a palace, and he has placed himself there.'

'Well, this has been a remarkable morning,' said Ferdinand Armine, as Lord Catchimwhocan set him down at his club. 'I am very much obliged to you, dear Catch!'

'Not a word, my dear fellow. You have helped me before this, and glad am I to be the means of assisting the best fellow in the world, and that we all think you. Au revoir! We dine at eight.'

CHAPTER XII.

Miss Grandison Makes a Remarkable Discovery.

IN THE mean time, while the gloomy morning which Ferdinand had anticipated terminated with so agreeable an adventure, Henrietta and Miss Grandison, accompanied by Lord Montfort and Glastonbury, paid their promised visit to the British Museum.

'I am sorry that Captain Armine could not accompany us,' said Lord Montfort. 'I sent to him this morning early, but he was already out.'

'He has many affairs to attend to,' said Glastonbury.

Miss Temple looked grave; she thought of poor Ferdinand and all his cares. She knew well what were those affairs to which Glastonbury alluded. The thought that perhaps at this moment he was struggling with rapacious creditors made her melancholy. The novelty and strangeness of the objects which awaited her, diverted, however, her mind from these painful reflections. Miss Grandison, who had never quitted England, was delighted with everything she saw; but the Egyptian gallery principally attracted the attention of Miss Temple. Lord Montfort, regardful of his promise to Henrietta, was very attentive to Miss Grandison.

'I cannot help regretting that your cousin is not here,' said his lordship, returning to a key that he had already touched. But Katherine made no answer.

'He seemed so much better for the exertion he made yesterday,' resumed Lord Montfort. 'I think it would do him good to be more with us.'

'He seems to like to be alone,' said Katherine.

'I wonder at that,' said Lord Montfort; 'I cannot conceive a happier life than we all lead.'

'You have cause to be happy, and Ferdinand has not,' said Miss Grandison, calmly.

'I should have thought that he had very great cause,' said Lord Montfort, enquiringly.

'No person in the world is so unhappy as Ferdinand,' said Katherine.

'But cannot we cure his unhappiness?' said his lordship. 'We are his friends; it seems to me, with such friends as Miss Grandison and Miss Temple one ought never to be unhappy.'

'Miss Temple can scarcely be called a friend of Ferdinand,' said Katherine.

'Indeed, a very warm one, I assure you.'

'Ah, that is your influence.'

'Nay, it is her own impulse.'

'But she only met him yesterday for the first time.'

'I assure you Miss Temple is an older friend of Captain Armine than I am,' said his lordship.

'Indeed!' said Miss Grandison, with an air of considerable astonishment.

'You know they were neighbours in the country.'

'In the country!' repeated Miss Grandison.

'Yes; Mr. Temple, you know, resided not far from Armine.'

'Not far from Armine!' still repeated Miss Grandison.

'Digby,' said Miss Temple, turning to him at this moment, 'tell Mr. Glastonbury about your sphinx at Rome. It was granite, was it not?'

'And most delicately carved. I never remember having observed an expression of such beautiful serenity. The discovery that, after all, they are male countenances is quite mortifying. I loved their mysterious beauty.'

What Lord Montfort had mentioned of the previous acquaintance of Henrietta and her cousin made Miss Grandison muse. Miss Temple's address to Ferdinand yesterday had struck her at the moment as somewhat singular; but the impression had not dwelt upon her mind. But now it occurred to her as very strange, that Henrietta should have become so intimate with the Armine family and herself, and never have mentioned that she was previously acquainted with their nearest relative. Lady Armine was not acquainted with Miss Temple until they met at Bellair House. That was certain. Miss Grandison had witnessed their mutual introduction. Nor Sir Ratcliffe. And yet Henrietta and Ferdinand were friends, warm friends, old friends, intimately acquainted: so said Lord Montfort, and Lord Montfort never coloured, never exaggerated. All this was very mysterious. And if they were friends, old friends, warm friends, and Lord Montfort said they were, and, therefore, there could be no doubt of the truth of the statement, their recognition of each other yesterday was singularly frigid.

It was not indicative of a very intimate acquaintance. Katherine had ascribed it to the natural disrelish of Ferdinand now to be introduced to anyone. And yet they were friends, old friends, warm friends. Henrietta Temple and Ferdinand Armine! Miss Grandison was so perplexed that she scarcely looked at another object in the galleries.

The ladies were rather tired when they returned from the Museum. Lord Montfort walked to the Travellers, and Henrietta agreed to remain and dine in Brook-street. Katherine and herself retired to Miss Grandison's boudoir, a pretty chamber, where they were sure of being alone. Henrietta threw herself upon a sofa, and took up the last new novel; Miss Grandison seated herself on an ottoman by her side, and worked at a purse which she was making for Mr. Temple.

'Do you like that book?' said Katherine.

'I like the lively parts, but not the serious ones,' replied Miss Temple; 'the author has observed but he has not felt.'

'It is satirical,' said Miss Grandison; 'I wonder why all this class of writers aim now at the sarcastic. I do not find life the constant sneer they make it.'

'It is because they do not understand life,' said Henrietta, 'but have some little experience of society. Therefore their works give a perverted impression of human conduct; for they accept as a principal, that which is only an insignificant accessory; and they make existence a succession of frivolities, when even the career of the most frivolous has its profounder moments.'

'How vivid is the writer's description of a ball or a dinner,' said Miss Grandison; 'everything lives and moves. And yet, when the hero makes love, nothing can be more unnatural. His feelings are neither deep, nor ardent, nor tender. All is stilted, and yet ludicrous.'

'I do not despise the talent which describes so vividly a dinner and a ball,' said Miss Temple. 'As far as it goes it is very amusing, but it should be combined with higher materials. In a fine novel, manners should be observed, and morals should be sustained; we require thought and passion, as well as costume and the lively representation of conventional arrangements; and the thought and passion will be the better for these accessories, for they will be relieved in the novel as they are relieved in life, and the whole will be more true.'

'But have you read that love scene, Henrietta? It appeared to me so ridiculous!'

'I never read love scenes,' said Henrietta Temple.

'Oh, I love a love story,' said Miss Grandison, smiling, 'if it be natural and tender, and touch my heart. When I read such scenes, I weep.'

'Ah, my sweet Katherine, you are soft-hearted.'

'And you, Henrietta, what are you?'

'Hard-hearted. The most callous of mortals.'

'Oh, what would Lord Montfort say?'

'Lord Montfort knows it. We never have love scenes.'

'And yet you love him?'

'Dearly; I love and esteem him.'

'Well,' said Miss Grandison, 'I may be wrong, but if I were a man I do not think I should like the lady of my love to esteem me.'

'And yet esteem is the only genuine basis of happiness, believe me, Kate. Love is a dream.'

'And how do you know, dear Henrietta?'

'All writers agree it is.'

'The writers you were just ridiculing?'

'A fair retort; and yet, though your words are the more witty, believe me, mine are the more wise.'

'I wish my cousin would wake from his dream,' said Katherine. 'To tell you a secret, love is the cause of his unhappiness. Don't move, dear Henrietta,' added Miss Grandison; 'we are so happy here;' for Miss Temple, in truth, seemed not a little discomposed.

'You should marry your cousin,' said Miss Temple.

'You little know Ferdinand or myself, when you give that advice,' said Katherine. 'We shall never marry; nothing is more certain than that. In the first place, to be frank, Ferdinand would not marry me, nothing would induce him; and in the second place, I would not marry him, nothing would induce me.'

'Why not?' said Henrietta, in a low tone, holding her book very near to her face.

'Because I am sure that we should not be happy,' said Miss Grandison. 'I love Ferdinand, and once could have married him. He is so brilliant that I could not refuse his proposal. And yet I feel it is better for me that we have not married, and I hope it may yet prove better for him, for I love him very dearly. He is indeed my brother.'

'But why should you not be happy?' enquired Miss Temple.

'Because we are not suited to each other. Ferdinand must marry some one whom he looks up to, somebody brilliant like himself, some one who can sympathise with all his fancies. I am too calm and quiet for him. You would suit him much better, Henrietta.'

'You are his cousin; it is a misfortune; if you were not, he would adore you, and you would sympathise with him.'

'I think not: I should not like to marry a very clever man,' said Katherine. 'I could not endure marrying a fool, or a commonplace person; I should like to marry a person very superior in talent to myself, some one whose opinion would guide me on all points, one from whom I could not differ. But not Ferdinand; he is too imaginative, too impetuous; he would neither guide me, nor be guided by me.'

Miss Temple did not reply, but turned over a page of her book.

'Did you know Ferdinand before you met him yesterday at our house?' enquired Miss Grandison, very innocently.

'Yes!' said Miss Temple.

'I thought you did,' said Miss Grandison, 'I thought there was something in your manner that indicated you had met before. I do not think you knew my aunt before you met her at Bellair House?'

'I did not.'

'Nor Sir Ratclifle?'

'Nor Sir Ratclifle.'

'But you did know Mr. Glastonbury?'

'I did know Mr. Glastonbury.'

'How very odd!' said Miss Grandison.

'What is odd?' enquired Henrietta.

'That you should have known Ferdinand before.'

'Not at all odd. He came over one day to shoot at papa's. I remember him very well.'

'Oh,' said Miss Grandison. 'And did Mr. Glastonbury come over to shoot?'

'I met Mr. Glastonbury one morning that I went to see the picture gallery at Armine. It is the only time I ever saw him.'

'Oh!' said Miss Grandison again, 'Armine is a beautiful place, is it not?'

'Most interesting.'

'You know the pleasaunce.'

'Yes.'

'I did not see you when I was at Armine.'

'No; we had just gone to Italy.'

'How beautiful you look to-day, Henrietta!' said Miss Grandison. 'Who could believe that you ever were so ill!'

'I am grateful that I have recovered,' said Henrietta. 'And yet I never thought that I should return to England.'

'You must have been so very ill in Italy, about the same time as poor Ferdinand was at Armine. Only think, how odd you should both have been so ill about the same time, and now that we should all be so intimate!'

Miss Temple looked perplexed and annoyed. 'Is it so odd?' she at length said in a low tone.

'Henrietta Temple,' said Miss Grandison, with great earnestness, 'I have discovered a secret; you are the lady with whom my cousin is in love.'

CHAPTER XIII.

In Which Ferdinand Has the Honour of Dining with Mr. Bond Sharpe.

WHEN Ferdinand arrived at Mr. Bond Sharpe's he was welcomed by his host in a magnificent suite of saloons, and introduced to two of the guests who had previously arrived. The first was a stout man, past middle age, whose epicurean countenance twinkled with humour. This was Lord Castlefyshe, an Irish peer of great celebrity in the world of luxury and play, keen at a bet, still keener at a dinner. Nobody exactly knew who the other gentleman, Mr. Bland-ford, really was, but he had the reputation of being enormously rich, and was proportionately respected. He had been about town for the last twenty years, and did not look a day older than at his first appearance. He never spoke of his family, was unmarried, and apparently had no relations; but he had contrived to identify himself with the first men in London, was a member of every club of great repute, and of late years had even become a sort of authority; which was strange, for he had no pretension, was very quiet, and but humbly ambitious; seeking, indeed, no happier success than to merge in the brilliant crowd, an accepted atom of the influential aggregate. As he was not remarkable for his talents or his person, and as his establishment, though well appointed, offered no singular splendour, it was rather strange that a gentleman who had apparently dropped from the clouds, or crept out of a kennel, should have succeeded in planting himself so vigorously in a soil which shrinks from anything not indigenous, unless it be recommended by very powerful qualities. But Mr. Bland-ford was good-tempered, and was now easy and experienced, and there was a vague tradition that he was immensely rich, a rumour which Mr. Blandford always contradicted in a manner which skilfully confirmed its truth.

'Does Mirabel dine with you, Sharpe?' enquired Lord Castlefyshe of his host, who nodded assent. 'You won't wait for him, I hope?' said his lordship. 'By-the-bye, Blandford, you shirked last night.'

'I promised to look in at the poor duke's before he went off,' said Mr. Blandford.

'Oh! he has gone, has he?' said Lord Castlefyshe. 'Does he take his cook with him?'

But here the servant ushered in Count Alcibiades de Mirabel, Charles Doricourt, and Mr. Bevil. 'Excellent Sharpe, how do you do?' exclaimed the Count. 'Castlefyshe, what bêtises have you been talking to Crocky about Felix Winchester? Good Blandford, excellent Blandford, how is my good Blandford?'

Mr. Bevil was a tall and handsome young man, of a great family and great estate, who passed his life in an imitation of Count Alcibiades de Mirabel. He was always dressed by the same tailor, and it was his pride that his cab or his vis-à-vis was constantly mistaken for the equipage of his model; and really now, as the shade stood beside its substance, quite as tall, almost as good-looking, with the satin-lined coat thrown open with the same style of flowing grandeur, and revealing a breastplate of starched cambric scarcely less broad and brilliant, the uninitiated might have held the resemblance as perfect. The wristbands were turned up with not less compact precision, and were fastened by jewelled studs that glittered with not less radiancy. The satin waistcoat, the creaseless hosen, were the same; and if the foot were not quite as small, its Parisian polish was not less bright. But here, unfortunately, Mr. Bevil's mimetic powers deserted him.

We start, for soul is wanting there!

The Count Mirabel could talk at all times, and at all times well; Mr. Bevil never opened his mouth. Practised in the world, the Count Mirabel was nevertheless the child of impulse, though a native grace, and an intuitive knowledge of mankind, made every word pleasing and every act appropriate; Mr. Bevil was all art, and he had not the talent to conceal it. The Count Mirabel was gay, careless, generous; Mr. Bevil was solemn, calculating, and rather a screw. It seemed that the Count Mirabel's feelings grew daily more fresh, and his faculty of enjoyment more keen and relishing; it seemed that Mr. Bevil could never have been a child, but that he must have issued to the world ready equipped, like Minerva, with a cane instead of a lance, and a fancy hat instead of a helmet. His essence of high breeding was never to be astonished, and he never permitted himself to smile, except in the society of intimate friends.

Charles Doricourt was another friend of the Count Mirabel, but not his imitator. His feelings were really worn, but it was a fact he always concealed. He had entered life at a remarkably early age, and had experienced every scrape to which youthful flesh is heir. Any other man but Charles Doricourt must have sunk beneath these accumulated disasters, but Charles Doricourt always swam. Nature had given him an intrepid soul; experience had cased his heart with iron. But he always smiled; and audacious, cool, and cutting, and very easy, he thoroughly despised mankind, upon whose weaknesses he practised without remorse. But he was polished and amusing, and faithful to his friends. The world admired him, and called him Charley, from which it will be inferred that he was a privileged person, and was applauded for a thousand actions, which in anyone else would have been met with decided reprobation.

'Who is that young man?' enquired the Count Mirabel of Mr. Bond Sharpe, taking his host aside, and pretending to look at a picture.

'He is Captain Armine, the only son of Sir Ratcliffe Armine. He has just returned to England after a long absence.'

'Hum! I like his appearance,' said the Count. 'It is very distinguished.'

Dinner and Lord Catchimwhocan were announced at the same moment; Captain Armine found himself seated next to the Count Mirabel. The dinners at Mr. Bond Sharpe's were dinners which his guests came to eat. Mr. Bond Sharpe had engaged for his club-house the most celebrated of living artists, a gentleman who, it was said, received a thousand a-year, whose convenience was studied by a chariot, and amusement secured by a box at the French play. There was, therefore, at first little conversation, save criticism on the performances before them, and that chiefly panegyrical; each dish was delicious, each wine exquisite; and yet, even in these occasional remarks, Ferdinand was pleased with the lively fancy of his neighbour, affording an elegant contrast to the somewhat gross unction with which Lord Castlefyshe, whose very soul seemed wrapped up in his occupation, occasionally expressed himself.

'Will you take some wine, Captain Armine?' said the Count Mirabel, with a winning smile. 'You have recently returned here?'

'Very recently,' said Ferdinand.

'And you are glad?'

'As it may be; I hardly know whether to rejoice or not.'

'Then, by all means rejoice,' said the Count; 'for, if you are in doubt, it surely must be best to decide upon being pleased.'

'I think this is the most infernal country there ever was,' said Lord Catchimwhocan.

'My dear Catch!' said the Count Mirabel, 'you think so, do you? You make a mistake, you think no such thing, my dear Catch. Why is it the most infernal? Is it because the women are the handsomest, or because the horses are the best? Is it because it is the only country where you can get a good dinner, or because it is the only country where there are fine wines? Or is it because it is the only place where you can get a coat made, or where you can play without being cheated, or where you can listen to an opera without your ears being destroyed? Now, my dear Catch, you pass your life in dressing and in playing hazard, in eating good dinners, in drinking good wines, in making love, in going to the opera, and in riding fine horses. Of what, then, have you to complain?'

'Oh! the damned climate!'

'On the contrary, it is the only good climate there is. In England you can go out every day, and at all hours; and then, to those who love variety, like myself, you are not sure of seeing the same sky every morning you rise, which, for my part, I think the greatest of all existing sources of ennui.'

'You reconcile me to my country, Count,' said Ferdinand, smiling.

'Ah! you are a sensible man; but that dear Catch is always repeating nonsense which he hears from somebody else. To-morrow,' he added, in a low voice, 'he will be for the climate.'

The conversation of men, when they congregate together, is generally dedicated to one of two subjects: politics or women. In the present instance the party was not political; and it was the fair sex, and particularly the most charming portion of it, in the good metropolis of England, that were subject to the poignant criticism or the profound speculation of these practical philosophers. There was scarcely a celebrated beauty in London, from the proud peeress to the vain opera-dancer, whose charms and conduct were not submitted to their masterly analysis. And yet it would be but fair to admit that their critical ability was more eminent and satisfactory than their abstract reasoning upon this interesting topic; for it was curious to observe that, though everyone present piqued himself upon his profound knowledge of the sex, not two of the sages agreed in the constituent principles of female character. One declared that women were governed by their feelings; another maintained that they had no heart; a third propounded that it was all imagination; a fourth that it was all vanity. Lord Castlefyshe muttered something about their passions; and Charley Doricourt declared that they had no passions whatever. But they all agreed in one thing, to wit, that the man who permitted himself a moment's uneasiness about a woman was a fool.

All this time Captain Armine spoke little, but ever to the purpose, and chiefly to the Count Mirabel, who pleased him. Being very handsome, and, moreover, of a distinguished appearance, this silence on the part of Ferdinand made him a general favourite, and even Mr. Bevil whispered his approbation to Lord Catchimwhocan.

'The fact is,' said Charles Doricourt, 'it is only boys and old men who are plagued by women. They take advantage of either state of childhood. Eh! Castlefyshe?'

'In that respect, then, somewhat resembling you, Charley,' replied his lordship, who did not admire the appeal. 'For no one can doubt you plagued your father; I was out of my teens, fortunately, before you played écarté.'

'Come, good old Fyshe,' said Count Mirabel, 'take a glass of claret, and do not look so fierce. You know very well that Charley learned everything of you.'

'He never learned from me to spend a fortune upon an actress,' said his lordship. 'I ave spent a fortune, but, thank heaven, it was on myself.'

'Well, as for that,' said the Count, 'I think there is something great in being ruined for one's friends. If I were as rich as I might have been, I would not spend much on myself. My wants are few; a fine house, fine carriages, fine horses, a complete wardrobe, the best opera-box, the first cook, and pocket-money; that is all I require. I have these, and I get on pretty well; but if I had a princely fortune I would make every good fellow I know quite happy.'

'Well,' said Charles Doricourt, 'you are a lucky fellow, Mirabel. I have had horses, houses, carriages, opera-boxes, and cooks, and I have had a great estate; but pocket-money I never could get. Pocket-money was the thing which always cost me the most to buy of all.'

The conversation now fell upon the theatre. Mr. Bond Sharpe was determined to have a theatre. He believed it was reserved for him to revive the drama. Mr. Bond Sharpe piqued himself upon his patronage of the stage. He certainly had a great admiration of actresses. There was something in the management of a great theatre which pleased the somewhat imperial fancy of Mr. Bond Sharpe. The manager of a great theatre is a kind of monarch. Mr. Bond Sharpe longed to seat himself on the throne, with the prettiest women in London for his court, and all his fashionable friends rallying round their sovereign. He had an impression that great results might be obtained with his organising energy and illimitable capital. Mr. Bond Sharpe had unbounded confidence in the power of capital. Capital was his deity. He was confident that it could always produce alike genius and triumph. Mr. Bond Sharpe was right: capital is a wonderful thing, but we are scarcely aware of this fact until we are past thirty; and then, by some singular process, which we will not now stop to analyse, one's capital is in general sensibly diminished. As men advance in life, all passions resolve themselves into money. Love, ambition, even poetry, end in this.

'Are you going to Shropshire's this autumn, Charley?' said Lord Catchimwhocan.

'Yes, I shall go.'

'I don't think I shall,' said his lordship; 'it is such a bore.'

'It is rather a bore; but he is a good fellow.'

'I shall go,' said Count Mirabel.

'You are not afraid of being bored,' said Ferdinand, smiling.

'Between ourselves, I do not understand what this being bored is,' said the Count. 'He who is bored appears to me a bore. To be bored supposes the inability of being amused; you must be a dull fellow. Wherever I may be, I thank heaven that I am always diverted.'

'But you have such nerves, Mirabel,' said Lord Catchimwhocan. 'By Jove! I envy you. You are never floored.'

'Floored! what an idea! What should floor me? I live to amuse myself, and I do nothing that does not amuse me. Why should I be floored?'

'Why, I do not know; but every other man is floored now and then. As for me, my spirits are sometimes something dreadful.'

'When you have been losing.'

'Well, we cannot always win. Can we, Sharpe? That would not do. But, by Jove! you are always in good humour, Mirabel, when you lose.'

'Fancy a man ever being in low spirits,' said the Count Mirabel. 'Life is too short for such bêtises. The most unfortunate wretch alive calculates unconsciously that it is better to live than to die. Well, then, he has something in his favour. Existence is a pleasure, and the greatest. The world cannot rob us of that; and if it is better to live than to die, it is better to live in a good humour than a bad one. If a man be convinced that existence is the greatest pleasure, his happiness may be increased by good fortune, but it will be essentially independent of it. He who feels that the greatest source of pleasure always remains to him ought never to be miserable. The sun shines on all: every man can go to sleep: if you cannot ride a fine horse, it is something to look upon one; if you have not a fine dinner, there is some amusement in a crust of bread and Gruyère. Feel slightly, think little, never plan, never brood. Everything depends upon the circulation; take care of it. Take the world as you find it; enjoy everything. Vive la bagatelle!'

Here the gentlemen rose, took their coffee, and ordered their carriages.

'Come with us,' said Count Mirabel to Ferdinand.

Our hero accepted the offer of his agreeable acquaintance. There was a great prancing and rushing of cabs and vis-à-vis at Mr. Bond Sharpe's door, and in a few minutes the whole party were dashing up St. James'-street, where they stopped before a splendid building, resplendent with lights and illuminated curtains.

'Come, we will make you an honorary member, mon cher Captain Armine,' said the Count; 'and do not say Lasciate ogni speranza when you enter here.'

They ascended a magnificent staircase, and entered a sumptuous and crowded saloon, in which the entrance of Count Mirabel and his friends made no little sensation. Mr. Bond Sharpe glided along, dropping oracular sentences, without condescending to stop to speak to those whom he addressed. Charley Doricourt and Mr. Blandford walked away together, towards a further apartment. Lord Castlefyshe and Lord Catchimwhocan were soon busied with écarté.

'Well, Faneville, good general, how do you do?' said Count Mirabel. 'Where have you dined to-day? at the Balcombes'? You are a very brave man, mon general! Ah! Stock, good Stock, excellent Stock!' he continued, addressing Mr. Million de Stockville, 'that Burgundy you sent me is capital. How are you, my dear fellow? Quite well? Fitzwarrene, I did that for you: your business is all right. Ah! my good Massey, mon cher, mon brave, Anderson will let you have that horse. And what is doing here? Is there any fun? Fitzwarrene, let me introduce you to my friend Captain Armine:' (in a lower tone) 'excellent garçon! You will like him very much. We have been all dining at Bond's.'

'A good dinner?'

'Of course a good dinner. I should like to see a man who would give me a bad dinner: that would be a bêtise,—to ask me to dine, and then give me a bad dinner.'

'I say, Mirabel,' exclaimed a young man, 'have you seen Horace Poppington about the match?'

'It is arranged; 'tis the day after to-morrow, at nine o'clock.'

'Well, I bet on you, you know.'

'Of course you bet on me. Would you think of betting on that good Pop, with that gun? Pah! Eh! bien! I shall go in the next room.' And the Count walked away, followed by Mr. Bevil.

Ferdinand remained talking for some time with Lord Fitzwarrene. By degrees the great saloon had become somewhat thinner: some had stolen away to the House, where a division was expected; quiet men, who just looked in after dinner, had retired; and the play-men were engaged in the contiguous apartments. Mr. Bond Sharpe approached Ferdinand, and Lord Fitzwarrene took this opportunity of withdrawing.

'I believe you never play, Captain Armine,' said Mr. Bond Sharpe.

'Never,' said Ferdinand.

'You are quite right.'

'I am rather surprised at your being of that opinion,' said Ferdinand, with a smile.

Mr. Bond Sharpe shrugged his shoulders. 'There will always be votaries enough,' said Mr. Bond Sharpe, 'whatever may be my opinion.'

'This is a magnificent establishment of yours,' said Ferdinand.

'Yes; it is a very magnificent establishment. I have spared no expense to produce the most perfect thing of the kind in Europe; and it is the most perfect thing of the kind. I am confident that no noble in any country has an establishment better appointed. I despatched an agent to the Continent to procure this furniture: his commission had no limit, and he was absent two years.

My cook was with Charles X.; the cellar is the most choice and considerable that was ever collected. I take a pride in the thing, but I lose money by it.'

'Indeed!'

'I have made a fortune; there is no doubt of that; but I did not make it here.'

'It is a great thing to make a fortune,' said Ferdinand.

'Very great,' said Mr. Bond Sharpe. 'There is only one thing greater, and that is, to keep it when made.'

Ferdinand smiled.

'Many men make fortunes; few can keep them,' said Mr. Bond Sharpe. 'Money is power, and rare are the heads that can withstand the possession of great power.'

'At any rate, it is to be hoped that you have discovered this more important secret,' said Ferdinand; 'though I confess to judge from my own experience, I should fear that you are too generous.'

'I had forgotten that to which you allude,' said his companion, quietly. 'But with regard to myself, whatever may be my end, I have not yet reached my acme.'

'You have at least my good wishes,' said Ferdinand.

'I may some day claim them,' said Mr. Bond Sharpe. 'My position,' he continued, 'is difficult. I have risen by pursuits which the world does not consider reputable, yet if I had not had recourse to them, I should be less than nothing. My mind, I think, is equal to my fortune; I am still young, and I would now avail myself of my power and establish myself in the land, a recognised member of society. But this cannot be. Society shrinks from an obscure foundling, a prizefighter, a leg, a hell-keeper, and an usurer. Debarred therefore from a fair theatre for my energy and capital, I am forced to occupy, perhaps exhaust, myself in multiplied speculations. Hitherto they have flourished, and perhaps my theatre, or my newspaper, may be as profitable as my stud. But I would gladly emancipate myself. These efforts seem to me, as it were, unnecessary and unnatural. The great object has been gained. It is a tempting of fate. I have sometimes thought myself the Napoleon of the sporting world; I may yet find my St. Helena.' 'Forewarned, forearmed, Mr. Sharpe.' 'I move in a magic circle: it is difficult to extricate myself from it. Now, for instance, there is not a man in the room who is not my slave. You see how they treat me. They place me upon an equality with them. They know my weakness; they fool me to the top of my bent. And yet there is not a man in that room who, if I were to break to-morrow, would walk down St. James'-street to serve me. Yes! there is one; there is the Count. He has a great and generous soul. I believe Count Mirabel sympathises with my situation. I believe he does not think, because a man has risen from an origin the most ignoble and obscure to a powerful position, by great courage and dexterity, and let me add also, by some profound thought, by struggling too, be it remembered, with a class of society as little scrupulous, though not so skilful as himself, that he is necessarily an infamous character. What if, at eighteen years of age, without a friend in the world, trusting to the powerful frame and intrepid spirit with which Nature had endowed me, I flung myself into the ring? Who should be a gladiator if I were not? Is that a crime? What if, at a later period, with a brain for calculation which none can rival, I invariably succeeded in that in which the greatest men in the country fail! Am I to be branded because I have made half a million by a good book? What if I have kept a gambling-house? From the back parlour of an oyster-shop my hazard table has been removed to this palace. Had the play been foul, this metamorphosis would never have occurred. It is true I am an usurer. My dear sir, if all the usurers in this great metropolis could only pass in procession before you at this moment, how you would start! You might find some Right Honourables among them; many a great functionary, many a grave magistrate; fathers of families, the very models of respectable characters, patrons and presidents of charitable institutions, and subscribers for the suppression of those very gaming-houses whose victims, in nine cases out of ten, are their principal customers. I speak not in bitterness. On the whole, I must not complain of the world, but I have seen a great deal of mankind, and more than most, of what is considered its worst portion. The world, Captain Armine, believe me, is neither so bad nor so good as some are apt to suppose. And after all,' said Mr. Bond Sharpe, shrugging up his shoulders, 'perhaps we ought to say with our friend the Count, Vive la bagatelle! Will you take some supper?'

CHAPTER XIV.

Miss Grandison Piques the Curiosity of Lord Montfort, and
Count Mirabel Drives Ferdinand Down to Richmond, Which
Drive Ends in an Agreeable Adventure and an Unexpected
Confidence.

THE discovery that Henrietta Temple was the secret object of Ferdinand's unhappy passion, was
a secret which Miss Grandison prized like a true woman. Not only had she made this discovery,
but from her previous knowledge and her observation during her late interview with Miss
Temple, Katherine was persuaded that Henrietta must still love her cousin as before. Miss
Grandison was attached to Henrietta; she was interested in her cousin's welfare, and devoted to
the Armine family. All her thoughts and all her energies were engaged in counteracting, if
possible, the consequences of those unhappy misconceptions which had placed them all in this
painful position.

It was on the next day that she had promised to accompany the duchess and Henrietta on a water
excursion. Lord Montfort was to be their cavalier. In the morning she found herself alone with
his lordship in St. James'-square.

'What a charming day!' said Miss Grandison. 'I anticipate so much pleasure! Who is our party?'

'Ourselves alone,' said Lord Montfort. 'Lady Armine cannot come, and Captain Armine is
engaged. I fear you will find it very dull, Miss Grandison.'

'Oh! not at all. By-the-bye, do you know I was surprised yesterday at finding that Ferdinand and
Henrietta were such old acquaintances.'

'Were you?' said Lord Montfort, in a peculiar tone.

'It is odd that Ferdinand never will go with us anywhere. I think it is very bad taste.'

'I think so too,' said Lord Montfort.

'I should have thought that Henrietta was the very person he would have admired; that he would
have been quite glad to be with us. I can easily understand his being wearied to death with a
cousin,' said Miss Grandison; 'but Henrietta,—it is so strange that he should not avail himself of
the delight of being with her.'

'Do you really think that such a cousin as Miss Grandison can drive him away?'

'Why, to tell you the truth, dear Lord Montfort, Ferdinand is placed in a very awkward position
with me. You are our friend, and so I speak to you in confidence. Sir Ratcliffe and Lady Armine
both expect that Ferdinand and myself are going to be married. Now, neither of us has the
slightest intention of anything of the sort.'

'Very strange, indeed,' said Lord Montfort. 'The world will be much astonished, more so than
myself, for I confess to a latent suspicion on the subject.'

'Yes, I was aware of that,' said Miss Grandison, 'or I should not have spoken with so much
frankness. For my own part, I think we are very wise to insist upon having our own way, for an
ill-assorted marriage must be a most melancholy business.' Miss Grandison spoke with an air
almost of levity, which was rather unusual with her.

'An ill-assorted marriage,' said Lord Montfort. 'And what do you call an ill-assorted marriage,
Miss Grandison?'

'Why, many circumstances might constitute such an union,' said Katherine; 'but I think if one of the parties were in love with another person, that would be quite sufficient to ensure a tolerable portion of wretchedness.'

'I think so too,' said Lord Montfort; 'an union, under such circumstances, would be ill-assorted. But Miss Grandison is not in that situation?' he added with a faint smile.

'That is scarcely a fair question,' said Katherine, with gaiety, 'but there is no doubt Ferdinand Armine is.'

'Indeed!'

'Yes; he is in love, desperately in love; that I have long discovered. I wonder with whom it can be!'

'I wonder!' said Lord Montfort.

'Do you?' said Miss Grandison. 'Well, I have sometimes thought that you might have a latent suspicion of that subject, too. I thought you were his confidant.'

'I!' said Lord Montfort; 'I, of all men in the world?'

'And why not you of all men in the world?' said Miss Grandison.

'Our intimacy is so slight,' said Lord Montfort.

'Hum!' said Miss Grandison. 'And now I think of it, it does appear to me very strange how we have all become suddenly such intimate friends. The Armines and your family not previously acquainted: Miss Temple, too, unknown to my aunt and uncle. And yet we never live now out of each other's sight. I am sure I am grateful for it; I am sure it is very agreeable, but still it does appear to me to be very odd. I wonder what the reason can be?'

'It is that you are so charming, Miss Grandison,' said Lord Montfort.

'A compliment from you!'

'Indeed, no compliment, dearest Miss Grandison,' said Lord Montfort, drawing near her. 'Favoured as Miss Temple is in so many respects, in none, in my opinion, is she more fortunate than in the possession of so admirable a friend.'

'Not even in the possession of so admirable a lover, my lord?'

'All must love Miss Temple who are acquainted with her,' said Lord Montfort, seriously.

'Indeed, I think so,' said Katherine, in a more subdued voice. 'I love her; her career fills me with a strange and singular interest. May she be happy, for happiness she indeed deserves!'

'I have no fonder wish than to secure that happiness, Miss Grandison,' said Lord Montfort; 'by any means,' he added.

'She is so interesting!' said Katherine. 'When you first knew her she was very ill?'

'Very.'

'She seems quite recovered.'

'I hope so.'

'Mr. Temple says her spirits are not what they used to be. I wonder what was the matter with her?'

Lord Montfort was silent.

'I cannot bear to see a fine spirit broken,' continued Miss Grandison. 'There was Ferdinand. Oh! if you had but known my cousin before he was unhappy. Oh! that was a spirit! He was the most brilliant being that ever lived. And then I was with him during all his illness. It was so terrible. I almost wish we could have loved each other. It is very strange, he must have been ill at Armine, at the very time Henrietta was ill in Italy. And I was with him in England, while you were solacing her. And now we are all friends. There seems a sort of strange destiny in our lots, does there not?'

'A happy lot that can in any way be connected with Miss Grandison,' said Lord Montfort.

At this moment her Grace and Henrietta entered; the carriage was ready; and in a few minutes they were driving to Whitehall Stairs, where a beautiful boat awaited them.

In the mean time, Ferdinand Armine was revolving the strange occurrences of yesterday. Altogether it was an exciting and satisfactory day. In the first place, he had extricated himself from his most pressing difficulties; in the next, he had been greatly amused; and thirdly, he had made a very interesting acquaintance, for such he esteemed Count Mirabel. Just at the moment when, lounging over a very late breakfast, he was thinking of Bond Sharpe and his great career, and then turning in his mind whether it were possible to follow the gay counsels of his friends of yesterday, and never plague himself about a woman again, the Count Mirabel was announced.

Mon cher Armine,' said the Count, 'you see I kept my promise, and would find you at home.'

The Count stood before him, the best-dressed man in London, fresh and gay as a bird, with not a care on his sparkling visage, and his eye bright with bonhomie. And yet Count Mirabel had been the very last to desert the recent mysteries of Mr. Bond Sharpe; and, as usual, the dappled light of dawn had guided him to his luxurious bed, that bed which always afforded him serene slumbers, whatever might be the adventures of the day, or the result of the night's campaign. How the Count Mirabel did laugh at those poor devils who wake only to moralise over their own folly with broken spirits and aching heads! Care he knew nothing about; Time he defied; indisposition he could not comprehend. He had never been ill in his life, even for five minutes.

Ferdinand was really very glad to see him; there was something in Count Mirabel's very presence which put everybody in good spirits. His lightheartedness was caught by all. Melancholy was a farce in the presence of his smile; and there was no possible combination of scrapes that could withstand his kind and brilliant raillery. At the present moment, Ferdinand was in a sufficiently good humour with his destiny, and he kept up the ball with effect; so that nearly an hour passed in amusing conversation.

'You were a stranger among us yesterday,' said Count Mirabel; 'I think you were rather diverted. I saw you did justice to that excellent Bond Sharpe. That shows that you have a mind above prejudice. Do you know he was by far the best man at the table except ourselves?'

Ferdinand smiled.

'It is true, he has a heart and a brain. Old Castlefyshe has neither. As for the rest of our friends, some have hearts without brains, and the rest brains without hearts. Which do you prefer?'

"Tis a fine question,' said Ferdinand; 'and yet I confess I should like to be callous.'

'Ah! but you cannot be,' said the Count, 'you have a soul of great sensibility; I see that in a moment.'

'You see very far, and very quickly, Count Mirabel,' said Ferdinand, with a little reserve.

'Yes; in a minute,' said the Count, 'in a minute I read a person's character. I know you are very much in love, because you changed countenance yesterday when we were talking of women.'

Ferdinand changed countenance again. 'You are a very extraordinary man, Count,' he at length observed.

'Of course; but, mon cher Armine, what a fine day this is! What are you going to do with yourself?'

'Nothing; I never do anything,' said Ferdinand, in an almost mournful tone.

'A melancholy man! Quelle bêtise! I will cure you. I will be your friend and put you all right. Now, we will just drive down to Richmond; we will have a light dinner, a flounder, a cutlet, and a bottle of champagne, and then we will go to the French play. I will introduce you to Jenny Vertpré. She is full of wit; perhaps she will ask us to supper. Allons, mon ami, mon cher Armine; allons, mon brave!' Ceremony was a farce with Alcibiades de Mirabel.

Ferdinand had nothing to do; he was attracted to his companion. The effervescence produced by yesterday's fortunate adventure had not quite subsided; he was determined to forget his sorrows, and, if only for a day, join in the lively chorus of Vive la bagatelle! So, in a few moments, he was safely ensconced in the most perfect cabriolet in London, whirled along by a horse that stepped out with a proud consciousness of its master.

The Count Mirabel enjoyed the drive to Richmond as if he had never been to Richmond in his life. The warm sun, the western breeze, every object he passed and that passed him called for his praise or observation. He inoculated Ferdinand with his gaiety, as Ferdinand listened to his light, lively tales, and his flying remarks, so full of merriment and poignant truth and daring fancy. When they had arrived at the Star and Garter, and ordered their dinner, they strolled into the Park, along the Terrace walk; and they had not proceeded fifty paces when they came up with the duchess and her party, who were resting on a bench and looking over the valley.

Ferdinand would gladly have bowed and passed on; but that was impossible. He was obliged to stop and speak to them, and it was difficult to disembarrass himself of friends who greeted him so kindly. Ferdinand presented his companion. The ladies were charmed to know so celebrated a gentleman, of whom they had heard so much. Count Mirabel, who had the finest tact in the world, but whose secret spell, after all, was perhaps only that he was always natural, adapted himself in a moment to the characters, the scene, and the occasion. He was quite delighted at these sources of amusement, that had so unexpectedly revealed themselves; and in a few minutes they had all agreed to walk together, and in due time the duchess was begging Ferdinand and his friend to dine with them. Before Ferdinand could frame an excuse, Count Mirabel had accepted the proposition. After passing the morning together so agreeably, to go and dine in separate rooms, it would be a bêtise. This word bêtise settled everything with Count Mirabel; when once he declared that anything was a bêtise, he would hear no more.

It was a charming stroll. Never was Count Mirabel more playful, more engaging, more completely winning. Henrietta and Katherine alike smiled upon him, and the duchess was quite enchanted. Even Lord Montfort, who might rather have entertained a prejudice against the Count before he knew him—though none could after—and who was prepared for something rather brilliant, but pretending, presumptuous, fantastic, and affected, quite yielded to his amiable gaiety, and his racy and thoroughly genuine and simple manner. So they walked and talked and laughed, and all agreed that it was the most fortunately fine day and the most felicitous rencontre that had ever occurred, until the dinner hour was at hand. The Count was at her Grace's side, and she was leaning on Miss Temple's arm. Lord Montfort and Miss Grandison had fallen back apace, as their party had increased. Ferdinand fluttered between Miss Temple and his cousin; but would have attached himself to the latter, had not Miss Temple occasionally addressed him. He was glad, however, when they returned to dinner.

'We have only availed ourselves of your Grace's permission to join our dinners,' said Count Mirabel, offering the duchess his arm. He placed himself at the head of the table; Lord Montfort took the other end. To the surprise of Ferdinand, Miss Grandison, with a heedlessness that was quite remarkable, seated herself next to the duchess, so that Ferdinand was obliged to sit by Henrietta Temple, who was thus separated from Lord Montfort.

The dinner was as gay as the stroll. Ferdinand was the only person who was silent.

'How amusing he is!' said Miss Temple, turning to Ferdinand, and speaking in an undertone.

'Yes; I envy him his gaiety.'

'Be gay.'

'I thank you; I dare say I shall in time. I have not yet quite embraced all Count Mirabel's

philosophy. He says that the man who plagues himself for five minutes about a woman is an idiot. When I think the same, which I hope I may soon, I dare say I shall be as gay.'
Miss Temple addressed herself no more to Ferdinand.

They returned by water. To Ferdinand's great annoyance, the Count did not hesitate for a moment to avail himself of the duchess's proposal that he and his companion should form part of the crew. He gave immediate orders that his cabriolet should meet him at Whitehall Stairs, and Ferdinand found there was no chance of escape.

It was a delicious summer evening. The setting sun bathed the bowers of Fulham with refulgent light, just as they were off delicate Rosebank; but the air long continued warm, and always soft, and the last few miles of their pleasant voyage were tinted by the young and glittering moon.

'I wish we had brought a guitar,' said Miss Grandison; 'Count Mirabel, I am sure, would sing to us?' 'And you, you will sing to us without a guitar, will you not?' said the Count, smiling. 'Henrietta, will you sing?' said Miss Grandison. 'With you.'

'Of course; now you must,' said the Count: so they did.

This gliding home to the metropolis on a summer eve, so soft and still, with beautiful faces, as should always be the case, and with sweet sounds, as was the present—there is something very ravishing in the combination. The heart opens; it is a dangerous moment. As Ferdinand listened once more to the voice of Henrietta, even though it was blended with the sweet tones of Miss Grandison, the passionate past vividly recurred to him. Fortunately he did not sit near her; he had taken care to be the last in the boat. He turned away his face, but its stern expression did not escape the observation of the Count Mirabel.

'And now, Count Mirabel, you must really favour us,' said the duchess.

'Without a guitar?' said the Count, and he began thrumming on his arm for an accompaniment. 'Well, when I was with the Duc d'Angoulême in Spain, we sometimes indulged in a serenade at Seville. I will try to remember one.'

A SERENADE OF SEVILLE.

I.

Come forth, come   forth, the star we love
Is high o'er Guadalquivir's grove,
And tints each tree with golden light;
Ah! Rosalie, one smile from thee were far more bright.

II.

Come forth, come forth, the flowers that fear
To blossom in the sun's career
The moonlight with their odours greet;
Ah! Rosalie, one sigh from thee were far more sweet!

III.

Come forth, come forth, one hour of night,
When flowers are fresh and stars are bright,
Were worth an age of gaudy day;
Then, Rosalie, fly, fly to me, nor longer stay!

'I hope the lady came,' said Miss Temple, 'after such a pretty song.'

'Of course,' said the Count, 'they always come.'

'Ferdinand, will you sing?' said Miss Grandison.

'I cannot, Katherine.'

'Henrietta, ask Ferdinand to sing,' said Miss Grandison; 'he makes it a rule never to do anything I ask him, but I am sure you have more influence.'

Lord Montfort came to the rescue of Miss Temple. 'Miss Temple has spoken so often to us of your singing, Captain Armine,' said his lordship; and yet Lord Montfort, in this allegation, a little departed front the habitual exactitude of his statements.

'How very strange!' thought Ferdinand; 'her callousness or her candour baffles me. I will try to sing,' he continued aloud, 'but it is a year, really, since I have sung.'

In a voice of singular power and melody, and with an expression which increased as he proceeded, until the singer seemed scarcely able to control his emotions, Captain Armine thus proceeded:—

CAPTAIN ARMINE'S SONG.

I.

My heart is like a silent lute
Some faithless hand has thrown aside;
Those chords are dumb, those tones are mute,
That once sent forth a voice of pride!
Yet even o'er the lute neglected
The wind of heaven will sometimes fly,
And even thus the heart dejected,
Will sometimes answer to a sigh!

II.

And yet to feel another's power
May grasp the prize for which I pine,
And others now may pluck the flower
I cherished for this heart of mine!
No more, no more! The hand forsaking,
The lute must fall, and shivered lie
In silence: and my heart thus breaking,
Responds not even to a sigh.

Miss Temple seemed busied with her shawl; perhaps she felt the cold. Count Mirabel, next whom she sat, was about to assist her. Her face was turned to the water; it was streaming with tears. Without appearing to notice her, Count Mirabel leant forward, and engaged everybody's attention; so that she was unobserved and had time to recover. And yet she was aware that the Count Mirabel had remarked her emotion, and was grateful for his quick and delicate consideration. It was fortunate that Westminster-bridge was now in sight, for after this song of Captain Armine, everyone became dull or pensive; even Count Mirabel was silent.

The ladies and Lord Montfort entered their britzka. They bid a cordial adieu to Count Mirabel, and begged him to call upon them in St. James'-square, and the Count and Ferdinand were alone.

'Cher Armine,' said the Count, as he was driving up Charing-cross, 'Catch told me you were going to marry your cousin. Which of those two young ladies is your cousin?'

'The fair girl; Miss Grandison.'

'So I understood. She is very pretty, but you are not going to marry her, are you?'

'No; I am not.'

'And who is Miss Temple?'

'She is going to be married to Lord Montfort.'

'Diable! But what a fortunate man! What do you think of Miss Temple?'

'I think of her as all, I suppose, must.'

'She is beautiful: she is the most beautiful woman I ever saw. She marries for money, I suppose?'

'She is the richest heiress in England; she is much richer than my cousin.'

'C'est drôle. But she does not want to marry Lord Montfort.'

'Why?'

'Because, my dear fellow, she is in love with you.'

'By Jove, Mirabel, what a fellow you are! What do you mean?'

'Mon cher Armine, I like you more than anybody. I wish to be, I am, your friend. Here is some cursed contretemps. There is a mystery, and both of you are victims of it. Tell me everything. I will put you right.'

'Ah! my dear Mirabel, it is past even your skill. I thought I could never speak on these things to human being, but I am attracted to you by the same sympathy which you flatter me by expressing for myself. I want a confidant, I need a friend; I am most wretched.'

'Eh! bien! we will not go to the French play. As for Jenny Vertpré, we can sup with her any night. Come to my house, and we will talk over everything. But trust me, if you wish to marry Henrietta Temple, you are an idiot if you do not have her.'

So saying, the Count touched his bright horse, and in a few minutes the cabriolet stopped before a small but admirably appointed house in Berkeley-square.

'Now, mon cher,' said the Count, 'coffee and confidence.'

CHAPTER XV.

In Which the Count Mirabel Commences His Operations with
Great Success.

IS THERE a more gay and graceful spectacle in the world than Hyde Park, at the end of a long
sunny morning in the merry months of May and June? Where can we see such beautiful women,
such gallant cavaliers, such fine horses, and such brilliant equipages? The scene, too, is worthy
of such agreeable accessories: the groves, the gleaming waters, and the triumphal arches. In the
distance, the misty heights of Surrey, and the bowery glades of Kensington.

It was the day after the memorable voyage from Richmond. Eminent among the glittering throng,
Count Mirabel cantered along on his Arabian, scattering gay recognitions and bright words. He
reined in his steed beneath a tree, under whose shade was assembled a knot of listless cavaliers.
The Count received their congratulations, for this morning he had won his pigeon match.

'Only think of that old fool, Castlefyshe, betting on Poppington,' said the Count. 'I want to see
him, old idiot! Who knows where Charley is?'

'I do, Mirabel,' said Lord Catchimwhocan. 'He has gone to Richmond with Blandford and the two
little Furzlers.'

'That good Blandford! Whenever he is in love he always gives a dinner. It is a droll way to
succeed.'

'Apropos, will you dine with me to-day, Mirabel?' said Mr. de Stockville.

'Impossible, my dear fellow; I dine with Fitz-warrene.'

'I say, Mirabel,' drawled out a young man, 'I saw you yesterday driving a man down to Richmond
yourself. Who is your friend?'

'No one you know, or will know. 'Tis the best fellow that ever lived; but he is under my
guidance, and I shall be very particular to whom he is introduced.'

'Lord! I wonder who he can be!' said the young man.

'I say, Mirabel, you will be done on Goshawk, if you don't take care, I can tell you that.'

'Thank you, good Coventry; if you like to bet the odds, I will take them.'

'No, my dear fellow, I do not want to bet, but at the same time————'

'You have an opinion that you will not back. That is a luxury, for certainly it is of no, use. I
would advise you to enjoy it.'

'Well, I must say, Mirabel,' said Lord Catchimwhocan, 'I think the same about Goshawk.'

'Oh, no, Catch, you do not think so; you think you think. Go and take all the odds you can get
upon Goshawk. Come, now, to-morrow you will tell me you have a very pretty book. Eh! mon
cher Catch?'

'But do you really think Goshawk will win?' asked Lord Cathimwhocan, earnestly.

'Certain!'

'Well, damned if I don't go and take the odds,' said his lordship.

'Mirabel,' said a young noble, moving his horse close to the Count, and speaking in a low voice,
'shall you be at home to-morrow morning?'

'Certainly. But what do you want?'

'I am in a devil of a scrape; I do not know what to do. I want you to advise me.'

'The Count moved aside with this cavalier. 'And what is it?' said he. 'Have you been losing?'

'No, no,' said the young man, shaking his head. 'Much worse. It is the most infernal business; I do not know what I shall do. I think I shall cut my throat.'

'Bêtise! It cannot be very bad, if it be not money.'

'Oh, my dear Mirabel, you do not know what trouble I am in.'

'Mon cher Henri, soyez tranquille,' said the Count, in a kind voice. 'I am your friend. Rest assured, I will arrange it. Think no more of it until to-morrow at one o'clock, and then call on me. If you like, I am at your service at present.'

'No, no, not here: there are letters.'

'Ha, ha! Well, to-morrow, at one. In the meantime, do not write any nonsense.'

At this moment, the duchess, with a party of equestrians, passed and bowed to the Count Mirabel.

'I say, Mirabel,' exclaimed a young man, 'who is that girl? I want to know. I have seen her several times lately. By Jove, she is a fine creature!'

'Do not you know Miss Temple?' said the Count. 'Fancy a man not knowing Miss Temple! She is the only woman in London to be looked at.'

Now there was a great flutter in the band, and nothing but the name of Miss Temple was heard. All vowed they knew her very well, at least by sight, and never thought of anybody else. Some asked the Count to present them, others meditated plans by which that great result might be obtained; but, in the midst of all this agitation, Count Mirabel rode away, and was soon by the very lady's side.

'What a charming voyage yesterday,' said the Count to Miss Temple. 'You were amused?'

'Very.'

'And to think you should all know my friend Armine so well! I was astonished, for he will never go anywhere, or speak to anyone.'

'You know him intimately?' said Miss Temple.

'He is my brother! There is not a human being in the world I love so much! If you only knew him as I know him. Ah! chère Miss Temple, there is not a man in London to be compared with him, so clever and so good! What a heart! so tender! and what talent! There is no one so spirituel.'

'You have known him long, Count?'

'Always; but of late I find a great change in him. I cannot discover what is the matter with him. He has grown melancholy. I think he will not live.'

'Indeed!'

'No, I am never wrong. That cher Armine will not live.'

'You are his friend, surely———'

'Ah! yes; but I do not know what it is. Even me he cares not for. I contrive sometimes to get him about a little; yesterday, for instance; but to-day, you see, he will not move. There he is, sitting alone, in a dull hotel, with his eyes fixed on the ground, dark as night. Never was a man so changed. I suppose something has happened to him abroad. When you first knew him, I daresay now, he was the gayest of the gay?'

'He was indeed very different,' said Miss Temple, turning away her face.

'You have known that dear Armine a long time?'

'It seems a long time,' said Miss Temple.

'If he dies, and die he must, I do not think I shall ever be in very good spirits again,' said the Count. 'It is the only thing that would quite upset me. Now do not you think, Miss Temple, that our cher Armine is the most interesting person you ever met?'

'I believe Captain Armine is admired by all those who know him.'

'He is so good, so tender, and so clever. Lord Montfort, he knows him very well?'

'They were companions in boyhood, I believe; but they have resumed their acquaintance only recently.'

'We must interest Lord Montfort in his case. Lord Montfort must assist in our endeavours to bring him out a little.'

'Lord Montfort needs no prompting, Count. We are all alike interested in Captain Armine's welfare.'

'I wish you would try to find out what is on his mind,' said Count Mirabel. 'After all, men cannot do much. It requires a more delicate sympathy than we can offer. And yet I would do anything for the cher Armine, because I really love him the same as if he were my brother.'

'He is fortunate in such a friend.'

'Ah! he does not think so any longer,' said the Count; 'he avoids me, he will not tell me anything. Chère Miss Temple, this business haunts me; it will end badly. I know that dear Armine so well; no one knows him like me; his feelings are too strong: no one has such strong feelings. Now, of all my friends, he is the only man I know who is capable of committing suicide.'

'God forbid!' said Henrietta Temple, with emphasis.

'I rise every morning with apprehension,' said the Count. 'When I call upon him every day, I tremble as I approach his hotel.'

'Are you indeed serious?'

'Most serious. I knew a man once in the same state. It was the Duc de Crillon. He was my brother friend, like this dear Armine. We were at college together; we were in the same regiment. He was exactly like this dear Armine, young, beautiful, and clever, but with a heart all tenderness, terrible passions. He loved Mademoiselle de Guise, my cousin, the most beautiful girl in France. Pardon me, but I told Armine yesterday that you reminded me of her. They were going to be married; but there was a contretemps. He sent for me; I was in Spain; she married the Viscount de Marsagnac. Until that dreadful morning he remained exactly in the same state as our dear Armine. Never was a melancholy so profound. After the ceremony he shot himself.'

'No, no!' exclaimed Miss Temple in great agitation.

'Perfectly true. It is the terrible recollection of that dreadful adventure that overcomes me when I see our dear friend here, because I feel it must be love. I was in hopes it was his cousin. But it is not so; it must be something that has happened abroad. Love alone can account for it. It is not his debts that would so overpower him. What are his debts? I would pay them myself. It is a heart-rending business. I am going to him. How I tremble!' 'How good you are!' exclaimed Miss Temple, with streaming eyes. 'I shall ever be grateful; I mean, we all must. Oh! do go to him, go to him directly; tell him to be happy.'

'It is the song I ever sing,' said the Count. 'I wish some of you would come and see him, or send him a message. It is wise to show him that there are some who take interest in his existence. Now, give me that flower, for instance, and let me give it to him from you.'

'He will not care for it,' said Miss Temple. 'Try. It is a fancy I have. Let me bear it.' Miss Temple gave the flower to the Count, who rode off with his prize.

It was about eight o'clock: Ferdinand was sitting alone in his room, having just parted with Glastonbury, who was going to dine in Brook-street. The sun had set, and yet it was scarcely dark enough for artificial light, particularly for a person without a pursuit. It was just that dreary dismal moment, when even the most gay grow pensive, if they be alone. And Ferdinand was particularly dull; a reaction had followed the excitement of the last eight-and-forty hours, and he was at this moment feeling singularly disconsolate, and upbraiding himself for being so weak as to permit himself to be influenced by Mirabel's fantastic promises and projects, when his door flew open, and the Count, full dressed, and graceful as a Versailles Apollo, stood before him. 'Cher ami! I cannot stop one minute. I dine with Fitzwarrene, and I am late. I have done your business capitally. Here is a pretty flower! Who do you think gave it me? She did, pardy. On condition, however, that I should bear it to you, with a message; and what a message! that you should be happy.'

'Nonsense, my dear Count'

'It is true; but I romanced at a fine rate for it. It is the only way with women. She thinks we have known each other since the Deluge. Do not betray me. But, my dear fellow, I cannot stop now. Only, mind, all is changed. Instead of being gay, and seeking her society, and amusing her, and thus attempting to regain your influence, as we talked of last night; mind, suicide is the system. To-morrow I will tell you all. She has a firm mind and a high spirit, which she thinks is principle. If we go upon the tack of last night, she will marry Montfort, and fall in love with you afterwards. That will never do. So we must work upon her fears, her generosity, pity, remorse, and so on. Call upon me to-morrow morning, at half-past two; not before, because I have an excellent boy coming to me at one, who is in a scrape. At half-past two, cher, cher Armine, we will talk more. In the meantime, enjoy your flower; and rest assured that it is your own fault if you do not fling the good Montfort in a very fine ditch.'

CHAPTER XVI.

In Which Mr. Temple Surprises His Daughter Weeping.

THE Count Mirabel proceeded with his projects with all the ardour, address, and audacity of one habituated to success. By some means or other he contrived to see Miss Temple almost daily. He paid assiduous court to the duchess, on whom he had made a favourable impression from the first; in St. James'-square he met Mr. Temple, who was partial to the society of a distinguished foreigner. He was delighted with Count Mirabel. As for Miss Grandison, the Count absolutely made her his confidante, though he concealed this bold step from Ferdinand. He established his intimacy in the three families, and even mystified Sir Ratcliffe and Lady Armine so completely that they imagined he must be some acquaintance that Ferdinand had made abroad; and they received him accordingly as one of their son's oldest and most cherished friends. But the most amusing circumstance of all was that the Count, who even in business never lost sight of what might divert or interest him, became great friends with Mr. Glastonbury. Count Mirabel comprehended and appreciated that good man's character.

All Count Mirabel's efforts were directed to restore the influence of Ferdinand Armine over Henrietta Temple; and with this view he omitted no opportunity of impressing the idea of his absent friend on that lady's susceptible brain. His virtues, his talents, his accomplishments, his sacrifices; but, above all, his mysterious sufferings, and the fatal end which the Count was convinced awaited him, were placed before her in a light so vivid that they engrossed her thought and imagination. She could not resist the fascination of talking about Ferdinand Armine to Count Mirabel. He was the constant subject of their discourse. All her feelings now clustered round his image. She had quite abandoned her old plan of marrying him to his cousin. That was desperate. Did she regret it? She scarcely dared urge to herself this secret question; and yet it seemed that her heart, too, would break were Ferdinand another's. But, then, what was to become of him? Was he to be left desolate? Was he indeed to die? And Digby, the amiable, generous Digby; ah! why did she ever meet him? Unfortunate, unhappy woman! And yet she was resolved to be firm; she could not falter; she would be the victim of her duty even if she died at the altar. Almost she wished that she had ceased to live, and then the recollection of Armine came back to her so vividly! And those long days of passionate delight! All his tenderness and all his truth; for he had been true to her, always had he been true to her. She was not the person who ought to complain of his conduct. And yet she was the person who alone punished him. How different was the generous conduct of his cousin! She had pardoned all; she sympathised with him, she sorrowed for him, she tried to soothe him. She laboured to unite him to her rival. What must he think of herself? How hard-hearted, how selfish must the contrast prove her! Could he indeed believe now that she had ever loved him? Oh, no! he must despise her. He must believe that she was sacrificing her heart to the splendour of rank. Oh! could he believe this! Her Ferdinand, her romantic Ferdinand, who had thrown fortune and power to the winds but to gain that very heart! What a return had she made him! And for all his fidelity he was punished; lone, disconsolate, forlorn, overpowered by vulgar cares, heart-broken, meditating even death———. The picture was too terrible, too harrowing. She hid her face in the pillow of the sofa on which she was seated, and wept bitterly.

She felt an arm softly twined round her waist; she looked up; it was her father.

'My child,' he said, 'you are agitated.'

'Yes; yes, I am agitated,' she said, in a low voice.

'You are unwell.'

'Worse than unwell.'

'Tell me what ails you, Henrietta.'

'Grief for which there is no cure.'

'Indeed! I am greatly astonished.'

His daughter only sighed.

'Speak to me, Henrietta. Tell me what has happened.'

'I cannot speak; nothing has happened; I have nothing to say.'

'To see you thus makes me quite unhappy,' said Mr. Temple; 'if only for my sake, let me know the cause of this overwhelming emotion.'

'It is a cause that will not please you. Forget, sir, what you have seen.'

'A father cannot. I entreat you tell me. If you love me, Henrietta, speak.'

'Sir, sir, I was thinking of the past.'

'Is it so bitter?'

'Ah! that I should live!' said Miss Temple.

'Henrietta, my own Henrietta, my child, I beseech you tell me all. Something has occurred; something must have occurred to revive such strong feelings. Has—has——— I know not what to say, but so much happens that surprises me; I know, I have heard, that you have seen one who once influenced your feelings, that you have been thrown in unexpected contact with him; he has not—he has not dared——-'

'Say nothing harshly of him,' said Miss Temple wildly; 'I will not bear it, even from you.'

'My daughter!'

'Ay! your daughter, but still a woman. Do I murmur? Do I complain? Have I urged you to compromise your honour? I am ready for the sacrifice. My conduct is yours, but my feelings are my own.'

'Sacrifice, Henrietta! What sacrifice? I have heard only of your happiness; I have thought only of your happiness. This is a strange return.'

'Father, forget what you have seen; forgive what I have said. But let this subject drop for ever.'

'It cannot drop here. Captain Armine prefers his suit?' continued Mr. Temple, in a tone of stern enquiry.

'What if he did? He has a right to do so.'

'As good a right as he had before. You are rich now, Henrietta, and he perhaps would be faithful.'

'O Ferdinand!' exclaimed Miss Temple, lifting, up her hands and eyes to heaven, 'and you must endure even this!'

'Henrietta,' said Mr. Temple in a voice of affected calmness, as he seated himself by her side, 'listen to me: I am not a harsh parent; you cannot upbraid me with insensibility to your feelings. They have ever engrossed my thought and care; and how to gratify, and when necessary how to soothe them, has long been the principal occupation of my life. If you have known misery, girl, you made that misery yourself. It was not I that involved you in secret engagements and clandestine correspondence; it was not I that made you, you, my daughter, on whom I have lavished all the solicitude of long years, the dupe of the first calculating libertine who dared to trifle with your affections, and betray your heart.'

"Tis false,' exclaimed Miss Temple, interrupting him; 'he is as true and pure as I am; more, much more,' she added, in a voice of anguish.

'No doubt he has convinced you of it,' said Mr. Temple, with a laughing sneer. 'Now, mark me,' he continued, resuming his calm tone, 'you interrupted me; listen to me. You are the betrothed bride of Lord Montfort; Lord Montfort, my friend, the man I love most in the world; the most generous, the most noble, the most virtuous, the most gifted of human beings. You gave him your hand freely, under circumstances which, even if he did not possess every quality that ought to secure the affection of a woman, should bind you to him with an unswerving faith. Falter one jot and I whistle you off for ever. You are no more daughter of mine. I am as firm as I am fond; nor would I do this, but that I know well I am doing rightly. Yes! take this Armine once more to your heart, and you receive my curse, the deepest, the sternest, the deadliest that ever descended on a daughter's head.'

'My father, my dear, dear father, my beloved father!' exclaimed Miss Temple, throwing herself at his feet. 'Oh! do not say so; oh! recall those words, those wild, those terrible words. Indeed, indeed, my heart is breaking. Pity me, pity me; for God's sake, pity me.'

'I would do more than pity you; I would save you.'

'It is not as you think,' she continued, with streaming eyes: 'indeed it is not. He has not preferred his suit, he has urged no claim. He has behaved in the most delicate, the most honourable, the most considerate manner. He has thought only of my situation. He met me by accident. My friends are his friends. They know not what has taken place between us. He has not breathed it to human being. He has absented himself from his home, that we might not meet.'

'You must marry Lord Montfort at once.'

'Oh! my father, even as you like. But do not curse me; dream not of such terrible things; recall those fearful words; love me, love me; say I am your child. And Digby, I am true to Digby. But, indeed, can I recall the past; can I alter it? Its memory overcame me. Digby knows all; Digby knows we met; he did not curse me; he was kind and gentle. Oh! my father!'

'My Henrietta,' said Mr. Temple, moved; 'my child!'

'Oh! my father, I will do all you wish; but speak not again as you have spoken of Ferdinand. We have done him great injustice; I have done him great injury. He is good and pure; indeed, he is; if you knew all, you would not doubt it. He was ever faithful; indeed, indeed he was. Once you liked him. Speak kindly of him, father. He is the victim. If you meet him, be gentle to him, sir: for, indeed, if you knew all, you would pity him.'

CHAPTER XVII.

In Which Ferdinand Has a Very Stormy Interview with His
Father.

IF WE pause now to take a calm and comprehensive review of the state and prospects of the
three families, in whose feelings and fortunes we have attempted to interest the reader, it must be
confessed that, however brilliant and satisfactory they might appear on the surface, the elements
of discord, gloom, and unhappiness might be more profoundly discovered, and might even be
held as rapidly stirring into movement. Miss Temple was the affianced bride of Lord Montfort,
but her heart was Captain Armine's: Captain Armine, in the estimation of his parents, was the
pledged husband of Miss Grandison, while he and his cousin had, in fact, dissolved their
engagement. Mr. Temple more than suspected his daughter's partiality for Ferdinand. Sir
Ratcliffe, very much surprised at seeing so little of his son, and resolved that the marriage should
be no further delayed, was about to precipitate confessions, of which he did not dream, and
which were to shipwreck all the hopes of his life. The Count Mirabel and Miss Grandison were
both engaged in an active conspiracy. Lord Montfort alone was calm, and if he had a purpose to
conceal, inscrutable. All things, however, foreboded a crisis.

Sir Ratcliffe, astonished at the marked manner in which his son absented himself from Brook-
street, resolved upon bringing him to an explanation. At first he thought there might be some
lovers' quarrel; but the demeanour of Katherine, and the easy tone in which she ever spoke of her
cousin, soon disabused him of this fond hope. He consulted his wife. Now, to tell the truth, Lady
Armine, who was a shrewd woman, was not without her doubts and perplexities, but she would
not confess them to her husband. Many circumstances had been observed by her which filled her
with disquietude, but she had staked all her hopes upon this cast, and she was of a sanguine
temper. She was leading an agreeable life. Katherine appeared daily more attached to her, and
Lady Armine was quite of opinion that it is always very injudicious to interfere. She
endeavoured to persuade Sir Ratcliffe that everything was quite right, and she assured him that
the season would terminate, as all seasons ought to terminate, by the marriage.

And perhaps Sir Ratcliffe would have followed her example, only it so happened that as he was
returning home one morning, he met his son in Grosvenor-square.

'Why, Ferdinand, we never see you now,' said Sir Ratcliffe.

'Oh! you are all so gay,' said Ferdinand. 'How is my mother?'

'She is very well. Katherine and herself have gone to see the balloon, with Lord Montfort and
Count Mirabel. Come in,' said Sir Ratcliffe, for he was now almost at his door.

The father and son entered. Sir Ratcliffe walked into a little library on the ground floor, which
was his morning room.

'We dine at home to-day, Ferdinand,' said Sir Ratcliffe. 'Perhaps you will come.'

'Thank you, sir, I am engaged.'

'It seems to me you are always engaged. For a person who does not like gaiety, it is very odd.'

'Heigho!' said Ferdinand. 'How do you like your new horse, sir?'

'Ferdinand, I wish to speak a word to you,' said Sir Ratcliffe. 'I do not like ever to interfere
unnecessarily with your conduct; but the anxiety of a parent will, I think, excuse the question I
am about to ask. When do you propose being married?'

'Oh, I do not know exactly.'

'Your grandfather has been dead now, you know, much more than a year. I cannot help thinking your conduct singular. There is nothing wrong between you and Katherine, is there?'

'Wrong, sir?'

'Yes, wrong? I mean, is there any misunderstanding? Have you quarrelled?'

'No, sir, we have not quarrelled; we perfectly understand each other.'

'I am glad to hear it, for I must say I think your conduct is very unlike that of a lover. All I can say is, I did not win your mother's heart by such proceedings.'

'Katherine has made no complaint of me, sir?'

'Certainly not, and that surprises me still more.'

Ferdinand seemed plunged in thought. The silence lasted some minutes. Sir Ratcliffe took up the newspaper; his son leant over the mantel-piece, and gazed upon the empty fire-place. At length he turned round and said, 'Father, I can bear this no longer; the engagement between Katherine and myself is dissolved.'

'Good God! when, and why?' exclaimed Sir Ratcliffe, the newspaper falling from his hand.

'Long since, sir; ever since I loved another woman, and she knew it.'

'Ferdinand! Ferdinand!' exclaimed the unhappy father; but he was so overpowered that he could not give utterance to his thoughts. He threw himself in a chair, and wrung his hands. Ferdinand stood still and silent, like a statue of Destiny, gloomy and inflexible.

'Speak again,' at length said Sir Ratcliffe. 'Let me hear you speak again. I cannot believe what I have heard. Is it indeed true that your engagement with your cousin has been long terminated?' Ferdinand nodded assent.

'Your poor mother!' exclaimed Sir Ratcliffe. 'This will kill her.' He rose from his seat, and walked up and down the room in great agitation.

'I knew all was not right,' he muttered to himself. 'She will sink under it; we must all sink under it. Madman! you know not what you have done!'

'It is in vain to regret, sir; my sufferings have been greater than yours.'

'She will pardon you, my boy,' said Sir Ratcliffe, in a quicker and kinder tone. 'You have lived to repent your impetuous folly; Katherine is kind and generous; she loves us all; she must love you; she will pardon you. Yes! entreat her to forget it; your mother, your mother has great influence with her; she will exercise it, she will interfere; you are very young, all will yet be well.'

'It is as impossible for me to marry Katherine Grandison, as for you yourself to do it, sir,' said Ferdinand, in a tone of calmness.

'You are not married to another?'

'In faith; I am bound by a tie which I can never break.'

'And who is this person?'

'She must be nameless, for many reasons.'

'Ferdinand,' said Sir Ratcliffe, 'you know not what you are doing. My life, your mother's, the existence of our family, hang upon your conduct. Yet, yet there is time to prevent this desolation. I am controlling my emotions; I wish you to save us, you, all! Throw yourself at your cousin's feet. She is soft-hearted; she may yet be yours!'

'Dear father, it cannot be.'

'Then-then, welcome ruin!' exclaimed Sir Ratcliffe, in a hoarse voice. 'And,' he continued, pausing between every word, from the difficulty of utterance, 'if the conviction that you have destroyed all our hopes, rewarded us for all our affection, our long devotion, by blasting every fond idea that has ever illumined our sad lives, that I and Constance, poor fools, have clung and clung to; if this conviction can console you, sir, enjoy it——

'Ferdinand! my son, my child, that I never have spoken an unkind word to, that never gave me cause to blame or check him, your mother will be home soon, your poor, poor mother. Do not let me welcome her with all this misery. Tell me it is not true; recall what you have said; let us forget these harsh words; reconcile yourself to your cousin; let us be happy.'

'Father, if my heart's blood could secure your happiness, my life were ready; but this I cannot do.'

'Do you know what is at stake? Everything. All, all, all! We can see Armine no more; our home is gone. Your mother and myself must be exiles. Oh! you have not thought of this: say you have not thought of this.'

Ferdinand hid his face; his father, emboldened, urged the fond plea. 'You will save us, Ferdinand, you will be our preserver? It is all forgotten, is it not? It is a lovers' quarrel, after all?'

'Father, why should I trifle with your feelings? why should I feign what can never be? This sharp interview, so long postponed, ought not now to be adjourned. Indulge no hopes, for there are none.'

'Then by every sacred power I revoke every blessing that since your birth I have poured upon your head. I recall the prayers that every night I have invoked upon your being. Great God! I cancel them. You have betrayed your cousin; you have deserted your mother and myself; you have first sullied the honour of our house, and now you have destroyed it. Why were you born? What have we done that your mother's womb should produce such a curse? Sins of my father, they are visited upon me! And Glastonbury, what will Glastonbury say? Glastonbury, who sacrificed his fortune for you.'

'Mr. Glastonbury knows all, sir, and has always been my confidant.'

'Is he a traitor? For when a son deserts me, I know not whom to trust.'

'He has no thoughts but for our welfare, sir. He will convince you, sir, I cannot marry my cousin.'

'Boy, boy! you know not what you say. Not marry your cousin! Then let us die. It were better for us all to die.'

'My father! Be calm, I beseech you; you have spoken harsh words; I have not deserted you or my mother; I never will. If I have wronged my cousin, I have severely suffered, and she has most freely forgiven me. She is my dear friend. As for our house: tell me, would you have that house preserved at the cost of my happiness? You are not the father I supposed, if such indeed be your wish.'

'Happiness! Fortune, family, beauty, youth, a sweet and charming spirit, if these will not secure a man's happiness, I know not what might. And these I wished you to possess.'

'Sir, it is in vain for us to converse upon this subject. See Glastonbury, if you will. He can at least assure you that neither my feelings are light nor my conduct hasty. I will leave you now.'

Ferdinand quitted the room; Sir Ratcliffe did not notice his departure, although he was not unaware of it. He heaved a deep sigh, and was apparently plunged in profound thought.

CHAPTER XVIII.

Ferdinand Is Arrested by Messrs. Morris and Levison, and
Taken to a Spunging-House.

IT MUST be confessed that the affairs of our friends were in a critical state: everyone interested felt that something decisive in their respective fortunes was at hand. And, yet, so vain are all human plans and calculations, that the unavoidable crisis was brought about by an incident which no one anticipated. It so happened that the stormy interview between Sir Ratcliffe and his son was overheard by a servant. This servant, who had been engaged by Miss Grandison in London, was a member of a club to which a confidential clerk of Messrs. Morris and Levison belonged. In the ensuing evening, when this worthy knight of the shoulder-knot just dropped out for an hour to look in at this choice society, smoke a pipe, and talk over the affairs of his mistress and the nation, he announced the important fact that the match between Miss Grandison and Captain Armine was 'no go,' which, for his part, he did not regret, as he thought his mistress ought to look higher. The confidential clerk of Messrs. Morris and Levison listened in silence to this important intelligence, and communicated it the next morning to his employers. And so it happened that a very few days afterwards, as Ferdinand was lying in bed at his hotel, the door of his chamber suddenly opened, and an individual, not of the most prepossessing appearance, being much marked with smallpox, reeking with gin, and wearing top-boots and a belcher handkerchief, rushed into his room and enquired whether he were Captain Armine.

'The same,' said Ferdinand. 'And pray, sir, who are you?'

'Don't wish to be unpleasant,' was the answer, 'but, sir, you are my prisoner.'

There is something exceedingly ignoble in an arrest: Ferdinand felt that sickness come over him which the uninitiated in such ceremonies must experience. However, he rallied, and enquired at whose suit these proceedings were taken.

'Messrs. Morris and Levison, sir.'

'Cannot I send for my lawyer and give bail?'

The bailiff shook his head. 'You see, sir, you are taken in execution, so it is impossible.'

'And the amount of the debt?'

'Is 2,800L., sir.'

'Well, what am I to do?'

'Why, sir, you must go along with us. We will do it very quietly. My follower is in a hackney-coach at the door, sir. You can just step in as pleasant as possible. I suppose you would like to go to a house, and then you can send for your friends, you know.'

'Well, if you will go down stairs, I will come to you.'

The bailiff grinned. 'Can't let you out of my sight, sir.'

'Why, I cannot dress if you are here.'

The bailiff examined the room to see if there were any mode of escape; there was no door but the entrance; the window offered no chance. 'Well, sir,' he said, 'I likes to do things pleasant. I can stand outside, sir; but you must be quick.'

Ferdinand rang for his servant. When Louis clearly understood the state of affairs, he was anxious to throw the bailiff out of the window, but his master prevented him. Mr. Glastonbury had gone out some two hours; Ferdinand sent Louis with a message to his family, to say he was about leaving town for a few days; and impressing upon him to be careful not to let them know in Brook-street what had occurred, he completed his rapid toilet and accompanied the sheriff's officer to the hackney-coach that was prepared for him.

As they jogged on in silence, Ferdinand revolved in his mind how it would be most advisable for him to act. Any application to his own lawyer was out of the question. That had been tried before, and he felt assured that there was not the slightest chance of that gentleman discharging so large a sum, especially when he was aware that it was only a portion of his client's liabilities; he thought of applying for advice to Count Mirabel or Lord Catchimwhocan, but with what view? He would not borrow the money of them, even if they would lend it; and as it was, he bitterly reproached himself for having availed himself so easily of Mr. Bond Sharpe's kind offices. At this moment, he could not persuade himself that his conduct had been strictly honourable to that gentleman. He had not been frank in the exposition of his situation. The money had been advanced under a false impression, if not absolutely borrowed under a false pretence. He cursed Catchimwhocan and his levity. The honour of the Armines was gone, like everything else that once belonged to them. The result of Ferdinand's reflections was, that he was utterly done up; that no hope or chance of succour remained for him; that his career was closed; and not daring to contemplate what the consequences might be to his miserable parents, he made a desperate effort to command his feelings.

Here the coach turned up a dingy street, leading out of the lower end of Oxford-street, and stopped before a large but gloomy dwelling, which Ferdinand's companion informed him was a spunging-house. 'I suppose you would like to have a private room, sir; you can have every accommodation here, sir, and feel quite at home, I assure you.'

In pursuance of this suggestion, Captain Armine was ushered into the best drawing-room, with barred windows, and treated in the most aristocratic manner. It was evidently the chamber reserved only for unfortunate gentlemen of the utmost distinction. It was amply furnished with a mirror, a loo-table, and a very hard sofa. The walls were hung with old-fashioned caricatures by Bunbury; the fire-irons were of polished brass; over the mantel-piece was the portrait of the master of the house, which was evidently a speaking likeness, and in which Captain Armine fancied he traced no slight resemblance to his friend Mr. Levison; and there were also some sources of literary amusement in the room, in the shape of a Hebrew Bible and the Racing Calendar.

After walking up and down the room for an hour, meditating over the past, for it seemed hopeless to trouble himself any further with the future, Ferdinand began to feel faint, for it may be recollected that he had not even breakfasted. So pulling the bell-rope with such force that it fell to the ground, a funny little waiter immediately appeared, awed by the sovereign ring, and having, indeed, received private intelligence from the bailiff that the gentleman in the drawing-room was a regular nob.

And here, perhaps, I should remind the reader, that of all the great distinctions in life none perhaps is more important than that which divides mankind into the two great sections of NOBS and SNOBS. It might seem at the first glance, that if there were a place in the world which should level all distinctions, it would be a debtors' prison. But this would be quite an error. Almost at the very moment that Captain Armine arrived at his sorrowful hotel, a poor devil of a tradesman who had been arrested for fifty pounds, and torn from his wife and family, had been forced to repair to the same asylum. He was introduced into what is styled the coffee-room, being a long, low, unfurnished sanded chamber, with a table and benches; and being very anxious to communicate with some friend, in order, if possible, to effect his release, and prevent himself from being a bankrupt, he had continued meekly to ring at intervals for the last half-hour in order that he might write and forward his letter. The waiter heard the coffee-room bell ring, but never dreamed of noticing it, though the moment the signal of the private room sounded, and sounded with so much emphasis, he rushed upstairs, three steps at a time, and instantly appeared before our hero: and all this difference was occasioned by the simple circumstance, that Captain Armine was a NOB, and the poor tradesman a SNOB.

'I am hungry,' said Ferdinand. 'Can I get anything to eat at this damned place?'

'What would you like, sir? Anything you choose, sir. Mutton chop, rump steak, weal cutlet? Do you a fowl in a quarter of an hour; roast or boiled, sir?'

'I have not breakfasted yet; bring me some breakfast.'

'Yes, sir,' said the little waiter. 'Tea, sir? Coffee, eggs, toast, buttered toast, sir? Like any meat, sir? Ham, sir? Tongue, sir? Like a devil, sir?'

'Anything, everything, only be quick.'

'Yes, sir,' responded the waiter. 'Beg pardon, sir. No offence, I hope, but custom to pay here, sir. Shall be happy to accommodate you, sir. Know what a gentleman is.'

'Thank you, I will not trouble you,' said Ferdinand; 'get me that note changed.'

'Yes, sir,' replied the little waiter, bowing very low as he disappeared.

'Gentleman in best drawing-room wants breakfast. Gentleman in best drawing-room wants change for a ten-pound note. Breakfast immediately for gentleman in best drawing-room. Tea, coffee, toast, ham, tongue, and a devil. A regular nob!'

Ferdinand was so exhausted that he had postponed all deliberation as to his situation until he had breakfasted; and when he had breakfasted, he felt dull. It is the consequence of all meals. In whatever light he viewed his affairs, they seemed inextricable. He was now in a spunging-house; he could not long remain here, he must be soon in a gaol. A gaol! What a bitter termination of all his great plans and hopes! What a situation for one who had been betrothed to Henrietta Temple! He thought of his cousin, he thought of her great fortune, which might have been his. Perhaps at this moment they were all riding together in the Park. In a few days all must be known to his father. He did not doubt of the result. Armine would immediately be sold, and his father and mother, with the wretched wreck of their fortune, would retire to the Continent. What a sad vicissitude! And he had done it all; he, their only child, their only hope, on whose image they had lived, who was to restore the house. He looked at the bars of his windows, it was a dreadful sight. His poor father, his fond mother, he was quite sure their hearts would break. They never could survive all this misery, this bitter disappointment of all their chopes. Little less than a year ago and he was at Bath, and they were all joy and triumph. What a wild scene had his life been since! O Henrietta! why did we ever meet? That fatal, fatal morning! The cedar tree rose before him, he recalled, he remembered everything. And poor Glastonbury—it was a miserable end. He could not disguise it from himself, he had been most imprudent, he had been mad. And yet so near happiness, perfect, perfect happiness! Henrietta might have been his, and they might have been so happy! This confinement was dreadful; it began to press upon his nerves. No occupation, not the slightest resource. He took up the Racing Calendar, he threw it down again. He knew all the caricatures by heart, they infinitely disgusted him. He walked up and down the room till he was so tired that he flung himself upon the hard sofa. It was intolerable.

A gaol must be preferable to this. There must be some kind of wretched amusement in a gaol; but this ignoble, this humiliating solitude, he was confident he should go mad if he remained here. He rang the bell again.

'Yes, sir,' said the little waiter.

'This place is intolerable to me,' said Captain Armine. 'I really am quite sick of it. What can I do?'
The waiter looked a little perplexed.
'I should like to go to gaol at once,' said Ferdinand.
'Lord! sir!' said the little waiter.
'Yes! I cannot bear this,' he continued; 'I shall go mad.'
'Don't you think your friends will call soon, sir?'
'I have no friends,' said Ferdinand. 'I hope nobody will call.'
'No friends!' said the little waiter, who began to think Ferdinand was not such a nob as he had imagined. 'Why, if you have no friends, sir, it would be best to go to the Fleet, I think.'
'By Jove, I think it would be better.'
'Master thinks your friends will call, I am sure.'
'Nobody knows I am here,' said Ferdinand.
'Oh!' said the little waiter, 'You want to let them know, do you, sir?'
'Anything sooner; I wish to conceal my disgrace.'
'O sir! you are not used to it; I dare say you never were nabbed before?'
'Certainly not.'
'There it is; if you will be patient, you will see everything go well.'
'Never, my good fellow; nothing can go well.'
'O sir! you are not used to it. A regular nob like you, nabbed for the first time, and for such a long figure, sir, sure not to be diddled. Never knowed such a thing yet. Friends sure to stump down, sir.'
'The greater the claim, the more difficulty in satisfying it, I should think,' said Ferdinand.
'Lord! no, sir: you are not used to it. It is only poor devils nabbed for their fifties and hundreds that are ever done up. A nob was never nabbed for the sum you are, sir, and ever went to the wall. Trust my experience. I never knowed such a thing.'
Ferdinand could scarcely refrain from a smile. Even the conversation of the little waiter was a relief to him.
'You see, sir,' continued that worthy, 'Morris and Levison would never have given you such a deuce of a tick unless they knowed your resources. Trust Morris and Levison for that. You done up, sir! a nob like you, that Morris and Levison have trusted for such a tick! Lord! sir, you don't know nothing about it. I could afford to give them fifteen shillings in the pound for their debt myself and a good day's business, too. Friends will stump down, sir, trust me.'
'Well, it is some satisfaction for me to know that they will not, and that Morris and Levison will not get a farthing.'
'Well, sir,' said the incredulous little functionary, 'when I find Morris and Levison lose two or three thousand pounds by a nob who is nabbed for the first time, I will pay the money myself, that is all I know.'
Here the waiter was obliged to leave Ferdinand, but he proved his confidence in that gentleman's fortunes by his continual civility, and in the course of the day brought him a stale newspaper. It seemed to Ferdinand that the day would never close. The waiter pestered him about dinner, eulogising the cook, and assuring him that his master was famous for champagne. Although he had no appetite, Ferdinand ordered dinner in order to ensure the occurrence of one incident. The champagne made him drowsy; he was shown to his room; and for a while he forgot his cares in sleep.

CHAPTER XIX.

The Crisis Rapidly Advances.

HENRIETTA TEMPLE began once more to droop. This change was not unnoticed by her constant companion Lord Montfort, and yet he never permitted her to be aware of his observation. All that he did was still more to study her amusement; if possible, to be still more considerate and tender. Miss Grandison, however, was far less delicate; she omitted no opportunity of letting Miss Temple know that she thought that Henrietta was very unwell, and that she was quite convinced Henrietta was thinking of Ferdinand. Nay! she was not satisfied to confine these intimations to Miss Temple; she impressed her conviction of Henrietta's indisposition on Lord Montfort, and teased him with asking his opinion of the cause.

'What do you think is the cause, Miss Grandison?' said his lordship, very quietly.

'Perhaps London does not agree with her; but then, when she was ill before she was in the country; and it seems to me to be the same illness. I wonder you do not notice it, Lord Montfort. A lover to be so insensible, I am surprised!'

'It is useless to notice that which you cannot remedy.'

'Why do you not call in those who can offer remedies?' said Miss Grandison. 'Why not send for Sir Henry?'

'I think it best to leave Henrietta alone,' said Lord Montfort.

'Do you think it is the mind, then?' said Miss Grandison.

'It may be,' said Lord Montford.

'It may be! Upon my word, you are very easy.'

'I am not indifferent, Miss Grandison. There is nothing that I would not do for Henrietta's welfare.'

'Oh! yes, there is; there is something,' said Miss Grandison, rather maliciously.

'You are really an extraordinary person, Miss Grandison,' said Lord Montfort. 'What can you mean by so strange an observation?'

'I have my meaning; but I suppose I may have a mystery as well as anybody else.'

'A mystery, Miss Grandison?'

'Yes! a mystery, Lord Montfort. There is not a single individual in the three families who has not a mystery, except myself; but I have found out something. I feel quite easy now: we are all upon an equality.'

'You are a strange person.'

'It may be so; but I am happy, for I have nothing on my mind. Now that poor Ferdinand has told Sir Ratcliffe we are not going to marry, I have no part to play. I hate deception; it is almost as bitter as marrying one who is in love with another person.'

'That must indeed be bitter. And is that the reason that you do not marry your cousin?' enquired Lord Montfort.

'I may be in love with another person, or I may not,' said Miss Grandison. 'But, however that may be, the moment Ferdinand very candidly told me he was, we decided not to marry. I think we were wise; do not you. Lord Montfort?'

'If you are happy, you were wise,' said Lord Montfort.

'Yes, I am pretty happy: as happy as I can well be when all my best friends are miserable.'

'Are they?'

'I think so: my aunt is in tears; my uncle in despair; Ferdinand meditates suicide; Henrietta is pining away; and you, who are the philosopher of the society, you look rather grave. I fancy I think we are a most miserable set.'

'I wish we could be all happy,' said Lord Montfort.

'And so we might, I think,' said Miss Grandison; 'at least, some of us.'

'Make us, then,' said Lord Montfort.

'I cannot make you.'

'I think you could, Miss Grandison.'

At this moment Henrietta entered, and the conversation assumed a different turn.

'Will you go with us to Lady Bellair's, Kate?' said Miss Temple. 'The duchess has asked me to call there this morning.'

Miss Grandison expressed her willingness: the carriage was waiting, and Lord Montfort offered to attend them. At this moment the servant entered with a note for Miss Grandison.

'From Glastonbury,' she said; 'dear Henrietta, he wishes to see me immediately. What can it be? Go to Lady Bellair's, and call for me on your return. You must, indeed; and then we can all go out together.'

And so it was arranged. Miss Temple, accompanied by Lord Montfort, proceeded to Bellair House.

'Don't come near me,' said the old lady when she saw them; 'don't come near me; I am in despair; I do not know what I shall do; I think I shall sell all my china. Do you know anybody who wants to buy old china? They shall have it a bargain. But I must have ready money; ready money I must have. Do not sit down in that chair; it is only made to look at. Oh! if I were rich, like you! I wonder if my china is worth three hundred pounds. I could cry my eyes out, that I could. The wicked men; I should like to tear them to pieces. Why is not he in Parliament? and then they could not take him up. They never could arrest Charles Fox. I have known him in as much trouble as anyone. Once he sent all his furniture to my house from his lodgings. He lodged in Bury-street. I always look at the house when I pass by. Don't fiddle the pens; I hate people who fiddle. Where is Gregory? where is my bell! Where is the page? Naughty boy! why do not you come? There, I do not want anything; I do not know what to do. The wicked men! The greatest favourite I had: he was so charming! Charming people are never rich; he always looked melancholy. I think I will send to the rich man I dine with; but I forget his name. Why do not you tell me his name?'

'My dear Lady Bellair, what is the matter?'

'Don't ask me; don't speak to me. I tell you I am in despair. Oh! if I were rich, how I would punish those wicked men!'

'Can I do anything?' said Lord Montfort.

'I do not know what you can do. I have got the tic. I always have the tic when my friends are in trouble.'

'Who is in trouble, Lady Bellair?'

'My dearest friend; the only friend I care about. How can you be so hard-hearted? I called upon him this morning, and his servant was crying. I must get him a place; he is such a good man, and loves his master. Now, do you want a servant? You never want anything. Ask everybody you know whether they want a servant, an honest man, who loves his master. There he is crying down stairs, in Gregory's room. Poor, good creature! I could cry myself, only it is of no use.'

'Who is his master?' said Lord Montfort.

'Nobody you know; yes! you know him very well. It is my dear, dear friend; you know him very well. The bailiffs went to his hotel yesterday, and dragged him out of bed, and took him to prison. Oh! I shall go quite distracted. I want to sell my china to pay his debts. Where is Miss Twoshoes?' continued her ladyship; 'why don't you answer? You do everything to plague me.'

'Miss Grandison, Lady Bellair?'

'To be sure; it is her lover.'

'Captain Armine?'

'Have I not been telling you all this time? They have taken him to prison.'

Miss Temple rose and left the room.

'Poor creature! she is quite shocked. She knows him, too,' said her ladyship. 'I am afraid he is quite ruined. There is a knock. I will make a subscription for him. I dare say it is my grandson. He is very rich, and very good-natured.'

'My dear Lady Bellair,' said Lord Montfort, rising, 'favour me by not saying a word to anybody at present. I will just go in the next room to Henrietta. She is intimate with the family, and much affected. Now, my dear lady, I entreat you,' continued his lordship, 'do not say a word. Captain Armine has good friends, but do not speak to strangers. It will do harm; it will indeed.'

'You are a good creature; you are a good creature. Go away.'

'Lady Frederick Berrington, my lady,' announced the page.

'She is very witty, but very poor. It is no use speaking to her. I won't say a word. Go to Miss Thingabob: go, go.' And Lord Montfort escaped into the saloon as Lady Frederick entered.

Henrietta was lying on the sofa, her countenance was hid, she was sobbing convulsively.

'Henrietta,' said Lord Montfort, but she did not answer. 'Henrietta, he again said, 'dear Henrietta! I will do whatever you wish.'

'Save him, save him!' she exclaimed. 'Oh! you cannot save him! And I have brought him to this! Ferdinand! dearest Ferdinand! oh! I shall die!'

'For God's sake, be calm,' said Lord Montfort, 'there is nothing I will not do for you, for him.'

'Ferdinand, Ferdinand, my own, own Ferdinand, oh! why did we ever part? Why was I so unjust, so wicked? And he was true! I cannot survive his disgrace and misery. I wish to die!'

'There shall be no disgrace, no misery,' said Lord Montfort, 'only for God's sake, be calm. There is a chattering woman in the next room. Hush! hush! I tell you I will do everything.'

'You cannot; you must not; you ought not! Kind, generous Digby! Pardon what I have said; forget it; but indeed I am so wretched, I can bear this life no longer.'

'But you shall not be wretched, Henrietta; you shall be happy; everybody shall be happy. I am Armine's friend, I am indeed. I will prove it. On my honour, I will prove that I am his best friend.'

'You must not. You are the last person, you are indeed. He is so proud! Anything from us will be death to him. Yes! I know him, he will die sooner than be under an obligation to either of us.'

'You shall place him under still greater obligations than this,' said Lord Montfort. 'Yes! Henrietta, if he has been true to you, you shall not be false to him.'

'Digby, Digby, speak not such strange words. I am myself again. I left you that I might be alone. Best and most generous of men, I have never deceived you; pardon the emotions that even you were not to witness.'

'Take my arm, dearest, let us walk into the garden. I wish to speak to you. Do not tremble. I have nothing to say that is not for your happiness; at all times, and under all circumstances, the great object of my thoughts.'

He raised Miss Temple gently from the sofa, and they walked away far from the observation of

Lady Bellair, or the auricular powers, though they were not inconsiderable, of her lively guest.

CHAPTER XX.

In Which Ferdinand Receives More than One Visit, and Finds
That Adversity Has Not Quite Deprived Him of His Friends.

IN THE mean time morning broke upon the unfortunate Ferdinand. He had forgotten his cares in sleep, and, when he woke, it was with some difficulty that he recalled the unlucky incident of yesterday, and could satisfy himself that he was indeed a prisoner. But the bars of his bedroom window left him not very long in pleasing doubt.

His friend, the little waiter, soon made his appearance. 'Slept pretty well, sir? Same breakfast as yesterday, sir? Tongue and ham, sir? Perhaps you would like a kidney instead of a devil? It will be a change.'

'I have no appetite.'

'It will come, sir. You an't used to it. Nothing else to do here but to eat. Better try the kidney, sir. Is there anything you fancy?'

'I have made up my mind to go to gaol to-day.' 'Lord! sir, don't think of it. Something will turn up, sir, take my word.'

And sooth to say, the experienced waiter was not wrong. For bringing in the breakfast, followed by an underling with a great pomp of plated covers, he informed Ferdinand with a chuckle, that a gentleman was enquiring for him. 'Told you your friends would come, sir.'

The gentleman was introduced, and Ferdinand beheld Mr. Glastonbury.

'My dear Glastonbury,' said Ferdinand, scarcely daring to meet his glance, 'this is very kind, and yet I wished to have saved you this.'

'My poor child,' said Glastonbury.

'Oh! my dear friend, it is all over. This is a more bitter moment for you even than for me, kind friend. This is a terrible termination of all your zeal and labours.'

'Nay!' said Glastonbury; 'let us not think of anything but the present. For what are you held in durance?'

'My dear Glastonbury, if it were only ten pounds, I could not permit you to pay it. So let us not talk of that. This must have happened sooner or later. It has come, and come unexpectedly: but it must be borne, like all other calamities.'

'But you have friends, my Ferdinand.'

'Would that I had not! All that I wish now is that I were alone in the world. If I could hope that my parents would leave me to myself, I should be comparatively easy. But when I think of them, and the injury I must do them, it is hell, it is hell.'

'I wish you would tell me your exact situation,' said Mr. Glastonbury.

'Do not let us talk of it; does my father know of this?'

'Not yet.'

''Tis well; he may yet have a happy day. He will sell Armine.'

Glastonbury shook his head and sighed. 'Is it so bad?' he said.

'My dearest friend, if you will know the worst, take it. I am here for nearly three thousand pounds, and I owe at least ten more.'

'And they will not take bail?'

'Not for this debt; they cannot. It is a judgment debt, the only one.'

'And they gave you no notice?'

'None: they must have heard somehow or other that my infernal marriage was off. They have all waited for that. And now that you see that affairs are past remedy; let us talk of other topics, if you will be so kind as to remain half an hour in this dungeon. I shall quit directly; I shall go to gaol at once.'

Poor Glastonbury, he did not like to go, and yet it was a most melancholy visit. What could they converse about? Conversation, except on the interdicted subject of Ferdinand's affairs, seemed quite a mockery. At last, Ferdinand said, 'Dear Glastonbury, do not stay here; it only makes us both unhappy. Send Louis with some clothes for me, and some books. I will let you know before I leave this place. Upon reflection, I shall not do so for two or three days, if I can stay as long. See my lawyer; not that he will do anything; nor can I expect him; but he may as well call and see me. Adieu, dear friend.'

Glastonbury was about to retire, when Ferdinand called him back. 'This affair should be kept quiet,' he said. 'I told Louis to say I was out of town in Brook-street. I should be sorry were Miss Temple to hear of it, at least until after her marriage.'

Ferdinand was once more alone with the mirror, the loo-table, the hard sofa, the caricatures which he hated even worse than his host's portrait, the Hebrew Bible, and the Racing Calendar. It seemed a year that he had been shut up in this apartment, instead of a day, he had grown so familiar with every object. And yet the visit of Glastonbury had been an event, and he could not refrain from pondering over it. A spunging-house seemed such a strange, such an unnatural scene, for such a character. Ferdinand recalled to his memory the tower at Armine, and all its glades and groves, shining in the summer sun, and freshened by the summer breeze. What a contrast to this dingy, confined, close dungeon! And was it possible that he had ever wandered at will in that fair scene with a companion fairer? Such thoughts might well drive a man mad. With all his errors, and all his disposition at present not to extenuate them, Ferdinand Armine could not refrain from esteeming himself unlucky. Perhaps it is more distressing to believe ourselves unfortunate, than to recognise ourselves as imprudent.

A fond mistress or a faithful friend, either of these are great blessings; and whatever may be one's scrapes in life, either of these may well be sources of consolation. Ferdinand had a fond mistress once, and had Henrietta Temple loved him, why, he might struggle with all these calamities; but that sweet dream was past. As for friends, he had none, at least he thought not. Not that he had to complain of human nature. He had experienced much kindness from mankind, and many were the services he had received from kind acquaintances. With the recollection of Catch, to say nothing of Bond Sharpe, and above all, Count Mirabel, fresh in his mind, he could not complain of his companions. Glastonbury was indeed a friend, but Ferdinand sighed for a friend of his own age, knit to him by the same tastes and sympathies, and capable of comprehending all his secret feelings; a friend who could even whisper hope, and smile in a spunging-house.

The day wore away, the twilight shades were descending; Ferdinand became every moment more melancholy, when suddenly his constant ally, the waiter, rushed into the room. 'My eye, sir, here is a regular nob enquiring for you. I told you it would be all right.'

'Who is it?'

'Here he is coming up.'

Ferdinand caught the triumphant tones of Mirabel on the staircase.

'Which is the room? Show me directly. Ah! Armine, mon ami! mon cher! Is this your friendship? To be in this cursed hole, and not send for me! C'est une mauvaise plaisanterie to pretend we are friends! How are you, good fellow, fine fellow, excellent Armine? If you were not here I would quarrel with you. There, go away, man.' The waiter disappeared, and Count Mirabel seated himself on the hard sofa.

'My dear fellow,' continued the Count, twirling the prettiest cane in the world, 'this is a bêtise of you to be here and not send for me. Who has put you here?'

'My dear Mirabel, it is all up.'

'Pah! How much is it?'

'I tell you I am done up. It has got about that the marriage is off, and Morris and Levison have nabbed me for all the arrears of my cursed annuities.'

'But how much?'

'Between two and three thousand.'

The Count Mirabel gave a whistle.

'I brought five hundred, which I have. We must get the rest somehow or other.'

'My dear Mirabel, you are the most generous fellow in the world; but I have troubled my friends too much. Nothing will induce me to take a sou from you. Besides, between ourselves, not my least mortification at this moment is some 1,500L., which Bond Sharpe let me have the other day for nothing, through Catch.'

'Pah! I am sorry about that, though, because he would have lent us this money. I will ask Bevil.'

'I would sooner die.'

'I will ask him for myself.'

'It is impossible.'

'We will arrange it: I tell you who will do it for us. He is a good fellow, and immensely rich: it is Fitzwarrene; he owes me great favours.'

'Dear Mirabel, I am delighted to see you. This is good and kind. I am so damned dull here. It quite gladdens me to see you; but do not talk about money.'

'Here is 500L.; four other fellows at 500L. we can manage it.'

'No more, no more! I beseech you.'

'But you cannot stop here. Quel drôle appartement! Before Charley Doricourt was in Parliament he was always in this sort of houses, but I got him out somehow or other; I managed it. Once I bought of the fellow five hundred dozen of champagne.'

'A new way to pay old debts, certainly,' said Ferdinand.

'I tell you—have you dined?'

'I was going to; merely to have something to do.'

'I will stop and dine with you,' said the Count, ringing the bell, 'and we will talk over affairs. Laugh, my friend; laugh, my Armine: this is only a scene. This is life. What can we have for dinner, man? I shall dine here.'

'Gentleman's dinner is ordered, my lord; quite ready,' said the waiter. 'Champagne in ice, my lord?'

'To be sure; everything that is good. Mon cher Armine, we shall have some fun.'

'Yes, my lord,' said the waiter, running down stairs. 'Dinner for best drawing-room directly; green-pea-soup, turbot, beefsteak, roast duck and boiled chicken, everything that is good, champagne in ice; two regular nobs!'

The dinner soon appeared, and the two friends seated themselves.

'Potage admirable!' said Count Mirabel. 'The best champagne I ever drank in my life. Mon brave, your health. This must be Charley's man, by the wine. I think we will have him up; he will lend us some money. Finest turbot I ever ate! I will give you some of the fins. Ah! you are glad to see me, my Armine, you are glad to see your friend. Encore champagne! Good Armine, excellent Armine! Keep up your spirits, I will manage these fellows. You must take some bifteac. The most tender bifteac I ever tasted! This is a fine dinner. Encore un verre! Man, you may go; don't wait.'

'By Jove, Mirabel, I never was so glad to see anybody in my life. Now, you are a friend; I feel quite in spirits.'

'To be sure! always be in spirits. C'est une bêtise not to be in spirits. Everything is sure to go well. You will see how I will manage these fellows, and I will come and dine with you every day until you are out: you shall not be here eight-and-forty hours. As I go home I will stop at Mitchell's and get you a novel by Paul de Kock. Have you ever read Paul de Kock's books?'

'Never,' said Ferdinand.

'What a fortunate man to be arrested! Now you can read Paul de Kock! By Jove, you are the most lucky fellow I know. You see, you thought yourself very miserable in being arrested. 'Tis the finest thing in the world, for now you will read Mon Voisin Raymond. There are always two sides to a case.'

'I am content to believe myself very lucky in having such a friend as you,' said Ferdinand; 'but now as these things are cleared away, let us talk over affairs. Have you seen Henrietta?'

'Of course, I see her every day.'

'I hope she will not know of my crash until she has married.'

'She will not, unless you tell her.'

'And when do you think she will be married?'

'When you please.'

'Cher ami! point de moquerie!'

'By Jove, I am quite serious,' exclaimed the Count. 'I am as certain that you will marry her as that we are in this damned spunging-house.'

'Nonsense!'

'The very finest sense in the world. If you will not marry her, I will myself, for I am resolved that good Montfort shall not. It shall never be said that I interfered without a result. Why, if she were to marry Montfort now, it would ruin my character. To marry Montfort after all my trouble: dining with that good Temple, and opening the mind of that little Grandison, and talking fine things to that good duchess; it would be a failure.'

'What an odd fellow you are, Mirabel!' 'Of course! Would you have me like other people and not odd? We will drink la belle Henriette! Fill up! You will be my friend when you are married, eh? Mon Armine, excellent garçon! How we shall laugh some day; and then this dinner, this dinner will be the best dinner we ever had!'

'But why do you think there is the slightest hope of Henrietta not marrying Montfort?'

'Because my knowledge of human nature assures me that a young woman, very beautiful, very rich, with a very high spirit, and an only daughter, will never go and marry one man when she is in love with another, and that other one, my dear fellow, like you. You are more sure of getting her because she is engaged.'

What a wonderful thing is a knowledge of human nature! thought Ferdinand to himself. The Count's knowledge of human nature is like my friend the waiter's experience. One assures me that I am certain to marry a woman because she is engaged to another person, and the other, that it is quite clear my debts will be paid because they are so large! The Count remained with his friend until eleven o'clock, when everybody was locked up. He invited himself to dine with him to-morrow, and promised that he should have a whole collection of French novels before he awoke. And assuring him over and over again that he looked upon him as the most fortunate of all his friends, and that if he broke the bank at Crocky's to-night, which he fancied he should, he would send him two or three thousand pounds; at the same time he shook him heartily by the hand, and descended the staircase of the spunging-house, humming Vive la Bagatelle.

CHAPTER XXI.

The Crisis.

ALTHOUGH, when Ferdinand was once more left alone to his reflections, it did not appear to him that anything had occurred which should change his opinion of his forlorn lot, there was something, nevertheless, inspiring in the visit of his friend Count Mirabel. It did not seem to him, indeed, that he was one whit nearer extrication from his difficulties than before; and as for the wild hopes as to Henrietta, he dismissed them from his mind as the mere fantastic schemes of a sanguine spirit, and yet his gloom, by some process difficult to analyse, had in great measure departed. It could not be the champagne, for that was a remedy he had previously tried; it was in some degree doubtless the magic sympathy of a joyous temperament: but chiefly it might, perhaps, be ascribed to the flattering conviction that he possessed the hearty friendship of a man whose good-will was, in every view of the case, a very enviable possession. With such a friend as Mirabel, he could not deem himself quite so unlucky as in the morning. If he were fortunate, and fortunate so unexpectedly, in this instance, he might be so in others. A vague presentiment that he had seen the worst of life came over him. It was equally in vain to justify the consoling conviction or to resist it; and Ferdinand Armine, although in a spunging-house, fell asleep in better humour with his destiny than he had been for the last eight months.

His dreams were charming: he fancied that he was at Armine, standing by the Barbary rose-tree. It was moonlight; it was, perhaps, a slight recollection of the night he had looked upon the garden from the window of his chamber, the night after he had first seen Henrietta. Suddenly, Henrietta Temple appeared at his window, and waved her hand to him with a smiling face. He immediately plucked for her a flower, and stood with his offering beneath her window. She was in a riding-habit, and she told him that she had just returned from Italy. He invited her to descend, and she disappeared; but instead of Henrietta, there came forward from the old Place——the duchess, who immediately enquired whether he had seen his cousin; and then her Grace, by some confused process common in dreams, turned into Glastonbury, and pointed to the rose-tree, where, to his surprise, Katherine was walking with Lord Montfort. Ferdinand called out for Henrietta, but, as she did not appear, he entered the Place, where he found Count Mirabel dining by himself, and just drinking a glass of champagne. He complained to Mirabel that Henrietta had disappeared, but his friend laughed at him, and said that, after such a long ride, leaving Italy only yesterday, he could scarcely expect to see her. Satisfied with this explanation, Ferdinand joined the Count at his banquet, and was awakened from his sleep, and his dream apparently, by Mirabel drawing a cork.

Ah! why did he ever wake? It was so real; he had seen her so plainly; it was life; it was the very smile she wore at Ducie; that sunny glance, so full of joy, beauty, and love, which he could live to gaze on! And now he was in prison, and she was going to be married to another. Oh! there are things in this world that may well break hearts!

The cork of Count Mirabel was, however, a substantial sound, a gentle tap at his door: he answered it, and the waiter entered his chamber.

'Beg pardon, sir, for disturbing you; only eight o'clock.'

'Then why the deuce do you disturb me?' 'There has been another nob, sir. I said as how you were not up, and he sent his compliments, and said as how he would call in an hour, as he wished to see you particular.' 'Was it the Count?'

'No, sir; but it was a regular nob, sir, for he had a coronet on his cab. But he would not leave his name.'

'Catch, of course,' thought Ferdinand to himself. 'And sent by Mirabel. I should not wonder, if after all, they have broken the bank at Crocky's. Nothing shall induce me to take a ducat.'

However, Ferdinand thought fit to rise, and contrived to descend to the best drawing-room about a quarter of an hour after the appointed time. To his extreme surprise he found Lord Montfort.

'My dear friend,' said Lord Montfort, looking a little confused; 'I am afraid I have sadly disturbed you. But I could not contrive to find you yesterday until it was so late that I was ashamed to knock them up here, and I thought, therefore, you would excuse this early call, as, as, as, I wished to see you very much indeed.'

'You are extremely kind,' said Captain Armine. 'But really I much regret that your lordship should have had all this trouble.'

'Oh! what is trouble under such circumstances!' replied his lordship. 'I cannot pardon myself for being so stupid as not reaching you yesterday. I never can excuse myself for the inconvenience you have experienced.'

Ferdinand bowed, but was so perplexed that he could not say a word.

'I hope, my dear Armine,' said his lordship, advancing rather slowly, putting his arm within that of Ferdinand, and then walking up and down the room together, 'I hope you will act at this moment towards me as I would towards you, were our respective situations changed.'

Ferdinand bowed, but said nothing.

'Money, you know, my good fellow,' continued Lord Montfort, 'is a disagreeable thing to talk about; but there are circumstances which should deprive such conversation between us of any awkwardness which otherwise might arise.'

'I am not aware of them, my lord,' said Ferdinand, 'though your good feelings command my gratitude.'

'I think, upon reflection, we shall find that there are some,' said Lord Montfort. 'For the moment I will only hope that you will esteem those good feelings, and which, on my part, I am anxious should ripen into sincere and intimate friendship, as sufficient authority for my placing your affairs in general in that state that they may in future never deprive your family and friends of society necessary to their happiness.'

'My lord, I am sure that adversity has assumed a graceful hue with me, for it has confirmed my most amiable views of human nature. I shall not attempt to express what I feel towards your lordship for this generous goodness, but I will say I am profoundly impressed with it; not the less, because I cannot avail myself in the slightest degree of your offer.'

'You are too much a man of the world, I am sure, my dear Armine, to be offended by my frankness. I shall, therefore, speak without fear of misconception. It does appear to me that the offer which I have made you is worthy of a little more consideration. You see, my dear friend, that you have placed yourself in such a situation that however you may act the result cannot be one completely satisfactory. The course you should pursue, therefore, as, indeed, all conduct in this world should be, is a matter of nice calculation. Have you well considered the consequences of your rushing upon ruin? In the first place, your family will receive a blow from which even future prosperity may not recover them. Your family estate, already in a delicate position, may be irrecoverably lost; the worldly consequences of such a vicissitude are very considerable; whatever career you pursue, so long as you visibly possess Armine, you rank always among the aristocracy of the land, and a family that maintains such a position, however decayed, will ultimately recover. I hardly know an exception to this rule. I do not think, of all men, that you are most calculated to afford one.'

'What you say has long pressed itself upon us,' said Captain Armine.

'Then, again,' resumed Lord Montfort, 'the feelings and even interests of your friends are to be considered. Poor Glastonbury! I love that old man myself. The fall of Armine might break his heart; he would not like to leave his tower. You see, I know your place.'

'Poor Glastonbury!' said Ferdinand.

'But above all,' continued Lord Montfort, 'the happiness, nay, the very health and life of your parents, from whom all is now concealed, would perhaps be the last and costliest sacrifices of your rashness.'

Ferdinand threw himself on the sofa and covered his face.

'Yet all this misery, all these misfortunes, may be avoided, and you yourself become a calm and happy man, by—for I wish not to understate your view of the subject, Armine—putting yourself under a pecuniary obligation to me. A circumstance to be avoided in the common course of life, no doubt; but is it better to owe me a favour and save your family estate, preserve your position, maintain your friend, and prevent the misery, and probable death, of your parents, or be able to pass me in the street, in haughty silence if you please, with the consciousness that the luxury of your pride has been satisfied at the cost of every circumstance which makes existence desirable?'

'You put the case strongly,' said Ferdinand; 'but no reasoning can ever persuade me that I am justified in borrowing 3,000L., which I can never repay.'

'Accept it, then.'

"Tis the same thing,' said Ferdinand.

'I think not,' said Lord Montfort; 'but why do you say never?'

'Because it is utterly impossible that I ever can.'

'How do you know you may not marry a woman of large fortune?' said Lord Montfort. 'Now you seem to me exactly the sort of man who would marry an heiress.'

'You are thinking of my cousin,' said Ferdinand. 'I thought that you had discovered, or that you might have learnt, that there was no real intention of our union.'

'No, I was not thinking of your cousin,' said Lord Montfort; 'though, to tell you the truth, I was once in hopes that you would marry her. However, that I well know is entirely out of the question, for I believe Miss Grandison will marry someone else.'

'Indeed!' exclaimed Ferdinand, a little agitated. 'Well! may she be happy! I love Kate from the bottom of my heart. But who is the fortunate fellow?'

"Tis a lady's secret,' said Lord Montfort. 'But let us return to our argument. To be brief: either, my dear Armine, you must be convinced by my reasoning, or I must remain here a prisoner like yourself; for, to tell you the truth, there is a fair lady before whom I cannot present myself except in your company.'

Ferdinand changed countenance. There wanted but this to confirm his resolution, which had scarcely wavered. To owe his release to Henrietta's influence with Lord Montfort was too degrading.

'My lord,' he said, 'you have touched upon a string that I had hoped might have been spared me. This conversation must, indeed, cease. My mouth is sealed from giving you the reasons, which nevertheless render it imperative on me to decline your generous offer.'

'Well, then,' said Lord Montfort, 'I must see if another can be more successful,' and he held forth a note to the astounded Ferdinand, in Henrietta's writing. It dropped from Ferdinand's hand as he took it. Lord Montfort picked it up, gave it him again, and walked to the other end of the room. It was with extreme difficulty that Ferdinand prevailed on himself to break the seal. The note was short; the hand that traced the letters must have trembled. Thus it ran:—

'Dearest Ferdinand,—Do everything that Digby wishes. He is our best friend. Digby is going to marry Katherine; are you happy? Henrietta.'

Lord Montfort looked round; Ferdinand Armine was lying senseless on the sofa.

Our friend was not of a swooning mood, but we think the circumstances may excuse the weakness.

As for Lord Montfort, he rang the bell for the little waiter, who, the moment he saw what had occurred, hurried away and rushed up stairs again with cold water, a bottle of brandy, and a blazing sheet of brown paper, which he declared was an infallible specific. By some means or other Ferdinand was in time recovered, and the little waiter was fairly expelled.

'My dear friend,' said Ferdinand, in a faint voice; 'I am the happiest man that ever lived; I hope you will be, I am sure you will be; Katherine is an angel. But I cannot speak. It is so strange.'

'My dear fellow, you really must take a glass of brandy,' said Lord Montfort. 'It is strange, certainly. But we are all happy.'

'I hardly know where I am,' said Ferdinand, after a few minutes. 'Am I really alive?'

'Let us think how we are to get out of this place. I suppose they will take my cheque. If not, I must be off.'

'Oh, do not go,' said Ferdinand. 'If you go I shall not believe it is true. My dear Montfort, is it really true?'

'You see, my dear Armine,' said Lord Montfort, smiling, 'it was fated that I should marry a lady you rejected. And to tell you the truth, the reason why I did not get to you yesterday, as I ought to have done, was an unexpected conversation I had with Miss Grandison. I really think this arrest was a most fortunate incident. It brought affairs to a crisis. We should have gone on playing at cross purposes for ever.'

Here the little waiter entered again with a note and a packet.

'The same messenger brought them?' asked Ferdinand.

'No, sir; the Count's servant brought the note, and waits for an answer; the packet came by another person.'

Ferdinand opened the note and read as follows:—

'Berkeley-square, half-past 7, morning.

'Mon Ami,—Best joke in the world! I broke Crocky's bank three times. Of course; I told you so. I win 15,000L. Directly I am awake I will send you the three thousand, and I will lend you the rest till your marriage. It will not be very long. I write this before I go to bed, that you may have it early. Adieu, cher ami.

'Votre affectionné,

'De Mirabel.

'My arrest was certainly the luckiest incident in the world,' said Ferdinand, handing the note to Lord Montfort. 'Mirabel dined here yesterday, and went and played on purpose to save me. I treated it as a joke. But what is this?' Ferdinand opened the packet. The handwriting was unknown to him. Ten bank notes of 300L. each fell to the ground.

'Do I live in fairyland?' he exclaimed. 'Now who can this be? It cannot be you; it cannot be Mirabel. It is wondrous strange.'

'I think I can throw some light upon it,' said Lord Montfort. 'Katherine was mysteriously engaged with Glastonbury yesterday morning. They were out together, and I know they went to her lawyer's. There is no doubt it is Katherine. I think, under the circumstances of the case, we need have no delicacy in availing ourselves of this fortunate remittance. It will at least save us time,' said Lord Montfort, ringing the bell. 'Send your master here directly,' he continued to the waiter. The sheriff's officer appeared; the debt, the fees, all were paid, and the discharge duly taken. Ferdinand in the meantime went up stairs to lock up his dressing-case; the little waiter rushed after him to pack his portmanteau. Ferdinand did not forget his zealous friend, who whispered hope when all was black. The little waiter chuckled as he put his ten guineas in his pocket. 'You see, sir,' he said, 'I was quite right. Knowed your friends would stump down. Fancy a nob like you being sent to quod! Fiddlededee! You see, sir, you weren't used to it.'

And so Ferdinand Armine bid adieu to the spunging-house, where, in the course of less than eight-and-forty hours, he had known alike despair and rapture. Lord Montfort drove along with a gaiety unusual to him.

'Now, my dear Armine,' he said, 'I am not a jot the less in love with Henrietta than before. I love her as you love Katherine. What folly to marry a woman who was in love with another person! I should have made her miserable, when the great object of all my conduct was to make her happy. Now Katherine really loves me as much as Henrietta loves you. I have had this plan in my head for a long time. I calculated finely; I was convinced it was the only way to make us all happy. And now we shall all be related; we shall be constantly together; and we will be brother friends.'

'Ah! my dear Montfort,' said Ferdinand, 'what will Mr. Temple say?'

'Leave him to me,' said Lord Montfort.

'I tremble,' said Ferdinand, 'if it were possible to anticipate difficulties to-day.'

'I shall go to him at once,' said Lord Montfort; 'I am not fond of suspense myself, and now it is of no use. All will be right.'

'I trust only to you,' said Ferdinand; 'for I am as proud as Temple. He dislikes me, and he is too rich for me to bow down to him.'

'I take it upon myself,' said Lord Montfort. 'Mr. Temple is a calm, sensible man. You will laugh at me, but the truth is, with him it must be a matter of calculation: on the one hand, his daughter's happiness, a union with a family second to none in blood, alliances, and territorial position, and only wanting his wealth to revive all its splendour; on the other, his daughter broken-hearted, and a duke for his son-in-law. Mr. Temple is too sensible a man to hesitate, particularly when I remove the greatest difficulty he must experience. Where shall I out you down? Berkeley-Square?'

CHAPTER XXII.

Ferdinand Meditates over His Good Fortune.

IN MOMENTS of deep feeling, alike sudden bursts of prosperity as in darker hours, man must be alone. It requires some self-communion to prepare ourselves for good fortune, as well as to encounter difficulty, and danger, and disgrace. This violent and triumphant revolution in his prospects and his fortunes was hardly yet completely comprehended by our friend, Ferdinand Armine; and when he had left a note for the generous Mirabel, whose slumbers he would not disturb at this early hour, even with good news, he strolled along up Charles-street, and to the Park, in one of those wild and joyous reveries in which we brood over coming bliss, and create a thousand glorious consequences.

It was one of those soft summer mornings which are so delightful in a great city. The sky was clear, the air was bland, the water sparkled in the sun, and the trees seemed doubly green and fresh to one who so recently had gazed only on iron bars. Ferdinand felt his freedom as well as his happiness. He seated himself on a bench and thought of Henrietta Temple! he took out her note, and read it over and over again. It was indeed her handwriting! Restless with impending joy, he sauntered to the bridge, and leant over the balustrade, gazing on the waters in charmed and charming vacancy. How many incidents, how many characters, how many feelings flitted over his memory! Of what sweet and bitter experience did he not chew the cud! Four-and-twenty hours ago, and he deemed himself the most miserable and forlorn of human beings, and now all the blessings of the world seemed showered at his feet! A beautiful bride awaited him, whom he had loved with intense passion, and who he had thought but an hour ago was another's. A noble fortune, which would permit him to redeem his inheritance, and rank him among the richest commoners of the realm, was to be controlled by one a few hours back a prisoner for desperate debts. The most gifted individuals in the land emulated each other in proving which entertained for him the most sincere affection. What man in the world had friends like Ferdinand Armine? Ferdinand Armine, who, two days back, deemed himself alone in the world! The unswerving devotion of Glastonbury, the delicate affection of his sweet cousin, all the magnanimity of the high-souled Mont-fort, and the generosity of the accomplished Mirabel, passed before him, and wonderfully affected him. He could not flatter himself that he indeed merited such singular blessings; and yet with all his faults, which with him were but the consequences of his fiery youth, Ferdinand had been faithful, to Henrietta. His constancy to her was now rewarded. As for his friends, the future must prove his gratitude to them.'

Ferdinand Armine had great tenderness of disposition, and somewhat of a meditative mind; schooled by adversity, there was little doubt that his coming career would justify his favourable destiny.

It was barely a year since he had returned from Malta, but what an eventful twelvemonth! Everything that had occurred previously seemed of another life; all his experience was concentrated in that wonderful drama that had commenced at Bath, the last scene of which was now approaching; the characters, his parents, Glastonbury, Katherine, Henrietta, Lord Montfort, Count Mirabel, himself, and Mr. Temple!

Ah! that was a name that a little disturbed him; and yet he felt confidence now in Mirabel's prescience; he could not but believe that with time even Mr. Temple might be reconciled! It was at this moment that the sound of military music fell upon his ear; it recalled old days; parades and guards at Malta; times when he did not know Henrietta Temple; times when, as it seemed to him now, he had never paused to think or moralise. That was a mad life. What a Neapolitan ball was his career then! It was indeed dancing on a volcano. And now all had ended so happily! Oh! could it indeed be true? Was it not all a dream of his own creation, while his eye had been fixed in abstraction on that bright and flowing river? But then there was Henrietta's letter. He might be enchanted, but that was the talisman.

In the present unsettled, though hopeful state of affairs, Ferdinand would not go home. He was resolved to avoid any explanations until he heard from Lord Montfort. He shrank from seeing Glastonbury or his cousin. As for Henrietta, it seemed to him that he never could have heart to meet her again, unless they were alone. Count Mirabel was the only person to whom he could abandon his soul, and Count Mirabel was still in his first sleep.

So Ferdinand entered Kensington Gardens, and walked in those rich glades and stately avenues. It seems to the writer of this history that the inhabitants of London are scarcely sufficiently sensible of the beauty of its environs. On every side the most charming retreats open to them, nor is there a metropolis in the world surrounded by so many rural villages, picturesque parks, and elegant casinos. With the exception of Constantinople, there is no city in the world that can for a moment enter into competition with it. For himself, though in his time something of a rambler, he is not ashamed in this respect to confess to a legitimate Cockney taste; and for his part he does not know where life can flow on more pleasantly than in sight of Kensington Gardens, viewing the silver Thames winding by the bowers of Rosebank, or inhaling from its terraces the refined air of graceful Richmond.

In exactly ten minutes it is in the power of every man to free himself from all the tumult of the world; the pangs of love, the throbs of ambition, the wear and tear of play, the recriminating boudoir, the conspiring club, the rattling hell; and find himself in a sublime sylvan solitude superior to the cedars of Lebanon, and inferior only in extent to the chestnut forests of Anatolia. Kensington Gardens is almost the only place that has realised his idea of the forests of Spenser and Ariosto. What a pity, that instead of a princess in distress we meet only a nurserymaid! But here is the fitting and convenient locality to brood over our thoughts; to project the great and to achieve the happy. It is here that we should get our speeches by heart, invent our impromptus; muse over the caprices of our mistresses, destroy a cabinet, and save a nation.

About the time that Ferdinand directed his steps from these green retreats towards Berkeley-Square, a servant summoned Miss Temple to her father.

'Is papa alone?' enquired Miss Temple.

'Only my lord with him,' was the reply.

'Is Lord Montfort here!' said Miss Temple, a little surprised.

'My lord has been with master these three hours,' said the servant.

CHAPTER XXIII.

Ferdinand Receives the Most Interesting Invitation to
Dinner Ever Offered to Him.

IS NOT it wonderful?' said Ferdinand, when he had finished his history to Count Mirabel.
'Not the least,' said the Count, 'I never knew anything less surprising. 'Tis exactly what I said, 'tis
the most natural termination in the world.'

'Ah, my dear Mirabel, you are a prophet! What a lucky fellow I am to have such a friend as you!'
'To be sure you are. Take some more coffee. What are you going to do with yourself?'

'I do not know what to do with myself. I really do not like to go anywhere until I have heard
from Montfort. I think I shall go to my hotel' 'I will drive you. It is now three o'clock.' But just at
this moment, Mr. Bevil called on the Count, and another hour disappeared. When they were
fairly in the cabriolet, there were so many places to call at, and so many persons to see, that it
was nearly six o'clock when they reached the hotel. Ferdinand ran up stairs to see if there were
any letter from Lord Montfort. He found his lordship's card, and also Mr. Temple's; they had
called about half an hour ago; there was also a note. These were its contents:—

'Grosvenor-square, Thursday.

'My Dear Captain Armine,

'I have prepared myself with this note, as I fear I shall hardly be so fortunate as to find you at
home. It is only very recently that I have learnt from Henrietta that you were in London, and I
much regret to hear that you have been so great an invalid. It is so long since we met that I hope
you will dine with us to-day; and indeed I am so anxious to see you, that I trust, if you have
unfortunately made any other engagement, you may yet contrive to gratify my request. It is
merely a family party; you will only meet our friends from St. James'-square, and your own
circle in Brook-street. I have asked no one else, save old Lady Bellair, and your friend Count
Mirabel; and Henrietta is so anxious to secure his presence, that I shall be greatly obliged by
your exerting your influence to induce him to accompany you, as I fear there is little hope of
finding him free.

'Henrietta joins with me in kindest regards; and I beg you to believe me,

'My dear Captain Armine,

'Most cordially yours,

'Pelham Temple.'

'Well, what is the matter?' said the Count, when Ferdinand returned to the cabriolet, with the note
in his hand, and looking very agitated.

'The strangest note!' said Ferdinand.

'Give it me,' said the Count. 'Do you call that strange? Tis the most regular epistle I ever read; I
expected it. 'Tis an excellent fellow, that Mr. Temple; I will certainly dine with him, and send an
excuse to that old Castlefyshe. A family party, all right; and he asks me, that is proper. I should
not wonder if it ended by my being your trustee, or your executor, or your first child's godfather.
Ah, that good Temple is a sensible man. I told you I would settle this business for you. You
should hear me talk to that good Temple. I open his mind. A family party; it will be amusing! I
would not miss it for a thousand pounds. Besides, I must go to take care of you, for you will be
committing all sorts of bêtises. I will give you one turn in the park. Jump in, mon enfant. Good

Armine, excellent fellow, jump in! You see, I was right; I am always right. But I will confess to you a secret: I never was so right as I have been in the present case. 'Tis the best business that ever was!'

CHAPTER XXIV.

Some Account of the Party, and Its Result.

IN SPITE of the Count Mirabel's inspiring companionship, it must be confessed that Ferdinand's heart failed him when he entered Mr. Temple's house. Indeed, had it not been for the encouragement and jolly raillery of his light-hearted friend, it is not quite clear that he would have succeeded in ascending the staircase. A mist came over his vision as he entered the room; various forms, indeed, glanced before him, but he could distinguish none. He felt so embarrassed, that he was absolutely miserable. It was Mr. Temple's hand that he found he had hold of; the calm demeanour and bland tones of that gentleman somewhat reassured him. Mr. Temple was cordial, and Count Mirabel hovered about Ferdinand, and covered his confusion. Then he recognised the duchess and his mother; they were sitting together, and he went up and saluted them. He dared not look round for the lady of the house. Lady Bellair was talking to his father. At last he heard his name called by the Count. 'Armine, mon cher, see this beautiful work!' and Ferdinand advanced, or rather staggered, to a window where stood the Count before a group, and in a minute he clasped the hand of Henrietta Temple. He could not speak. Katherine was sitting by her, and Lord Montfort standing behind her chair. But Count Mirabel never ceased talking, and with so much art and tact, that in a few moments he had succeeded in producing comparative ease on all sides.

'I am so glad that you have come to-day,' said Henrietta. Her eyes sparkled with a strange meaning, and then she suddenly withdrew her gaze. The rose of her cheek alternately glowed and faded. It was a moment of great embarrassment, and afterwards they often talked of it.

Dinner, however, was soon announced as served, for Mirabel and Ferdinand had purposely arrived at the last moment. As the duke advanced to offer his arm to Miss Temple, Henrietta presented Ferdinand with a flower, as if to console him for the separation. It was a round table; the duchess and Lady Bellair sat on each side of Mr. Temple, the duke on the right hand of Miss Temple; where there were so many members of the same family, it was difficult to arrange the guests. Ferdinand held back, when Count Mirabel, who had secured a seat by Henrietta, beckoned to Ferdinand, and saying that Lady Bellair wished him to sit next to her, pushed Ferdinand, as he himself walked away, into the vacated seat. Henrietta caught the Count's eye as he moved off; it was a laughing eye.

'I am glad you sit next to me,' said Lady Bellair to the Count, 'because you are famous. I love famous people, and you are very famous. Why don't you come and see me? Now I have caught you at last, and you shall come and dine with me the 7th, 8th, or 9th of next month; I have dinner parties every day. You shall dine with me on the 8th, for then Lady Frederick dines with me, and she will taste you. You shall sit next to Lady Frederick, and mind you flirt with her. I wonder if you are as amusing as your grandfather. I remember dancing a minuet with him at Versailles seventy years ago.'

'It is well recollected in the family,' said the Count.

'Ah! you rogue!' said the little lady, chuckling, 'you lie! I like a lie sometimes,' she resumed, 'but then it must be a good one. Do you know, I only say it to you, but I am half afraid lies are more amusing than truth.'

'Naturally,' said the Count, 'because truth must in general be commonplace, or it would not be true.'

In the meantime, Ferdinand was seated next to Henrietta Temple. He might be excused for feeling a little bewildered. Indeed, the wonderful events of the last four-and-twenty hours were enough to deprive anyone of a complete command over his senses. What marvel, then, that he nearly carved his soup, ate his fish with a spoon; and drank water instead of wine! In fact, he was labouring under a degree of nervous excitement which rendered it quite impossible for him to observe the proprieties of life. The presence of all these persons was insupportable to him. Five minutes alone with her in the woods of Ducie, and he would have felt quite reassured. Miss Temple avoided his glance! She was, in truth, as agitated as himself, and talked almost entirely to the duke; yet sometimes she tried to address him, and say kind things. She called him Ferdinand; that was quite sufficient to make him happy, although he felt very awkward. He had been seated some minutes before he observed that Glastonbury was next to him.

'I am so nervous, dear Glastonbury,' said Ferdinand, 'that I do not think I shall be able to remain in the room.'

'I have heard something,' said Glastonbury, with a smile, 'that makes me quite bold.'

'I cannot help fancying that it is all enchantment,' said Ferdinand.

'There is no wonder, my dear boy, that you are enchanted,' said Glastonbury.

'Ferdinand,' said Miss Temple in a low voice, 'papa is taking wine with you.' Ferdinand looked up and caught Mr. Temple's kind salute.

'That was a fine horse you were riding to-day,' said Count Mirabel, across the table to Miss Grandison.

'Is it not pretty? It is Lord Montfort's.'

'Lord Montfort's!' thought Ferdinand. 'How strange all this seems!'

'You were not of the riding party this morning,' said his Grace to Henrietta.

'I have not been very well this day or two,' said Miss Temple.

'Well, I think you are looking particularly well to-day,' replied the duke. 'What say you, Captain Armine?'

Ferdinand blushed, and looked confused at this appeal, and muttered some contradictory compliments.

'Oh! I am very well now,' said Miss Temple.

'You must come and dine with me,' said Lady Bellair to Count Mirabel, 'because you talk well across a table. I want a man who talks well across a table. So few can do it without bellowing. I think you do it very well.'

'Naturally,' replied the Count. 'If I did not do it well, I should not do it at all.'

'Ah! you are audacious,' said the old lady. 'I like a little impudence. It is better to be impudent than to be servile.'

'Mankind are generally both,' said the Count.

'I think they are,' said the old lady. 'Pray, is the old Duke of Thingabob alive? You know whom I mean: he was an émigré, and a relation of yours.'

'De Crillon. He is dead, and his son too.'

'He was a great talker,' said Lady Bellair, 'but then, he was the tyrant of conversation. Now, men were made to listen as well as to talk.'

'Without doubt,' said the Count; 'for Nature has given us two ears, but only one mouth.'

'You said that we might all be very happy,' whispered Lord Montfort to Miss Grandison. 'What think you; have we succeeded?'

'I think we all look very confused,' said Miss Grandison. 'What a fortunate, idea it was inviting

Lady Bellair and the Count. They never could look confused.'

'Watch Henrietta,' said Lord Montfort.

'It is not fair. How silent Ferdinand is!'

'Yes, he is not quite sure whether he is Christopher Sly or not,' said Lord Montfort. 'What a fine embarrassment you have contrived, Miss Grandison!'

'Nay, Digby, you were the author of it. I cannot help thinking of your interview with Mr. Temple. You were prompt!'

'Why, I can be patient, fair Katherine,' said Lord Montfort; 'but in the present instance I shrank from suspense, more, however, for others than myself. It certainly was a singular interview.'

'And were you not nervous?'

'Why, no; I felt convinced that the interview could have only one result. I thought of your memorable words; I felt I was doing what you wished, and that I was making all of us happy. However, all honour be to Mr. Temple! He has proved himself a man of sense.'

As the dinner proceeded, there was an attempt on all sides to be gay. Count Mirabel talked a great deal, and Lady Bellair laughed at what he said, and maintained her reputation for repartee. Her ladyship had been for a long time anxious to seize hold of her gay neighbour, and it was evident that he was quite 'a favourite.' Even Ferdinand grew a little more at his ease. He ventured to relieve the duke from some of his labours, and carve for Miss Temple.

'What do you think of our family party?' said Henrietta to Ferdinand, in a low voice.

'I can think only of one thing,' said Ferdinand.

'I am so nervous,' she continued, 'that it seems to me I shall every minute shriek, and leave the room.'

'I feel the same; I am stupefied.'

'Talk to Mr. Glastonbury; drink wine, and talk. Look, look at your mother; she is watching us. She is dying to speak to you, and so is some one else.'

At length the ladies withdrew. Ferdinand attended them to the door of the dining-room. Lady Bellair shook her fan at him, but said nothing. He pressed his mother's hand. 'Good-bye, cousin Ferdinand,' said Miss Grandison in a laughing tone. Henrietta smiled upon him as she passed by. It was a speaking glance, and touched his heart. The gentlemen remained behind much longer than was the custom in Mr. Temple's house. Everybody seemed resolved to drink a great deal of wine, and Mr. Temple always addressed himself to Ferdinand, if anything were required, in a manner which seemed to recognise, his responsible position in the family.

Anxious as Ferdinand was to escape to the drawing-room, he could not venture on the step. He longed to speak to Glastonbury on the subject which engrossed his thoughts, but he had not courage. Never did a man, who really believed himself the happiest and most fortunate person in the world, ever feel more awkward and more embarrassed. Was his father aware of what had occurred? He could not decide. Apparently, Henrietta imagined that his mother did, by the observation which she had made at dinner. Then his father must be conscious of everything. Katherine must have told all. Were Lord Montfort's family in the secret? But what use were these perplexing enquiries? It was certain that Henrietta was to be his bride, and that Mr. Temple had sanctioned their alliance. There could be no doubt of that, or why was he there?

At length the gentlemen rose, and Ferdinand once more beheld Henrietta Temple. As he entered, she was crossing the room with some music in her hand, she was a moment alone. He stopped, he would have spoken, but his lips would not move.

'Well,' she said, 'are you happy?'

'My head wanders. Assure me that it is all true,' he murmured in an agitated voice.

'It is all true; there, go and speak to Lady Armine. I am as nervous as you are.'

Ferdinand seated himself by his mother.

'Well, Ferdinand,' she said, 'I have heard wonderful things.'

'And I hope they have made you happy, mother?'

'I should, indeed, be both unreasonable and ungrateful if they did not; but I confess to you, my dear child, I am even as much astonished as gratified.'

'And my father, he knows everything?'

'Everything. But we have heard it only from Lord Montfort and Katherine. We have had no communication with anyone else. And we meet here to-day in this extraordinary manner, and but for them we should be completely in the dark.'

'And the duchess; do they know all?'

'I conclude so.'

"Tis very strange, is it not?'

'I am quite bewildered.'

'O mother! is she not beautiful? Do you not love her? Shall we not all be the happiest family in the world?'

'I think we ought to be, dear Ferdinand. But I have not recovered from my astonishment. Ah, my child, why did you not tell me when you were ill?'

'Is it not for the best that affairs should have taken the course they have done? But you must blame Kate as well as me; dear Kate!'

'I think of her,' said Lady Armine; 'I hope Kate will be happy.'

'She must be, dear mother; only think what an excellent person is Lord Montfort.'

'He is indeed an excellent person,' said Lady Armine; 'but if I had been engaged to you, Ferdinand, and it ended by my marrying Lord Montfort, I should be very disappointed.'

'The duchess would be of a different opinion,' said Ferdinand.

Lady Bellair, who was sitting on a sofa opposite, and had hitherto been conversing with the duchess, who had now quitted her and joined the musicians, began shaking her fan at Ferdinand in a manner which signified her extreme desire that he should approach her.

'Well, Lady Bellair,' said Ferdinand, seating himself by her side.

'I am in the secret, you know,' said her ladyship.

'What secret, Lady Bellair?'

'Ah! you will not commit yourself. Well, I like discretion. I have always seen it from the first. No one has worked for you as I have. I like true love, and I have left her all my china in my will.'

'I am sure the legatee is very fortunate, whoever she may be.'

'Ah, you rogue, you know very well whom I mean. You are saucy; you never had a warmer friend than myself. I always admired you; you have a great many good qualities and a great many bad ones. You always were a little saucy. But I like a little spice of sauciness; I think it takes. I hear you are great friends with Count Thingabob; the Count, whose grandfather I danced with seventy years ago. That is right; always have distinguished friends. Never have fools for friends; they are no use. I suppose he is in the secret too.'

'Really, Lady Bellair, I am in no secret. You quite excite my curiosity.'

'Well, I can't get anything out of you, I see that. However, it all happened at my house, that can't be denied. I tell you what I will do; I will give you all a dinner, and then the world will be quite certain that I made the match.'

Lady Armine joined them, and Ferdinand seized the opportunity of effecting his escape to the piano.

'I suppose Henrietta has found her voice again, now,' whispered Katherine to her cousin.

'Dear Katherine, really if you are so malicious, I shall punish you,' said Ferdinand.

'Well, the comedy is nearly concluded. We shall join hands, and the curtain will drop.'

'And I hope, in your opinion, not an unsuccessful performance.'

'Why, I certainly cannot quarrel with the catastrophe,' said Miss Grandison.

In the meantime, the Count Mirabel had obtained possession of Mr. Temple, and lost no opportunity of confirming every favourable view which that gentleman had been influenced by Lord Montfort to take of Ferdinand and his conduct. Mr. Temple was quite convinced that his daughter must be very happy, and that the alliance, on the whole, would be productive of every satisfaction that he had ever anticipated.

The evening drew on; carriages were announced; guests retired; Ferdinand lingered; Mr. Temple was ushering Lady Bellair, the last guest, to her carriage; Ferdinand and Henrietta were alone. They looked at each other, their eyes met at the same moment, there was but one mode of satisfactorily terminating their mutual embarrassments: they sprang into each other's arms. Ah, that was a moment of rapture, sweet, thrilling, rapid! There was no need of words, their souls vaulted over all petty explanations; upon her lips, her choice and trembling lips, he sealed his gratitude and his devotion.

The sound of footsteps was heard, the agitated Henrietta made her escape by an opposite entrance. Mr. Temple returned, he met Captain Armine with his hat, and enquired whether Henrietta had retired; and when Ferdinand answered in the affirmative, wished him good-night, and begged him to breakfast with them to-morrow.

CHAPTER XXV.

Which, Though Final, It Is Hoped Will Prove Satisfactory.

OUR kind reader will easily comprehend that from the happy day we have just noticed, Ferdinand Armine was seldom absent from Grosvenor-square, or from the society of Henrietta Temple. Both were so happy that they soon overcame any little embarrassment which their novel situation might first occasion them. In this effort, however, they were greatly encouraged by the calm demeanour of Lord Montfort and the complacent carriage of his intended bride. The world wondered and whispered, marvelled and hinted, but nothing disturbed Lord Montfort, and Katherine had the skill to silence raillery. Although it was settled that the respective marriages should take place as soon as possible, the settlements necessarily occasioned delay. By the application of his funded property, and by a charge upon his Yorkshire estates, Mr. Temple paid off the mortgages on Armine, which, with a certain life-charge in his own favour, was settled in strict entail upon the issue of his daughter. A certain portion of the income was to be set aside annually to complete the castle, and until that edifice was ready to receive them, Ferdinand and Henrietta were to live with Mr. Temple, principally at Ducie, which Mr. Temple had now purchased.

In spite, however, of the lawyers, the eventful day at length arrived. Both happy couples were married at the same time and in the same place, and Glastonbury performed the ceremony. Lord and Lady Montfort departed for a seat in Sussex, belonging to his father; Ferdinand and Henrietta repaired to Armine; while Sir Ratcliffe and his lady paid a visit to Mr. Temple in Yorkshire, and Glastonbury found himself once more in his old quarters in Lancashire with the duke and duchess.

Once more at Armine; wandering once more together in the old pleasaunce; it was so strange and sweet, that both Ferdinand and Henrietta almost began to believe that it was well that the course of their true love had for a moment not run so smoothly as at present, and they felt that their adversity had rendered them even more sensible of their illimitable bliss. And the woods of Ducie, they were not forgotten; nor, least of all, the old farmhouse that had been his shelter. Certainly they were the happiest people that ever lived, and though some years have now passed since these events took place, custom has not sullied the brightness of their love. They have no cares now, and yet both have known enough of sorrow to make them rightly appreciate their unbroken and unbounded blessings.

When the honeymoon was fairly over, for neither of them would bate a jot of this good old-fashioned privilege, Sir Ratcliffe and Lady Armine returned to the Place, and Glastonbury to his tower; while Mr. Temple joined them at Ducie, accompanied by Lord and Lady Montfort. The autumn also brought the Count Mirabel to slaughter the pheasants, gay, brilliant, careless, kind-hearted as ever. He has ever remained one of Ferdinand's most cherished friends; indeed, I hardly think that there is any individual to whom Ferdinand is more attached. And after all, as the Count often observes, if it had not been for Ferdinand's scrapes they would not have known each other. Nor was Lord Catchimwhocan passed over. Ferdinand Armine was not the man to neglect a friend or to forget a good service; and he has conferred on that good-natured, though somewhat improvident, young nobleman, more substantial kindness than the hospitality which is always cheerfully extended to him. When Ferdinand repaid Mr. Bond Sharpe his fifteen hundred pounds, he took care that the interest should appear in the shape of a golden vase, which is now not the least gorgeous ornament of that worthy's splendid sideboard. The deer have appeared again too in the park of Armine, and many a haunch smokes on the epicurean table of Cleveland-row.

Lady Bellair is as lively as ever, and bids fair to amuse society as long as the famous Countess of Desmond,

Who lived to the age of a hundred and ten,

And died by a fall from a cherry tree then;

What a frisky old girl!

In her annual progresses through the kingdom she never omits laying under contribution every establishment of the three families, in whose fortunes she was so unexpectedly mixed up. As her ladyship persists in asserting, and perhaps now really believes, that both matches were the result of her matrimonial craft, it would be the height of ingratitude if she ever could complain of the want of a hearty welcome.

In the daily increasing happiness of his beloved daughter, Mr. Temple has quite forgotten any little disappointment which he might once have felt at not having a duke for a son-in-law, and such a duke as his valued friend, Lord Montfort. But Ferdinand Armine is blessed with so sweet a temper that it is impossible to live with him and not love him; and the most cordial intimacy and confidence subsist between the father of Henrietta Temple and his son-in-law. From the aspect of public affairs also, Mr. Temple, though he keeps this thought to himself, is inclined to believe that a coronet may yet grace the brow of his daughter, and that the barony of Armine may be revived. Soon after the passing of the memorable Act of 1828, Lord Montfort became the representative of his native county, and an active and influential member of the House of Commons. After the reform, Mr. Armine was also returned for a borough situate near the duke's principal seat, and although Lord Montfort and Mr. Armine both adhere to the Whig politics of their families, they have both also, in the most marked manner, abstained from voting on the appropriation clause; and there is little doubt that they will ultimately support that British and national administration which Providence has doubtless in store for these outraged and distracted realms. At least this is Mr. Temple's more than hope, who is also in the House, and acts entirely with Lord Stanley. The Montforts and the younger Armines contrive, through mutual visits and a town residence during the Session, to pass the greater part of their lives together; they both honestly confess that they are a little in love with each other's wives, but this only makes their society more agreeable. The family circle at Armine has been considerably increased of late; there is a handsome young Armine who has been christened Glastonbury, a circumstance which repays the tenant of the tower for all his devotion, and this blending of his name and memory with the illustrious race that has so long occupied his thoughts and hopes, is to him a source of constant self-congratulation. The future Sir Glastonbury has also two younger brothers quite worthy of the blood, Temple and Digby; and the most charming sister in the world, with large violet eyes and long dark lashes, who is still in arms, and who bears the hallowed name of Henrietta. And thus ends our LOVE STORY.

Printed in Great Britain
by Amazon